Relics

Relics Series, Volume 1

K. A. Moore

Published by K. A. Moore, 2020.

This is a work of fiction. Names, characters, businesses, places, events, locales, and incidents are either the products of the author's imagination or used in a fictitious manner. Any resemblance to actual persons, living or dead, or actual events is purely coincidental.

Book cover design by Betibup

Editing by Jessica at Bookhelpline

First Edition: June 2015

Second Edition: May 2020

ISBN 9781733236232 (ebook)

ISBN 9781957223131 (paperback)

Also by K. A. Moore

Relics Series

Relics

The Key

The Chosen

Standalone

Watching Her Sleep

Sentinel

Weeping Widow's Heirloom

For my Parents who have always believed in me.

One

"Thank you for your business. Please come again." Casey turned from the well-worn counter toward the back of the store to put away the last shipment of new books. She noticed several had damaged corners as she pulled them from the box. *We'll sell those at a discount.*

"You ready to close, Casey?" Monica yelled from the back office. Casey glanced up from the box as Monica poked her head around the doorway. "You can put the shipment away tomorrow. It's been a long day. Go ahead and go home."

"Sure. Let me lock the door and close the register."

The deadbolt silently slid home on the front door, and the faded open sign—chipped in the lower corner—faced in to announce to all who may be outside the business had closed. The bell rang on the register as the cash drawer sprung forward, breaking the silence in the deserted store. She scurried to the back office, the coins jingling with every step. After the deposit was locked in the safe for Monica to take in the morning, a fight ensued with her coat as she tried to wriggle her arms into the sleeves just before she hollered, "Bye. See you tomorrow."

"Yeah. See ya."

Casey's right foot slipped on the mostly frozen, brown slush that had frozen over as the cool, brisk night air hit. She flung her arms out to her sides as if on a tight rope.

Another slight slip caused her to pinwheel her arms to keep upright. A smile crept across her face until she grinned ear to ear. She darted a quick glance around and inwardly cheered when she found there were no witnesses to her near fall. She had escaped another embarrassing moment. Of course, who would come out in this weather to brave the subfreezing temperatures and exposure to the negative degree windchill? The only reason the last customer graced them with their presence was a last-minute need for study supplies.

Short, quick, shuffled steps took her to the car. Shivers racked her body, and her breath escaped in billows of steam. The windows fogged in an instant when she closed the door and sighed, relieved she made it to the car in one piece. With the turn of the key, the car engine sputtered several times before it groaned to life. She rubbed her hands against each other, waiting for the engine to warm up.

The tires spun on the ice as they searched for traction when she pulled out of the parking space. She cautiously pulled onto the road. With her car pointed toward home, her headlights splashed across the road and reflected off the mountainous piles of snow left from the city plows. The streets were void of any life, from humans to animals. No one endured the brunt of the cold to go anywhere. As she pulled into her driveway, a dark shadow moved past the windows in the living room. Her foot punched the brakes harder than she intended. The seatbelt pinned her back into her seat, locking in place. Her wide, panicked eyes were glued to the front window waiting for any movement.

Nothing.

A flash of light caught her attention. Her heart raced as her hands tightened on the steering wheel, her knuckles turning white. Oh, wait. She'd left the television on for Mason. She'd never known a television to project shadows the way it did tonight. Casey chuckled at herself and swore the shadow was three dimensional as if a person sauntered past. Her headlights illuminated the gaping open garage door, beckoning her to come in. She released the brake and inched her car into the garage. The ticking of the engine was louder than usual as she shuffled to the mailbox, while the icy surface underneath the snow taunted her to fall.

Mason jumped and spun in mid-air in the backyard. "Hey, big boy. How's it going?" Casey glanced past the side of the house, her Rottweiler's rapt attention on her. Another shadow moved across the front window, and a lump formed in her throat, making it difficult to swallow. The television? Casey shook her head. Lurking shadows danced in her mind as she envisioned intruders in the dark recesses of her home. Mason charged toward the stairs at the back of the house, and within seconds, his enormous paws thudded on the front windows. The steam from his breath became marred by nose prints on the glass. He barked once to tell her to come inside. Of course, no one was in her house. She entered through the garage into the shadowy confines of the basement. The heat from the furnace that warmed the eternally chilly, unfinished concrete basement helped dispel the impression of someone being in her home.

Mason stuck his head around the corner, smiling as his tongue lolled to the side while she trudged up the stairs. Mason would never let anyone close to the house ever since she took him to obedience and protection dog training, much less wander around inside. How could she think that someone would be in here? She shook her head to clear her wandering mind.

Casey listened at the top of the stairs for any sound that didn't belong. Mason nudged her hand that clutched her purse with a cold nose. She shooed him as she took in the living room and kitchen. Nothing was out of place or missing that she could tell. The light in the spare bedroom showed the dust-laden furniture, reminding her she needed to dust again, but it didn't give away any stranger lurking in the corners. Her bedroom also dispelled any thoughts of a stranger being in her house when no one was in the closet. She even looked under the bed.

A thud echoed throughout the bedroom when she dropped her purse into the bottom drawer of the nightstand. With her shoes off, she shuffled toward the kitchen. The glare of empty shelves in the refrigerator blinded her. They were as ravenous for food as she was. She had forgotten to stop at the grocery store on the way home. She dug around in a drawer and looked for the menu to the local pizza place. When she found it, she grabbed her phone, dialed, and placed the order.

Twenty-five minutes later, the dependable driver rang the doorbell sending Mason into a rant of low, throaty barks. "It's okay, Mason. Go lie down." He plopped on his bed and waited patiently as she paid for the pizza. She threw a couple of slices on a plate, the cheese stringing across the edge of the box before she closed it. Mason trotted next to her as she sat down, waiting for the crust to be his. Casey tucked her feet under a blanket and sat back into the soft plush pillowed back of her old couch—it had seen better days judging by the frayed edges, reminiscent of the seventy's clothes fashions with fringe—and enjoyed the pizza. Before she blinked, half of it was gone. She slowed down to savor the last piece as her thoughts drifted to shadows in the living room. *Stop it.* Why was her imagination running wild tonight? She tossed the last crust to Mason, who inhaled it without chewing and shook her head as she carried the plate to the sink.

On the way to her room, movement at the end of the hall stopped her cold. Her heart caught in her throat once again as beads of sweat formed on her brow. She barely made out the shape of something at the end of the hall. Or was it some*one*?

Was someone in the living room earlier when she pulled into the driveway? Wouldn't Mason let on if someone was in the house? Could they be in here all day much less the couple of hours since she had been home? Casey reached out, ever so slowly, for the light switch. She slid her fingers across the grainy paint-textured wall that was in desperate need of a new coat of paint, feeling for the light switch. The sound of her searching fingers echoed down the hall. Her hand hit the switch, illuminating the hallway with such a blinding glare, no dark corner for a shadow to hide was left.

There was nothing besides her reflection in the mirror at the far end of the hallway. Why was she so jumpy tonight? The mirror's been there since the day she bought the house. Hoarse laughter escaped as she berated herself for acting like a scared four-year-old. She left the light on as she got ready for bed.

When she sunk under the soft down comforter, small pockets of air dispelled, causing the comforter to puff up in certain spots. Mason warmed her feet as he stretched his body the width of the bed.

Her thoughts drifted to the dreams of the past week. Almost every night, she dreamed of this man with the most amazing blue eyes. Would he visit her dreams tonight? His eyes could rival the Caribbean Sea. Always in the distance, he worked his way closer and closer, making her think maybe this time she might speak to him. The blackness engulfed her.

Two

Someone chased her, but she couldn't see them. Thunderous footfalls told her they were gaining, but she couldn't run fast enough. Someone ahead urged her on, but she was tired. She couldn't keep going. Fatigue plagued her until she gave in to the exhaustion. She collapsed, her lungs screaming in pain as she gulped air.

Heavy, quick, booming footsteps thudded on the pavement from whoever chased her. She turned toward the footsteps as they grew closer, and someone grabbed her from behind under the arms and yanked her off the rain-soaked ground. Drops of rain fell from his hair onto her, and she shivered. "Run." His gruff voice mesmerized her. She froze, unable to move. He wrenched her around a building and into a doorway as a barrage of bullets ricocheted off the bricks around the doorframe, sending pieces of brick and dust in every direction. His arm snaked around her waist, swinging her around as he closed the door behind them. He engaged the lock, then turned toward her.

"This door won't hold for long." He took her hand and raced across the dilapidated wood floor that crumbled from their footfalls. His touch energized her enough to follow. Goosebumps raced across her smooth skin as he tugged her around yet another corner. He glanced at her, then skidded to a stop. His eyes were the most astonishing blue. He yanked his jacket off and draped it over her shoulders. Maybe he thought she was cold. He grabbed her hand, and they took off at a sprint. The warmth of his jacket from his body heat chased away the last of the goosebumps. His scent intoxicated her. She inhaled as if her lungs had no boundaries, not wanting to let any of his clean-shaven-meets-outdoors-real-man scent escape. She finally gave in and exhaled.

As her alarm sounded, she rolled over and reached for the snooze. Oh, to go back to dreamland. Seven more minutes, please. Seven more minutes to go back to the one place where she could change—herself, her destiny. Seven minutes of being able to change events and actions that she was unable to with the boring, groggy events in her own life. Sleep settled back in, and she drifted off into the action-packed world, yet again ensconced in the dream where she'd left off.

She dashed across the warehouse, trying to miss the large holes in the floor big enough to lose a car through. She attempted to catch him. He no longer held her hand. He disappeared around the corner. She hurried because she didn't want to lose track of him. When he made eye contact with those amazing blue eyes, she swore a light pierced her heart, stopping it from beating in a mere split second.

Beep, beep, beep. "No." She sighed as the alarm clock ripped her from the more appealing life of her dreams into the shocking reality of her dull, real-life existence. Goosebumps sprang up on her legs as she slid them out from under the toasty warm blankets. Her knees hit the carpet next to the bed, and she started her day in prayer as she had done for years. "Dear Heavenly Father, thank You for today. I'm alive and have more than most—a roof over my head, the love of my family, an adorable dog, and a job to pay the bills. Keep my heart open today. Let me see people the way You do, that they need to find You, and if possible, let me be able to share the story of Your love for them. Give me patience. Your plan's always perfect, and everything happens in Your timing. In Jesus Christ's name, amen."

She dragged her feet to the bathroom to get ready for her day. Yes, you could dream about people you never met—usually actors or celebrities on television, magazines at the checkout counter, and television commercials. They're embedded in your daily thoughts before you go to bed. This was different. She had never seen him before, and he wasn't a celebrity. If he were, she would have watched everything that featured him, whether it was on television or in the movies. She would've never forgotten those eyes, the ones that bore through you and melted your heart in a single glance. This tall, dark stranger who graced her dreams for the past couple of weeks filled her thoughts.

She didn't know what it meant, but at this stalled-out point in her life, she didn't care. She didn't worry about being hurt by a dream. The fact he was always out of reach frustrated her. It never failed when she was at an exhilarating point, her utterly dependable alarm clock ripped her from her dreams.

Ever since she was a little girl, a nagging voice in the back of her mind told her something great would happen. Each passing year, lightness in her chest grew at what God had planned for her, and why she was here. Now, with another year closing, her heart sank that she was still unsure where God wanted her.

She worked a dull job. How many wrong turns had she taken to end up where she was? If she could undo some of those turns, she would. Was this where God wanted or needed her, though? At least working in a small Christian bookstore, she didn't fret about the big daily song and dance of corporate office atmosphere with all its drama and politics. She dreaded the annoying alarm clock, which seemed to enjoy its morning ritual of ripping her from her sleep into a world where she didn't think she would ever belong. Maybe today would be different. Maybe today something would happen. Maybe God would tell her how He could use her to do His work.

She couldn't shake the image of his piercing blue eyes. She tried to recall the touch of him when he held her hand. Why couldn't someone in real life look at her like that? Sure, dreams weren't real, and nothing would come of this, but why did she dream of this man who didn't exist?

She backed out of the garage. The sides of the car cleared the opening inch by inch with barely enough room. She slammed on the brakes. Her purse was still in the house. She turned the car off, jumped out, and bolted up the basement stairs two at a time. How'd she miss grabbing her purse? She had never done that before. Next, she would forget her shoes or something equally stupid. Mad at herself, she raced down the hall and yanked open the bottom drawer to the nightstand.

Her hair stood up on the back of her neck, and she straightened. Something felt off. She scanned the room, but nothing was out of place or missing.

Then a scent hit her.

Something about it was familiar. Then a stark realization hit—she wasn't alone! A shadow moved from the open door of the closet into the bedroom. She lunged toward the hallway, but her legs didn't move fast enough. Her keys slipped from her hand as his arm slid around her waist, lifting her off the ground as the other one clamped over her mouth. Her blood-curdling scream fell on deaf ears, muffled under this man's hand, not reaching beyond the secure walls of her house.

In the far reaches of her mind, she tried to recall the self-defense class she took years before, and she drove the heel of her tennis shoe into his shin. He didn't flinch. She attempted to ram her head back to catch his chin, maybe throw him off balance. Nothing happened except the back of her head thudded against his well-defined chest. He stepped toward the closet, taking her with him as she clawed at his hands. Mason stood in the doorway with his tongue hanging out the side of his slobbering mouth and panting as if a spectator at an event.

He murmured in her ear, "I won't hurt you. Let me explain."

"Mmph!" She shook her head back and forth.

Panic set in. Her heart raced as she tried to slow her breathing. The longer he held her, the harder it was to keep a clear head with an overpowering question. Why the closet? She threw her elbow back into his ribs. He sucked in air and grunted. It was the first sign her attempt to fight might pay off. Yet his hold on her didn't loosen. In fact, he did the exact opposite. His hand over her mouth pulled her head back, pinning her to his chest as he quickly released her waist. He lowered her to the ground before he grabbed her right arm, wrapped it around the front of her waist, picking her up in one fluid motion.

"Calm down. You're going to injure yourself. It's okay. I have to take you somewhere." His voice was a husky whisper.

She tried to shake her head back and forth again. "Mmph!"

"If I take my hand off your mouth, will you promise not to scream?" He hunched over her.

She furiously nodded her head.

His hand slid off her mouth. "I need you to come with me." He took a step toward the closet.

She screamed and tried to pull away. He clamped his hand back over her mouth.

With a step closer to the closet, she held her breath as a strange light seeped through the slats in the doors. Not the closet light, but dimmer, as if a nightlight were stuck behind clothes letting out such a small amount. It didn't access all the closet but only increased the shadows. He kicked the door open the rest of the way.

Her eyes widened as a shiver coursed down her spine. A small, one-foot area of wavering haze as if fog from a harbor rolled into shore hovered against the back of the closet, several feet off the floor. The edges—always changing and not easily defined—almost pulsed. His breath and lips grazed her ear as he said, "We're not going to hurt you. We need your help. I don't mean to scare you."

Something about his voice was familiar. Was it supposed to put her at ease? Because the fact he mentioned "*we*" made the panic almost unbearable. She was outnumbered. Where was the "*we*?" No one occupied the closet. Her captor took another step forward, and she kicked her legs, catching the doorframe. Her leg muscles strained as she pushed back against him. He staggered back several feet. She kept the closet out of reach. He started forward again, seemingly determined to continue as she kicked with her legs, aiming for the doorframe. The light frightened her more than the man who held her.

"Stop. You're going to injure yourself." His lips brushed her ear.

Lord, please help me out of this, she cried in her mind. Why wasn't Mason doing anything? Was this man in her house last night? Did he do something to Mason do keep him from attacking? She tried to scream again, but his hand muffled the sound.

The man spun around and stepped backward, pulling her with him. "I'm sorry, but this will be weird. Breathe through it."

Casey grasped with her free hand in a frantic attempt to hold onto the doorframe when there was a pull at her waist. Did he really need to tighten his steel grip on her? His arms firmly held her when he pulled her so close to him. She thought they would merge into each other. He muffled her blood-curdling scream against his hand as she shook her head from side to side. The light pulled them into it. She tried to scream again as everything faded to dark.

She floated, but she wasn't alone. With his arms around her, a dizzying jerk wrenched them into a room. People stared at her with wide eyes. A woman yelped and ran to a man in the doorway. The room spun as if Casey were in a drunken stupor. Her captor removed his hand from her mouth and moved them down, so they hugged her waist. He turned her toward him as she placed her hands on either side of her head.

"It will pass in a minute. Breathe through it." Her legs wobbled, so she grasped his upper arms to steady herself. She leaned her perspiring head on his chest. The energy she exerted fighting him took its toll. Perspiration started a downward trek from her forehead to her temples and eyebrows. After several minutes, her double vision subsided, she put weight on her legs and found they still worked.

"Are you okay?" His voice mesmerized her.

Casey nodded, which made the room spin again. She steadied herself by tightening her hold on his arms. He was stronger than she thought. Her eyes widened when she lifted her head. It was him—the man who entered her dream world not even a week ago and occupied her thoughts, even in her waking hours.

She pushed away from him and stumbled to the wall. She held up her hand as if that could stop him. Casey shook her head to clear his image out of her mind. "You!" she hissed.

How was this possible? His scent was the same as in her dream—clean-shaven combined with outdoorsman. It was as if he had been there, physically standing in front of her while she was in dreamland. How do you dream about a scent? The voice from her dream was also unerringly the same.

The young woman brought over a glass of water and motioned to a stool. As the man stepped toward her, Casey sat but refused the water. Did they think she would drink something after they kidnapped her? Was this the "we" he spoke of? But how did she get here? Did he drug her? Her hands violently shook as she clenched them together. The more she tried to stop the shaking, the worse it got.

He smiled as he took the glass from the woman, then squatted in front of her. "The water helps."

Casey shook her head and tensed her muscles. Her hands clenched into fists.

A man lurked in the doorway, and she glanced at him. His short, cropped, military hairstyle gave away his role in this group. Muscles strained under his plain tan t-shirt with no insignia as he crossed his arms and stood with his feet shoulder-width apart. His intense eyes locked on hers, and his eyebrows drew together on his finely chiseled face. He glanced at the man in front of her and raised his left eyebrow.

She wrung her hands. "Where am I, and why did you bring me here?"

Casey wasn't sure which she was more afraid of—being taken or the adrenaline rush from being in the same room with the man from her dreams. Here he knelt in front of her, concern on his face, eyes piercing into her the same as in her dreams.

How do you dream of someone who you've never met, but who had now pulled you through a threshold of some kind? Was she still dreaming? If she wasn't, how could she explain what happened? Would he tell her what he had done and why? Would it be the truth? There were so many questions rolling around in her mind, and she couldn't grasp just one.

"First, my name's Ben." He motioned to the others as if they were meeting at a restaurant or gathering. "This is Clint and Amanda."

Casey shifted on the stool, and her chin trembled. Her heart raced, and her knuckles turned white as she gripped the edges of the stool. A door slammed somewhere in the building, and she flinched before her eyes darted to the doorway.

Amanda smiled and waved to her as if they had known each other for years and passed each other in the hall at work. What was wrong with these people? This was no casual meeting. They'd kidnapped her! The seriousness of the situation was lost by these three. Clint only nodded his head, but a slight smile touched the corners of his mouth. The nerve of these three. Her hands no longer shook but balled into fists. Ben knelt in front of the stool she sat in and gently placed his hand on her arm. She jumped and yanked her arm away.

"Sorry. I didn't mean to do this. We never intended to take you from your home." Ben begged for forgiveness. "But when we finally found you, I couldn't take the chance of losing you. We need your help."

Before she could stop herself, she blurted out. "Help?"

"We'll get to that, but we need you checked out in the infirmary now."

Her eyes widened. "No!"

"This place...is a little different than when you're from, so we need to make sure we take care of anything that can hurt you. There are different strains of colds, different types of flu, and airborne pathogens we have vaccines for that you need."

"Vaccines? Vaccines don't exist for the common cold." Were they going to do some weird laboratory testing on her? She fought the urge to run. Long, drawn-out, methodical breaths helped slow her racing heart.

"Not in the time you're from. I'll explain later, but we need to get you to Doc."

"You're not injecting me with anything!" she blurted. Her breathing quickened again.

Ben glanced at Clint. Clint tilted his head in acknowledgment, walked over to a cabinet, and turned around with a strange apparatus. Liquid sloshed against the sides of a vial attached to the top. The dented silver aluminum stool clattered loudly to the floor when she shoved it backward. Its hollow legs echoed and rang out like organ pipes when they bounced off the floor. A quick swipe at the water glass knocked it from his hand. It shattered as it hit the cold, slick linoleum floor. Shards of glass scattered every direction, and water ran toward the door on the uneven floor. With her back to the wall, she observed the muscles under Clint's shirt tense as he moved his finger to the trigger. "We don't need to use this. Just come with us to Doc."

Ben held his hands up. "It's to keep you safe. We can't take the chance of you getting sick. The colds here are not the same as your body's used to." He took a tentative step toward her.

Amanda scrambled past Clint into the hall. She shook her head, and her bangs swished back and forth across her forehead. Casey backed away from them and tested her legs. She stumbled sideways against the wall. Clint sidestepped to the doorway he had leaned against earlier as Ben stepped around to her other side. They put her between them. Clint took several steps forward. Was it to distract her so Ben could grab her from behind? "We won't hurt you."

Three quick steps took her closer to Clint. It startled him, and Casey darted around to the right, putting her in arms reach of the door. He swept his hand toward her as she sprinted for the hall. Two more steps, and she was around Clint. Her knees buckled, and she fell into the far wall escaping his attempt to grab her as his fingers swiped the fabric of her shirt.

Amanda tried to block her. "We're not going to harm you."

Casey pulled back a fist, and Amanda cringed, yelped, and ducked out of the way. She took a quick step around Amanda, then spun around and shoved Amanda into Clint, taking them both down. Casey clumsily took off and focused her eyes on the swaying hallway in front of her. Ben and Clint scrambled behind her, yelling for her to stop. She wouldn't stop for anyone. Maybe someone could help her so that she could go home. As she picked up speed, fully alert now that her adrenaline had kicked in, the rapid squeaks from her tennis shoes bounced off the walls.

"If she gets out of this building, it will kill her." Clint's voice carried down the hall. "Casey, please stop."

Ben stepped over Clint's legs. "I know!"

Three

"What were you thinking, Ben?" Amanda argued.

"I'll explain later. We have to find her."

"This better be a really good explanation, Ben. This could ruin everything." Clint scrambled off the floor and untangled himself from Amanda.

Ben shook his head and offered Clint his hand. He yanked him off the floor, spilling Amanda on her side. They jumped over her and darted around the corner Casey had disappeared around. They stopped and stared at the two different hallways she could've taken. Ben shrugged his shoulders just before he darted down the hall on the left, Clint on his heels. Their thick, rubber-soled boots thundered down the hall, the sound echoing off the walls.

"Hey, we need to talk about this. What were you thinking, grabbing her like that?" Clint kept pace with Ben as he jogged to the next door.

"Can't we talk about this later?"

"Well, I say we talk about it now while we try and find her. If she gets out of this building, it could kill her and ruin everything! We have to keep her safe."

"Trust me, I know." Ben grabbed a doorknob and jiggled it—locked.

Clint seized the next one across from Ben to find his locked, too. He was glad they kept these unused rooms locked. That meant fewer rooms to clear, giving them a quicker chance of finding her. Ben glanced back and locked eyes with Clint. How would he explain this to his best friend?

"Well?"

"How long have we known each other?" Ben grasped the next cold industrial steel doorknob—locked. "Since we were kids. Trust me. I needed to bring her here."

"Of course, I trust you, but that doesn't tell me why you did this. We talked about this. She was never supposed to know about us. You were supposed to go there, grab evidence, and leave, letting her live her life, never knowing about us. Now she's at risk along with everyone in the warehouse."

Ben whispered, "I know."

"Why did you bring her here and take the chance of getting her killed? We need to keep her safe and away from this."

Ben stopped and hung his head and ran his hand through his hair. He couldn't tell Clint yet. He whipped around to face his best friend since childhood. His friend, who he almost lost in the wars and the aftermath they now dealt with daily. No, Ben couldn't tell him how he disregarded their promise to keep her out of it or why he decided while in her house that he would never let her go, no matter the cost.

"Hey, are you okay?" Clint clasped Ben on the shoulder.

"Yes. Please trust me. She needs to be here." Ben pleaded with his eyes.

"Yeah, okay. Just tell me when you're ready. You won't convince your sister that easily." Clint smirked and continued down the hall.

"Yeah, tell me about it." Ben and Clint reached the end of the hall.

"She took the other hallway," they said in unison and took off at a sprint.

Four

As Casey darted around the next corner, two hallways beckoned her. Which one should she choose? Halfway to the one on the right, heavy footsteps echoed behind her. She scampered to the right, but several doors on either side of the hallway made it difficult to decide which way to go. Was this how a rat felt in a maze? Not being able to glimpse above the walls to the people outside?

The third door on the left was the first one she found unlocked. She closed the door quickly yet quietly behind her. She fumbled with the doorknob and found there was no lock on the door, which explained why it was unlocked in the first place. It wouldn't take them long to realize she won't be in any of the locked rooms. She tried to slow her breathing and racing heart as she clutched her chest and leaned against the door, resting her head against the cold metal. She wanted more excitement in her life, but this was ridiculous!

The light from the hall shone through the frosted glass in the door. She spun to the right, then to the left as her eyes settled on several pieces of equipment lurking in the dark on tables. The chemistry lab from college popped into her mind, but this equipment was on a whole new level. She wished she hadn't come into this room. On her way back to the door, footsteps in the hall made her stop midstride.

Frantic, she scanned the room when she noted another door on the far side. A few quick steps and she yanked the door open to find a storage room. Cold darkness suffocated her as she closed the door behind her. She couldn't turn on the light, or it might be visible under the door.

Careful not to bump into anything, small, shuffled steps took her to the back of the room. The back wall would seal her fate if she couldn't hide or find another way out. She squeezed behind one of the shelving units. As her eyes adjusted to the dark, she could make out the shape of the shelves. If they came in, she might be able to knock the shelves over on top of them. The thought of hurting Ben startled her with an instant rush of dizziness. *Stop it!* She couldn't think that way—she had to get out of here. They'd kidnapped her and brought her here. She couldn't trouble herself about that since they didn't hesitate to kidnap and drug her to bring her to this building.

"Please help me, God."

Air rushed down from the ceiling. Was there a vent she could hide in? The rickety shelving threatened to bend and collapse as she scaled the side. It was a drop ceiling. Her heart jumped. Maybe she would be able to fit through one of the tile sections, and there'd be enough room to crawl. If so, she would be able to make her way along the bearing walls undetected.

Casey hoisted herself through the hole next to the vent, trying not to put any weight on the ceiling and pulled herself along the wall at the back of the storage room. Once she lowered the tile back in place, the narrow wall offered little room for error if she were to misplace her hands. Lights from other rooms filtered through the tiles and lit the space well enough for her to see. A shiver ran down her back as she tried not to think of the spiders that may call this ceiling home. She would put that phobia on the back burner if she wanted to survive this.

Her heart thundered so loud she was unsure if anyone could hear it as she tried to peer into the dark, cobweb-infested corners of the ceiling. Someone opened the door to the storage room she had climbed out of and turned on the light. The instant flood of light through the vent hit her like a spotlight, and she held her breath. Clint made his way through the rows of shelves. A few seconds later, Ben joined him. She gawked and peered through the unattached vent next to her, wondering why they didn't think to look in the air duct.

"Anything, buddy?" Ben paced back and forth.

"No, and I don't understand where she could've gone. She has to be scared. She won't understand how bad it is outside." Clint stomped out of the room.

"Clint, we need to find her!"

"I know. Before it's too late."

Their footsteps faded as they continued searching for her. Carefully picking her way, making turns when the wall did, she dead-ended at a concrete wall which continued well above her head. This must be an outer wall of the building. What she might find outside made her knees shake.

Would one of the rooms below these tiles lead her outside? She was hesitant to lift a tile to look at what was below, afraid she might alert someone to her presence. She wasn't sure how long she was in the ceiling, but she had to take a chance. Casey lowered her ear toward the tiles. Several agonizing minutes passed before she mustered the courage to raise a tile.

With her weight on the wall, she lifted a corner of the tile. Several tables littered the room below. Light streamed in from a window and showed the room to be vacant. With the tile slid to the side, she lowered herself onto the desk below her, then replaced the tile. If she needed to hide again, she didn't want them to be alerted to where she'd hid before.

She raced to the window. An overcast, rainy day, with several buildings clustered together was the backdrop to a dreary scene. It was a warehouse district, with other buildings damaged. Most had more broken windows than not. Were they abandoned? If she made it out of the building, would there be anyone outside to help her? Not a single soul was in sight, and she half expected a tumbleweed to roll past. She grasped the lock to turn the lever. It wouldn't turn.

As much as three coats of paint caked around the lock secured it in place. With this much paint, she wouldn't be surprised if the windows were intentionally painted shut. She stifled a cry behind her fist as she spun on her heels toward the door, ready for them to barge in. There was no way to be quiet while opening this window. She hoped they were on the far side of the building, and she could escape before they found her.

A desk at the front of the room gave her hope. She yanked open drawers one by one but found nothing useful. The far side of the room held another desk. In the first drawer that she slid open, a metal ruler glinted as the light hit it. Grasping the ruler, she scraped down the edges of the window. It was as though she worked at a snail's pace to cut through the paint, releasing the window from the death grip. She worked feverishly to penetrate the layers, as every gouge of the ruler echoed through the room and no doubt down the hall.

"OKAY, THIS DOESN'T make sense. There's only one room she could be in with all the others locked." Clint scratched his head, then smoothed out his short-cropped hair.

"Did she double back to here?" Ben glanced down the hallway.

They jogged to the lab to find Amanda locking up. "Where is she?"

"Did she come back this way?" Clint eyed the other end of the hall.

"No. Ben, what were you thinking?" Amanda put her hands on her hips. "Why on earth would you bring her here?"

Clint smirked. "Told you."

"Amanda, don't start. Just trust me. I had to." Ben grabbed a roll of paper off the top of a filing cabinet and, in one swift snap of his wrist, unrolled it on the lab table.

"Okay, we checked this hall and that one. None of the doors were unlocked, so unless she can pick locks with her fingers, we need to move farther into the building to find her." Clint traced the hallways they cleared.

"But with the doors locked, how would she be at the other end of the warehouse?" Amanda peered around Clint's shoulder.

Ben and Clint spun to each other. "The ceiling," they said in unison.

"Ceiling? What are you? Crazy? How could she be in the ceiling?" Amanda yelled as they took off from the lab, but not before Clint swiped a set of keys off the lab table.

They sprinted to the end of the hallway on the right, where Clint used the keys to unlock the door giving them access to the rest of the building. This part of the building was dangerous. They couldn't keep people from breaking into this part of the warehouse when they relocated to the warehouse district. Between the ones addicted to drugs, to the gangs, or even murderers, they hoped there weren't any unwanted guests today.

Halfway down the old, dilapidated hall, ugly ceiling tiles stained various shades of yellows and browns showed the areas of the warehouse where the roof leaked. Several lights flickered as they hung from the ceiling with exposed wires. Faint sounds of water dripped somewhere, breaking the deafening silence.

Clint raised his hand with his fist closed. He turned his head, first to the right then to the left. A smile plastered on his face, and he drew the apparatus with the serum and motioned for Ben to follow with his hand that held the keys, making sure they didn't jingle.

Ben jogged to keep up. He didn't make a sound. He wasn't sure what Clint smiled about, but he also trusted his long-time friend. The military had trained him well. A slight scraping sound caught his attention, which explained why Clint took off in this direction.

Clint stopped outside another office door where the glass had been painted over, barring anyone from looking inside except a small corner about the size of a dime. He studied the room and nodded to Ben, who put his eye to the scratched off part of the glass. Casey worked at the window. She appeared so small as she fiercely scraped along the edges of the window. Pain in the back of his throat sparked for bringing her here. She was scared, and the fact it was because of him broke his heart. Clint tapped him on the shoulder.

"We need to do this quiet, so we don't alert her. I don't want her hurt. She'll be scared, so she may do anything to escape. With the Monarchs outside, she wouldn't stand a chance," Clint whispered.

Ben took the keys, found the one for the door, and removed it from the ring before shoving the rest in his pocket. With a nod at Clint, he slipped the key into the lock.

Several agonizing seconds went by before he heard her return to the window. Did she hear them? Clint motioned for Ben to grab her from behind and wrap her arms around to keep her from harming herself. He nodded to Clint, who motioned with the injector to say he would do the rest.

Ben turned the doorknob, and they both slid into the room, leaving the door ajar. Ben edged past the desk outside of her peripheral vision as he glanced back at Clint. A few calculated steps forward, and he was ready. Then he motioned to Clint, who started forward.

Five

Hands grabbed Casey from behind as an ear-piercing scream erupted from her. Both of her wrists disappeared into Ben's large hands as he folded her arms around her into a bear hug, pulling her in tight before she finished her scream. With a simple lift of his arms, her legs swung free several inches off the floor. Her head hit his chest as she thrashed around.

"Casey, calm down. You're going to get hurt. I know we haven't given you a reason to trust us, but we need to get you to Doc." Ben's calm voice was in her ear.

Clint added, "Then we can sit down and talk and tell you what's happening."

She thrashed around and kicked out with her feet. How could she trust someone who kidnapped her?

Clint strode over and jammed the injection gun to her neck.

She screamed, "No!" and kicked out in front of her. Her foot glanced off Clint's leg as he sidestepped in a single motion and pulled the trigger on the gun. Everything faded as her arms and legs became heavy. Her head fell forward. Ben tried to swing her into his arms, but she lurched forward and stumbled to the closest desk.

"Did you inject her?" Ben stepped to the right.

"Yes. She was going to hurt herself. We are on the unsecured side of the warehouse, and we are putting everyone's lives on the line being over here. She shouldn't be awake, much less able to walk!"

"What...what...did you do?" She stumbled a few more steps before her legs gave out, and she sank to her knees.

"Calm down. We aren't going to harm you. Please, we have to get you to Doc, or you could get very sick or die." Ben took another step to the right, bringing himself close enough to grab her, but hesitated.

She gingerly touched her neck; the smallest drop of blood dotted her finger. Her head swayed. There was no getting away this time. Her hair tumbled back and forth over her shoulders as she shook her head and blinked several times to force her eyes to focus on the blurry dot on her finger.

They grabbed her at the same time, as she stared at the drop of blood. She sluggishly raised her head and narrowed her eyes at Clint. When did he get so close? She shoved against his chest with both her hands as she staggered to her feet. Ben steadied her with a hand around her waist. She couldn't focus on his hands. The room spun as her vision blurred. Her movements and the room were in slow motion.

Casey shook her head. "Wait, I—"

"Come on. Let's get you to Doc." Clint tried to guide her toward the door.

She grabbed the lamp on the desk and hurled it through the window, snatched a glass shard that landed on the desk, and sliced toward them as Ben ducked and Clint jumped back.

"Woah, calm down." Ben thrust his hands out in front of him. His eyes met Clint's.

"Let me go," Casey slurred. The glass blurred in front of her eyes as her head drooped.

"Casey, drop the glass, you're going to cut yourself." Clint reached around his back.

Her eyes widened. "Are you going for a gun?"

Blood dripped from her hand and splattered on the floor as the ragged glass shard punctured her palm. She shook her head. What did they inject her with? Ben moved at her right. She swung at him with the glass shard again.

Casey squealed as Clint grabbed her and pinched a pressure point in her wrist. She dropped the glass from the pain and weakness and tugged at his hand, trying to peel his fingers off her throbbing wrist.

Ben yanked off his outer shirt and tried to stop the blood pouring from her hand. She pulled back and tried to shove him with her free hand. Clint grabbed her wrist and twisted it around her back, pulling up enough that she could only comply as he slowly but firmly guided her face down on the desk. Ben quickly ripped his shirt into several strips and tied them around her hand as she yelped, pulling away.

Clint applied pressure to her shoulder. He pulled the apparatus from his back pocket, put it up to her neck, and pulled the trigger a second time. The room blurred as her vision faltered. Tears fell, marring the layers of dust that had collected on the smooth metal surface of the industrial desk next to her footprints from when she lowered herself from the ceiling.

Six

"Was that necessary?"

"She would have cut herself worse if I didn't. Did you bandage her hand?" Clint released Casey's arm. She didn't move as he brushed the hair off her forehead.

Ben picked her up and cradled her in his arms. He tightened his arms as he stared at her face. He wanted to wipe away the tears and dust smeared on her cheek. He turned his back on Clint and started for the other side of the warehouse.

"She'll be okay. We just need to make sure Doc takes care of her." Clint caught up to Ben with long, steadfast strides. "We need to talk about getting her home. She can't stay here. Doc can pull blood so we can test it and find what we're looking for. Ben...we need to take her home."

Ben ignored Clint and kept his pace. All he cared about was Doc making sure she was okay. He didn't tell Clint he wouldn't take her home. He would never let her go, not after what happened in her house. They wouldn't understand. It may take some time for them to accept it, but he didn't care. He would do anything for her.

The only sound between them as they left the unsecured side of the warehouse and brought Casey to the infirmary were their thick-soled boots thudding on the concrete floor. Doc waited for them with Amanda at his side. Ben asked her to fill him in on what happened. The disappointment written on Doc's face bothered Ben. Doc motioned with his hand to an empty bed as frown lines creased his weathered forehead.

Ben laid Casey down as Clint grabbed the restraint on the side of the bed and cinched it around her wrist. Ben frowned but didn't say anything as he grabbed for the one on the other side, restraining that wrist.

"You're gonna be okay." Ben leaned down next to Casey. "I'm sorry we had to do this. If you made it outside without the vaccines, you could've died." His fingers brushed her skin as he moved the strands of hair off her forehead. Casey shook her head, and Ben stepped back as Doc wedged himself between Ben and the bed.

"How long has she been here?" Doc put the stethoscope in his ears.

"At least forty-five minutes to an hour," Clint volunteered.

Casey's voice came out in a hoarse whisper, "Please, Father, help me through this."

"Geez, Clint. Did you need to dose her twice?" Ben snapped

Clint crossed his arms. "Calm down, Ben. She tried to slice you with a piece of broken glass."

"Yeah, but look at her! Maybe we could have restrained her without the second dose." Ben motioned to Casey with a sweep of his hand.

"Doc, if you can, sew up the gash in her hand." Clint peered around Ben.

Ben sighed, "Sorry...you know how important she is. She's the key."

"I know how important she is, but I didn't bring her here and put her in danger." Clint shifted his weight.

Ben punched a wall, and Amanda flinched. "We're supposed to keep her safe. One dose should have dropped her! How was she still standing?"

"Maybe it has to do with this being such a different world than when she's from, and it affects her differently," Amanda offered. Then she turned to Clint and grimaced. "Two doses? Really?"

"Yeah, she did just come through the threshold. Maybe that has something to do with it," Clint reasoned. "Hey, Doc. How long's this gonna take?"

Doc's voice was stern as he said, "At least a couple of hours. I need time to do some tests to make sure she didn't contract any viruses, and for the vaccines to take effect, so she'll be safe to roam around."

"Thanks, Doc. I'm going to go board up that window. Ben, you coming?" Clint stepped past Ben, stopped, and clasped a hand on his shoulder. Ben ignored him.

"No, I'm staying here in case she wakes." Ben lurked in the hall, then propped himself against the wall and slid to a seated position.

"Suit yourself." Clint stalked away.

Seven

Casey attempted to open her eyes, but it felt as if hundred-pound weights held them closed. Talk about the weirdest dream. She struggled to pull her hands to her face, but they refused to budge. She hated when her arms went to sleep, and she couldn't move them when she first woke. Now those horrible pins and needles would be next.

"Hey, there you are. You gave us a scare being out for so long."

Casey flinched. It wasn't a dream.

"You're in the infirmary. We had to sedate you. You were a danger to yourself and others." Someone's hand brushed across her forehead, and she flinched at their touch.

"Ben?" She tried to open her eyes.

Ben leaned toward her. "Yes, I'm here."

"Hey, is the sleepyhead awake?" Amanda chimed in from somewhere past her feet.

"Sort of. She's still trying to wake up," Ben murmured.

Amanda lowered her voice. "Did Doc find out anything?"

"Yes, but later," Ben whispered.

Casey slurred, "Why am I so sleepy?"

"Sorry. We had to give you a double dose of the sedative. Never done that before. Do sedatives not work on you?" Ben cringed.

"I don't know. It's not every day that I'm kidnapped and sedated to compare it to!" Casey blew out her breath.

Ben lowered his voice, "I'm sorry. Let me explain a few things."

After several tries, she victoriously opened her protesting eyes. Ben sat next to her bed, and his smile caused her heart to race. She grimaced as the beeping rhythm on the heart monitor sped up.

Her restrained wrists came into focus as her eyes adjusted. She glanced from Ben to Clint. What was next? What did they want with her? No one kidnaps someone as a good thing.

"Sorry. They're for your own safety until the vaccines take hold," Ben calmly justified the restraints as if that made it all better.

"And you came close to hurting Ben," Clint's no-nonsense comment made her bite her lip.

"Where am I?"

"You're in a warehouse. And this is going to be hard to understand, but you're about thirty-five years in the future." Ben lowered his voice when he mentioned the part about the years as if to lessen the blow.

"What?" Her voice caught in her throat as she tried to swallow past the lump that formed.

"There was an uprising when the president took office. No one was aware of how connected he was to a terrorist group. He opened the borders to anyone who wanted the freedom to live in America. His terrorist cell, called the Monarchs, took over the east coast, pushing us back toward the Midwest. They released several biological weapons, killing a lot of Americans. Some great scientists on our side created vaccines. Those of us who survived are now in hiding from the Monarchs." Ben waved his hand around the room. "They are cruel, and don't hesitate to kill us."

"What year is it?" Casey inched away from Ben.

Ben pressed his lips together. "Twenty forty-eight."

"Time travel doesn't exist! I'm not stupid." She yanked up on her wrists and winced as pain shot through her right hand.

Ben flinched but continued, "We stumbled across something that let us. When we went underground years ago, in old warehouses, we discovered several tunnels used during the mob days for smuggling guns and money in and out of the city. Ground-penetrating radar showed a hollow space on the other side of a section of wall on one of our scouting trips. After we were able to determine the whole place wouldn't collapse with the removal of part of the wall, we started the tedious task of removing what we could without causing damage to the surrounding walls."

Ben continued. "Finally, after a couple of days, we had an opening large enough to walk through. We found an ancient Native American sanctuary with the most amazing drawings. The tunnels continued for miles underground and led to several different tunnels with additional rooms off those. The relics and artifacts we found, we preserved, so when all this ends, we can place them in a museum."

Ben glanced at Clint as Amanda continued, "The most amazing part is the drawings were a combination of Egyptian hieroglyphics and Native American symbols.

According to history books, Egyptians never came to this continent."

"When we thought we were done exploring the rooms, Clint found a lever built into the wall. After engaging the lever, there was movement on the far end of the room. The hidden door pulled away from the wall, exposing two more chambers off the newly created hallway." Ben's leg bounced up and down.

Clint chuckled. "And a lot of dust."

Ben smiled. "The room on the right appeared to be used primarily for burial preparation, but the room on the left had us in awe. These strange relics no one had ever seen in association with Native Americans or even Egyptians were said to have powers. They're housed in crystal cases. A parchment revealed four relics linked to bloodlines are to be used for God's service."

"What do you mean powers?" The question was out before she could stop herself. She couldn't take her eyes off him. How had she dreamed of him before this? It sounded like a book from where she worked. She pictured the author signing autographs, explaining the thoughts behind their ideas.

"We'll show you," he said, interrupting her thoughts. "But we have a problem. The relics are said to be linked to certain family lines. No one here could make this one relic work or even turn on. We brought several different people from a large network of underground communities to see if they could elicit a reaction from it. After several months passed, the sphere scanned through timelines on its own and stopped on you. The relic glowed. We weren't sure if it was the sphere being active or you on the other side of the timeline that activated the relic."

"Sphere?" What was wrong with these people? Were they crazy? She took short, quick gasps of air, unable to breathe. This was worse than she thought. She shut her eyes.

"Well, one of the relics—a small handheld sphere—lets you view and even travel to different timelines. The edges of the parchment show symbols for this dialect's alphabet. Running the symbols through a cryptogram program, we were able to translate the letters to the symbols and combinations in the text. Amanda was able to decipher the parchment about the prophecy. Each relic is unique to certain people and passed down through generations. We found a ring, some sort of weapon, a shield, and a healing stone. Only descendants from those families can operate them. It also said that God has Chosen Ones appointed to use and defend His people from total annihilation so they may spread His word and His love."

Ben nodded to Amanda.

"The prophecy states there are four Chosen Ones to carry out God's work. Three will be close, and the fourth will come from a different time and place. The fourth will be alone to be united with the other three before the prophecy's fulfilled," Amanda clarified.

"There are four distinct relics attuned to the four Chosen Ones, along with other relics to be used by any of the Chosen Ones." Ben's eyes met hers.

Amanda played with the cuffs on her sleeves, stretching them out of shape. "We didn't know how to activate the sphere. Then it turned on one day as Ben held it. The symbols on the sphere, as far as I can figure, are dates that we could use to change the time to the past by running our fingers across the symbols in different orders. It led us to believe we're only able to go back in time, not forward. Ben surmised this because the future hasn't been written yet."

"Anyway, every occasion the relic turned on, was when the sphere scanned by itself to your time. You were at home one day as I held the sphere. A wavering green light framed the display of you. When I touched the display, it transported me to your house." Ben diverted his eyes.

Wow, he was in her house? Who were these people? She held back a scream and took slow, deep breaths. She closed her eyes. She needed out of here! She pulled up on her wrists again, but the restraints didn't falter.

Ben studied his shoes and bounced his leg. "The sphere created a phased-out field on the other side to get back through. The parchment said it would only be distinctive to the person who went through. So, it was a way back as long as the sphere was with the person who went through. Since the day I was transported to you, the sphere never scanned to a different date than yours. No matter which one of us turned it on, you were all it would display. Amanda and Clint tried to go through, but it never let them, only me."

"The relics are in cases made from an amazing material which keeps them from activating when the Chosen One for a certain relic is near, at least until you open the lid. They don't do anything but glow so far, so we've been unable to figure anything out on how to make them work. We also figured out certain ones glow specifically for a certain person." Amanda smiled at Casey.

Ben wouldn't meet her gaze. "We agreed I would go again and find out as much about you as possible and find a descendant of your bloodline. But every time I came back with any information, we hit dead-ends with no link to you here. The last time I went through, I was supposed to gather a blood sample or another source to run a profile on you through the national database and find a relative to turn on the relic. A few hidden, large corporate allies help us. But you came back to the house, and I didn't know what to do. The moment you figured out I was in your house, I grabbed you and pulled you through to now."

"I dreamed about you for several days now," she confessed before she could stop herself.

"How's that possible?" Clint stepped into the room, leaving the doorframe to hold itself up.

"In every dream, you were always out of reach." She refused to admit how he made her emotions soar every time she dreamed about him. Maybe if she could convince them she believed them, she could sneak out from wherever "here" was, go home, and tell the police about these people and this place.

"Do you think the sphere linked us together?" Ben glanced at Amanda as she walked around the corner of the bed.

"Since we don't know how the relics work. Anything's possible. We're unsure what the sphere is capable of. Since you were the only one able to go to her, then maybe." Amanda sat on the edge of the bed.

Doc came in and ordered everyone out so he could check her vitals. "How are you feeling?"

"Fine." Casey looked toward the three huddled in the hallway.

"Any nausea, upset stomach, or aching muscles?" Doc listened to her lungs.

Casey shook her head. "No."

"Any headaches?" He took her pulse at her wrist while he observed the secondhand tick by on his watch.

"No."

"Well, your temp's normal, blood pressure's great, and you're getting your color back. I'm giving you a clean bill of health as soon as the final blood work is back to make sure the vaccines are working, then you're safe to leave the building."

"Okay."

Doc patted her leg and smiled. "You can come back in now."

She tried to smile back, but it was a lame attempt, and her smile disappeared as soon as her kidnapper walked back in. Everything she'd known and her instincts yelled at her to not believe what they told her. This must be a dream. Time travel didn't exist, much less something maybe even early tribes of Native Americans had used before Columbus.

"WE NEED TO SHOW HER the relics. I think she's having a hard time believing us." Ben put his back to the door and talked in hushed tones.

Clint balked. "No! Not after she tried to cut you!"

"She really tried to cut you?" Amanda rocked back on her heels.

"Think about how scared she is. Maybe if we include her, she'll open up to what we tell her." Ben didn't answer Amanda's question.

"Gee, I wonder why she's so scared, I would be too. Imagine if someone took me like this. Why did you take her, Ben? You don't keep things like this from us, not with how the world is. What are you hiding? I don't care if you are my brother, you can't keep this from us."

"Later. I'm going to show Casey the relics." Ben turned his back on the other two.

Amanda and Clint shared a look and furrowed their brows at Ben. They had never known him to be secretive about anything. "Did she really try to cut my brother?"

Clint nodded. "That's how she cut her hand. She used a lamp to break a window and grabbed one of the shards. We had a dose of sedative in her before she tried."

"Wait. She had a dose in her when she went after my brother?" Amanda glared.

"Yes," Clint stared at the back of Ben and shook his head. Ben's eyes were glued to Casey's sleeping form when he sat by her bed all night last night. This wouldn't end well. He had fallen for Casey.

Doc called them back into the room, Ben was the first one through the door, as the other two stood back and whispered quickly between themselves.

Ben smiled at Casey, "Hey, you up for a walk?"

"Maybe?"

"We want you to see something, and why I brought you here."

"Okay," Casey shrugged. She stared at the restraints. Clint joined them at her bed, but he wasn't sure he was ready for her to be free of them just yet. Would they be able to place them back on her if they needed to without hurting her? There would be a fight on their hands if it came to that.

Ben unfastened the restraint on her left wrist as Clint unfastened her right. She swung her legs over the side of the bed and stood. Her knees wobbled, threatening to buckle as he rushed around the bed. He wanted the two of them by her if she tried something. She closed her eyes and grabbed in front of her. Ben and Clint each grabbed a hand, but she tensed under their grasp and pulled back. Clint tightened his hold. He didn't trust her to not try to run.

She had put everyone in the warehouse in danger when she tried to get out yesterday. He nodded to Amanda, so she stood in the doorway. The color drained from her face as Clint got ready to catch her. He had seen that look just before someone passed out. Her grip on his hand tightened as she fought to stay upright and conscious. With a smile plastered on her ashen face, she opened her eyes wide, blew out a breath, then nodded. Clint gripped Casey's hand hard enough to remind her of his ability to immobilize her earlier. He hoped to deter her enough from trying anything as she glanced at him out of the corner of her eye. Along with her clammy, trembling hands, and her false smile, he wanted to get her home where she was safe from this world.

Eight

"Follow me, kids," Amanda joked as she led the parade out of the infirmary.

They took several twists and turns in hallways with more turns than Casey could remember. Would she find her way back? All the hallways were the same. Finally, they approached a door, and Amanda smiled a mischievous smile when they stopped.

"Ladies and gentlemen, would you like to see what's behind door number one?" Amanda gestured as if in a game show.

"Come on, Amanda, open the door. Always the dramatic one," Clint scolded.

Amanda's frown was so genuine Casey was unsure if it was real, but she had to tell herself she was in on this kidnapping or whatever this was. But what was between those two?

Ben glanced at Clint then to her. "Are you ready?"

"Um. I think so?"

Strange cases littered the lab tables. Crystalline boxes resembled small pirate treasure chests that cast prismatic rainbows on the walls as the fluorescent lights shone down on them. She half expected music and a disco ball to drop from the ceiling to announce she was at a weird time-warp disco.

"We've been unable to decipher all the markings yet, but one of the items is a weapon," Amanda stepped back as Casey took in her surroundings. The only door out of the room was the one they came through. That didn't give her a lot of options to make a run for it. She kept her eyes downcast as she surveyed the room while pretending to study the relics.

"One had a life of its own when the sphere displayed you, so we keep the case closed. It was enough to keep from switching on when we focused on you. Different ones react to different people." Ben opened the lid for a ring, the stoned glowed.

As Casey finally let her eyes come to rest on the crystalline boxes, she saw the most beautiful objects she had ever seen. Each box held a different item, including a bracelet made of silver with a large, opaque white stone in the middle, a ring with a yellow stone around the entire band, and a small sphere small enough to fit in the palm of your hand. The one that caught her eye was a large chunk of black rock, with a brilliant blue stone protruding from the middle as if someone had been in the process of chiseling it out, yet never finished.

A loud shriek erupted out of nowhere. Casey covered her ears with her hands as she doubled over, cringing from the pain in her head. Ben and Clint grabbed her elbows.

"What's wrong?" Ben and Clint asked almost in unison.

"Don't you hear that?" she screamed.

Clint squinted at Ben, who shrugged.

Out of the corner of her eye, the blue stone swirled and glowed as if churning water in a brook, and pierced through the closed crystal lid of the case. Was it pulsing?

"Look! It shouldn't be glowing in the case," Ben snapped at Amanda.

"Even with the sphere dialed into her time and the relic in the case, it's never done that."

Ben's eyes were glued to the stone. "How can it be glowing?"

"I don't know! Hold on."

"No, don't!" Ben yelled, but not before Amanda raised the lid, easing it back on the single brass hinge that ran across the back of the box.

High volume shrieks dropped Casey to her knees. How come it didn't affect them? A sharp pain shot through her brain. Her eardrums roared as the shriek got louder.

She yelled, "Turn it off!"

Clint put his hand on the small her back and knelt to check on her when it stopped. She opened her eyes and stood. They all looked at her, turned to each other, then back at her again.

Casey was happy that her ears stopped ringing, "What happened? You made it stop."

"We didn't do anything," Amanda raised her eyebrows to Clint.

She stepped forward countering, "But the buzzing stopped. Wow! It's beautiful."

"This is the one we think we've deciphered as The Healing Stone. Not sure how it works, though," Ben narrowed his eyes as he studied her.

The closer she got, the brighter the glow emanated from the rock. She bumped into Clint's arm as he threw it out in front of her to keep her from the relic.

She turned to him as he declared, "I don't think that's a good idea. We're not sure what'll happen, or if it'll do something to you."

"I agree. Until we can find a descendant to bring here and help with the testing, we shouldn't do anything that can put you in danger," Ben's hands clamped down on her shoulders as he stood behind her. He pulled back just enough to discourage her from venturing too close.

"There has to be a way to figure some things out without putting her in harm's way," Amanda interjected.

He was awful protective of someone he only kidnapped yesterday. Casey shrugged out of his grasp.

Ben let his hands slip off her shoulders. "Do you have any suggestions?"

"Maybe we can come up with one together," Clint stepped forward and peered into the case.

Amanda gawked at her brother. "We need to take her back to her time since we don't know the consequences of her staying in this one. Doc has her DNA and is running it again to see if the results are the same."

"What do you mean if the results are the same? What results?" What weren't they telling her? Why were they testing her DNA? Everything she knew screamed at her that this wasn't real. She wanted to go home, and the first chance she got, she would look for a way out of this building. Time travel, relics with powers. How could they imagine anyone falling for this? Was everyone here deranged where they all believe the same delusion? How could so many people be pulled into this madness? Did they all use drugs? How else could she explain it?

CLINT TOOK A FEW STEPS toward Ben, continuing the conversation only quieter. Casey took a single step toward the case when the stone shot into the air and hovered for a split second before a blue shaft of light raced at her heart. Her feet left the floor as it lifted her into the air. A blood-curdling scream of pain escaped as she arched her back.

Clint rushed forward and grabbed her leg, then yanked his hand back. He rubbed his hands together and exclaimed, "She shocked me!"

The beam surged into Casey as Amanda shielded her eyes and hid behind a table, peeking over the top. Casey fell, but Ben and Clint caught her before she hit the floor, almost taking them with her.

"Casey?"

Ben cradled her lifeless body in his arms. He knelt and set her on his bent leg as he patted her face trying to wake her.

"Take her to Doc!" Amanda whimpered.

Ben scooped Casey into his arms as Amanda gazed at the case. The blue stone no longer glowed. Amanda snatched the case off the table as Ben bolted for the door, sprinting down the hall. He glanced back at her before darting around the hallway to the right. They ran to the infirmary and told Doc what happened.

"Doc, what's going on?" Ben's voice broke.

Amanda edged around the corner, her hands hidden behind her back.

"Give me room to work, Ben," Doc urged. "Clint, take him outside."

"Come on, Ben. Let the Doc do his job," Clint pulled a reluctant Ben out of the room.

"How could you lift the lid of the case, Amanda?" Anger burned in Ben's narrowed eyes.

"I didn't know that would happen," Amanda muttered.

"Still, we don't know enough about these things to take any chances with her."

Clint squared his shoulders. "Ben, why did you bring her here? She wouldn't be at any risk if you left her where she belongs."

Ben spun around, turning his back on him. "I don't want to talk about it."

"Well, I think we deserve an answer because we can't take her home now!"

"I guess not."

"You guess not! You need to start talking, and I mean now!" Clint had never raised his voice to Ben as he did now. Amanda shrunk back out of the line of fire.

"Guys, I—I just had to bring her here."

"That's not good enough, nowhere *near* good enough a reason. I see how you look at her."

Ben's head snapped up. He glanced between his sister and his best friend. He turned his back to them again as he stared at Casey. He twisted around. They didn't say a word as they waited for him. "God told me to never let her go."

"God did what?" Clint stepped forward.

"I heard a voice. I knew it was God. He told me to never let her go. I grabbed her and brought her with me. Clint, she was so scared, and it was because of me! My heart broke for her." Ben glimpsed the box Amanda hid behind her back.

"Are you sure what you heard?" Clint eyed Amanda.

"Yeah, I'm sure. After I grabbed her, I almost let her go. I hated being the cause of that much fear, but God told me again not to let her go. I tried to talk to her first, but she was too scared to listen."

"Who are you to argue with God?" Amanda produced the case she had hidden behind her back.

"What are you doing?"

"Ben, look. I wanted to show you. It is—I guess—dead."

Sure enough, they all stared at the very ominous black rock that no longer showed any signs of life. The blue part of the stone was no longer blue, but also black. Ben glanced in at the bed where Casey lay unconscious. What did this mean?

Clint tugged at the belt loops on the side of his well-fit jeans, a nervous habit he'd done since high school, causing the lower edges of the loops to tear away from the waistband.

"Let's put it next to her," Clint's eyes never left Casey's bed.

"No!" Ben's frantic voice filled the hallway.

Amanda raised her eyebrows at him. "I think Clint's right. I think we need to try. We'll go slow and see what happens." Amanda opened the lid of the case.

Nothing. Ben silently prayed, *Father, if she's supposed to be here with us and I was supposed to bring her here, guide us in the direction you want us to go.*

Now in the doorway, Amanda shook her head no, the block of dead rock still appeared dead. Several more steps, and she was next to Casey. She extended her hands and sat the case on the bed. Her wide eyes matched those of Ben and Clint. "I'll take it back to the lab and lock everything up for the night." As she left, Ben saw her lock eyes with Clint but didn't glance at him.

Nine

"Hey, she's awake for now. Not sure how long it will last, though. Don't stay too long. She needs to sleep before any more of your adventures." Doc draped his stethoscope around his neck.

"Sure, Doc." Clint apparently volunteered to hold up the doorframe as he leaned his hulking shoulders against it.

"Hey, if it isn't the floating woman," Ben smiled as he walked to the bed. "You okay?"

"Yes. Tired."

"Well, Doc said to let you rest until tomorrow."

"Until tomorrow? What do you mean until tomorrow? NO! I want to go home now!" She fought to kick the blankets off.

"It's eight forty-five." Ben's eyes never left hers.

"No, no, you're lying!" She bit her tongue as she held back what else she wanted to say.

"You were out for several hours." Ben cleared his throat as he drew his eyebrows together.

"Why am I so tired? Are you drugging me to keep me here?" she spat out.

"No, not at all. We would never do that! We're not sure why you're tired, but you need to rest for tonight, and we'll check on you in the morning."

"No, I need to go home. I can't stay the night. My dog will be hungry and wondering why I'm not home yet." She attempted to sit up.

"Casey, we can't let you go home until we find out what the stone did to you." Ben's hand on her shoulder applied enough pressure that it stopped Casey.

"Did to me?"

"We think it transferred the healing power to you. It isn't glowing anymore. Please just give us a chance to see what happened. This could be dangerous. We want to study the parchment to see if it says anything about this."

"I don't care! You kidnapped me! What gives you the right to do this to someone? You can't take someone from their life!" She couldn't hold back her anger. She swung her legs over the side of the bed and shoved Ben's hand off her shoulder. She wavered from a head rush. Ben stepped forward as she yelled, "No, I'm going home! You can't keep me here!"

Ben tilted his chin down at Clint, who whispered around the corner. "Casey, we can't take you home yet. We don't know what the stone did, if you're okay, or if there are any lasting effects."

"Casey, calm down. I understand why you're so upset. Let us see what we can find out first." Clint stepped across from Ben to the other side of the bed. He stood, his jean-clad legs now shoulder-width apart. His worn black military boots were planted firmly in place. Arms crossed over his chest, his light gray t-shirt strained even more against the tensed muscles in his massive arms and chest. An officer who arrested a guy who lunged at him in front of her one day had that same stance. The officer subdued the man without breaking a sweat.

Maybe if she made enough noise and ruckus, they would realize she was not worth whatever they brought her here for.

"Casey, I'm sorry. We can't let you go home. Too much is at stake to take you home and lose this advantage the relic gives us." Ben took a single step toward her.

"And how did you come to this conclusion?" she spat out at him.

"Well, when you were unconscious, Amanda brought the case here. The stone was black. Clint suggested bringing it in the room to see if it'd turn back on. I was against it, but they convinced me they'd be careful. Let's say it didn't glow even when they set it on the bed next to you."

"How do we find out what it did?" She only thought of home and Mason.

"Amanda has a few ideas, but I'm not ready to try them yet."

"What ideas? I want to go home." She refused to admit the attraction toward Ben when she gazed into his eyes.

"Well, we believe that relic has healing powers. If one of us were injured, you could heal us to see if it transferred the powers to you. The downside is how to access the power. We don't want to take a chance it won't work."

Her eyes shimmered as blue flecks danced through her field of vision and filtered over her hazel irises. Warmth spread down her arm. "I wouldn't know how to try to heal someone. And if I did, would I be healing or hurting them.

I don't think that's a good idea." She swiped at her forehead, her hand glowing blue.

"Your hand is blue!" Ben stepped back.

She turned her hand over several times. "What's happening?"

Ben held his hand out to her. She shrunk back toward the edge of the bed as he continued to hold his hand out. Seconds later, she held her trembling hand out palm up. Ben nodded. He wrestled off the bandage Doc wrapped around her hand only hours ago. Layers of bandages later, he exposed the cut on her palm. Her skin stitched itself together in front of them, pushing the stitches through her skin until they lay in her palm.

Clint dropped his arms. He stepped back to the doorway and shook his head to whoever was down the hall.

"What was that?" She couldn't believe what happened. They would never let her go now.

"I would say that was the healing power of the stone you absorbed." Clint crossed his arms again as he blocked the doorway.

She swung her legs up on the bed, the stitches in her hand no longer held the wound closed. Ben grabbed her hand, ran his finger over the stitches as they fell away. She didn't pull her hand away but let him hold it.

"Casey, you need some sleep, but we'll get you in the morning and figure out what this means."

"Okay." Maybe she could let them think she would stay tonight.

"Don't worry, we're going to work on this, I promise." Ben placed the covers over her as she sunk into the pillows and closed her eyes. Long, slow breaths helped her relax. Would they think she had fallen asleep?

"Should we keep someone in here with her in case something happens?" How could he be so concerned? Doesn't he realize he kidnapped her?

"She should sleep through the night," Doc's voice sounded from somewhere outside the room.

Amanda muttered. "Should we give her a sedative?"

"I would prefer to not sedate her," Doc scolded.

She tensed at the mention of a sedative. She told herself to relax and hoped no one spotted her reaction. Casey forced herself into slow, methodical breaths.

"Well, she looks like she's out anyway. Let her sleep. We can go back and see if anything mentions what the stone did to her or how to reverse it." Clint's voice was no longer in the room. Casey resisted the urge to peek and kept her eyes closed.

Ten

"Ben, we've been through everything twice," Amanda countered.

"I don't care! We'll go through it as many times as it takes to figure out what it did to her, and if she's in danger!" Ben's long, determined steps led him away from the infirmary.

"Ben, take a breath, man." Calm as always, Clint tried to deescalate the situation.

Amanda quickly shuffled her feet. Her jeans swished as she walked. "You said you were told to bring her here. What if this is what was supposed to happen?"

"How can you say that?" Ben turned, glanced toward the infirmary, then spun back around.

"What is it?" Amanda stopped in the hallway, blocking their way to the lab.

"You didn't see what Clint and I saw, but I think you may be right. Let's look at that parchment again." He hooked his arm around Amanda's shoulders and pulled her along until she laughed.

Clint smiled, showing his perfect, straight, brilliant white teeth. They only made his dimples stand out even more. He reached around the back of the waistband, his hand glancing over the gun he never went anywhere without. Gun in place, he yanked down his gray t-shirt. Even though the gun was against his back, he had a habit of checking. He was the self-appointed protector, and he knew everyone trusted him with that task.

The parchment was rolled out on the table as Clint meandered into the room. His best friend and sister talked back and forth. It was almost normal if only the unconscious woman in the infirmary and the now-dead healing relic didn't mess that up. He tried to work out what he thought of her. He couldn't imagine someone taking him from home like that. He could see she struggled to understand what happened to her. He didn't like that she took a swipe at his friend, though. He would keep a close eye on her until he could decide if he could trust her with his friends' lives or not. His thick military boots thudded on the floor as he joined his friends.

"See? I told you. This right here," Amanda beamed at the discovery.

"What did you find out?" Clint squinted at the strange symbols on the page.

"She is the key. The one who releases the rest of the relics."

This didn't mean Clint trusted her. "So, you were supposed to bring her here. And with what we saw—"

"Yes, I guess so. I just wish she would have let me talk to her and explain everything. The way I did it was wrong." Ben sank down onto the stool.

Amanda stalked to Clint. "What did you see?"

"I say we check on her, then go to sleep, see what we can find in the morning. Maybe we can convince her we won't hurt her. You have to remember that Casey is going through a trauma. This isn't something she's going to be okay with anytime soon." Clint started for the door.

"I know that, but—Wait," She tugged on his arm, "what did you guys see?"

Clint crooked his arm around Amanda's neck, pulled her to him, and kissed the top her head. "She healed her hand. Now go to bed, you goof. We'll check on Casey."

"I knew it! See you in the morning." She saluted him.

With a smirk on his face, he turned to Ben. "You like her, don't you?"

"I don't know what you're talking about." Ben placed the relics in a file box and lumbered to the storage closet. A couple of seconds later, he reappeared and locked the door behind him.

Clint rocked back on his heels. "You forget, I've known you our whole lives."

"And you don't like her." Ben put his hands on his hips.

Clint shook his head. "No, I don't trust her yet—big difference. You know we have more than just us in the warehouse. We are also protecting the others who are hiding with us. I want us all to get out of this alive. I'm trying to keep everything in perspective and work on possible scenarios of what we could be dealing with."

Ben blew out a sigh and sauntered to the door. "Let's check on her. Tomorrow will be a mess, and I'm not sure how to start to fix this."

"Maybe if you didn't like her so much, you could think clearer."

Ben stopped and glared at him. Clint paused and shrugged his shoulders. He struggled with his emotions over

Casey. He would be ready when Ben wanted to talk. Clint had to jog to catch up before they got to the door to the infirmary.

Eleven

Darkness took over as she started to drift off to sleep, her fingernails dug into her palms as she struggled to keep herself awake. One of her nails cut into the soft tissue of her hand.

Waking with a start, she glanced around the room. No one was there, and the dark hallway gave her hope. Casey swung her legs over the side of the bed. They were steady when she put weight on them, unsure if she had any ill effects from the stone that she absorbed.

So far, so good. She bounced up and down a few times on the balls of her feet to make sure. Her clothes were neatly folded on the chair in the corner. The hospital scrubs they had her in, she shoved under the pillow. She tiptoed to the doorway as she perused the room for her shoes. Where were her shoes? What would they gain by taking them? She bent at the waist, lifted the edge of the blanket and peered under the bed, still no shoes.

They were in for a shock. She didn't need shoes to sneak out of a building and make her way to her house. Although not sure what she should do if she had no idea where she was. What about transportation? She prayed God would show her where to go and what to do and that she was close enough to walk if necessary.

With a quick peek around the door frame, her heart dropped at the darkness that grew darker, the longer she stared at it. No one was out there that she could see. Unsure which way led to a door leading outside, or if they had guards in the hallways or rooms, she almost scared herself out of trying. No, she needed out of this building and away from these people.

Several steps into the hall, she cocked her head to the side, listening for any sounds to alert her that someone waited in the dark for her to try to escape. The silence was deafening. She would need to be quiet because if everyone were asleep, it'd be a short trip if she woke them. She had no clue to the size of the building, and she hoped she wouldn't choose the wrong direction and travel the length of the building, diminishing her chances of escape.

She found a dimly lit stairwell after opening several doors. Now, which way? Go up or down? Not sure, she headed down a flight then paused outside the door. With the door open an inch, she pressed her ear up to it to figure out if she should chance it with this hallway. With the eerie darkness, she was astounded at the silence as she stepped into the barren, vacant hall. The door closed quietly behind her, with the only sound being the click of the latch. Several locked doors later, she tried the door by the lit emergency light halfway down the hall, her heart dropped as it was also locked.

The doors were spaced farther apart on this level. By the time she reached the fourth door and found it also locked, she regretted her decision to go down a flight. With only one door left to check, if locked, she would run back and try the floor above the one she started on. She twisted the knob with such force she almost fell into the room when the door opened.

As Casey stumbled through the doorway, her heart froze, then pounded in her chest. She was thrown into a vast wasteland of darkness save for the emergency exit light from the hall. From the looks of it, there didn't seem to be any windows. With the door held open by her foot wedged up against it, she let her eyes grow accustomed to the dark. Slowly they adjusted to the room's immense, empty space.

On the far wall, she could barely make out large overhead doors. Maybe this was the loading dock for the building. There must be a regular door somewhere. After several steps into the loading dock, she screamed as the door she'd just come out of slammed behind her with a thunderous crash that rattled the door frame and shook the walls.

Her hands flew to her mouth. *Did they hear her? Did they hear the door*? Her eyes adjusted to the suffocating darkness. She didn't move an inch but took deep breaths to slow her racing heart that hammered in her chest.

Much to her astonishment, no running feet came after her. As her eyes focused, she could make out the doors again. Once at the back wall, she found a walk-through door to the left of the overhead doors. Just as she thought, all loading docks usually had a pedestrian entrance. She extended her hand toward the push bar. As it glanced across the ice-cold steel, she snatched it back and clutched it to her chest. What if there was an alarm? Rooted in place, she gradually applied just enough pressure on the bar to disengage the latch and prayed, "Father, please don't let there be an alarm."

As no sound signaled the opening of the door, she pushed harder and, at long last, found herself outside. She gulped in a huge lung full of air, waiting for the relief of fresh air to hit her and cringed. The assault her on senses was horrific. Her hand flew to cover her mouth and nose as bile stirred in her stomach. The stale air had a putrid stench to it. Where was she?

"CLINT, THE DOOR'S OPEN!" Ben jogged to the room. The bed was empty, no Casey, no clothes in the chair. He spun to Clint, who closed his eyes and dropped his head forward.

"Okay, I'll grab a sedative from Doc, something different than before. I'll meet you back here." Clint bolted around the corner, his shoes thudding on the cold linoleum floor.

"Casey!" Ben hissed under his breath. He pinched his lips together. Here we go again. He rubbed the back of his neck then threw his hands in the air. He blinked, and his lips started to tremble. This world was not what she would expect. In a matter of minutes, she could be dead, and the stark realization of that rooted him to the floor unable to move. The blue scrubs sticking out from under the pillow only confirmed his apprehension that she would try and escape from the building.

Clint emerged around the corner as he shoved something in his inside jacket pocket. "Ben, you don't look good. What's wrong?"

"She doesn't know how dangerous it is out there!"

"I know, buddy. Let's find her before they do."

Clint and Ben took off at a jog. From this room, there was only one way they could think she would go to get out of the building. Ben's heart hammered in his chest at the thought of losing her. He hated himself for putting her through that kind of dread, but he couldn't tell his heavenly Father "no." God told him to take her with him. He had hesitated just before he lunged out of Casey's closet for her.

A thunderous bang alerted them that they at least headed in the right direction. That could only come from one door in the warehouse. They sprinted around the next corner.

Twelve

Casey glanced around to get her bearings. Besides a couple of streetlights, only dark, lifeless buildings were in her line of sight. She stared at the building she staggered out of. Dark, vacant windows stared down at her. How was that possible? She gawked at it; it was more intimidating outside than it was inside.

Approximately fifteen floors made the building larger than she thought. The urge to turn and run blindly in any direction weakened her knees. To keep herself from even more trouble than she was in, she studied her surroundings. She listened for cars, people—any sound to give her a hint of a direction to go. Maybe if she could find a road, she could flag down a ride to a police station.

She couldn't wait to go home and see Mason again. Hopefully, she wouldn't be far, and would never dream of Ben again, because after this she wasn't sure they would be good dreams where he saved her but instead hunted her.

The silence was deafening. Her heart started to fall as she spun on her heels in search of bright lights that would lead her to people. Could this area be as deserted as it appeared from the window earlier? There was no sound, no traffic, or even crickets, but a complete absence of noise.

Her bare feet were chilled from the unforgiving gravel in the parking lot, but she headed toward the lights in the distance. What kept her reeling and questioning everything was the fact she had been dreaming of Ben, and now he was a real person she met, talked to, and touched. How could her mind create someone, and they turn out to be real?

"Learn to trust him."

"What?" She twisted in several different directions but didn't see anyone.

"Learn to trust him."

"Who's there?" She shook as she scanned for who spoke to her.

Frozen in place for several agonizing minutes, she waited to hear it again and tried to clear Ben from her thoughts. Why would she think of him when someone said to trust him? She looked around, checking the area, but it was void of life. The voice was so quiet as if someone whispered it to her, yet that would make them close enough to touch her.

She wrapped her arms around herself as her nerves frayed. The industrial park was endless. She edged around the building and only found more buildings devoid of any architectural design or embellishments. They were here to serve a purpose, not for admiring.

Once around the edge of the building, voices from where she escaped reached her. Wait. Was it someone from inside messing with her? It sounded like...no wait! It was Ben! How'd they figure out she'd gotten out? Did they hear the door when it crashed into the door frame?

"Learn to trust him."

She stifled a cry behind her hand as tears filled her eyes. Who was doing this? Wait. Father? She searched the heavens. Could He be speaking to her?

"Learn to trust him."

This time it was in her heart. Tears spilled over on her cheeks. Who could He be talking about? No one was around. Was there someone she was supposed to trust? Was that what He was telling her—to trust the person He sent her no matter what?

Either way, she was never so close to her Heavenly Father than she was in that instant. Her eyes closed, and more tears spilled down her cheeks as she treasured the moment. She wanted to hear Him again. Knowing He was with her, guiding her through this, she knew He would never leave her nor forsake her. All she had to do was follow Him.

Quick steps took her to the back of the next building, putting further distance between her and Ben. She bumped into a dumpster with the lid open. It crashed down with such force it echoed into every depth of the industrial area. No! How could she be so stupid?

"Clint, this way!" Ben half-whispered. No one's around. Why was he whispering?

"Learn to trust him."

"Wait, Father, you want me to trust Ben?" Love from her Heavenly Father rushed over her. She sunk to her knees, unable to pull in air. "Father, I want to go home. I need to go home where I'm safe. Please, I can't let Ben in. He kidnapped me, and I can't trust him! My heart isn't safe with him. Yes, I wanted to share my life with someone, but now that You're telling me who that someone is, I'm scared. I can't do this. I'm not strong enough for this!" She crouched behind the dumpster and held her breath as Ben and Clint jogged past, the gravel crunched under their shoes.

CLINT STOPPED. "IT came from this direction."

"If they catch her, they'll kill her!" Ben's whisper raised an octave.

"She can't explain what she's doing here. If she tries, they won't hesitate to execute her."

"Not before they torture her to find out what she knows. We'll all be in danger!" Ben hissed.

Ben turned as Casey crept out from behind the dumpsters that they'd just ran past. He grabbed Clint by the arm and pointed to Casey's small figure darting around the side of the warehouse. They jogged in her direction as Clint pulled a gun from his waistband. Ben hid at the corner and peered around the building then pulled his head back. He nodded to Clint, mouthed *car,* and backed up enough for him to squeeze between him and the corner of the building.

Clint peered around the edge as Casey stepped backed to their location. A Monarch's car loomed ahead of her. The gun turret mounted on the top was armed by someone dressed in all black. This had one of two ways of going down, bad or *really* bad. Clint switched places with Ben. They had to time it right, or Casey's scream would alert the Monarchs. They would run from the safety of the warehouse to lead them away from everyone else who lived there, including his sister. More than likely, out of Ben and Clint, one or both would be killed.

Ben closed his eyes as Clint put a hand on his shoulder. Gun in hand, Clint nodded to Ben as Casey's small frame came into view. Ben's feet crunched on the gravel when he lunged forward and grabbed one of her wrists, wrapping it around her waist as the other stifled her scream under his hand that he clamped down over her mouth. A quick yank and they were on the side of the warehouse hidden from view of the Monarchs. Casey started to kick when Ben whispered, "Quiet, or they'll kill us all!"

He picked her up by the waist as his hand kept her mouth covered from alerting the Monarchs. Clint opened the warehouse door and motioned them in. Clint slipped the lock in place and yanked a large injector from his inside jacket pocket. Casey's eyes widened.

Thirteen

Ben's hot breath in her ear as he carried her back to the warehouse sent an onslaught of goosebumps along her skin. He never loosened his grasp on her mouth, and she was too scared from his comment to make a noise. She clamped her hands on each of his wrists. Her fingers turned white as she held on. Her eyes were wide after seeing the car the way it was decked out with weapons she'd only read about.

Clint made it to the warehouse door first and opened it for Ben. Clint bolted it from inside and glared at her as she squeezed her eyes shut. Sure, it would be the last time she went outside, her heart raced as she gasped for air.

"Shh, it will be okay, but we have to be quiet, or the Monarchs will hear us. Everyone in the warehouse could be killed. Do you understand?" Ben loosened his grip slightly.

She nodded. Ben let go of her mouth but kept his arm around her waist. "Please, let me go."

"We still need to figure out what the stone did so we know how to fix it. Give us some time."

"How long are we talking about?"

Ben released her, and she turned to him. Her heart hammered in her chest when she thought about what God told her. Clint joined Ben. "I honestly don't know, but Amanda's going over the prophecy again."

The engine of the car outside caught their attention as it rumbled past, gravel crunching under the tires. A piece of gravel shot out and hit the side of the roll-up door. She leaped back and jostled into Ben and Clint.

"Watch out!" Clint's gruff voice cautioned as she felt his hand push against her back, milliseconds before she felt a prick in her shoulder as she continued back from the momentum. She turned around, wide-eyed her hand slowly felt over her shoulder.

"I'm sorry." Clint stood dumbfounded. "You backed into the injector."

Pain shot through in her chest. Her lungs burned, and she screamed. Clint threw the injector, and his face drained of color. Ben grabbed Casey and twisted her to him.

"Casey!" Ben sounded far away.

"Ben lay her down!" Clint grabbed her legs to lay her on the cold, rigid concrete floor.

"Casey! Breathe!"

"Ben, what's happening?" Clint uttered as he stepped back.

Ben lowered his head. "Dear Heavenly Father, please help her. Father, You told me to bring her here and to trust her with my heart. Please, Father, please save her!"

Trust her? Wait. God told him to bring her here? She thought God told her to trust Ben. Her eyes closed as the pain knotted in her chest. "Father, please take me home."

Blue light flooded her vision. It was beautiful, almost a royal blue but with flecks of free-floating diamonds. Everything sparkled. It warmed her, and she was no longer on the cold floor. It was as if the concrete was gone, and she floated on a cloud above the pain.

"Ben?" Clint gasped.

"I see it. It's like her hand, but all over."

The ash color in her skin faded away as blue radiated down her arms and legs, engulfing her entire body, which now glowed a radiant pink.

"Clint, she's warm."

Ben's hand caressed her cheek. She didn't resist.

"Ben, we need to get her to Doc." Clint didn't move to pick her up.

Ben gingerly placed one arm under her knees and the other under her shoulders as he pulled her into his arms, the wool of his navy-blue sweater scratched her face, but she didn't mind.

"Ben, is this the healing stone in her?" Clint jogged to catch up.

"I don't know, but she's beautiful. She looks almost angelic!"

"*Trust him.*"

She mumbled, "I can't, Father."

"What, Casey?" Ben glanced at Clint, who shrugged.

Did she say that out loud? There was peace in the light. All her worries were gone, and everything would be okay. This was where she was meant to be.

"What happened?" Amanda's voice climbed several octaves as she caught up to them after they passed her in the hall.

"We caught her before they did, but it was close, then she backed into the injector. In the meantime, we need to be careful for the next few days and cancel the food run. They were parked outside our building," Clint barked.

"Got it. I'll run over and tell them so we can ration the food supply." Amanda's shoes echoed in the hall.

"What happened now?" Doc's face tightened as he ambled after them.

"The sedative you gave Clint. She grabbed at her chest and collapsed. This blue light spread from her shoulder where she backed into the injector." Her head sunk into the pillow on the hard mattress Ben lowered her on.

"Blue light? All I see is a young lady I told you guys to take care of," Doc berated Ben.

"Doc the blue light's all around her," Clint straightened into his military stance as he reached around his back.

"Clint, what blue light? Are you two all right?" The stethoscope was cold through her shirt as Doc listened to her heart and lungs. "What I gave you wouldn't do this to her or drop her heart rate like this."

She didn't interrupt. She wanted to stay in this blue aura and enjoy the peace that washed over every inch of her and swelled in her heart. The only explanation was this was from God.

Fourteen

"Doc, I'm sorry, but she's enveloped in blue light. You can't tell me you can't see it. Clint and I both do." Ben stalked to the doorway Clint towered in. He turned on his heels and stalked back to the bed. The pain in her face haunted him. Would he ever be to a point where he didn't scare her? Unsure of God's plans for her, he hoped in his heart this wouldn't be all God had for them.

"Well, Ben, I'm sorry, but all I see is her—no blue light, but someone in bad shape."

"How bad?"

"Her heart rate's twenty-seven beats per minute, and her breathing barely registers."

Ben paced back and forth across the open doorway. "Is she going to be okay?"

"I'm sorry. I need some time with her. Please wait outside." Doc limped around to the other side of the bed.

"Doc, don't leave me in the dark. Is she going to be okay?"

"Give me a couple of minutes, okay?" Doc waved his hand at him.

"Why can't Doc see her glowing?" Ben whirled to Clint.

"Not sure, but I think Amanda saw it. We'll ask her when she's back."

Ben turned back to the room. "Did you look at her face?"

"You don't need to remind me. I saw the pain and agony after she backed into the injector I should have put away. I'll never forget the fact I caused it, and it may kill her."

"No, Clint. After, when the blue light surrounded her. I've never seen anyone with such contentment and peace on their face. She was beautiful, and she isn't going to die. She can't!"

Clint raised an eyebrow. "You think she looks beautiful, anyway."

"This time, she was angelic." Ben glanced at Clint, "I mean—"

"Too late. You're attracted to her. Why wouldn't you tell me?"

"No, I'm not. What are you talking about?" Ben huffed. "So, Doc can't see the blue aura she's bathed in."

"Okay, guys. Everything's canceled, and we're good on the food stored, so no worries there." Amanda jogged to the guys. At least a foot shorter than they were, her pink hoodie stood out in contrast to their muted earth-toned clothes.

"Hey, good to hear. Amanda question for you." Clint leaned a shoulder against the wall opposite the doorway.

"Shoot. What is it?"

"What did you see when we brought Casey to Doc?"

"Well, gee, I would say the fact Ben carried her, and she didn't walk in on her own. What else? Well, besides a brilliant blue, sparkly light surrounding her, nothing at all. Why do you ask?"

Clint shoved her arm. "Okay, ornery. Doc doesn't see it."

"What do you mean? How can he not?" Amanda peered around the doorway at Casey, her eyes closed and bathed in the blue aura.

"Ben, you thinking what I'm thinking?" Clint gave a single swift nod.

"Only the Chosen Ones can see it?" they said in unison.

"Bingo. Since a relic reacts to each of us, maybe it makes us in tune with what happens to her when the healing stone activates."

Doc stepped into the hall, interrupting the conversation. "Okay, you can see her. Her vitals are back to normal, but she must be allergic to what I gave you. Her heart almost stopped, and her lungs should've seized up. She shouldn't be awake, much less alive. You can thank God for that."

"Ben, did you want a minute alone with her?" Clint arched his left brow.

"No, let's check on her, then I'm going to bed. The sun will be up soon." Ben stepped around Clint. "Hey, how are you?"

Casey shrunk away from Ben, "I'm okay. What did you guys do to me?"

"We're sorry, there was a reaction. When you backed into the injection apparatus, the sedative injected into your skin. There's a quick-release on that, so if you press against someone, it automatically injects them, so you don't have to pull the trigger." Clint studied the ground.

"Would those guys in the car really kill me?"

Clint's head snapped up as he locked eyes with Casey. "Yes, without a moment's hesitation."

"The stone!" Casey exclaimed as her eyes popped open.

"Yeah, we think so, too." Ben started to reach for her hand but stopped when she flinched. "Get some sleep."

They stood in the hall as Clint locked the door but not before he snatched a chair out of the room and positioned it across from the secured door. Ben knew Casey didn't stand a chance of getting past him and alerting the Monarchs.

The other two didn't say a word, but Amanda tugged on her brother's arm to coax him away from the room. Clint would keep watch tonight, and there would be no arguing with him. His hand skimmed the butt of the gun just under the back of his shirt. Ben watched him wrench it out of his waistband, check the chamber and clip, and return it tucking it away and hiding it from sight. Clint settled in for the night. Ben had heard stories from Clint how he had stayed up on watch more times than he could count when he was deployed on missions.

Fifteen

The next morning, Ben walked Casey to the lab, where Amanda huddled over the parchment. It was the morning after her failed escape attempt, and she was still groggy. The only thing on her mind was home, all her family and friends, and, of course, her dog. The sound of running feet stopped them. She glanced around but didn't see Clint.

"He declared martial law!" a kid yelled as he slid to a stop in the doorway, out of breath.

"What?" Ben slammed his fist against the black-coated top to the table. "The broadcast we got out must have put him in a panic."

"Curfew's at six and anyone caught out after that will be shot on sight as a traitor and terrorist." The kid gasped as if a goldfish at the top of water gulping air.

"He can't think people will put up with this," Ben huffed.

"Let's make sure we stay here, no one outside the building at all," Clint grunted from the doorway.

"I need to finish warning the rest of the group," yelled the young kid as he raced away.

"Sure, thanks, Marcus," all three answered.

"Ben, are we going to be safe here?" Amanda's voice broke.

"You bet, sis. We'll be fine. God's on our side."

"Sis?" Casey glanced between the two.

"Yep, he's my *big* brother." Amanda regarded her brother in awe as only a little sister could.

"Nice, rub it in that you're younger than me, but only by three years." Ben smiled at her.

"Still makes you older. Clint is Ben's age, and since we grew up together, it was like having two older brothers looking out for me."

"Yeah, and with the trouble you got yourself in, you needed two brothers to handle it." That explained the brotherly protectiveness from Clint that she mistook for something else earlier.

"How bad is it going to be around here?" They already live in abandoned warehouses. She tried to slow her breathing.

"We should be okay for now, but we need to figure out what happened with the crystal, what it did to you, and why we can't find any of your family's descendants to operate the relics." With concern etched on Ben's face, she saw that these relics were their answer to prayer.

"Does it say anything on the parchment about ways to reverse it?" she whispered.

"No. Amanda was up all night but was unable to find any references to it."

"Excuse me, Clint. You got a moment?" A young girl who didn't look old enough to be out of high school, clutched several pages in a white-knuckled grip as she hid behind the wall to the lab. She darted a quick, worried glance at Casey, then hung her head then darted out of sight.

"Sure, Chloe. What'd you find? Come on in. It's okay."

"Are you sure? I think I need to speak to you out here." She motioned with her head to the hallway.

"Okay. Ben, do you want to join us?" Clint turned to Ben, avoiding eye contact with Casey.

"Yeah, I'll be right back." Ben sauntered out.

Sixteen

"Well?" Ben put his hands on his hips and glanced toward the lab they had walked a few steps away from.

"Something changed when you brought her here." The crinkled pages rustled, and her hands shook when she handed them to Clint.

Clint perused the pages, flipped through them again, and stared at Chloe. "This can't be right."

"This wasn't there the last time my uncle searched for her." Red flashed through her cheeks.

"Wait, what changed?" Ben tried to snatch the pages out of Clint's hand. Clint was too fast, and Ben swiped at air.

"This isn't good. We have to take her back." Clint narrowed his eyes at Ben.

"Would you give me those?" Frantic, Ben grabbed the pages and flipped through them as a couple floated to the floor. "No, no, this isn't right."

"My uncle said this appeared yesterday when you had me call him to check again on what he could find. He would've never missed something this big when he ran her the first time." Chloe chewed on her fingernail and paced back and forth. The soles of her green tennis shoes squeaked on the yellowing, worn linoleum with each turn, and her too-long jeans swished across the floor. She tugged on the sleeves on her olive-green sweater that was several sizes too large.

"No, this didn't happen. This is wrong. How could this change?"

"You changed this by bringing her here! Thanks, Chloe. We'll take it from here. Tell your uncle, thanks. We owe him yet again." Clint smiled as he dismissed her.

"Do you really think—"

"No, I *know* that's why this happened! How do we explain this to her? This will crush her." Clint waved the pages he picked up off the floor at Ben. He read them again, shook his head.

Ben knew when she found out she'd fight them to go back. "But we can't take her back."

"How do we know we can't? She doesn't belong here. How could you, Ben? We all agreed you would gather information and bring that back, not her! That wasn't the mission!"

"Mission? This isn't a military operation!" Ben hissed.

"You know what I meant. Ben, look at what you did! Your feelings for her are clouding your judgment." Clint lowered his voice to a whisper as he glanced toward the lab.

"What do we do?" Ben told himself to relax and released the pent up air in his lungs slowly.

"We take her back where she belongs. Let's grab lunch, and we can tell Amanda on the way." Clint snatched the papers out of Ben's shaking hands.

"We can't. She has the healing stone in her."

"We find a way to extract it from her and take her back, but this can't be on your head." Clint waved the pages at Ben.

"What if she's supposed to be with us."

"Stop it! Do you want her to deal with this for the rest of her life? That you bringing her here is the cause of this?"

"Clint, she's the key."

"Only because you want her to be. We need to send her back after we figure a way to put the healing power back in the stone." Clint stormed off, the pages crinkling as he clenched his fists.

Seventeen

"You'll be fine here if we can't take you back." Amanda eyed Clint as he walked into the room. He shook his head, then diverted his eyes when Casey glanced at him.

"I'm sorry, but I want to go home."

Ben wouldn't look at her, and Clint didn't lift his head as he walked around the tables.

"What happened?" Amanda's concern set Casey on edge.

"Later," Ben whispered. "Did you guys find anything?"

Casey rubbed her hands up and down her arms. "What's going on?"

"Nothing. Just things about the martial law." Ben wouldn't make eye contact but shuffled over to Amanda and talked animatedly to her in hurried whispers.

Her heart fell. Something upset them, and it wasn't about martial law. They didn't want to share it with her. She understood she was an outsider, and they had so much going on here. There was no way she could fathom what they went through daily. Now, with the announcement of martial law, stress levels were through the roof. She let it drop and joined them around the parchment. She would never forget them, but with time they would become just a memory of a strange time in her past. With a tight chest at the thought for her family, there was a small part of her that didn't want to leave Ben. He had grown on her. She couldn't imagine never seeing him again.

"All it says is a Chosen One will possess the power of healing once released from the crystal, and the four will be united." Amanda's finger skimmed the symbols as she read.

A shrill of sirens outside the building made her jump. "This state is now in martial law. Anyone found outside the designated living areas will be detained and questioned. Anyone found out after the curfew of six o'clock will be shot on sight as an aggressor of terrorism. No warning will be given. If anyone wishes to surrender now, we'll be lenient and escort you to a detention center to be questioned before we move you to a designated living area of your choosing."

The message repeated. The heavy droll of the large diesel engine penetrated the walls of the warehouse. As the message started to fade, they all breathed again. Maybe she needed to go home. After all, she wasn't supposed to be here. In twenty forty-eight, she would be in her seventies or with her Heavenly Father. Wait, did she just suggest to herself the time travel story?

Clint broke the silence. "Okay, I say we need a lunch break. Who's buying?"

"You are since you brought it up," Amanda joked.

"Oh, I am, am I?" Clint tugged Amanda's hair.

"Yep, and I'm getting a double helping." Amanda laughed as she swatted his hand.

They headed toward the lunch area, again taking several turns losing her and any possibility she would be able to find her way back to the lab.

Their makeshift cafeteria was smaller than the one at her church. Electric stoves from several different manufacturers lined one wall with refrigerators in the same range of manufacturers on the adjoining wall. Folding tables were set as counters with a wide array of food on them, and by the smell of it, good home-cooked food.

Behind Amanda in line, Casey grabbed a plate then followed her. A ham and cheese sandwich, potato salad, and baked beans soon filled her plate. She trailed behind Amanda to a table in the back of the room. Ben and Clint followed shortly after. They ate in silence during most of the meal. The tension was enough to make her want to scream and ask what they talked about with the young girl.

"So, what's your brother's name?" Amanda's question caused Ben to drop his fork, and Clint stared at her, his mouth gaping.

"Matt. Amanda asked about him while you two were in the hall outside the lab." Casey studied them, lips slightly parted, unsure why they reacted that way at the mention of her brother.

"Oh." Ben snatched her plate as she finished the last bite, then held the plate for her to put her fork on it. Clint grabbed his and Amanda's as they headed to the dishwashing area. Amanda shrugged her shoulders and shoved her chair away from the table.

Clint caught up to Casey, while Amanda fell behind to walk with Ben just out of earshot.

"So, younger or older brother." Clint startled her. The fact that he probably didn't even like her threw her off because he was making small talk.

"Matt's younger by eleven months."

"Wow, close in age."

"When we were young, a lot of people thought we were twins." Casey glanced behind her.

"I wasn't lucky enough to have siblings, but with Ben and Amanda, it was like they were my brother and sister."

"It's good you had them." Ben and Amanda lagged even further behind. Maybe they were talking about the announcement over the loudspeaker, and he was making sure she didn't go outside and put herself in danger. Didn't she say she got herself in trouble a lot?

"What about your parents?" The question pulled her back to her conversation with Clint.

"My dad's William and my mom was Maddie."

"Was?" Clint locked eyes with her.

"She died in a car accident when I was in high school. Driving home after Bible study, a drunk driver crossed a double yellow line and hit her head-on, killing her instantly."

"I'm so sorry."

"Thanks, but I'll see her when I get to heaven. I said goodbye a long time ago."

"I understand, but it still had to be hard to lose your mom at such a young age."

"Thanks. I guess my brother took it harder than I did. He rebelled for about a semester before Dad took him to a counselor from the church. Matt got back on track with his life and has been ever since."

Amanda and Ben caught up at the door of the lab. Amanda stalked in first.

"We need to talk," Amanda said so quietly—just above a whisper—then lowered her eyes.

"What about?" Something was wrong.

Eighteen

"We need to talk to you about something we found out today." Ben edged closer to Casey.

"Guys, could this jeopardize our time?" Clint shook his head at Ben.

"We need to tell her, especially if Amanda's right about the prophecy." Ben and Amanda pulled chairs into a circle.

"First, let me start by saying I agree with Amanda and her take on the prophecy. You're the one sent to us from another time and place." Ben stalled.

"We recruited Chloe to do a little research when you were first in the sphere, and the crystal glowed. When we found that I could go through and be in the same time you were, I found out who you were, and we tracked your family to find a descendant who might be able to make the healing crystal work." Ben recited the information, and sadness filled his eyes. Ben cleared his throat. "I ran into you at your house and decided to grab you. Clint didn't agree with my judgment call and thought we needed to take you back, immediately."

Amanda continued. "I deciphered the text as the Chosen One from a different moment and place, and when you were here, and the crystal did what it did, I took another look at the text. It says someone from a different time, not moment. I told Ben my suspicions, but he didn't agree. I didn't know he started believing me until his meeting with Clint and Chloe today."

"Our meeting with Chloe was the outcome of her research into your family descendants, so to speak." Ben wrung his hands.

Casey blurted. "Okay, you guys are scaring me. What happened today?"

"To be correct, what happened thirty-five years ago," Ben murmured.

"What are you trying to tell me?"

"When you disappeared thirty-five years ago, two days ago for you. Your neighbor called your brother to tell him your car was in the driveway with the garage open. Matt came over and saw your car and the door open to your house. Your keys were on the floor of your bedroom. Mason hadn't been fed, so he called the police, which was how we were able to find such details of the days after you disappeared. They listed you as 'missing under suspicious circumstances.' After a week, they scheduled a vigil at your house. They had the news stations standing by to do a live feed on the evening news for any tips on your whereabouts. Something happened when Matt got to your house. Police filed it as an accident and didn't find any foul play, but there was a gas explosion. Your brother and his family died." Ben blurted.

"No, you're wrong. Matt's fine, and so are his kids." Casey stood as tears started a slow trek down her face. She gritted her teeth as she swiped at them.

Ben reached for her. She slapped his hands away. "A police report stated nothing was left of the house. They said it was faulty gas pipes to the water heater."

"My dad's all alone. Send me back. He needs me." Casey stepped back. Tears blurred her vision. She spun around. "If I go back now, I can stop my brother from ever needing to go to my house, and they'll be all right. I need to go back now! How do I turn on the sphere?" She started toward the lab table where the sphere lay dormant and nodded her head.

"You can't go back yet. We don't know what it'd do with everything that's happened since you got here." Ben stepped in front of her.

"Since I got here? Don't you mean since you kidnapped me?"

Ben stepped back half a step. Was she really this angry with him? Ben's face fell, and his shoulders dropped as a vein pulsed on the side of her neck.

Ben shook his head. "Casey, we can't let you go back. Chloe said there are no descendants to operate the healing relic, and since the power was transferred into you, we need to investigate whether we can transfer it back into the crystal."

"How are we supposed to do that when I don't know how to access the powers? You need to fix this. This is all because I'm missing, if I go back, there may be descendants to operate the relic, or maybe I can find a way to pass this through the family member who's supposed to be here."

Ben raised his voice. "Casey, it says the person from another time and place."

"Ben, stop. Please. I have to be there for Dad. He doesn't have anyone but his kids."

"When your brother and his family died, your father didn't take the news well and lived in seclusion for several years before a heart attack hit, and he didn't recover." Ben's voice was flat. "He was gone within a few hours."

"Stop, okay? Stop!" Casey covered her ears with her hands and searched for a way out of the room. She was like a ticking time bomb, and the smallest thing could push her over the edge. "I need to lie down. I want to go lie down."

Ben started to follow her out of the lab. She spun around and held out her hand as she yelled, "No, you leave me alone! You've done enough!"

CLINT CLENCHED HIS jaw. He hated that she wounded his friend with her words. He couldn't blame her but the fact that she had just dealt such a vicious blow to his best friend, he stepped forward as she turned to him. With a motion of his hand, he pointed her in the right direction toward the women's sleeping quarters. Not able to figure out which way to go, she stalled in the hallway when he motioned for her again which direction to go. It didn't help tears blurred her vision. Any hesitation, and he directed her again. Her cries of anguish filled the air before she closed the door behind her. He started to reach out as the latch secured the door.

Sobs broke and bounced off the cold, unforgiving concrete walls and reached Clint, who slid down the wall outside her room and took up watch over her. His heart broke for her, and her wailing ripped at him.

The wall made a great support for Clint as he leaned back and crossed his arms. He was ready for a fight. Fighting he could handle, but somehow this was worse. She broke. He would never have predicted that, or for the urge to protect her that roared through him in a wave of heat. Something tugged at his heart, and in that instant, he knew he couldn't let her go back. Energy pulsed from the room. With it came an overwhelming urge to fight for their Heavenly Father. She was their hope in turning this war around. Another pulse surged from her room.

Ben lurked at the corner. Clint didn't look up, ignoring his friend. Amanda crept around the corner and joined Clint, with a smirk on her face she leaned back, crossed her arms and mimicked Clint's posture.

"Really? I think you need to grow about a foot before you come close to being as cool as me."

Ben smiled as he joined them. Nervous energy filled the hall as they stared at the door. Behind it was someone Clint knew Ben had started to develop feelings for.

"How is she?" Ben gazed straight ahead.

"This broke her. She finally stopped crying, or at least it doesn't penetrate the door anymore. She's dealt with a lot in the last couple of days. It was enough to break anyone." He frowned as he tilted his head to listen.

Amanda glanced at her brother. "What do we do?"

"We take her back," Ben finally admitted.

Clint leaned his head back against the wall and closed his eyes for a split second. "We can't."

Ben's head snapped to Clint, "Wait, what?"

"She's the key." Clint tilted his head to the side.

"But you said we had to take her back!"

"She's the key. Can't you feel it?" Clint raised from the floor in one fluid motion, sauntered to the door, closed his eyes, and placed his strong hand on the gray, cold industrial metal door.

"So, we don't take her back?"

"Ben, you sound like you're excited to keep a puppy." Amanda laughed.

"No, I don't!" He snapped.

Three simple steps took Amanda to Clint's side. "She can't go back."

"What's gotten into you two?"

"You feel it don't you, Amanda?" Clint peeked down at her.

"Is that her?" Amanda closed her eyes as another energy pulse surged through them.

"Okay, what are you two doing? This is ridiculous. What am I supposed to touch the door, too?"

"No, you don't need convincing to accept she's the key." Clint turned from the door as a smile played at the corners of his mouth.

"You know, don't you? God told me to bring her here."

"Yes. Go get some sleep. I'm staying here. I'll keep an eye on her and keep her safe," Clint murmured.

Amanda nodded and shuffled toward her room. Ben lingered. Clint wasn't sure Casey'd be able to forgive Ben for what he did, bringing her here as her family suffered like they were about to. Would he be able to forgive someone if they did that to him? All he could do was pray for the forgiveness he wanted for his friend. They stood there for another hour before Ben finally sauntered off toward his room without a word.

Clint walked to the door and placed his hand on it again. He took the key out of his pocket and unlocked the door and saw Casey lying curled in a heap on the floor between the bed and the wall. He quietly slipped in and took off her shoes, set them next to the bed without making a sound. He lifted her into his strong arms and placed her on the bed, covering her with the blanket from the end of the bed. She stirred, and he almost tripped over a chair as he tried to back out of the room before she woke.

With the door locked, he slid down the wall across from her room. He spun the key on the floor in circles for hours. How would they tell her they couldn't send her home? How would she react? He would fight with everything he had to go home if it was him.

"Protect her."

"I will, Father."

Nineteen

Several hours later, Casey woke to a pitch-black room. For a split second, she imagined it was just a dream. Her hand skimmed the top of the nightstand for a light to find she was still in her concrete tomb. Someone had come in, taken off her shoes, put her in bed, and covered her with a blanket. She never heard them.

Dried tears pulled at the skin around her eyes. She cringed as the puffy, sensitive skin yelled at her when she rubbed them. Not sure how late it was, she turned the door handle as quiet as possible. Her skin tingled, and her heart raced. The door was unlocked. She squinted at the brightness of the hall lights, unable to open her eyes all the way as she held her hand up to shield her eyes from the intensity. Ben loomed in the hall with Clint and Amanda.

"You okay?" Ben asked as they all turned.

"No," she croaked in a raspy, rough voice. She cleared her throat. "I need you to send me home to fix this."

"We've been praying for what to do, and we don't think we're supposed to send you back." Ben hung his head. "We think this is what's supposed to happen, and this is God's plan."

"God's plan is for me to lose my entire family? To be here in a time where, if I came this far like a normal person, I'd be in my seventies?" Casey glared at them as she clenched her fist, ready for a fight.

"We think you're the one in the prophecy." Amanda eyed her fists, then inched around behind Clint as he wrapped his arm behind him to shield her.

"No, No, No. How's this possible?"

"Casey, we're sorry, but it's too dangerous to send you back without knowing what you can or can't do." Clint's muscles tensed under his shirt, and they pushed at the fabric, stretching it further.

She marched off toward the lab, hoping she took the correct turns and hallways. She stunned herself when she turned the corner and the lab was in front of her. The other three were behind her. She searched for the sphere. "Where is it?"

"Casey, we can't let you go back. We moved it." Ben placed his hands on her shoulders.

She shrugged free from his grip. "You can't expect me to let my family die."

"I'm so sorry. Please believe me. I didn't know this would happen."

With swift steps to the side, he stepped in her way as she tried to go around him. She clenched her fist and stepped around to the other side, where he again stepped in her way. Casey shoved Ben in the chest. He didn't budge but instead wrapped his arms around her in a bear hug. Sobs racked her body as her legs turn to jelly, and she sank into his embrace as the emotions and torment from the last couple of days weighed on her.

"Shh," Ben whispered in her ear. "Maybe I can go with her to warn her family, and we both can come back until we figure this out."

Tears streaked her red, blotchy face. "I'll come back and stay as long as you want. Just don't let my family die. I'll leave them forever if it means they live."

She turned to Clint and Amanda. "We can give it a try, can't we?"

"I don't see why not. Amanda, go ahead and get it. Ben, you can't let her out of your sight. Casey, you must be quick. Make them understand you're okay, and you can't tell them now, but you will one day." Clint was in mission mode.

A quick nod of her head told him yes. She could stop this and save her family. For the first time in days, she had hope.

A loud explosion shook the building, and objects on the tables bounced around. All the lights went out. Ben pulled Casey into a crouching position while he hovered over her in the doorway, his arm a vice grip around her waist.

"Amanda!" Clint raced down the hall, his hand skimming the wall for direction in the dark.

Ben grabbed Casey's hand and pulled her along with him.

A FLASHLIGHT BEAM ILLUMINATED the room at the far end of the dark hallway. Amanda tossed more flashlights on the bed, where they bounced a couple of times before coming to rest. Ben and Clint kept Casey between them as they made their way to Amanda's room. A flashlight set on its end served to brighten the room from its position on the nightstand. Amanda pulled open the second drawer in her armoire that held the sphere. Ben took it from her, his brow furrowed, and his eyes narrowed.

"This should've turned on by now." Ben turned the sphere over from one hand to the next, and the hairs stood on the back of his neck.

"Hey, is everyone alright?" Marcus yelled from the hall.

"Yes, we're all okay. What happened?" Clint's voice had an edge as he pointed his flashlight at Marcus's feet.

"Think they set off an EM pulse. It shut down everything electronic in the vicinity."

"Great. What about the backup systems?"

"Hank's working on them."

"Okay, Thanks."

"Sure thing." Marcus's flashlight bounced off any reflective surface as he ran down the hall.

Casey whirled around to the others. "Does it mean they know where we are?"

"No." Clint's voice was monotone. "Since it only knocked out the power to anything turned on, it was close enough to do damage but still far enough to tell us we're safe."

"Clint, could that knock out the sphere?" Ben's eyes bored into the sphere as if he could will the thing to turn on.

"Don't know, man. It's not my area of expertise. These relics have a power source that doesn't need to be recharged, so I'm not sure how it'd react to an attack."

"I think we need to go to the lab and check on the other relics."

"Amanda, can you check on how Hank's doing?"

"Sure thing. I'll be right back." As she passed, she touched Casey's shoulder.

Clint took the lead, and Ben kept Casey in front of him as they made their way back to the lab, with the use of the flashlights, to retrieve the relics.

"Clint, the hand-shaped one with the green stone in the center always glowed when you were near it, see if it will glow again."

Clint marched to the far end of the table, and opened the case, triggering the green stone as it pulsed, coming to life. "This one works." Clint held the relic. Suddenly three sides of the relic shifted, and circular rings erupted from the sides—one side with three rings and the other two sides with one ring on each. Clint almost dropped it. His three center fingers slid into the three rings. His thumb fit perfectly into the one on one side of the relic. The third side didn't stay circular but wound around the back of his hand to connect between his thumb and first finger. The center stone turned from green to clear as the relic camouflaged itself to his skin.

"Ya think?" Ben stifled a laugh behind his fist as he arched an eyebrow at Casey.

"Knock it off. How are we supposed to tell about the—" Clint spun around and faced Casey.

Twenty

"What?" Casey stepped back and bumped into Ben, who placed his hands on her shoulders. She tensed and stepped away.

"What if they didn't turn on because the key wasn't here yet?" Clint's eyes locked on hers. Chills ran down Casey's spine as Clint intently stared at her with piercing eyes.

"I can't be the one that sets this in motion," She waved her arm around the room. She was no one. How could she be the start of the turning point in a revolution for these people? The obsession in Clint's eyes unnerved her.

"Maybe when the stone released into you, it sent out a signal to the other relics you were here. They glowed before but nothing close to this." Clint studied her and held up his hand.

Ben raised his eyebrows and locked his steely blue eyes on her.

"Clint, I think you're wrong. Ben, tell him it doesn't say anything in the prophecy about me being the catalyst for the other relics." Casey stepped back. They would never let her go if they thought she was the answer they had been looking for.

"I'm not the expert on the prophecy. We'll ask Amanda when she's back."

"What else?" Clint whipped around to the other relics on the table. His hand glanced over the cases

"There are four of these. What are they supposed to do?" Casey peered at a tray with four curled metal pieces, as if they were shavings taken from drilled metal, and pushed them around with her finger.

"I think we've figured out they're communication devices, but Amanda hasn't been able to work them."

"Well, there are four relics other than the sphere along with these communication devices, right? If your theory's correct, they have to be activated by her?" A smile played at the corners of their mouths, as Ben turned toward Casey.

"Did it say how to use them?" How were these communication devices?

"They're supposed to fit in your ear, I think, but it wouldn't stay in Amanda's ear."

They stared at the tray. Casey gingerly touched one, and a faint vibration ran through her fingers. She lifted it to her ear to listen if any sound came from it. Ben grabbed her wrist.

"Why did you stop me? They're turned on. You can feel them." The minutest vibration was unmistakable as she held her hand out to Ben, who took the device.

His eyes grew wide and gleamed as his face lit up. He placed one in his ear and winced, scrunching up his nose and eyes. He sucked in air as his hand flew to his ear.

Amanda strolled in. "Lights should be on in about half an hour. You guys look like you were caught with your hand in the cookie jar. What's up?"

Ben glanced at Clint, who seized his. Amanda arched her eyebrow at them, glanced at the tray then Casey. Ben handed one to Amanda, who didn't hesitate to put it in. She yelped.

Ben smiled. "Wimp."

"Do we talk normal, or should one of us go to another room?" Clint shifted from one foot to the other.

"Go into the hall and test it."

Clint bumped his shoulder into Ben as he left. "Can you hear me?"

Casey heard him in the hallway. Ben and Amanda smirked as they nodded as if Clint watched them from around the corner, then chuckled when they turned, and no one stood behind them.

"Loud and clear, what about you?" Ben converted to commando mode, and Casey pictured them as kids with big walkie-talkies, running around the neighborhood.

"These work great," Clint stepped in the room.

Ben held up the last one for Casey, she shook her head, inching back she put the lab table between her and Ben. "No, I want to go home. You'll need that for the fourth person in your little group."

"Casey, you're the key. This one is for you. You're the fourth person." Ben stepped to the right as Clint pulled Amanda behind him, so she was out of the way.

"Guys, I think we need to talk about this." Amanda's eyes darted between Clint and Casey as she chewed on her lower lip.

"No, I'm not the key. I want to go home. You can't force me to join your delusional group!"

"We aren't delusional, and neither are you. You can't deny what you've seen."

"Yes, I can. You drug me whenever it's convenient for you!" She slid over, edging behind another lab table. The only way out of the lab was past the three of them, which was impossible. Her hands ran over the blacktopped corner of the lab table as if it were her only defense with it between her and them. Quick, furtive glances to the door made Clint narrow his eyes.

Ben inched around the first table, closing the space between them as her heart raced. Clint mimicked his movements and closed the gap to her right. Beads of sweat collected on her forehead as her mind flashed to when she tried to escape, and Ben pulled her into the closet. His strong arms that held her a few days ago seemed to grow and push at the fabric of his shirt as her mind screamed that it was an ill-conceived notion to even try, much less fight her way out.

Clint's muscles flexed under his shirt; she could only surmise he was ready for her to fight. Casey's rapid breaths fill the room as she tried to figure out her next move.

"Casey, you're hyperventilating. You need to slow your breathing." Ben held out his hand.

He was right. The room spun, and she panicked. Clint bolted over the table, and she threw her hands up in defense. He grabbed her wrists before she could blink, and the room swayed. With a quick twist, he spun her around and looped his arm around her neck. Her fingernails dug into his arms as she clawed frantically. Ben lunged and grabbed her wrists as Clint's massive arm applied just the smallest amount of pressure on the side of her slender neck. Small droplets of blood appeared where her fingernails broke the surface of the skin on his muscled forearms. She tried to gulp down air. Panic set in, and Ben turned into a blur. Her huge, wide eyes no longer focused as the room faded to black.

Twenty-One

Casey went limp. The only thing keeping her from hitting the ground was Clint's arm around her neck. Her head lolled forward, draping her hair over his arm seconds before he removed his arm from her neck and wrapped it around her tiny waist as he checked her pulse, placing two fingers on the side of her neck. Her limp, lifeless arms swayed over his arm. Ben stretched over the first table and snatched the last communicator off the tray. Amanda's mouth dropped open. They tilted Casey's head to the side and carefully swept her hair back, exposing her ear.

"Guys, why are you doing this?" Amanda shrieked.

"She's the one. You were outside her door the other night. You can't deny that!" Clint held Casey up and nodded to Ben.

"But can't we let her make this decision?"

"If Ben takes her back, we can keep in constant contact with her and what she's doing. That is if the sphere will work," Clint reasoned.

Amanda placed both hands on the table and leaned toward them. "Yeah, but forcing her to do this, won't she hate us even more than she does?"

Ben glanced at his little sister. "That's a chance we take.". His hand poised near Casey's ear.

"Don't do it this way. Let her make the choice."

"We don't have time to wait for her to make that choice." Ben's hand inched closer to Casey's ear.

"Ben, if you make this decision for her, she may never trust you or forgive you. Isn't she supposed to be the key? We need her. If you force this on her, she may never fight with us." Amanda arched her eyebrows and raised her hands.

Ben stared at his sister as Clint drooped his shoulders. Amanda was right; they couldn't force Casey into this. She was the key, and he would wait for God's timing for her to join them of her own free will.

"Wait, the sphere works?" Amanda ran her hands over the symbols.

Clint patted Casey's cheek. "Come on, wake up." He shifted her to his other arm and grabbed a water bottle from the table. Condensation splattered in small droplets on the floor. The coolness as he rested the bottle on her neck brought her around, and she started to fight. Clint dropped the bottle on the table.

"Let me go!" Casey tried to lunge out of his hold.

"I'm going to let you go." Clint released her wrists from the death grip his enormous hands had on them. Then he snatched the bottle off the table and chugged half of it. Casey pawed at her ear until Ben dropped the communicator on the tray. The metal glinted from the overhead fluorescent lights. Clint eyed her before joining the other two.

Ben sighed as he grabbed the sphere from Amanda's hand and pushed several symbols. His shoulders sagged when nothing happened.

Amanda pressed her lips together. "What about the other relics?"

"The relic for Clint came to life, you could say. He thinks because Casey activated the healing relic, it communicated to the rest and turned them on, including the communication devices. Not sure why the sphere doesn't work." Ben acted as if what ensued a few minutes before never happened.

"What about the bracelet and ring, anything from them yet?" Amanda carried them over.

"Haven't tried those yet. Maybe we can reboot the sphere?"

"I'll check if the parchment says anything else about the sphere, but I don't remember off the top of my head reading about a reset button listed as one of the options on this model. We may need to upgrade." Amanda cringed then mouthed sorry to Casey.

Two steps back put distance between Casey and the others. Clint listened to Ben and Amanda discuss the relics and the possibilities of what the activated relics could mean for their group while he matched Casey's steps. Casey took another step toward the door, her eyes glued to the other two. Clint matched her next step quietly as she focused on Ben and Amanda, who faced the door. Ben looked up at Clint. With a quick flurry of motion, she turned on her heels to bolt out of the room but ran into Clint instead. He folded his arms across his chest. No one ever got past him when he was determined to stand in their way. Casey's face fell as he stood between her and escape. Concern etched his furrowed brow.

"I just want to go for a walk." Casey's shoulders drooped.

"I can walk you back to your room. Amanda and I got some clothes for you. They're in the dresser." Clint suggested.

"What about the sphere? Is it working?"

"No, we're going to call it a night and crash."

"You can't give up yet." Casey shook her head.

"Yeah, sorry it's been such a bad day, but we promise we're going to spend all day tomorrow trying to figure this out and why it won't work." Ben reached for her but pulled his hand back at the last second. Ben reached up to his ear as she eyed the tray with the last communicator on it. "Hey, question. How do we remove the communicators?"

Amanda grabbed a flashlight and scaled a stool to look at Ben's ear. "Wow, big brother, do you ever clean your ears?"

Ben playfully punched her throwing her off balance. Clint grabbed her elbow to steady her before she fell, leaving his post at the door.

"Talk about abuse. This is what I had to grow up with." She continued to give Ben a hard time as he laughed.

Clint studied Casey, not sure how much more she could take.

"Do you see anything or not?" Ben tried to sound serious as he scrunched his face.

"Do you want me to answer? Not sure how you got through school with a brain this small."

"My grades were higher than yours. Don't you forget it."

"I don't see anything. Did you take it out?" Amanda turned off the flashlight and hopped off the stool. Clint started to move as if to keep her from falling.

"We'll ask Doc to take a look. We may need an x-ray to figure out how far it went and if we can remove it." Clint rubbed behind his ear, then stopped. "Hey, I think I found something."

Ben folded his earlobe forward and followed Clint's finger to a small round bump about the size of the head of a pin.

"It won't come off, so I pushed it, and it vibrated in my ear. I wonder if it turned it off or something?"

Ben found his first and pushed it, "Whoa! Yeah. Mine vibrated. Hold on, and I'll go to the hall to figure out if you can hear me."

"Found mine. I'll leave it alone and wait to see what happens." Amanda perched on the stool.

After several seconds Ben walked in the door. "Anything?"

"Nope." Amanda pushed hers.

"Guess we can check with Doc in the morning." Ben grabbed for a flashlight as the lights flickered on in the hallway.

Clint eyed Casey, hoping she'd be okay if they met back in the morning to work on the sphere. Her eyes were glued to the sphere. She wouldn't let this go for the night, so he brushed past her and snatched it off the table.

Twenty-Two

"Take a flashlight in case something happens, and you need to find us." Ben handed her one, and their fingers brushed against each other.

"Thanks." Her cheeks flushed crimson as she turned just before Amanda turned off the lights.

"See you in the morning." Amanda linked her arm through Casey's and tugged her through the door as Casey angled her head away from Amanda and arched an eyebrow.

Amanda gave Casey a quick hug just before she closed the door to her room. Clint stood at the entry of the hallway to the women's rooms. She couldn't help but shudder at what they almost did to her. Would she ever be able to trust them? Did they only want to use her for their cause and could care less about getting her home? She sank down on the bed and couldn't help but think she would never save her family. She stalked to the door and reached for the doorknob, stopped herself, but instead placed her hand on the door knowing Clint or Ben were standing guard outside her room. Was this what her life was going to be like? She spun on her heels and threw herself on the bed. Sleep crept to her from the dark corners of the room.

Images of her younger brother and his family dying filled her thoughts, jarring her awake as she bolted upright in bed. She imagined them dying over and over, her dad alone through it all. There must be a way back to save them from their future deaths that she was the cause of if she could heal the sphere.

The clock announced it was only four thirty-eight. Her head dropped back on the pillow. Everyone would still be asleep except whoever got the dreaded task of watching her. She didn't care. She swung her legs over the side of the bed and resolved to borrow the sphere. Not sure where Clint's room was, she was sure she could find something in the lab to help her fix the sphere. She told herself if it worked, she would go back, save her family, and come back like she promised.

She approached her bedroom door with the knowledge she was about to go behind everyone's back. She didn't like it, but there was no other option for what she needed to do. Her family came first. Her hand froze on the doorknob. Would it even be unlocked? The doorknob turned beneath her sweating palms. With a quick scan of the hallway, she was shocked to find it unguarded. She left her door open a crack, so no one would be alerted of her coming or going.

Casey crept through hallways to the lab and peeked around the corner to find it void of anyone. The large double doors were intimidating, but she grabbed the door handle and turned it. Nothing happened. It was locked, she jiggled the handle several times, then snatched her hand away. Her chin lowered to her chest, and her hands hung limp at her sides. She shuffled down the hall. Would she be able to make the sphere work again or not?

"Casey?"

Her hand flew to her mouth as she gasped and whirled to see Ben lurk in the open doorway. "Ben? What're you doing? It isn't even five."

His eyes narrowed. "I could ask you the same question."

"I wanted to take a second look at the possibility of fixing the sphere. I don't know. Maybe I can do something."

"Come on in. I couldn't sleep thinking about it and if I could figure anything out." Ben stepped to the side and gestured with a sweep of his hand for her to join him.

The lifeless sphere rested on one of the lab tables, and her breath caught in her throat. She hoped they would keep the sphere in the lab, and Clint grabbing it in his massive hand earlier was to distract her from trying to find it. She picked it up, stared intently at it, but the lifeless sphere lay dead in her hands. When nothing happened, she heaved a huge sigh. She was not sure what she expected. If only she could will it to work. Yet if she activated the other relics, why couldn't she activate this? With her eyes closed, she wrapped her hands delicately around the sphere.

Strong hands on her shoulders caused her to jump. She deposited the sphere back on the table, then turned away. "Sorry, I didn't mean to jump." She cast her eyes to the floor and her sock-covered feet, remembering she didn't put shoes on so she could sneak to the lab. A blush rose on her cheeks as she covered one foot with the other one.

"Casey, you don't need to apologize." Ben's eyes searched hers.

"Can I take the sphere back to my room and work on it for a little while?"

Ben sat on a stool and crossed his arms. "We want someone with you in case the sphere starts working again."

"No problem. I understand." She turned and rushed toward the door.

"Casey, please stop. Talk to me." Ben lunged off the stool and caught her upper arm; his fingers easily wrapped around it, stopping her in her tracks.

"Ben, don't." She shrugged out of his grasp.

He took several hurried steps and blocked the door.

"Ben, let me go back to my room." She stared at the floor so she wouldn't be pulled in by his eyes. She couldn't trust herself to stay focused on getting home to her family when he was this close.

"Casey, I'm sorry you're going through this. If you need to talk..." Ben stood his ground and peered down at her.

She shook her head. "No offense, but I don't want to talk to you about it. You wouldn't understand."

"Try me. I'm a pretty good listener."

"Oh, you want to know how I'm doing? Do you really?" Casey put her hands on her hips.

"Yes," he pleaded with her.

"Okay, I miss my family. I was stolen away from everyone I know and love. I was dragged away, kicking and screaming, fighting with everything I had because I thought you were going to kill me. I thought when you grabbed me, that if I didn't get away, I would never see my family again. You ripped me from my world, you tore my life apart, and now I lost my family. In two days, my brother and his entire family die at my house, and I can't stop it. Do you know how defeated that makes me feel?" Her words tumbled out.

"No, and I'm sorry." Ben stepped closer.

"No, stay away." She turned and marched to the opposite wall as Ben took several steps with her. "You don't get to be sorry. You don't get to...to try and understand what it's like for me. I have no one. I'm alone in this...this world. I don't belong here. So, an 'I'm sorry' from you won't fix this. Nothing will except getting the sphere to work so I can save my family from the hurt and pain *you* caused. Are you just waiting for me to make a wrong move for a reason to kill me?"

She snatched the sphere off the table. She regretted what she said, but the thought of losing her family tore at her. With the sphere clutched to her chest, she turned to leave the lab as Clint blocked the door. The sphere dropped from her hands as she gasped at the sight of Clint. He reached for it, but his fingers only grasped air. The sphere hit the ground with a shattering blow.

Casey stumbled back to the lab table. The sphere lay in seven large pieces on the floor. "No. No, this can't be happening." She cried in anguish as she sprinted for the door. "No! No! No!"

"Casey, stop." Clint stepped in front of her, and she collided with him.

"Move. Let me through." She clenched her jaw as Clint grasped her upper arms in his massive hands.

"No, you don't know how bad this hurts Ben. He carries a huge amount of guilt around with him every day because of this. He made a split-second decision that brought you here. And no one here wants to kill you, so get that through your head!"

"Please stop." She gaped over her arms at the shattered sphere that lay on the floor.

"Casey, Ben cares deeply about you. We don't know what you're going through, but we're here for you. Have you ever thought maybe this is where God wants you?"

"Where God wants me? Thirty-five years in the future, alone, no family, no friends? Hiding from persecution for what I believe and who I am? No. This was because of a decision Ben made—a man, not God." She tried to wrench her arms out of his iron grip and failed.

"You ever thought Ben made the decision because God told him to?" He let her go.

Casey staggered several steps to keep her balance as she spun on her heels and scowled at Ben. "God told you to bring me here? To scare me half to death by kidnapping me instead of talking to me and telling me about this?" She spread her hands out and made a half-turn motion to the room.

"Not exactly. And I tried to talk to you. He told me you were the one. We needed you here." Ben wouldn't look at her.

"What Ben was told—"

"Clint, don't." Ben glared at him.

"Don't what? Is there another reason I was brought here? And it was too late to try to talk to me after you already grabbed me." She had every right to ask why her life fell apart.

"It isn't your place to tell her." Ben narrowed his eyes at Clint.

"Fine. I'll let you be the one to tell her. Casey, you shouldn't be so hard on Ben. We didn't know why until he told us." Clint stepped to the side.

"What else is there?" She glared at Ben.

Ben snatched a tray to pick up the shattered pieces from the sphere. "Not right now, Casey."

"Not right now? No, don't keep me in the dark. I have a right to know, especially since I'll never go home because of this decision." She choked as she balled up her fist. Her cheeks heated as she clenched her jaw.

"I'm sorry, but I can't tell you yet." Ben rose from picking up the pieces, strode over to a table, and attempted to piece the sphere back together as if it were a jigsaw puzzle.

Casey stared daggers at his back. She envisioned punching Ben and took a step forward. She glanced at Clint, who stared at her fists and shook his head.

"Sorry," Clint joined Ben.

She rushed out the door. Unsure why God chose her to endure this, she would need to rely on Him now more than ever. As the realization sank in that she would never go home, her heart ached to hug her brother and dad one last time.

"SHOULD WE GO AFTER her to make sure she goes to her room and not outside?" Ben closed his eyes as he released the pent-up air in his lungs.

"She knows what's out there now with the martial law announcement from the Monarchs and what happened today. I don't think she would risk it." Clint understood she was stronger than he thought. When she clenched her fists, he was sure he would need to come between her and Ben. He smiled at her gumption while still having restraint. She had no chance of doing any sort of damage to Ben without a weapon, but the fact she was going to give it a shot told him she just might make it in this world.

They worked on the sphere for an hour, discussing their options if they got it to work. Amanda sauntered in, hair wet from a shower, wearing a red hoodie and jeans that now seemed too big when they once fit her perfectly. Clint smirked as he looked down. Red fuzzy slippers adorned her tiny feet.

"Nice."

"They're comfortable. Casey was crying when I walked past her door. Oh, my gosh! What happened to the sphere?" Amanda's eyes grew wide as her mouth hung open.

"There was a little incident. Casey dropped it when she tried to take it out of the room and I stopped her." Clint dropped a piece back onto the tray.

"She can't go home and save her family," Amanda whispered.

"No, she can't, and she blames Ben. She's hurting. I'm glad she's in her room, though."

"Wait, one of you didn't make sure she went to her room?"

"Well, she's not twelve and grounded." Clint saw Amanda's scowl. "No. With what happened today, she wouldn't attempt an escape again after the last scare. She's a fighter, though. She was ready to take a swing at your brother."

"What do you mean?"

He smirked. "She almost punched Ben."

"No, she didn't." Ben swiveled around to face them.

"Oh, yeah, she did. She had her fist balled up, ready to strike. She's a fighter. She's exactly where God wants her to be. I can help her learn how to fight."

"She really hates me, doesn't she?" Ben whirled back around and tossed the piece of the sphere in his hand on the tray. "This is no use."

"She doesn't hate you. You didn't see her face when she yelled at you—the regret, it was all there. Brother, you'll have your hands full with her." Clint clasped Ben on the shoulder.

"We need to keep her safe. Maybe she'll come around. What are the odds that the Monarchs are getting closer to finding us here?" Amanda plopped down next to her brother and slid the tray over in front of her.

"I think they're just taking shots to scare anyone out into the open. I think we still have time. We need to focus on this. This is what's going to change the tide of this war. We may be America's only hope of taking this country back with these." Clint swept his hand over the relics, and his glowed in the case.

Twenty-Three

Sobs shook her body as her back hit the wall, where she slid to the floor and pulled her knees to her chest. There was no going back, and she did it to herself. She blamed Ben for his part in this, but if she hadn't let her emotions run away, the sphere wouldn't have broken. She had no one to blame for breaking it except herself. But she wouldn't be in this situation if not for Ben. How could she be so frustrated and angry with someone but wish for his touch at the same time?

It was after seven when she finally pulled herself off the floor. She wanted to take another shot at the sphere. Her stomach growled as she reached for the doorknob—maybe food first.

They all stood there. "Do you want to join us for breakfast, Casey?" Amanda smiled as she bounced up and down in her fuzzy slippers. Her shoulders sagged when Casey shook her head.

"No, thanks." Casey pulled the door closed behind her, then marched past them. Her heart ached, and she didn't trust herself to keep from yelling at them in the middle of the cafeteria.

Ben's long steps caught her, but Clint and Amanda walked several paces behind.

"Casey—"

"Stop. Leave me alone. I don't want to be around you."

"Casey, you need to talk to someone. What about Amanda?"

"So she can run and tell you and Clint everything so I can be 'poor Casey' who everyone needs to feel sorry for? I've taken care of myself for a long time. I don't need anyone. Leave me alone." She quickened her pace, and Ben fell behind to wait for Clint and Amanda.

"She wants to be alone," Ben told the other two.

"It's not your fault. She needs some time alone." Amanda's love for her brother only made it worse, knowing what was in store for her own.

"I don't think she should be alone. She's hurting too bad. We need to be there for her," Ben argued.

Clint tried to keep his voice quiet. It still reached Casey's ears. "We will, but when she's with us, all she sees is that we took her away from what she's grieving for. Amanda's right. She needs to work through this on her own, and when she's ready, we'll be there for her. All we can do now is pray."

She walked to the food line, grabbed a saran-wrapped bowl of cereal, milk, and a spoon, and stormed out of the cafeteria. Several sets of eyes followed her as she didn't join the other three for breakfast. She didn't care, and she marched back to her room. She couldn't come to terms with the fact that they kept a secret from her. There was another reason Ben grabbed her and pulled her into this time. As she ate her cereal, she reached for the Bible she found on her nightstand and held it as she finished her breakfast. The Bible comforted her in so many ways.

Clint was right—God had her here for a reason, but Casey wasn't sure she would ever truly know why. She would trust Him like she had so many times in the past and knew that He was here with her.

The lack of sleep from the night before hit her. She had nothing else to do in this cell she now lived in, so she crawled under the covers with thoughts of her family on her mind.

Twenty-Four

Behind the closed doors of the lab, they met to discuss Casey. They had passed the point of no return. She could no longer go back and save her family. This could cripple her. They needed her help, but this wouldn't convince her to fight with them. Clint threw his feet on the desk as he leaned back, perfectly balancing his chair with his feet as an anchor.

"What's going to happen when we need to move?" Amanda played with the pieces of the sphere.

Ben stared at the ring in the case as the crystalline top swirled. "I think she'll fight. She doesn't know anyone around here, but this warehouse is the only thing she knows. She may not want to let that go when we move."

"Well, she won't have a choice. We sedate her if necessary to keep her with us and safe." Amanda spun one of the shards of the sphere on the tray.

"No. I refuse to put her through that again. Amanda, you didn't see what it did to her the last time. That's not an option."

"I'm with Ben on that. Doc said she shouldn't have survived the last sedative, and that one was my fault."

"What? Take her kicking and screaming so she can alert everyone where we are?" Amanda tucked her hair behind her ears.

"How do we know she would resist moving? If she's too scared to go out there with the Monarchs threatening to shoot people and moving means getting away from that, who's to say she wouldn't be all-too-happy to go?" Ben suggested as Clint steepled his fingers.

"I hate to say this, but if she does resist, I can, if all else fails, subdue her again. It won't help her trust us. We need to keep her with us and keep her safe, though." Clint shoved his chair away from the desk. He paced back and forth, shaking his head.

"What? You mean choke her out?" Amanda's jaw dropped.

"You can't be serious!" Ben slid off the stool.

"Hey, I'm just saying if we need to, it may come down to that again. Ben, would you rather take the chance on another sedative, maybe killing her this time? I didn't hurt her last time. It would be the same. I'd never hurt her."

"No! I just can't."

"What if we see how the next couple of days go and talk to her. We've never sat her down and talked to her. Ben, I think it needs to come from you. If we try to as a group, it may overwhelm her like she's being attacked." Amanda spun on her stool until she faced her brother.

"Ben, what do you think? Amanda has a point. Also, let's lock up the relics. With her being the key and activating the relics, maybe she can *heal* the sphere. We can't chance she's able to heal it and then leave through it. Moving is a good reason to give."

They pondered what their next move would be and what they needed to do to keep Casey and the three of them safe as the Chosen Ones from the parchment. They agreed for Chloe to check with her uncle on how the move was coming along and when they could leave the warehouse district. They arranged to meet with Casey the next day since it could be the worst day of her life with the loss of her brother. Everyone would try to keep her busy and her mind off the fact she couldn't go home. With a plan in motion, they went to their respective rooms to sleep.

Twenty-Five

"Go away," Casey answered hoarsely to the person who knocked.

"Casey? It's Clint."

"What?" she mumbled from under the covers.

The hinges groaned as he pushed the door open. "Can I talk to you?"

The comforter pulled her hair down over her face as she uncovered her head and nodded for him to come in. With a swipe of her hand, she swept her hair from her face.

"Casey, we're worried about you. You haven't left this room except for food in two days. Please talk to someone even if it isn't one of us." Clint's genuine concern made her stomach quiver that she secluded herself from these three.

"Clint, today's the day my brother and his family die. I don't want to be around anyone. Unless you've miraculously repaired the sphere and I can jump back to save them, I don't want to be around you either." Her shoulders slumped as she rubbed her hand over her upper arm.

Clint stepped in a little farther. "Ben's devastated by this. He wants to make sure you're going to be okay. Today's not the day you want to be asked if you're okay, but we don't want to leave you alone either."

"I don't want to be around anyone. I might say something like I did to you and Ben the other night. Leave me alone." A flurry of static sparks raced through her hair as she tugged the covers over her head. Maybe he would leave.

"We understood how upset you were and didn't take it personally, but we don't want you to go through this alone."

She flipped the covers off her head and frowned at him as her chin trembled.

"Oh, Casey." Giant steps took him to the side of the bed, where he held out his arms and pulled her to him, wrapping his massive arms around her when she reached for him. Her sobs shook them.

"I'm so sorry, Casey." Clint squeezed tighter. She clutched at him, not able to stop the flow of tears as all the anguish and pain poured out. Clint never loosened his strong arms that engulfed her. The sobs finally subsided several minutes later, and she was able to let go. When she raised her head, Ben and Amanda lingered in the doorway.

"Ben, I'm sorry for going off on you the other day." She could see the pain in his eyes.

Ben took a couple of steps into the room. "Don't worry about it. It's already forgotten."

"Would you like to join us for breakfast?" Amanda diverted her eyes.

"Sure, let me...I'll meet you there in half an hour." Casey shrugged.

Tears soak through Clint's shirt, where they came to rest. She cringed but didn't think she could stop the torrential downpour that built up over the past couple of days.

"Okay, we'll meet you there." Clint stepped into the hallway, then disappeared around the corner.

She grabbed her bag for the shower and tossed in clothes she pulled from the dresser. They had supplied her with several articles of clothing when she moved to the room. She was about to be the sole survivor of her family, and she didn't want to be alone today.

The quiet tension at the table made her stomach knot from her decision to meet them for breakfast. "Sorry, guys. I can't do this...I just can't." The walls closed in. She couldn't pull in enough air. She stumbled around the corner of the doorway from the cafeteria before the walls began to blur into a taupe blob. Her hands searched for the wall as she tried to stay on her feet. She plastered herself against the wall while taking slow, lumbering steps. The cool gloss finish of the painted surface felt good against her face.

"Casey!" Ben knelt beside her. "Casey, listen to me." His hand grabbed hers as his other hand took hold of her elbow.

She pulled away from them. "Matt."

"Casey, you need to slow your breathing. Take in a deep breath and hold it." Clint guided her away from the wall, so he and Ben flanked her. "You need to slow your breaths. Ben, talk to her."

"Casey, come on. Slow your breathing. Just slow breaths and hold them in for the count of five." Ben's voice was close to her ear.

Darkness filtered into her field of vision. The hallway spun out of control as if the floor rushed up at her. She gasped loudly as her breathing quickened. "Matt!"

"Casey, you're breathing too fast."

Casey turned her head from Ben to Clint, unable to focus as they blurred together. She could no longer tell them apart. Her world ebbed away as blackness rushed at her. She fell when her legs gave out. "Matt."

BEN SWEPT CASEY INTO his arms as she lost consciousness. Clint placed his hand on her forehead and smoothed the hair away from her face. Ben pulled her close and started off to her room while Amanda and Clint closely followed.

Amanda frowned. She wasn't sure Casey would make it through this. "Is she going to be all right?"

Clint was several steps ahead of her. "It will take time. Imagine what she's been through in such a short time. All we can do is pray for her and put it in God's hands. I saw a fighter in the lab the other night, and I think she's strong enough to handle this. But that's a lot to take in, in such a short time frame."

"Clint," Amanda whispered and waved her hand for him to come to her when she stopped in the hallway.

"What?" Clint glanced toward Ben, who continued to Casey's room.

"Is Ben going to be okay? I know he adores her."

"We'll be there for both of them." Clint draped his arm around her shoulders.

"I'm not mistaken, though, am I? I'm not blind to his reactions when she's in the room with him. He's never been this bad before." Amanda stopped and stared at her brother's back.

Clint tugged her arm to keep her walking. "No. You're not mistaken. He's fallen for her. It will crush him if he either loses her or worse, she rejects him."

"That isn't going to happen. I see how she looks at him then looks away." Amanda peered up at Clint.

"Yeah, but with what we put her through, what if she can't let go of that?" Clint's hand on Amanda's shoulders kept her walking.

"Oh, man. I didn't think of that. Maybe with enough time, she'll let him in?"

"Maybe. I hope she does. Otherwise, we'll be picking up the pieces of Ben's heart for years." Clint motioned for her to move faster.

They casually caught up to Ben, who made it to Casey's room and gingerly held her—in her pale pink sweater and dark blue jeans—as Amanda yanked back the coarse, drab, brown blanket. He lowered her slowly as if he didn't want to put her down. Clint and Amanda exchanged a knowing look. Amanda covered Casey with the blanket as Ben pulled the chair in the corner over to the side of the bed. His eyes were glued to her small frame. He smoothed the side of the blanket. How did it come to this? Amanda knew this could break her brother if it ended badly. Clint tugged at her elbow.

Amanda and Clint backed up to the door. She didn't want to say anything, but they needed to work on a few things they had scheduled. "Ben, we're going to meet with Chloe and a few others to discuss our options in the meeting we scheduled today. Are you staying with her or coming?"

“I’m not leaving her.” Ben leaned his broad shoulders back into the chair and crossed his arms over his chest.

Clint and Amanda slipped quietly out and partially closed the door behind them. Amanda cringed as her tennis shoes squeaked on the linoleum floor as they headed to the meeting.

Twenty-Six

A massive explosion jolted Casey out of a restless sleep, and she tumbled out of bed and ran toward Amanda's room. Two more explosions shook the building before she got there. Large fissures spread across the walls like spider webs, and the lights flickered, dimmed, then flickered again before going out.

It had been several weeks since the sphere was destroyed, and the ability to go home and save her family passed. The tension between her and the other three was still there, but they had started becoming friends while they worked on the relics. They found out the sphere stopped working because once the healing stone sensed the fourth person, it sent the healing power into her and activated the other relics. The sphere was meant to bring her to the other three and shut down. The explosion they thought disabled the sphere was from the sphere itself, sending out the signal to the other relics that the fourth had been found.

Amanda opened the door as Casey reached for the handle. "Okay, that was close."

"Hey, wait." Casey reached behind her ear, she gave in and took a communicator about a week ago. "You guys there?"

Ben was the first to respond. "Yeah. You okay, Casey? Is Amanda with you?"

"Yes, she's with me and we're fine, but not sure about the building. Stress fractures are on the walls over here."

"Yeah, here, too," Clint piped in.

"Do you guys want to meet at the lab?" Casey glanced at Amanda, who nodded as she tugged on a sweater over her t-shirt.

"Be there in two," Ben answered.

The guys were already at the lab when the girls got there, with the relics in a satchel to transport if they evacuated.

"You guys okay?" A woman who Casey hadn't met yet loomed in the doorway.

"Yeah, we're all in one piece in here," Ben stated then introduced them.

"Nice to meet you," they chorused.

She continued down the hall to check on other people in the building.

Casey turned to the others. "How many people are here?"

Clint studied the ceiling and mouthed numbers as he counted in his head, but Amanda answered before he could, "About fifteen."

Ben added, "Any more puts us at risk. We've lost so many as it is, so we try to stay in small groups."

"What were the explosions?"

"The Monarchs try to scare us out in the open, so they set off discharges. Some of the surrounding buildings are now unsafe. When people run for safety, they capture them." Ben didn't seem to be as concerned as she thought he should be.

"We've been lucky so far, only because God's on our side. We haven't taken a direct hit to this building yet. We pray God will keep us safe so we can continue His work. We were driven into the Midwest. Congregating and worshipping what anyone believes in the open was outlawed, so we're not able to share our faith, or they execute us." Clint lowered his head. Casey reached out and touched his arm.

How could this be? What happened to the United States of America? The country with freedom everyone in all the other countries wanted—the freedom of religion, freedom of speech, or the right to peaceably assemble. She didn't want this world. A president elected into office with strong ties to terrorist groups wanted to destroy America.

"You mean to tell me we can't go to church and praise God anywhere without being killed?" Her mouth fell open.

"Sorry to say it's true." Ben shook his head.

"I never thought this would happen in my life before God sends His Son back for His children." Casey shuddered.

"Neither did we, and the hard thing is it's even harder to find a Bible that's not reprinted in their propaganda and disguised in the bindings of our Bibles to produce more converts to their side. They give up the small cluster of communities, so we move every so often to keep from being found and massacred." Ben plopped down on a stool. The legs bounced when the rubber caps on the bottom of the legs skidded across the floor.

"But, a Bible is in my room." Casey motioned to the side of the warehouse where her room was. "Is there enough for everyone?"

"Yes. An underground group reproduced the Bible the way God intended it and got it back out in circulation. It just isn't printed on the onionskin paper everyone's used to. The word of God helps us be closer to Him."

"How can people shut Him out of their life or say He doesn't exist? I count my blessings every day that I had parents who found God when I was a little girl, so I grew up in church singing hymns and listening to people who love Him. Anyone can look around and see all the wonders He's made and the amazing miracles He performs." Casey had a faraway look in her eyes as they glazed over at the memories that flooded her thoughts.

Ben smiled. "You don't have to tell us. We're there with you on that one."

A commotion from the hall startled them. Ben rushed to the door. "Jason's been injured." He darted out the door. The rest of them followed.

There in his father's arms, a boy of about six years old had a large piece of ugly, rust-coated rebar impaled in his abdomen. His father had a death grip on him as he ran, cradling him, to the infirmary. Silent tears in the father's wide eyes threatened to spill over as he clutched his lifeless son whose eyes were open but not seeing.

The urge to follow them overpowered Casey. Doc waited for them when they reached the hallway to the infirmary. Someone had a gurney, and the boy's father placed him gingerly on it, trying not to jar him. As they wheeled him into the room, Casey pushed past Ben, Clint, Amanda, and several other people in the doorway. Maybe she could help. Maybe she could save this father from outliving his son.

There kneeling next to his bed, his father prayed while clutching his son's hand. "Dear Heavenly Father, I place my son in Your hands. Only You know what Your plans are for him. He's only on loan to me but belongs to You. I ask you, Father, to spare his life. After losing his mother and sister, I'm not sure how I can go through the loss—" His voice caught in his throat as the sobs he tried to hold in shook his body as he rocked back and forth.

Tears threatened her eyes as she listened to the father's prayer, and she walked to the foot of the bed to place her hand on the small child's foot. With her eyes closed, she said a silent prayer. *Father, You have a special purpose in mind for me, and I'm here to make a difference in these peoples' lives. You chose me to help and to use these amazing gifts You've given me. Please show me how to use this healing power if I'm supposed to save this little boy. If this is where You want and need me to be, use me now.* A rush of heat raced from her heart down her arm, through her hand into the boy's foot. She opened her eyes, blue light raced up his legs and over the rest of his body.

"My child, tell them to remove the rebar."

Goosebumps raced down her arms. She knew that voice and smiled as she closed her eyes, cherishing the closeness to Him. "Doc, pull out the rebar," she whispered.

"Casey, we need an operating room. It could be piercing something vital, and he could bleed out when we remove it. We need the right equipment before we can do that!" Doc's voice rose several octaves.

"Trust me. It's okay to remove it." Blue light surrounded them.

Ben stepped to the bed next to the father. "Doc, do it. I think he'll be fine."

"No, I'm not taking any chances of losing someone else in my care," Doc almost whispered.

The father stood and smiled. "He'll be fine. We need to remove the rebar."

"Are you guys sure about this?" Doc hesitated, his hand inched closer toward the ugly rusted metal protruding from the boy's abdomen.

"I think we need to trust Casey." Ben studied her, the blue light reflected in his eyes.

"Okay, but we need to be ready in case he starts bleeding. Amanda, grab several packages of cotton bandages and be ready," Doc snapped. "Clint, when I tell you, pull straight up."

"Sure." Amanda walked around the bed to a cabinet stocked full of bandages, ready for Doc's orders. She, too, stared at Casey in awe. A smile tugged at the corners of her mouth as she winked.

"Now."

Clint pulled the rebar straight up, showing four inches covered in blood, and the skin stitched itself closed. Gasps filled the room as the wound disappeared before their eyes. Exhaustion reared its ugly head as Casey held on.

She closed her eyes as her Heavenly Father's love and peace washed over her. Ben gasped, and Casey opened her eyes. He stared at her as he took a breath. Blue light receded down the boy's legs and to her arm. The boy opened his eyes and smiled at his father, who wrapped his arms around him, rocking him back and forth as he murmured how much he loved him in his ear.

Casey started to fall back from the exertion of healing him. Ben guided her to a chair. "I'm okay—a little tired. I think it saps part of my energy." She smiled.

Amanda hurried to Casey, hugging her. "You're amazing!"

"That was all God."

"Amen" echoed through the room. They all witnessed a miracle and the love of Jesus. Everyone rejoiced in the knowledge that Jesus was in the room with them.

"Casey, I'd like to introduce Mark and his son Jason." Ben lead them to her.

"Nice to meet you," she said as she stood with Ben's help and extended her hand to Mark.

Mark stepped past her hand and crushed her ribs in a bear hug. "Extremely nice to meet you."

Jason threw his arms around her neck. "Jesus told me you were coming." Silence filled the room.

"What?" She pulled her head back and stared into the pure innocence in his large round eyes.

"He told me someone special was coming, and He has special plans for you." Jason leaned forward and whispered between his hands as he cupped them around her ear, "He said to open your heart to save him." He leaned back and locked eyes with her. "Thank you for coming so God could heal me through you."

"You're welcome, sweetie." The urge to protect this little boy engulfed her.

"My name's Jason, not sweetie." He scrunched his nose.

Everyone laughed. After several of them shook her hand and introduced themselves, the room cleared out.

"Wow. Look who's the instant celebrity." Amanda perched on the arm of the chair. "You don't look so hot."

Ben glanced at Clint and Amanda then to Casey. "You look flushed. You okay?"

"Yeah. I'm just tired."

Amanda placed her hand on Casey's forehead. "You're feverish. Hey, Doc."

"No. I want to go lay down for a bit." Her eyes drooped.

"I think maybe Doc should check you out," Ben insisted.

"No, I want to go back to my room."

"We'll take you." Ben took her by the elbow.

"Do you mind if Amanda walks me?" Casey widened her eyes and raised her eyebrows at Amanda.

Once they were around the next hallway, her legs were sluggish to respond to her mind telling them to keep walking. The farther they got, the more she leaned on Amanda. Her eyes blurred as she yawned, and her eyelids drooped. Every time she yawned, Amanda yawned, then it started all over. They laughed by the time they were back at her room.

Amanda opened the door. "You want company for a little?"

"No, thanks. I didn't want anyone fussing over me. Thanks for walking me. I'm going to crash for a couple of hours," Casey mumbled.

"Okay, do you want me to wake you, say, in two hours?"

"Sure."

"You look beautiful when you're in the blue aura." Amanda winked and nodded toward the side of the warehouse that the lab was on.

"Wait, you see the light?" Casey looked around to make sure no one heard them.

"Yes, but I think only the four of us can. Doc can't, and I don't think anyone else in the room was able to either. I'm sure someone would have said something." Amanda shrugged.

"Wonder what it means that no one else can." Casey furrowed her brow.

"Not sure, but I'll be back in two hours."

As she closed the door, Casey kicked her shoes off then crawled over the foot of the bed toward her pillows. When her head landed on the soft downy pillow, the world disappeared as she sank into the darkness of sleep.

Twenty-Seven

Ben, Amanda, and Clint stared at the relics. Was Casey the key to activating them? Never could they fathom that just a couple months ago, when they found the relics and their hopes had ignited at the thought of being able to turn the course of this war, that Casey would be the key to that hope. Amanda held the bracelet in her hands as she turned it over and over. The stone in the bangle shimmered as she clutched it. Swirls of diamond flecks swished through the stone as it came to life. She took a quick step back, and she thrust her hands further away from her body.

Ben dropped the ring back in the case as his sister held the bracelet. She raised her eyebrows and shrugged at him as she slid the bangle on. It sprung to life, and tendrils wrapped around her arm and camouflaged into her skin. With her right arm outstretched, Ben grabbed her hand and studied her arm. The stone blended in with her skin.

Marcus raced into the room, and they all spun on their heels toward the doorway. A bubble engulfed all three of them. Ben and Clint turned to face Amanda. She held her hands up as she shrugged her shoulders almost to her ears, then smiled when the bubble disappeared.

Marcus glanced from one to the other, waiting for one of them to speak.

"Yeah. Sorry. Whatcha got, Marcus?" Clint wandered to the door. Ben and Amanda turned her arm over as the bangle shimmered again. She smirked when the shield appeared around her and Ben. He tilted his head at his sister, who only smiled wider as the shield disappeared.

Clint strolled back to the other two, watching the exchange between them. "Okay, show off. How'd you do that?"

"Not sure. Just thought it and it happened. Marcus scared me when it appeared the first time, then I made it go away by thinking about it, so I tried to make it appear the same way and, well, there you go."

"Hold on. Let me grab mine." Clint snatched the weapon out of the case. It wrapped around his hand and camouflaged with his skin, and the stone in the middle shimmered like Amanda's bracelet. A pulse shot out and traveled the length of the room, knocking a binder off the desk at the far end. The corners of his mouth twitched just before he smiled, and he turned his hand over to study the relic molded to his palm.

"Now, who's the showoff?" Ben dropped on the closest stool to him.

"I think Casey's the key. None of these relics did anything until the healing stone surged into her." Clint admitted, "She has to be the catalyst to this. Maybe now is our time to start taking our country back." Clint stood, planting feet shoulder-width apart with his hands clasped behind his back.

"So, we make sure she's safe, and nothing happens to her. If she started this, what happens if she's injured or worse?"

Ben rubbed the back of his neck. She was more important than they thought. His affection toward her had only grown since the issue with the shattered sphere, and there was no sending her back to her time. His shoulders heaved as he sighed.

With his attraction to Casey, there was no going back now, and Amanda and Casey only grew closer over the past couple of weeks. Ben caught Clint on more than one occasion laughing at something Casey said. Clint admitted to Ben one night he needed to protect her. The only thing he could explain was that maybe he was her guardian assigned by God to keep her safe. She had stolen Ben's heart, though he kept it from her.

Amanda waved her hand in front of his face. He had missed the question she asked. "Hello, earth to Ben. What's going on?"

"I think Ben's right. What if something happens to her? Does it deactivate the other relics?" Clint scowled.

Amanda snatched a soda can out of the trash, with a slight tilt of her head back to Clint, she tossed it to him. A field shot out from his raised hand and deflected the can with a crushing blow as it hit the empty aluminum, hurtling it into the cabinets. Amanda turned to Clint and smiled. Their hopes were up for the first time in years. Could this really help with their dire situation that they had dealt with for the past decade? Maybe this was the turning point they had been waiting for.

"Nothing's going to happen to her. We come up with our next move so we can do some damage to the Monarchs and remove them from our country." Amanda glanced at her watch. "I need to wake Casey. She wanted to be woken up in two hours. It is just after that now."

Ben hopped off his stool, "I'll go." He disappeared into the hall before the other two could respond.

"He's got it bad, doesn't he?" Amanda sidled up to Clint.

"Yes. We can't lose her no matter what. It would devastate him," Clint mumbled.

Ben shook his head as he loitered outside the lab door, he didn't know they were aware of his attraction for her, but this told him he was horrible at hiding it from them. He rushed down the hall to Casey's room.

Twenty-Eight

A soft knock on the door woke Casey. It was dark, and she couldn't tell what time it was. "Come in," she called, fumbling with the light on the nightstand.

Ben opened the door. "Did I wake you? Amanda said she was going to wake you in two hours. I can come back if you're still tired."

"I need to get up, or I won't sleep tonight." Casey tossed back the covers.

"Want to join us for a little testing of the other relics?" Ben smirked and his eyes teased with a raise of a single eyebrow.

"Sure. Hold on. Let me grab my shoes." She managed to pull her shoes on as she hopped across the room.

"Jason can't stop talking about the pretty lady God sent to save him." Ben tilted his head to her and raised his eyebrows.

Casey waved him away. "He's such a cute little boy."

"He's the youngest child here. There's also an eight and fourteen-year-old."

Casey shook her head. "It is a shame these kids live like this and grow up in the world the way it is. I remember being a kid and not having a care in the world. My parents were always there, and we never worried about bombs dropping or buildings collapsing around us."

"At least they're alive. Many were lost or orphaned when the wars broke out." Ben shoved his hands in his pockets.

"God's going to raise His people up. Everyone will realize how they misjudged so many things, and God always keeps His word to His people. He always said in the Bible that he would avenge his people."

"I'm glad we found you. Even in the darkest of times when you need God, He's there for you. It helps when your family's with you, but it helps to know you'll be with them even after the end of everything, in Heaven." Ben nudged her arm.

Casey stopped and met his eyes. "How old were you when you accepted Jesus into your heart?"

"Fifteen. And you?" Ben pulled his hands out of his pockets.

"Seven." Casey studied him for a second, then continued. "So, have you been able to use any of the other relics?"

Ben grinned and faced Casey, walking into the lab backward. "Funny you should ask."

Amanda pulled out safety goggles as Casey glanced at the desk overturned in the corner. "I suggest being behind there if I were you."

Casey scrambled to climb behind the desk.

"What are you two up to?" Ben raised an eyebrow at Clint.

The goggles were huge as Casey put them on, covering half her face. Amanda lined several cans on a desk at the other end of the room, then joined Casey and Ben behind the desk.

Clint faced them. "You three ready?"

Casey's eyebrows raised at Ben and Amanda, who shrugged to Clint they were ready. With the relic weapon molded around his hand, Clint pointed it toward the cans lined on the desk at the far end of the room. A strange energy pulse shot across the room, knocking the can on the far right off the desk. It ricocheted back at them, and Casey ducked out of the way.

"Wow, can you do that every time?" Casey was impressed.

"Yeah. Think about what you want it to do, and, well, extend it to the relic." Clint seemed pleased he was able to operate the device at will.

"Okay. If the cans ever decide to attack, we can win hands down. How do we find out what it does in a battle against people?" Casey smiled at Amanda, who laughed at her. "I'm serious. We can't test it on people here. So how do we find out what it does?"

Ben and Clint exchanged an outlandish look between them.

"Tell me you didn't try it on one another?" Would they try something so extreme?

"No, but it gives me an idea of going out there and trying it on them." Ben motioned with his head toward the outside of the warehouse.

"No, that's too dangerous!" Casey couldn't help but think about what Jason told her earlier—to give her heart to him. Did he mean Ben? She wasn't ready to admit her attraction to him. She needed more time to work through this, paranoid any look or action would give it away. She blushed every time he looked at her with those amazing eyes of his.

"Yes, but we need to go out anyway and make our food pickup." Worry wasn't a word used in Clint's vocabulary, with the thought of going out there, where anyone not in the terrorist group was a target. It must be his military training because she was scared to death of what lay beyond the walls of the warehouse.

"We use a car at the other end of one of the tunnels under the warehouse, so we don't leave by way of this building." Ben continued, "We've done this for a long time, so no big deal, and we've never lost anyone doing our monthly food pickup."

"Okay. I want to come along," she insisted.

"No!" Ben snapped his head around, his eyebrows drawn together. The fire in his eyes made her heart race.

"I agree. It isn't a good idea." Clint yanked off his goggles.

"Wait, you said it wasn't a big deal, and you do it all the time. So, what's the harm of me coming along?"

"First, we never send more than one person out at a time. Second, we can't take the chance of you being wounded. If one of us is hurt, you can heal us, but who would heal you?" Ben tossed his goggles on the table. They slid several inches then teetered on the edge. How could he act this way when he was the reason her life was in shambles?

"So, I can go by myself. Amanda, do you ever go on food pickups?"

Amanda glanced at Ben, then Clint before she nodded.

"What's the difference between Amanda or me going? Didn't I heal myself when I reacted to the sedative?"

"Well, yes, but with one difference—she's been here since the beginning and has done a pickup before. The possibility of losing you isn't an option." Ben exhaled.

"Yes, but I can't go home, right?"

"So?"

"I need to contribute somehow, or am I supposed to stay here, do nothing, and let you guys take all the risks?"

Amanda offered her support by saying, "Ben, she has a point."

"Don't start!" Ben snatched the trash can off the floor and dropped the cans in one by one.

Clint defected to her side. "Maybe we should give her a chance."

"Not you, too. I don't like the fact she hasn't been out there yet." Ben gestured to outside the warehouse. He didn't seem to realize this was going to be a losing battle for him.

"Point taken. But if she wants to, I don't see the harm in it. Is she supposed to stay cooped up in a building for the rest of her life? What about when we move again? She's going to go out there sooner or later." Amanda could provoke her brother more than anyone.

Casey was glad Amanda was on her side. With a smile, she said, "What do I do, and when do I leave?"

"Fine, if you want to do this, you do exactly what we say, or it won't work." Ben pointed his finger at her. "Meet back here tomorrow. And Amanda, go with her to find some dark clothes."

"Sir, yes, sir!" Amanda gave a sloppy salute and marched with high steps toward the hall.

Casey didn't look at Ben as she walked past. When she met Amanda, they rushed out of the room.

"He doesn't want anything to happen to you. He isn't being a chauvinist or anything like that. My brother was taught to always protect women, and he's trying to do that." Amanda shrugged.

Casey shuffled her feet as she walked. "I didn't take it that way, but I wonder what the world is like since I haven't seen it in what? Thirty-five years?"

"Oh, right. I wonder how it used to look." Amanda had a faraway look.

Casey snorted. "Gee, thanks. You make me sound ancient."

"Well, you're around seventy-one years old. You have to be careful of brittle bones and all the other good stuff like that at your age."

Casey forced an exaggerated frown. "Rude."

They reached her door, and Amanda leaned over to give her a hug. "I'm glad you're here. Sorry you're separated from your family, but I am glad you're with us. Want to meet for breakfast?"

"Sure, I'm glad I got to meet you guys, also. I hate that I took it out on Ben, but I wanted to save my family." Her voice caught in her throat.

"He understands, and he feels horrible. I'll see you tomorrow and help you pick out your outfit." Amanda turned abruptly on her heels.

Casey sank down in the corner chair and stared at the wall. How did she end up here? One day she was going through her normal boring life and now wished to go back there. She never imagined she would miss her simple life. Sink into the sofa to watch a couple of television shows, read a good book, or play with Mason. Grill out for dinner, enjoy it on the deck, and watch the sun set between the houses.

She snatched the Bible off the nightstand and plopped back into the chair. The lamp behind her illuminated the walls with a hue of amber, creating a soft glow, and she curled her feet under her. This Bible meant more to her than any other she owned. The thought of not being able to worship God and Jesus openly was a concept she couldn't wrap her head around. After a while, her head fell to the side.

Several hours later, she woke, unfolded her feet from under her, and crawled into bed.

Twenty-Nine

Ben stalked back and forth in the lab. This was not how he planned on keeping Casey safe. Her being out there without anyone with her scared him more than he ever imagined. His shoes left black smudge marks on the blue speckled linoleum floor with each turn. Clint perched on a stool. His chin rested on top of his hands that were folded together and held up by his elbows on the black molded top to the lab tables. Ben ignored him and made another turn leaving another smudge as the floor took the brunt from his pacing.

"I'm here if you need to talk." Clint cracked his neck in each direction with the help of his hand under his chin to give it that final stretch as Ben cringed.

"I'm fine!" Ben pinched his lips together.

"Yeah, I see that."

Ben faced Clint, opened his mouth, closed it again, and continued pacing. "It is just that—"

"You love her and don't want her hurt." Clint finished for Ben.

"Of course...wait, I never said I loved her!" Ben rubbed the back of his neck.

Clint crossed his ankle over his knee and held his leg with both hands. "No, you didn't. I've known you your whole life. It's obvious to me—and Amanda, in case you're wondering."

"Does Casey know?" Ben's shoulders tensed.

"I don't think so. I think she's struggling with her own emotions about you."

The corners of Ben's mouth twitched. "What? Do you think?"

"Yes, now can we call it a night? Tomorrow will be hard enough...at least for you."

"No, I can't sleep." Ben made another pass by Clint and turned.

"Come on, brother, you need to sleep. What if she needs you to be ready for anything tomorrow? What if you fail her because you're too tired?" Clint pressed his lips together, and the corners of his mouth twitched.

Ben narrowed his eyes. "You're just wrong, man. I don't want her to go if something could happen to her."

"Something could happen to her at any time, or to me, or anyone here. That's the world we live in. You know this." Clint's arms tensed.

"It doesn't mean we can't do everything to keep her and everyone else safe."

"We will, and we do. Let her do this run. We'll check with Chloe on how soon we can move out of this area. The Monarchs are destroying more and more buildings out here. It is just a matter of time before this one crumbles." Clint leaned down, grabbed a bottle of water out of the mini-fridge that was on its last leg, struggling to keep even the smallest number of items they could fit in it cold.

Clint held up the bottle to Ben, who nodded, then caught the bottle that Clint hurled at him. "I hate how my emotions run rampant when I'm around her. What am I supposed to do?"

"How about we sleep? We need to be there for her tomorrow." Clint stretched his arms over his head.

"Yeah, yeah, I know." Ben chugged the rest of his water and tossed the empty bottle toward the trashcan. It hit the rim, bounced off the other side, then dropped out of sight.

"Ben, trust your gut on this one. God sent her to you for a reason. Go for it! Don't let another moment go without telling her. Would God put her in your life, the extreme way he did, if it wasn't supposed to be this way?" Clint dropped his bottle in the trash, and he hit the switch for the lights throwing the room into complete darkness.

Ben strolled to the hall as Clint locked the door. "For the first time, I'm scared. I've never been so unsure about anything in my entire life. Not that God put her in my life for a reason, but of rejection. I'm not sure I can handle being turned down by her...especially not her." He mumbled more to himself than to his best friend.

"Put it in God's hands and leave it there. He knows what He's doing. You might be surprised by her answer."

"What do you mean? Do you know something?" Ben smoothed his shirt down with his hands.

"Just go to bed. We'll talk more tomorrow. I'm tired." Clint walked into his room as Ben continued to his. A light click from the latch on the doorknob securing the doors was the only sound on that side of the building.

Ben dropped on his bed and lay back, staring at the ceiling. “Father, I give this to you.”

Thirty

In the morning on Casey's way out of her room, when she turned toward Amanda's, a figure in the hallway caused her to let out a yelp. Uneasy laughter filled the halls when her mind recognized it was Amanda.

Amanda held up her hands. "Sorry. I didn't mean to scare you."

"I didn't expect someone to be standing there. I don't do well with someone sneaking up on me. Bad memories." Casey blew out a breath.

Amanda winced. "I'm so sorry. I never thought of that. Well, I'm an early riser, always have been. Ben's not, so he's probably still asleep."

The smell of breakfast wafted down the hall as they got closer to the cafeteria. Biscuits and gravy were on the menu today, and they didn't hesitate to load their plates.

"So, did you ever imagine Clint as more than sort of an adoptive big brother?" Casey recalled her first impression of the two of them.

Amanda took a sip of her orange juice before she answered. "I did have a crush on him when I was in my early teens, but never told him."

"You never told him?"

"Would you?" Amanda pressed her lips together.

Casey shook her head. "No, I guess I wouldn't, either."

"Well, I wrote it in my diary, and my brother being a brat when he was younger read it one day and told Clint." Amanda sighed.

Casey's fork stopped halfway to her mouth, "What'd you do? I would've been mortified."

"Oh, I was. I avoided him for months and didn't talk to him."

"I couldn't imagine. My brother was a little monster, but I never kept a diary, so I didn't agonize about anyone finding it." Casey had a far off look in her eyes.

"I never kept a diary again. Ben felt so bad that he kept doing my chores for me." Amanda whispered.

"Good morning, ladies." Clint set a heaping plate of biscuits and gravy in front of him. "What're you talking about this morning?"

"Nothing," both replied, glanced at each other, and roared with laughter.

"Now, why do I not believe that?" Clint squinted.

"No clue. It sounds like a personal problem to me." Amanda laughed.

"Whatever troublemaker," Clint turned toward Casey, "You ready for today?"

"I guess. Is there anything to do to be ready?"

"No, as long as you know how to drive, you should be good to go." Clint shoveled a massive fork-full of biscuits into his mouth.

"My license might be a little expired, but other than that, I can drive."

"Look who's got jokes!" Clint laughed. "Well, the car's ready to go, and the directions on how to get to the food pickup location are ready."

"Okay, when do I leave?"

"About nine tonight."

They strolled to the dishwashing area and dropped off the trays. They almost ran Ben over on his way in for breakfast.

"You guys leaving?" Ben turned and walked backward as they passed him in the hall.

"Yeah, some people wake at a semi-normal hour, big brother." Amanda smirked.

Ben scoffed. "I was up late working on some things, so don't talk to me about getting up later than you when you went to bed several hours earlier."

"Well, we're heading to the lab if you want to join us." Amanda turned her back on her brother and smiled at Casey.

"Sure, let me grab something to eat, and I'll meet you there."

CLINT, AMANDA, AND Casey walked to the lab, and Ben was there before they could turn around. He chewed on a breakfast wrap with potatoes, bacon, and eggs threatening to spill from the side he ate from. "Look, I'm still here the same time you guys are."

"Okay, let's go over the plan." Clint unrolled a map on the table. "You'll need to access the car by use of the tunnels below this building, but one of us will go with you. From there, you'll be alone. This street will take you out of the warehouse district, from there follow the back roads we highlighted. If you go off these, they may find you. Our allies keep an eye on the roads, so you should be fine. Once you make it to the pickup location, the password's King James. They'll load the groceries."

"Take the same route you took there. If, for any reason, you come across another vehicle, don't stop. If they start to turn around, floor it and take one of these streets that we marked on the map, and whoever's on those streets will be able to help you." Clint pointed out where she could find shelter.

"Do you think I'll run into anyone?" Casey clasped her hands tightly together as she gawked at the map.

"No, but we want you to know what to do in case. It never hurts to be prepared. We'll be able to find you quickly and test out the relics if something happens. We also have backups in case Ben or I need them." Clint pulled a black, matte-finish handgun out of the back waist of his pants, and Ben lifted his shirt to show he also had one.

Ben and Amanda were silent as Clint explained everything with the maps on the desk. Casey nodded.

"You'll need to memorize this map because we can't take the chance that you're caught with it. The Monarchs would come knock on our front door. We'll go over it several more times to make sure you know it." Clint placed his hand on her shoulder.

"Don't let her go."

Clint glanced at Casey, and his heart raced. He looked at Ben, but he wasn't close enough to whisper anything to him.

They studied the map several times when Clint took it away and quizzed her on the streets and the side streets if she needed to run.

"Don't let her go."

Clint glanced around the room, looked at Ben then back at Casey. Ben narrowed his eyes.

After several hours, she was able to quote the directions step by step and give all the side streets in order whether she was coming or going from the pickup. Clint nodded and smiled.

"Okay, I think she has it." Clint beamed.

"Don't let her go."

Clint frowned as he looked down at Casey. The urge to protect her sent his heart racing.

"I'm going to go change into a darker outfit unless a relic can make me invisible."

"I'll come with you." Amanda bounded out of her chair, following Casey.

"What gives? I know that look." Ben locked eyes with Clint.

Clint narrowed his eyes. "Did you say something?"

"What do you mean." Ben leaned against the table.

"Something's wrong."

"Then, she doesn't go."

"We can't tell her no now."

"Why not?" Ben raised his eyebrows.

"We'll be ready to act fast if something goes wrong."

"Be ready? How about we don't let her go! If you are having doubts about her going, we need to stop her. You've never been wrong about your gut instincts."

"It's not an instinct." Clint didn't want to sound crazy to his friend, so he didn't mention the voice he heard when he went over the maps with Casey.

"What?"

"Nothing. Drop it. Let's get ready." Clint grabbed his relic, and it camouflaged into his hand. He pulled his gun, checked the clip, reached up behind a box on the top shelf of a storage cabinet to grab an extra clip and handed Ben one, also. Ben wouldn't like his answer, but he would deal with it. Ben would be on alert since Clint said something was off, and that was exactly what Clint needed, was his best friend concerned.

Thirty-One

Once outside in the hallway, the girls pushed behind their ears to turn off their communication devices. Amanda turned to Casey. "You don't need to do this if you aren't ready."

"I'm a little nervous—never had to deal with anything like this before. My action-packed days used to consist of trying not to fall on the ice while crossing the parking lot to the car after work."

"Wow, now that could be dangerous." A mischievous smile played at Amanda's lips.

"What?" Casey tugged at her right earlobe.

Amanda stopped and stared at her. "Do you not know?"

"Know? Know what?" Casey stuttered.

"He doesn't want you to go and take the chance of you being caught or hurt."

"Clint?" Casey diverted her eyes.

Amanda bumped her shoulder into Casey's. "No. Ben."

Heat rushed across her cheeks as she studied the floor. "Stop it. I've only been here for a little while. He's being nice and thinks he's responsible for keeping me safe since he brought me here."

"You're right. He does think he's responsible for you." Amanda scuffed her feet along the floor, the frayed hem of her jeans trailed behind her shoes.

"I can handle myself. I'm not incompetent." Casey clenched her jaw.

"We were raised in a strict Christian home. Our parents taught us that men take on the dangerous things and look after the women even in this day and age when women are so self-sufficient." Amanda jammed her hands in her pockets and shrugged her shoulders.

Casey gazed down the hall. "Such a rarity even back in my time, but let him know I can take care of myself."

"I want you to know, being his sister, I know him better than anyone, with maybe Clint as an exception. Ben's never been so protective toward anyone, not even me."

"He's a nice guy, but I'm not sure he feels the way you think he does toward me. Plus, I don't think of him that way," Casey lied, but she couldn't take the chance she would say something and have Ben find out. She'd be crushed if it wasn't mutual.

"He's attracted to you, and I see the way you look at him. With the dangerous world we live in, imagine finding someone here with how often we move." The tattered hem of Amanda's jeans swished along the floor as they continued down the hall.

"I can't imagine living like this for as long as you. Who would have thought anything like this could be possible?" Casey opened the door to her room and waved Amanda in.

Casey tossed several black articles of clothing on the bed as she yanked them out of dresser drawers. Her stomach tightened as she surveyed her options. Small beads of sweat emerged on her forehead, and she swiped at them. What was she thinking? She swallowed hard past the lump in her throat, then gulped in air. Casey stared at the clothing on the bed.

Amanda jerked her back to reality. "I would go with the black pants, black long sleeve shirt, and black boots."

Amanda closed the door behind her as Casey changed into the clothes she suggested. Amanda tossed a hair tie Casey's direction and a hairbrush. With her hair piled on top of her head, she threw the brush over her shoulder, where it landed and bounced on the bed. They ambled down the hall toward the lab as they turned on their communication devices. Casey slowed down. Her heart raced.

"I don't like it. I don't think she's ready! Maybe someone should go with her. You said something was off and didn't want her to go!" Ben snapped at Clint. Casey looked straight ahead and didn't react as she caught up to Amanda.

"She'll be fine. She has an advantage we never had before. We can hear everything through our communication devices," Clint reassured Ben.

"Hey, guys. We're ready to go on our end." Amanda interrupted their exchange and smiled at Casey as they made the last turn to the lab.

"Great, let's head to the tunnels." Clint was halfway out the door with a flashlight in hand.

Amanda and Casey fell in behind Clint and tried to keep up with his long, lumbering steps. Ben didn't follow. About three flights of stairs later, they came to a solid concrete wall.

"The car at the end of the tunnel has a key hidden in the visor on the passenger side. If you pull the mirror on the right top corner, it will expose a hidden compartment." Clint turned and stared at her.

"This is where I leave you two." Amanda threw her arms around Casey and squeezed as tight as she could. "Good luck, and see you soon. I'll pray constantly for you until you're back."

"Thanks. I'll be back in no time." Casey forced a smile that was more like a grimace as her stomach flip-flopped, and nausea hit. Her breathing quickened as she rubbed the back of her neck and bit her lip.

"Our communicators are on. If you're lost, say where you are, and we'll feed you the directions." Clint glanced down at her.

"If we can do it that way, why did I spend time learning the map?" Casey glanced at the tunnel Amanda had disappeared through.

"Hey, is everything okay?" Clint glanced down the tunnel following Casey's eyes.

"Yeah, I'm fine."

"We don't know the range on these things. If they can't go past this building, we didn't want to take a chance of you not knowing how to get back or where to go for help.

"That makes sense. Guess I get to test the distance on these." She tapped her ear as her chin quivered.

Clint pushed a concrete block, and the wall pulled away from them on the left side, exposing a hallway. She jumped at the loud sound of grinding concrete that revealed a tunnel so hidden, you had to know which concealed block to push to open it. Several agonizing minutes later, they came to a metal rung ladder bolted to the side of the wall.

Clint stopped and faced her. "You find yourself in any trouble, head to one of the side streets, and keep going.

Someone from our group will help you. We don't expect any problems but also remember the curfew. Turn the headlights off when you don't need them. Hey, don't do this if you don't want to."

"I'll be back as soon as I can." She turned to climb the ladder as Clint touched her shoulder. When she turned around, he wrapped his massive arms around her.

She shook as Clint hugged her. She turned around, squared her shoulders, blew out her breath, then started her climb. When she got to the top, there was a whirring noise. Her adrenaline spiked as part of the concrete above her shifted over to the side and slid out of place so she could finish the climb to the top. As she stood there, she saw several cars spanning the length of the garage. She looked for the black sedan and found only one. She slid into the drivers' seat, pulled down the visor over the passenger side, and tugged at the top right corner, which folded on a hinge exposing the key to the ignition.

As she sat there, she took a deep breath, closed her eyes, and turned the key in the ignition. The car purred beautifully as if someone had taken special care of it. She lowered her head and prayed for the strength and courage to complete this task and get back safely. The engine was almost silent as she eased onto the street. Quick, furtive glances told her no one was in sight. How many sets of eyes watched her? Her heart raced for a split second with the urge to drive and find out where it took her and maybe find her way home. Several blocks from the warehouse, she tested their built-in walkie-talkies.

"Testing, testing one, two, three." She chuckled.

"Loud and clear," Clint answered. Was Ben still upset that she took this little mission even after his protest? Also, why didn't Clint try to stop her after what Ben said earlier, and again in the tunnel?

"I'm several blocks away, so not too bad on reception." Casey clenched the steering wheel. Her hand sweated as her heart thundered in her chest.

"I agree. It sounds like you're in the room with us." Clint's voice comforted her.

"Is everyone there?" Casey checked the rearview mirror.

"Sure are—Amanda, Ben, and even Chloe. She's curious about the distance on these things."

She wondered why Ben didn't talk to her. "Got it. I'll check in after a little farther."

"Sure thing. You okay so far?" Clint sounded as if he sat next to her. She half expected to see him in the passenger seat when she checked the next cross street.

"As quiet as a mouse out here." The streets were deserted, and she craned her neck, looking up and down the alleys she passed.

"That's a good thing." She could hear the smile in Clint's voice.

"Yeah, I know." Her knuckles turned white as she clutched the steering wheel.

Buildings rushed past in a blur. She hit the brakes and listened for a couple of seconds. An engine to a large vehicle sounded in the distance. She slammed the car in reverse and backed into an alley next to another car, turned off the engine, and sank in the seat below window level as her heart thundered in her ears. "Guys have a problem here."

"What kind of problem?" A hard edge crept into Ben's voice.

"A large vehicle in the area. I pulled down a side street." Casey's breath quickened.

"Did they see you?" Clint's calm helped her to slow her breathing.

Casey sank lower in the seat. "Not so far. Hold on. They're passing by on the main street."

A bright beam of light flashed over the windshield of the car, illuminating the interior above her head. Her hand found the key, ready to start the engine and run if they approached the alley. A split second later, the light panned past the windshield to the next car. She peered over the dashboard, and she dropped in the seat as they continued to scan the area. Did they know she was there? As the seconds ticked by, her roaring heart only beat louder.

"Casey, what's happening?" Ben practically yelled, almost causing her to scream.

"Hold on," she whispered.

"Clint, we shouldn't have let her go. You even agreed!" Ben hissed.

"She'll be fine. We'll give it a minute to find out if they will move on." Clint's calm voice in her ears gave her hope.

"But I still don't like that she's out there by herself."

"Let's wait and see what happens. If they spot her, we'll go get her. Amanda, grab the relics in case we need to go." There was a clatter as she pictured Amanda scrambling to the cases with the relics. The unmistakable sound of someone slamming a clip into the butt of a gun filled her ears.

"So, we're going to wait until they find her? I say we grab another car and go out to her. We'll wait for the food pickup on another day." Ben's voice raised an octave.

"You know we can't. What if it was one of us out there? Ben, would you want the ones back here to risk everything, the warehouse, everyone who's here to rescue one person in trouble?"

Ben sighed. "No, I wouldn't. And neither would you, but this is different. We can't risk *her* like this."

The Monarchs continued to scan the area for several minutes. With the combination of the cool night air and her hot, steamy breath, the inside of the windows showed a build-up of steam. It started at the corners, then crawled its way across the glass as if to say, "She's in here! Come find her." She lifted the collar of her shirt over her mouth and nose, frantic as the steam spread on the windows. It continued to rise but not as fast as a few minutes ago. It stopped its ascent.

The only obstacle between her and the outside was the molded vinyl dashboard as she edged ever closer to peek over it. No signs of the other vehicle shocked her as she stared at the empty alley void of Monarchs. Able to catch her breath, she exhaled, which caused an explosion of traitorous steam to crawl several inches across the windows.

After a quick glance around in every direction, her heart was able to beat a normal rhythm again. The engine came to life as she turned the key. With an eye out for any kind of movement, she inched her way toward the intersection she ran from to hide.

"All clear, guys," she informed the group.

"Casey, you okay?" Clint's calm voice came through her ear.

"Yes, just a close call." Casey watched her trembling hands and tried to stop the shaking.

"Okay, where are you at?"

Casey searched for the street sign. "Back on the main road, Pine Street."

"Good, not much farther," Clint informed her.

The siren behind her made her jump. She clutched her chest as she gasped. Where did they come from? "Clint, they're behind me. It's too late for me to run. What do I do?"

"Nothing. Keep communications open, and we'll get to you. Ben?"

"Step out of the vehicle and put your hands on the trunk of the car!" a man bellowed.

She closed her eyes and said a quick prayer before stepping out. The wind disturbed wisps of her hair and constricted the capillaries draining all color from her cheeks. Hands up, she inched toward the back of the car. Once at the trunk, she placed her hands on the cold dew-covered metal. She didn't want to make any sudden movements and get shot for being out after curfew.

"Do exactly what they tell you!"

Two men walked up behind her, and the hair on the back of her neck stood on end. She had no clue what would happen or what to expect. Would they question her or just shoot? If they took her somewhere, would Ben and Clint be able to find her? One of the two men pushed on her upper back, pinning her to the trunk as the ice-cold metal of a gun was shoved against her temple. The other one patted her down and found nothing. Anyone on a food pickup went without any papers to give away where they were from or where they were going. He grabbed her wrists, wrapped them around her back, and put on plastic ties. He pulled on her wrists toward the sky, too far in her opinion than what was needed, and she cried out in pain. They laughed and pushed and tugged her to keep her off balance as they dragged her to the rear of a large van.

"CASEY! CLINT, LET'S go get her. She said she was back on Pine Street. How fast can we get there?"

"We need a plan first. They have a lot more firepower than we do to try a rescue out in the open. What if they have snipers covering the area?"

Ben and Clint studied the map. Clint had his weapon molded to his hand, and Amanda slid on her bracelet. Clint bolted down the hall, and Ben and Amanda waited for him to return. Ben clenched his fists, yanked the gun out of his waistband, checked the clip, and, once satisfied, returned the gun to his waistband. Clint bounded back into the room with a duffle bag he tossed on a table. He pulled out guns of all shapes and sizes. Ben handed Amanda the handguns she was familiar with. She checked to make sure they were loaded before slinging a holster around her shoulders that was capable of holding the two.

Ben grabbed a shotgun and added another handgun to his waistband, while Clint grabbed the rifle, slinging it over his shoulder. The bag contained numerous clips that went to each of the guns they had chosen. With a quick nod of his head, Clint stepped in front of Ben.

"Out of my way!" Ben's face reddened.

"Take a breath. We're going to get her back. I need to know you're not going to go in shooting wildly. I won't hesitate to leave you here if I think you can't handle this."

"Move!"

"Listen, we're going to get her back. But to do that, I need you with a level head. If you go in shooting, you could hit her." Clint pointed his finger at Ben.

Ben stopped and locked eyes with Clint, "I won't—"

"We all want her back. I will die to save her. But I need you there *with* me, not working against me. We keep our heads on this one." Clint's steely gaze was enough for Ben to nod and step back. Amanda put a hand on her brothers' arm.

"Okay, tell me what you want me to do." Ben expelled his breath.

Thirty-Two

Her shins smacked the bumper as they tossed her into the back of the van. They locked the door, leaving her alone with her thoughts. The two front door hinges creaked as the men opened them just before the van's diesel engine roared to life. She fell to the side as they pulled away from her car left on the side of the road, where the keys dangled from the ignition. Blood trickled down her shins.

The only light in the back of the dank, dark van, with a crudely soldered metal panel separating the front seats from the back, came from a scratched off area of the painted over back windows. Glimpses of street signs as they passed gave her hope. Plastic ties that restrained her hands behind her made it a task to keep upright with every drastic turn of the van. With each fall, she had to fight her way back to the windows. The arguing in her ears distracted her.

She interrupted their rescue plan. "Can you guys stop long enough for me to say something?"

"Casey, what's going on?" Ben's words bit into her ear.

"Okay, the streets we've taken so far are a right on Summit, left on Monroe, left on not sure, a right on Johnson. We just took a right on Cardinal and are around some houses in a residential area. Left on Crossing."

"Great job. I know right where you are. Keep feeding us directions. We're on our way." Clint's calm voice helped her to slow her breathing and gave her hope this wouldn't be a long, drawn-out process of rescuing her.

"Right on Madison. Woah!" Casey fell over, and her head bounced off the side of the van.

"Casey!" Ben and Clint's voices intermingled.

"I'm fine. They took a turn a little faster than I expected. Clint, they turned left on Roanoke. We're at a large brick building."

"Ben, they took her to the school. Casey, you're in an abandoned school, so hold on until we get there."

"Sure thing. I'll wait right here in case you're wondering."

"Amanda's rubbing off on her." Ben's gruff voice broke through.

The doors to the back of the van opened. She squinted and lowered her head against the setting sun that flooded the back of the van. They each grabbed an arm and tugged her out. Her feet barely touched the ground as they hauled her across the parking lot. The plastic ties around her wrist gouged into her skin. Blood ran into her hands, off her fingers, and dripped to the ground. They passed through a set of glass doors and up a flight of stairs. Classrooms lined both sides of the hallway.

Screams from the classrooms seeped into the hall. She couldn't even begin to fathom what was being done to them. Her heart raced as the screams echoed in the hall. They stopped in front of one of the classrooms, and the guy on her left fumbled with keys with large, calloused hands. Would she be able to hold out until Ben and Clint found her, or would she be the downfall to everyone in the warehouse?

The florescent lights blinked and flickered, then came to life as the small hum announced the electrical current running through them.

On the far wall, the chalkboard still hung neglected from the years the school had been closed. When was the last time a teacher or student graced its presence with the light, smooth texture of a piece of chalk? The memory of the smell of the chalk with small particles of dust collecting in the tray under the edge of the board flooded her senses. It was sad to think no one had been taught in this room for who knew how long. Knowledge was put on hold because of the terrorist group that now held her.

"Get in there!" They shoved her into the discarded room with peeling paint. Her feet tripped over each other and tangled in the chaos. The floor rushed at her, and her eyes grew wide. They grabbed her hair, yanking up at the last second, saving her from the certain pain of broken bones in her face.

The desks were shoved to the side to make enough space in the middle of the room for a chair that resembled an ancient electric chair from a prison. Hospital restraints replaced the leather straps. Jagged cut edges of wires protruded from several parts of the chair. One of the men spun her around, and she cried out. They chuckled as they viciously cut off the plastic ties embedded in her wrists. A shove into the chair caused it to tilt back, but their foot stopped it before it tipped over, slamming the legs to the floor. One held her arms down as they cinched restraints around her wrists. Her ankles were next.

"Casey, you okay? Answer if you can." Ben's hoarse voice came out in a whisper.

"Are those too tight?" one of the men asked, but they didn't care about her well-being. It did give her a chance to answer Ben.

"Yes." She smiled. They had no clue that she communicated with someone several miles away. She was relieved by the connection with her friends.

The men left the room, so she was free to speak in secret if there weren't any listening devices in the room.

"Casey? We aren't far from you." Amanda was a welcome voice.

"Great. I'm in a room on the second floor about five doors on the left if you come through the glass doors from what looked like a rear parking lot."

The door opened, and an unshaven, dirty man walked in. He spat tobacco on the floor, splattering brown sludge across the dirty linoleum. "What's your name?"

"Monica Stewart." She used her old boss's name.

"What are ya doing out after curfew and outside the designated livin' areas? We shoulda shot you." He smiled to reveal tobacco-stained teeth, and the worst breath she had ever encountered wafted out. Bile rose in her throat.

"I don't know anything about any curfew. I don't own a television."

He slapped her across her cheek. She sucked in air. She didn't trust herself not to cry out, so she bit her lip instead as tears stung her eyes.

"Why are ya out after curfew and outside the designated livin' area?"

She didn't say anything, hoping she wouldn't receive the same treatment. The back of his hand met her cheek again, and she screamed. She had never been hit before. With her eyes squeezed shut, the ache in her cheek deepened, and stars crossed her vision.

"Guys, we have to get her out of there." Amanda distracted her for a split second.

"Now, tell me why you're out of the livin' area and out after curfew?" His voice deepened, and his face turned red. Sweat stains grew on his two-sizes-too-small, plaid, blood-stained shirt. What if he escalated the interrogation?

For the third time, the back of his hand struck her cheek, and she cried out. Blood trickled toward her chin as she trembled. He never gave her a chance to say anything before striking her.

"We can stop this at any time if you tell me what I want." The evil in his eyes chilled her blood.

With a glance at the ceiling, she hoped it wouldn't give him an easy target. He grabbed her by the hair and yanked her head forward to hit her again. The swollen cheek obstructed her view when she looked to her left.

He turned and stormed out the door. She looked at her wrist. Could she lean forward enough to undo the buckles with her mouth? Unable to touch the buckle with her teeth, she pushed up with her feet to angle herself closer to the buckle. Still not enough to reach. She gripped the arm of the chair and yanked up. There was no give, but wait—her fingers brushed across a nail on the side of the worn, wooden arm. With her thumb and forefinger, she wiggled the nail back and forth. It moved a fraction of an inch. A little more wiggling and the nail slid out some more.

Voices in the hall startled her. Somewhere out there, someone screamed. She shivered, but the voices continued past her door. Grasping the nail, she wriggled it free. She twisted her wrist around until it faced up in the restraint. The nail was barely long enough to edge under the strap, but with a few lifts with the nail, the strap looped up several inches almost through the metal ring on the buckle.

The doorknob twisted, and her eyes widened as the door opened. A man's back was to her, and he spoke in hushed tones to someone in the hall. Someone screamed. Casey jumped and dropped the nail. It jingled when it hit the ground, and her mouth fell open as she watched the door. A loud voice yelled down the hall. The man slammed the door behind him, and his heavy footsteps continued down the hall.

She glanced down and tried to flex her wrist toward the strap, straining to touch the loop with her fingers, but it was too far. Maybe the loop was high enough to grasp the end with her teeth. Straining forward, she bit into the leather and tilted her head away from the buckle. It was enough to release the latch. She yanked her right hand free from the restraint. Her left hand was free in a matter of seconds, leaving only her ankles. She was out of the chair faster than she thought possible.

With her ear pressed to the space between the flimsy wooden door and the doorframe, Casey listened. She turned the knob and was shocked to find it was unlocked. The small squeak it made stopped her dead. She was sure it echoed through the entire building, but no running footsteps alerted her that anyone heard it. She edged the door open, sure that the hinges would give her away.

Out in the hallway, a quick glance both ways told her there was no one to alert them of her escape. Voices poured out from under the doors to the hall. They were muffled, so it was unknown which direction they came from. One of the voices sounded familiar. How did she know that voice? Then it hit her—it was President Polson. She recalled his voice from news broadcasts in the warehouse.

Polson's grisly voice penetrated the hall. "We need his contributions, or we can't offer him protection. Did you tell him this? We need to make sure he understands, and if he doesn't, make sure one of his own is the bearer of the message."

"I done told him, but he won't budge. He said he won't bow to your commands and refuses to contribute. He won't support a known terrorist conspirator." An unknown voice whimpered in response.

"Well, make him understand if he doesn't want to keep his obligations, the Monarchs won't protect him. The Grables need to understand that if they don't pay, they lose. Take his daughter out, and maybe he'll contribute." His raspy voice hissed through the door.

She couldn't believe a President of the United States ordered a hit on some innocent daughter.

"We'll take care of it, sir. You can count on us. Our plans for pressing forward in advancing the territories farther west is going according to schedule." She pictured the man on his knees, groveling to the president.

She needed to get out of the building. What kind of world was she brought to where the President ordered hits and helped terrorist groups take over America? Footsteps approached from around the corner behind her, so she sprinted toward the stairs at the end of the hall and to the dark night outside, where she hoped to hide until her friends arrived. "Guys, I'm on my way out a door. How far away are you?"

"What? How did you get out of the room?" Ben was no help.

"We're around the corner if you can hide until we can get to you. Amanda, Ben, we're going to try and grab her on the run."

"They're right behind me!" She headed to the stairs in front of her.

She hurdled the flight of stairs as they closed in on her from above, shouts for reinforcements reached her. She hit the door at a dead run. It slammed against the brick wall to the left. The glass shattered, throwing shards everywhere, but she didn't stop. The lights in the parking lot illuminated the area in a soft amber glow as fog reached down touching the ground.

She was at the first row of vehicles when a sharp pain hit her right shoulder. A small metal cylinder protruded out of her shirt. With her left hand, she yanked it out, but it was too late. The edges of her vision grew fuzzy. The bumper of a car in front of her took out her knees as she crumpled on the hood. She crouched and stumbled between vehicles to stay out of their line of sight. Where were they? She lumbered to the fifth row of cars before she dropped to her knees, unable to focus. “Guys, I need you. Ben?”

“I’m on my way, hold on.” Ben’s voice faded.

Someone grabbed her from behind around her upper arms and yanked her into a standing position. She clawed at his hands. He let go, but only long enough for her to stumble to the next row of cars. This time when he grabbed her, he slugged her across the face. The fire from her cheek spread as she fell backward. He caught her before she hit the ground, and tossed her over his shoulder as if she was a ragdoll, putting her upside down.

His cold and sweaty face brushed her arm. Chills spread down her spine, and she shivered. She wouldn’t escape this time. Someone helped him when he tossed her off his shoulder. They snapped plastic ties around her wrists, and her cries pierced the night as they cut into her still raw skin.

Ben was right. She shouldn’t have gone. She was caught on what she thought would be a simple trip for food. They were almost back at the doors to the old high school, converted into their operations building. They wouldn’t make a mistake with her again.

Thirty-Three

"There she is!" Ben grabbed the door handle before the car came to a stop.

Clint placed a hand on his friends' shoulder. "Wait, let's be smart about this."

Amanda's foot slammed on the brakes, and they slid to a stop next to the men who carried Casey. Clint held out his hand, and his relic sent a pulse radiating away from them. The men collapsed, dropping Casey, whose head bounced off the curb.

Ben and Clint jumped out as three men race out of the building. Clint yelled for the men to back up as he aimed the rifle at them. Six other men appeared from around the side of the building as Ben reached Casey. Amanda's eyes grew wide at the men, and she deployed the shield to cover them. Several Monarchs had their guns trained on them. Ben pulled his two handguns, which he pointed one at the group of six and one at the group of three, as he knelt over Casey's lifeless body.

Another man ran around behind the six and took down two with a piece of lumber as two more lunged at him, taking him to the ground. He rolled to his right, catching another's legs, knocking them out from under him. He managed to land a punch to the back of the other's knee. He went down, screaming as he clutched his dislocated knee cap. Just as he stood, a punch to his jaw knocked him back. He landed on the piece of lumber he used before, then took out the last two.

Clint kept his rifle on the three who exited the building, "Ben, grab her, and let's go. Who knows how many are in that building!"

"Ben, come on!" Amanda squealed from behind the steering wheel.

Ben shouted for the man who helped them to get in the front seat

Clint slid into the back behind Amanda, and Ben handed Casey to him before sliding in next to them while the mystery guy lunged into the front. The shield covered the car as Amanda spun the tires as she accelerated out of the parking lot. The Monarchs shot at them as they fishtailed onto the street. Ben and Clint threw themselves on top of Casey.

"She's going to need stitches." Ben's voice shook.

Clint poured water over her wrists that he placed on a towel. "Her wrists are torn up."

"Is she okay?" Amanda sped through the streets, yet glanced in the rearview mirror as Casey drifted in and out of consciousness.

"What's your name?" Ben held a cloth to the back of Casey's head and eyed the man in the seat in front of him.

"James is the name, James Malloy." A gap showed between his front teeth. His disheveled, long blonde hair swept across his forehead. Dark brown eyes that were too close together glanced every which way.

"Nice to meet you, James. Glad for the help back there."

Clint placed gauze around Casey's wrist and began the tedious task of gently wrapping them. She jerked her hands back, and a small gasp escaped at the last knot.

"Sorry, too tight?" Clint rechecked the knots.

"No, I'm okay. He was in there." Her eyes closed as she talked.

"Who?" Ben leaned away from her.

"Polson," she mumbled.

Ben leaned in close, and his lips brushed against her ear as he whispered, "We'll talk later. Don't say another word."

"Can we drop you somewhere, James? Is there a place close by?" Clint wiped the blood off Casey's fingers with alcohol and cotton, checking for injuries.

James turned in the passenger seat. "Anywheres along the way to where you're going, so I can figure out my next step."

Clint stopped his hand poised over Casey's. "Don't you have a place to go or people to meet?"

"No, I pretty much stay to myself. That way, I don't worry about who to trust." James turned and rubbernecked out the side window.

Amanda raised her eyebrows at Ben and Clint through the rearview mirror. They exchanged a look.

"You want to come back with us? There are a few of us who do okay and keep out of the Monarch's way." Clint continued cleaning Casey's hands.

"Well, I don't know. I gots no problem jumping in back there to help. I don't like the Monarchs no more than anyone else. But to join a group? Not sure I want that." James slung an arm across the back of his seat, his chin resting on the top. He raised an eyebrow as he looked at Casey.

"It won't be a problem, but we'll need to know before we go much farther, and we'll need to blindfold you for our safety." Clint tossed the scraps of bandages into a bag.

Ben finished the knot to the bandage on the back of Casey's head. He cracked open a cold pack and placed it over the bandage. The cut on her cheek continued to bleed, so he held a bandage over it. He let Clint question James, so they didn't overwhelm him with everyone interrogating him.

"What if I wants to leave? Can I leave whenever?" James drummed his fingers on the console.

"No problem. We'll drop you wherever you need. But until we know more about you or where your loyalties lie, we need to take the necessary precautions to protect the group we take care of and make sure they're safe." Clint met Ben's eyes, and he shrugged just his right shoulder.

James ran a hand through his hair. He seemed to think for a minute, then answered. "Sounds like you care about these people in your group. I think I'll accept your offer if you're this protective. Maybe this is where I needs to be."

Clint pulled a box out from under the seat in front of him and produced a blindfold.

"Close your eyes," Ben leaned Casey against Clint, slid forward in the seat to wrap the bandana around James's eyes, and knotted it twice. He motioned to Amanda, who backtracked several streets. A left here and right there, the same streets again, but this time rights and lefts in the opposite direction. Fifteen minutes later, they were back to where they started when Ben had blindfolded James.

In the parking garage that Casey had left a few hours earlier, Ben and Clint got out of the car as Amanda popped the hood. Clint removed the distributor cap along with two sparkplug wires, placed them in a backpack, which he slung over his shoulder. Amanda walked to the passenger door. Ben slung the bag with medical supplies over his shoulder.

"Follow me, please." She took James by his hand to lead him toward the stairs. Ben leaned back in the car to help Casey out, and Clint closed both back doors. Clint met Ben around the side as Ben lifted her into his strong arms and walked in the direction Amanda led James.

"James, there are some stairs here, so we'll go slow." Amanda started down the first step.

Ben carried Casey down the stairs. The effects of the tranquilizer dart started to wear off, and she wrapped her arms around his neck and rested her head on his shoulder.

"I thought Amanda was bad at getting herself in trouble. She's got nothing on you," Clint teased.

They made it the five flights of stairs and continued through a dark, claustrophobic, damp tunnel. Once they were about fifty feet from what looked like the dead-end of the corridor, Ben kept an eye on Amanda ahead of them, with James attached to her elbow and hand to be led into the unknown. He didn't seem to be bothered with being blindfolded for the length of time he had been.

Clint reached out his hand to push a cement block. It moved in, and on the left, a hidden door opened. Once on the other side, Clint engaged a cement block no different than any of the other ones around it, and the door closed, hiding the secret underground tunnels. James turned his head from side to side, listening to the grinding concrete as the door closed.

They made the long walk toward the metal ladder bolted into the cement wall that led to the lower level of the warehouse. Amanda descended first, and James followed with Amanda's assistance. She helped him when he reached the bottom rung to stand on the cold, unforgiving, dirt-packed floor. Clint was next, then Casey climbed down, and Ben followed. Casey paused several times, and Clint held out his hands to catch her if she fell. Ben guided her the last two rungs while Clint grabbed her by her waist and lifted her off the ladder as if she didn't weigh a thing. Ben jumped off the third rung from the bottom, checked the bandage on the back of Casey's head, and put another one on top, wrapping it quickly as she clung to Clint's arm for support.

"Ready to go." Ben picked Casey up and headed through the hall with her.

They climbed the three floors to the main level of the warehouse when Amanda stopped for the others to join her. She untied James's blindfold, and he rubbed his eyes, squinting in the light.

"I'll show you to a room you can use. We don't go outside, so if you need anything, ask, and we'll find it for you if we don't have it. If you want to leave, we'll take you out the same way you were brought in. Are there any questions?" Clint studied James.

"Thank you, guys, for letting me come here. I can live by those rules." James followed Clint around the corner toward the men's side of the warehouse.

"Let's get you to Doc and look at that head of yours." Ben wasn't out of breath even though he carried Casey the entire way.

Thirty-Four

Warmth spread over Casey as she opened her eyes to the blue light, starting at her heart as it enveloped her.

"Amanda," Ben whispered.

Amanda inhaled sharply. "I see it."

Warmth spread over Casey's whole body.

"I want to go to my room," Casey said in a tone to let them know there was no other option.

Ben looked at her. "Don't you want Doc to look at you?"

Casey pleaded with her eyes. "I want to go to my room."

Ben didn't argue. "Sure."

"Clint, we're headed to Casey's room," Amanda declared.

"Wait. Why?" Clint's voice was in Casey's ear.

"Looks like she'll be healing herself," Ben responded as he pulled Casey closer.

"Okay. I'll meet you there as soon as I get James settled in."

They reached her room in a couple of minutes. Ben set her on the edge of her bed, where she held out her hands, palms up. "Can you remove the bandages?"

Amanda reached for her left wrist as Ben took her right. They unwrapped each wrist from Clint's professional and efficient bandaging.

As Ben removed the last of the gauze, Clint rounded the corner of the doorway and walked into the room. He stared at her from the doorway, "Since when do you have blue eyes?"

"Well, since never. They're hazel like my dad," she mumbled.

"Uh, well, I beg to differ. They're vibrant blue." Clint smiled.

The cuts on her wrists stopped bleeding as her skin knit itself closed. Ben gently unwound the bandage from her head.

She winced. Guess it didn't magically take the pain away while she healed herself.

Ben cringed. "Sorry! Are you okay?"

"Yeah, please keep going." Casey closed her eyes and blew out a breath.

Faint scars where the cuts on her wrists once were, were all that remained. Ben tilted her head forward to look at the back of her head.

"How bad is it?"

"Honestly, not sure how you're going to heal." Ben pressed his lips together and shook his head.

Clint furrowed his brow. "I say we need Doc to check you over, Casey."

"No, I want to find out what I can do first." She closed her eyes and wrinkled her brow. The blue aura brightened as it surrounded her, washing her with peace.

"Trust him."

"What?" She opened her eyes.

"Um, no one said anything." Amanda looked at Ben then turned toward Clint.

"Nope, nothing said here," Ben confirmed.

"Trust him."

Tears fell as she closed her eyes. The overwhelming love from her Heavenly Father was too much. They cascaded down her face, leaving trails through the blood-caked on her cheeks.

"Casey! What's wrong?" Ben knelt in front of her and placed his hands on the sides of her face. "Amanda, go get Doc!"

"Trust him."

"No, I'm okay." Casey smiled.

"But, you're crying."

"I'm okay," she insisted as she laid her hand on Ben's. She closed her eyes, and tears dropped on her legs.

The throbbing pressure in the back of her head subsided. After a few minutes, only the memory of the pain remained. Prying her eyes open, the blue aura rushed back down her limbs and retracted until it was a small blue pinprick over her heart, just before it winked out.

"Hey, your eyes aren't blue anymore," Clint stated in a hushed tone.

Tired but overall fine, she twirled her wrists around and was amazed at the absence of any pain. She cringed at all the caked-on blood matted in her hair on the back of her head. "Gross! I need a shower." She stood, and Ben moved to help her. "I'm okay. The pain's gone. I'm just tired."

She grabbed her shower bag with a change of clothes and started for the door. "Guys, I'm okay." She smiled as all three looked at her as if she was a fragile porcelain doll.

"Amanda's going with you to make sure," Ben demanded. She didn't argue.

The warm water from the shower turned pink from the blood as she washed her hair. Pink suds splattered on the shower floor when she washed her hair a second time. She traced every inch of her face bracing herself for the possibility that it was deformed from being hit so many times. A small line ran lengthwise along her cheekbone. Oh, no! She was concerned about how bad the scar looked. For an instant, she wished she was back home and had never been brought here. Her heart ached for her family, her lost days of innocence, and this violence surrounding her that she'd never before been exposed to. She would never be the same. This world pulled at her heart to help stop the viciousness, and she sank to her knees and prayed.

Once out of the shower, she cinched her fluffy cotton pastel pink robe around her waist. She hesitated before stepping in front of the mirror to check out the damage to her face. Her fingers trembled as she traced the delicate six-inch scar that ran the length of her cheekbone. "Great," she muttered.

"Oh, it doesn't look bad. It will even fade over time," Amanda volunteered.

She spun on her heels, and her hand clutched her throat. "Yeah, you're right." She tried to slow her racing heart. She tugged her clothes on as quickly as she could, then snatched her bag off the sink. Amanda followed her as they rounded the corner for her room. Ben and Clint were still there when they got back.

"Wow, you look no worse for wear." Clint's massive arm slid around her shoulders and gave her a quick squeeze.

"Thanks." She laughed. When she was with them, she didn't want to leave, but alone at night curled under the covers, her family flooded her thoughts and sobs racked her body. The urge to go home scared her to the point of escaping and running away.

"Are you okay?" Ben's eyes locked with hers, and she couldn't look away. Heat rose in her cheeks as he gingerly traced the scar on her cheek with his finger.

"Yes."

"Well, I don't know about you, but I'm ready to crash for the night." Amanda gave Casey's shoulder a squeeze as she left her room. She grabbed Clint by the arm and yanked him in the direction she headed.

"Me, too. See you in the morning." Clint waved from the door.

"Well, good night," She awkwardly shifted from one foot to the other as Ben stood there.

"Go to bed. I don't want to leave you alone tonight." Ben walked to the corner and plopped down on the chair. He threw his feet up toward the end of the bed, and they thudded heavily as they landed on the old, beaten-up footboard.

Casey sighed. "Ben, I don't need a babysitter."

"I didn't say you did. But I won't sleep unless I know someone's here with you."

"Seriously, go back to your room. God will watch over me."

"I'll feel better knowing someone is close by if you need them. Would you feel better if I were outside?" Ben pointed to the hall.

She nodded and stared at his deep blue eyes. Her heart raced, and she was unable to make her feet move. He smiled and picked up the chair and set it outside the room. The thought of him being that close sent goosebumps racing down her arms. She took a deep breath as her eyes started to droop. All she could do was crawl into bed. Did he see the panic on her face? She tried to slow her breathing, certain he would hear her racing heart. As soon as she closed her eyes, darkness took over and pulled her into sleep and a deep hole she couldn't climb out of.

Thirty-Five

"Ben!" Casey screamed.

Ben's heart raced as he rushed off the chair to see she'd lurched upright and thrown her arms out in front of her. He took giant steps to her bed and wrapped her in his arms. "You're okay. You're safe."

"Ben? I'm sorry. I was...it was so real."

"I'm here. It wasn't real." Ben held her as she lay her head on his wrinkled, slept-in shirt. The urge to kiss the top of her head engulfed him. He closed his eyes and laid his cheek on the top of her head. With his arms wrapped around her, he never wanted her to go on a food run again. He didn't want her out of his sight where he couldn't keep her safe.

"Go get some sleep. You didn't need to stay." Casey cringed as her stomach growled.

"Do you want me to bring you something to eat?" Amanda chimed in from the doorway.

"We can all go grab something if you guys want." Casey swung her legs over the side of the bed. "Thanks for coming to rescue me yesterday. I didn't think I would make it." Her voice broke as tears flooded her eyes.

"Nothing to it. Ben wouldn't leave you out there long even if he had to go alone to get you." Clint peeked around the door.

"Oh, I almost forgot. I need to tell you what President Polson said."

"How about after breakfast when we can be in the lab, safe and secure from any prying ears." Clint motioned for them to head for breakfast, and Ben stiffly stood from the side of the bed. He and Clint headed down the hall while Amanda and Casey followed. He glanced back, not liking the distance he was from her. Clint glanced at him and raised an eyebrow, but Ben ignored him and kept walking.

"Can't believe how much of a mess I was yesterday. I've never been through anything like that before. Seriously, I don't know what I would've done if you didn't come after me." Casey shook her head.

Amanda smiled. "Hey, you should've seen me. Once I was out for almost four days. I went out to pick up some computer equipment. They chased me into an alley, so I had to ditch the car. Fell through a manhole and broke my leg. Several lacerations needed stitches. I was there without food or water for two days before our guys were able to find me. I was sure the Monarchs would come back, so I stayed awake the entire time. I didn't sleep for two days before that because it was a rough time, and we were on the verge of discovery."

"How horrible! How long has it been this way since Polson was elected into office?"

"He's been in office for ten years." Ben peered over his shoulder.

Casey shook her head. "No, that's not right. Presidents can only serve two four-year terms at most, shouldn't someone else be elected into office by now?"

"No, he had the laws changed during his first term. If the President deems it necessary for the safety of the country, he can enact a new law that states he can suspend elections until the threat's believed unsubstantiated or neutralized. Blah blah blah." Amanda rolled her eyes.

"Guess he hasn't deemed it so."

Amanda laughed. "Exactly."

"I can't believe no one's been able to change anything to remove him from office," Casey muttered under her breath.

Casey joked with Clint and Amanda while they ate. Hope churned in Ben for the first time since he brought her here. He glanced over, locking eyes with her hazel ones, that had the slightest hint of emerald specks, and winked. The other two bantered back and forth. He pressed his lips together when a blush rose in her cheeks. She lowered her gaze to the bowl of cereal that was in front of her. He smiled as she swirled the spoon in the lukewarm milk that covered the bottom. He listened to her jeans swish against the leg of the chair as she bounced her leg up and down.

CLINT CLOSED THE DOOR to the lab after they all meandered in. "Okay, tell us what you heard."

"Polson's voice, and he ordered a hit on someone's daughter."

"What? He ordered a hit?" Clint's back stiffened, his muscles rigid as he frowned.

Casey nodded. "Yes. He said if he didn't want to contribute, he would lose his daughter."

"Oh, if only we had a chance to record it." Clint's shoes scuffed the floor as he paced.

She continued. "I'd gotten out of the room where they held me, and I recognized his voice. At first, I couldn't place it because it sounded so familiar, but I wasn't sure if it was someone from my past, or from this time. It was from the news broadcasts from here, and it was Polson. He was talking about someone named Grables who didn't contribute his share or something to that nature. He told another person if he didn't want to pay his contributions to take out his daughter, and they would see how he would react."

"What? Grables? Oh, we need to put a stop to this." Clint huffed as he marched out.

Casey watched Clint leave. "Oh, no. What did I say? And who are the Grables?"

"You didn't say anything wrong. We needed to know before anything happened. The Grables are a wealthy family from before the fall of eastern America, and they're a huge influence in the movement against Polson and donated to our cause to bring him down. They support us not only in keeping our secret but financing whatever we need to keep going. We need to warn him that Polson ordered a hit on his daughter. Clint went to talk to Chloe so she could send a message out priority Lion's Den." The concern in Ben's eyes bothered her.

"What's Lion's Den?" Casey loved the biblical codes they used.

"It means someone's in immediate danger. If he's risking exposure at the Monarchs's headquarters by conducting a meeting on this here, then something's happened where he needs money." Amanda absently twirled her hair around her finger.

Ben hung his head as he paced back and forth in the lab. "Maybe James knows something about the Monarchs we can use."

Clint's large frame blocked most of the doorway. "Ben, I don't trust this James. I think the fact that he was around at the time we rescued Casey is a little too convenient. He doesn't have a place to go. Everyone knows that being outside of the living areas is a crime, and to be caught means interrogation, death, or both. Why would someone be that close to their building at night after curfew and risk exposure? I think he jumped in to make us think he was helping, but he's secretly part of the Monarchs."

Ben glanced at Clint. "I'm not sure. He didn't have to help, and there were enough of them that, if he is one of them, they could have taken us out, recaptured Casey, and taken Amanda."

"I don't trust him. My gut instinct says there's something wrong. When have I ever been wrong, when I have this feeling?" Clint held up his hands.

"Never. I've known you long enough. You wouldn't bring something like this up if you weren't sure." Ben pulled a stool away from the table but didn't sit.

"You can't be serious. They hit him pretty hard. Would they hit one of their own like that if he was in league with them?" Amanda stared at Clint.

Clint pointed at Amanda and raised his eyebrows. "How far would they go to kill us? They've searched for us for years, yet we're always a step ahead of them because God's on our side. How far would they go to take us out?"

"What do we do now? Send him away?" Amanda glanced toward the hall.

"No. I think we can feed him information to see if it gets back to them to know for sure which side he's on." Clint rounded one of the lab tables and stared at the relics.

Amanda joined Clint. "What information do we feed him, so we know it came from James?"

"Not sure. It has to be something distinctive so that it couldn't come from any other source but him." Clint opened the lid to the weapon relic.

"Why can't we use the ring and ask about the Monarchs and Polson?" Ben piped in.

"The ring? One of the relics you found?" Casey edged closer. What could a ring do?

Ben reached around Amanda; tugged a ring out of one of the cases, and slid it on his first finger. It was a silver band with strange symbols on it, and in the center section, a yellow stone shaped into a continuous circle fit inside. It was an amazing piece of work and had probably taken many painstaking hours to cut the stone and fashion it into the center of the band.

There was a slight twinkle from the stone. Ben placed his hand on Clint's shoulder and smirked at Amanda. "When we were kids, did you break the window on old man Shepard's house?"

Clint stared across the room, his gaze unfocused. "It was an accident. I was throwing a baseball in the air and swinging my bat to try to connect with the ball to work on my hand-eye coordination to beat Billy Tannon. I swung as hard as I could thinking I could hit it farther when I connected with the ball, and it sailed over the fence through the window."

Amanda cackled, and Casey's jaw dropped. She could tell these were the closest of friends. Her family flashed through her mind—her niece and nephew, their infectious giggle when she tickled them. Her dad watching them play with a content smile on his face, full of pride for his children. The history of these three was from early childhood, something she'd never have with them. Her heart ached. She shoved her hands in her pockets as she sucked in her bottom lip.

"Ha! You're such a horrible liar, and I still can't believe Mr. Shepard believed you when you said you didn't do it." Ben sounded as if he won a long-running bet and high-fived his sister.

"Would you quit it? It's not fair that you asked me that. You don't think I didn't feel guilty when it happened?" Clint hopped off the stool.

"Oh, calm down, you big cry baby. He knew the whole time. He was giving you a chance to come clean, maybe when you grew up a little more." Amanda took a swing with an imaginary bat.

Clint wadded up a piece of paper and tossed it at Amanda, who ducked gracefully, then curtsied.

"What do you mean, 'he knew?'" Ben's mouth hung open as his eyes grew wide.

"He saw Clint do it. I was in my room, sick. Mom wouldn't let me go out and play. When I heard the crash, I ran to my window. Mr. Shepard was talking to Clint. When you walked away, he smiled, so later I asked him why he smiled if his window was broken. He said it took him back to when he was a kid, and a similar thing happened to him."

"I can't picture Mr. Shepard being a kid with him living next door all those years, and even when we were little, he still was so much older than everyone on the block." Ben's eyes had a faraway look.

"You were always scared to go into his yard when we hit the ball or lost a Frisbee over there. I still don't know anyone who can scale a galvanized, six-foot chain-link fence as fast as you." Amanda looked like she was in her element, reminiscing about the better times of their childhood.

Casey blew out her breath. She darted into the hallway and rapidly blinked as she thought about Matt. She couldn't let them see her like this. It'd upset Ben, especially since she told him she blamed him for this. She couldn't bear to hurt him again. He was so important to her now, and her attraction grew stronger with each passing day.

"How do we know what question to ask James, and know he's telling the truth? And Clint, did you know you told the truth when Ben asked the question?" Casey asked as she sidestepped into the lab and busied herself with an object on the desk as if she had never left.

"Yes, but I couldn't stop myself from answering."

Amanda raised both eyebrows at her. Maybe one day she'd be able to let these three in and talk about what bothered her. Not yet, though. Not when the loss of her family was so raw and painful.

"At least the ring works." Casey wondered what question they would be able to ask James about Polson.

"There you are." Doc stood in the doorway. "Rumor has it you were involved in a pretty bad incident yesterday." He checked over Casey's healed injuries. "I was going to ask why you didn't come to me, but it doesn't look like you needed a doctor."

"It was the healing relic. She can also heal herself." Amanda smiled wide.

"Amazing. I wish I had those options when treating patients."

"Come on, Doc. You'd eventually be out of a job. Then what would you do?" Clint clasped him on the shoulder.

"I would rather be bored than work on injured friends and loved ones any day."

"I hear ya, but we still need a doctor. We're glad you're one of the good guys doing God's work." Clint towered over Doc's worn body that was hunched with age.

"Amen. Yous guys heading to lunch?" Doc ambled to the doorway.

"Wow, is it that late?" Clint double-checked his watch against the clock on the wall.

"Yep. Time flies, don't it?" Doc disappeared.

Clint turned to the others. "You guys hungry?"

"Big time." Amanda looped her arm through Casey's as they headed toward the door together. It was more Amanda tugging her along, and Casey helpless to do anything but follow.

"Meet you there. We need to lock up here first." Ben had the relics on a tray as he headed toward a door at the back of the lab she hadn't been through yet.

"You okay?" Amanda's question pulled her back from her thoughts.

"What?"

"You looked sad back there when we were joking around."

"I was thinking of my brother and how close we are—or were—and how much I miss him, Dad, and my friends." She averted her eyes.

"I couldn't imagine being taken from everything and everyone I know and love."

"It's harder during times like today." Casey pressed her lips together.

"I'm sorry. We shouldn't carry on like that. Sometimes we don't realize what we're saying and how it could affect you." Amanda leaned into Casey

"No need to apologize, and don't change who you are when you're around me. I think of you as my friends, and I don't want you uncomfortable and not sure what to say. It'd only make it worse if I made you guys uneasy."

"We're so glad you're here. I see you as a sister, and not only in Christ but a real sister if I had one." Amanda squeezed Casey's arm with the one she had linked through hers.

Casey smiled. "Me too. I miss my family and would go back if I could, but couldn't wish for a better group of friends while I'm going through this."

"Ben is guilt-ridden for what you've been through because of him." Amanda dropped her arm.

Casey's heart quickened at the mention of Ben's name. She had spent a couple of hours with him in the lab, self-conscious of being caught looking at him for too long. Yet being away from him for this small amount of time, the mention of his name made her heart flutter like a schoolgirl with a crush. He was different than anyone she had ever known. She didn't want to get her hopes up, yet her heart raced at the possibilities.

"Hello, earth to Casey." Amanda waved a hand in front of Casey's face.

Casey blinked. "Sorry, I was thinking of something."

"Or someone?"

Casey glanced at her and smiled. "Please don't tell him. I don't want him to know."

"I won't tell Clint." Amanda smirked.

"Clint? No. Ben."

Amanda nudged her and grinned. Her resemblance to Ben shocked her.

Casey shifted her eyes away from Amanda as she shuffled her feet. "There's something different about him. I can't describe it."

"Yes, there is. Why wouldn't you want him to know? It isn't like God didn't put you two together or anything. He's kind of figured that part out."

"The guys I dated in the past either liked me more than I like them or vice versa. We could never seem to meet in the middle. There were days the loneliness swallowed me whole, and I couldn't breathe. On other days, I was fine alone and couldn't imagine anyone in my life. I came to the conclusion that maybe God's plan for me didn't include finding someone. I gave everything over to Him instead of trying to make things happen how I wanted them. I was a lot happier, and a lot less stressed. Now I need to delve back into that frame of mind. God's in control, but I'm scared to let go of the reins."

Amanda stopped and turned to Casey. "He's amazing that way, isn't He? I can't imagine going through what's happened here because of this President and not having God in control, guiding me through life during all of this. There were a lot of deaths and suicides when the Monarch's first attacked. The people who lost loved ones were so distraught they took their own lives because they didn't have a personal relationship with God. All they need to do is lean on Him, and He'll always catch them."

"Did you lose anyone close?"

Amanda shook her head. "No. Ben and I were lucky. Our parents had moved to the West Coast years before. We chose to stay in the Midwest because we don't like hot weather. They're safe. They asked us to join them, but we've explained we need to stay and fight for God's people. We pray for them all the time."

"At least you two and Clint are together through this. Maybe it'd be easier to make it through with each other reminding you God's here with you."

"Yes, it does. I couldn't imagine being alone—well, I guess like you are. We're here for you no matter what, whether it's a friend to talk to or anything. Have you thought you're here for a reason? Why else would you dream of Ben weeks before all this?" Amanda continued down the hall.

"I miss talking to my friends, but I'll admit I'm crazy about Ben, but you can't tell him. I'm not ready to let him in yet. I don't think my heart can take any more pain."

"Casey, I think you need to tell him. You may be shocked at what develops between the two of you. And who says there will be pain? It keeps him awake at night, which, of course, keeps me awake because he comes to talk to me about it. I think he would like to know."

"Who would like to know what?" Ben and Clint joined them. Ben clad in his usual navy-blue t-shirt—the fabric stretched to its limits around his biceps and complimented by jeans and boots.

Thirty-Six

Ben studied the blush that spread across Casey's cheeks but kept it to himself. He could probably guess what the two of them talked about. She appeared so fragile when they brought her back to the warehouse yesterday.

"No one. Didn't your mother ever teach you not to eavesdrop on someone's conversation?" Amanda scowled at him.

"Well, since I had the same mother as you, yes, she did. But we weren't eavesdropping. We were joining you for lunch like we said we were going to." Ben snarled at his sister. She looped her arm through Clint's and walked on ahead.

Ben startled her. "You okay? You look pale."

"No, I'm okay. It just startled me when you walked up behind us." She gaped after Clint and Amanda.

"Sorry about that. I bet you're a bit jumpy from what you went through."

"Nothing to be sorry about. I'll be fine." Casey stiffened.

Ben reached for her, then stopped. "Good, we want you to feel like one of the family."

Casey gazed down at her feet. "It'll take a little getting used to, is all."

"Well, Amanda's grown attached to you and thinks of you as a sister."

"I like her, as well. If I could have chosen anyone to go through this with, it'd be you guys. You mean a lot to me, and we'll be together in eternity, but I'm glad I know you before Heaven." She glanced at Ben.

Ben slung his arm around her shoulders and squeezed. "Well, thanks. We're glad you're here. If you need something, let us know."

Casey cleared her throat. "Thanks. I appreciate it. There are several times I think about calling a friend or my brother when it hits me that they're gone, and I can't. I didn't realize how much I leaned on them. I should've told them before I lost them how much they meant to me."

"I'm so sorry." Ben took a step away from her.

"I'm here for a reason, but...I still think about home. Although I'm not sure my friends would've been able to pull off a rescue or dealt with the situation as you did. Not sure if I told you thanks."

A smile crept across Ben's face. "No need to thank us. If not for us, you wouldn't have been in that predicament. I have a confession."

Casey flinched as Clint and Amanda's laughter reached them.

"Your eyes are blue again, and your scars are almost gone, although this time you aren't glowing. I wonder if your emotions are tied in with how you heal. You flinched when they laughed."

"What? My eyes are blue? I didn't tense up, I mean I did but not because—" Casey's cheeks flushed red, as Ben's brow furrowed.

"Well, if your eyes are a glimpse of your emotions, I hope it isn't because you're still upset with me. I hope you know how important you are to us."

Casey's chin trembled. Ben grabbed her by the shoulder, she tensed and jumped.

Ben pulled his hand away "I didn't mean to upset you."

"No, it meant a lot to me what you said. I'm not upset." Casey averted her eyes.

"Sorry, did I hurt you?" Ben dropped his hands to his sides.

"You didn't. I was startled. I'm not used to people touching me...caring for me. I never let anyone past my walls." The words tumbled out. "Hey, let's catch up to Clint and Amanda." Casey marched away from Ben as she rubbed her hands over her arms. They had a lot of work to do to convince her she was important to them. He could picture the wall she had around her. He would do what he needed to keep her safe and alive. They needed her probably more than she needed them.

Her leaving him in the hall gave him a reprieve of telling her why he brought her here. His heart raced at the thought that she would tell him to never talk to her again.

"HELLO, EARTH TO CASEY. You going to join us?" Amanda waved at Casey from across the table. Casey was off in her own little world.

"Sorry, thinking."

Ben smirked. "Oh, hey, Amanda. You don't know what that's like, do you?"

She tossed a French fry at Ben, who caught it in mid-air, tossing it back at her hitting her forehead before she could blink.

Casey howled with laughter, and Clint joined her. Amanda stared at Ben with her mouth open. Soon Ben and Amanda joined in. Casey laughed so hard tears streamed down her face as the stress of the last several weeks found an outlet. The torment of yesterday, and the possibility she could have died, found a release and used her laughter to escape.

Finally, the hysterics died down, and they were able to finish lunch without so much as a flying French fry or any other food. With their molded plastic lunch trays dropped off at the wash station, they decided to do more work in the lab.

As they were about to turn the corner of the hallway to the lab, Clint held his fist up in military fashion and motioned everyone back against the wall. Ben joined him at the front, where they strained to listen to what was going on around the corner. Soon Casey heard why they had stopped, metal on metal scraping sounds reached her ears, she raised her eyebrows to Amanda, who only shrugged.

Clint peeked around the corner but pulled his head back so fast Casey wasn't sure he saw anything. He held up a single finger to show them there was only one person. He motioned, in military fashion again, to stay where they were, and he and Ben went around the back way to the lab.

Amanda inched closer to the corner and swatted Casey's hand away as she tried to grab her arm to stop her. Inching ever closer, she stopped and leaned far enough forward Casey was sure she would tumble into the middle of the hallway and expose them both.

After what seemed like hours but was only a couple minutes, Ben and Clint rejoined them, looking a little dirtier than they had when they left. They strolled around the corner to the lab. Amanda and Casey joined them.

"He didn't find anything, but he was looking." Clint surveyed the lab.

"Who?" Amanda looked around, checking her pages of notes.

"James. Good thing we keep everything locked in the closet. Ben and I went through the vents to the storage room in the back. James went through your notes, Amanda, and looked around as if searching for something."

"Did he take anything?" Amanda rubbed the back of her neck.

"No, he didn't even find the relics. He's here on a mission. Otherwise, he wouldn't need to break in while we were at lunch." Clint knelt to study the lock on the door and frowned. "This would take an expert to pick, and you can hardly tell it has been touched."

"How much of an expert, and how worried should we be?" Ben joined Clint at the door.

"We'll need to keep the relics with one of us at all times. I would say we need to look at moving from the warehouse district."

"Move?" Amanda violently chewed on her fingernail.

"Are we in danger?" All the moving conversation, and James being an expert at picking locks, put her on edge. Casey had one run-in with the Monarchs. She didn't want another.

"Yes, if we can't stop him from getting out and telling the Monarchs where we are. They've tried to take down the cells we established all over the Midwest, but failed so far." Clint marched over to the closet, pulled a key out of his pocket, and unlocked the door. The hinges screamed and groaned as if asking to be oiled as the door opened.

Ben joined Clint and pulled the relics off the top shelf, where they were hidden behind some binders. He slid the ring on, handed the bracelet to Amanda, then the weapon to Clint.

Amanda piled several pages of notes on top of the parchment, which she slid into a satchel. The worn brown leather bag concealed their secrets from prying eyes as she slung the strap over her shoulder.

Leaving the lab with the relics hidden in plain sight, on their bodies, and all documentation with them, they headed toward the women's side of the warehouse and Amanda's room. Once inside, she moved the nightstand away from the wall and pressed a secret compartment which slid open a thin drawer hidden under the top edge of the nightstand. Sliding the papers out of the satchel, she placed them in the hidden drawer then wrestled with it to slide it back in place.

BEN WATCHED CLINT RUB his chin as he strode to the door and peered out, scanning the hallway. Clint's actions told him something was off. He wondered if it was James. "We need to find a way to get James out of the way, and everyone and everything moved to the new location before we let him go."

"You have a new location?" Casey perched on the end of the bed.

"Yes. We have numerous houses in a suburb. We secretly worked on them for the last few months to route an underground network of hidden tunnels connecting to each house so we can move back and forth."

Casey wrapped her arms around herself. "How far away is it?"

"Not far, about twenty miles at most." Ben parked himself on the arm of a chair, similar to the one in Casey's room.

"Will we need to take all the furniture, clothes, and food?" Casey frowned.

"No, furniture is in the homes, but we'll need to pack the clothes and food. We can't take a chance we run out of food before a new pickup location for our reserves is set up." Clint patrolled the doorway.

"How do we lure James out of here?" Amanda stretched across her bed, her head hanging off one side and her feet off the other.

Ben frowned as Clint made another pass by the door. It was wrong to allow James to join their group. What were they thinking, inviting him? "We'll start packing now while someone distracts him, so we know where he is in the warehouse at all times. We'll move our things out immediately, and when we're safe in the new houses, we'll come back and release him. I don't want to let him go and try to move because it would only make for a smaller possibility of getting everyone out."

"Don't worry. We've had to do this before, and with no warning." Amanda's voice carried to Ben from his right.

"Okay, let's pass the word to pack and that we'll be moving today or the next. I need Doc to give us a sedative and find a way to slip it to James before he finds out too much about us. Amanda, go ahead and pull out the storage boxes and start packing yours and Casey's room immediately. Ben, stay with them." Clint nodded at Casey.

Ben rose from the chair and gently brushed his hand over Casey's shoulder. He looked down and smiled as goosebumps ran rampant up and down her arms.

"Come on, Casey. You can help me pull boxes out of storage so we can start with your room and finish mine after dinner." Amanda grabbed Casey's hand, pulling her off the bed. They were in the hall before she could protest.

They heaved open heavy metal double doors to reveal a large storage room filled with boxes from floor to ceiling. Amanda walked to the right and pulled boxes off a pile tossing several on the ground. She slid several rolls of tape over her hand up her arm then grabbed markers.

"Grab those, would you?" She nodded her head at the first stack she'd piled on the floor. Grabbing them, Casey followed her into the hall, closing the doors behind them. Ben kept an eye on them to make sure James didn't trouble them. He couldn't shake the sensation that they were being watched. As soon as Casey and Amanda were safe in Casey's room, Ben jogged to catch up to Clint.

Thirty-Seven

They finished with the last box, and Casey grabbed the unused boxes while Amanda grabbed the tape and markers. Both reached for the doorknob at the same time. Amanda stopped and shook her head to Casey. With her ear pressed against the door, she motioned Casey to put the boxes down that she carried.

There was a light knock on the door, and Amanda stepped back. She concealed the markers and tape in a drawer. She leaned the boxes in her hand against the wall behind the door where Casey's boxes were. Amanda motioned for her to open the door to whoever was on the other side. Casey reached for the doorknob as it started to turn. She opened the door as if she didn't know someone tried to open it from the other side. James stood there with a fake plastered smile that sent chills down her spine. There was something in his smile she didn't trust.

"Yes? Can I help you, James?" Casey held the door partially open. Her knuckles turned white.

James smiled, his eyes dark. "Yeah, I was looking for Amanda. Ben said she wanted to have dinner with me tonight, and I thought I would find her to accept her invitation."

"Oh, great. Glad you'll be joining us for dinner." Amanda stepped from behind the partially open door.

"Us?" James glanced down the hall.

"Yeah, thought it'd be nice since we haven't seen much of you after you helped with Casey."

"Oh, sure. By the way, the damage was worse than that." He waved his hands up and down in front of Casey, motioning from her head to her feet.

"I'm a fast healer. I inherited it from my dad. He always healed fast."

"No, there was blood everywhere. You needed stitches." He reached forward and tried to touch the back of her head. She jerked away.

"Sorry, still jumpy after the whole ordeal. I was drugged, so it looked worse than it was. Doc did a good job cleaning my wounds." She smiled as she took a step back.

"Oh, understandable why you'd be jumpy. I'm glad it's not as bad as it looked." James took a step forward.

"Thanks. So I guess we'll see you at dinner?" Amanda's eyes darted to the hall.

"Um, sure. Meet you at dinner." James stepped forward again.

Casey swallowed past a lump in her throat as she balled her hands into fists. She didn't like the fact he was invading her personal space. She blew out her breath as Amanda glanced at her fists.

"So, Casey and I need to go."

James never acknowledged Amanda but took another step toward Casey. Amanda's eyes grew wide. James stared at Casey as a smirk twitched at the corners of his mouth.

"Yup...dinner," James stepped back, not taking his eyes from Casey.

Casey closed the door, leaned back, and sighed as she looked at Amanda. "Don't you think Ben could have warned you he was using you in this little setup?"

"I think he would've if he could, but you did great. If I didn't know how you were healed, I would have believed your story."

"Well, he had no ground to stand on since no scars can prove otherwise."

"No, you did great."

Another small knock on the door had her hair standing up on the back of her neck. She opened the door a mere sliver and smiled. Ben and Clint stood there, and Clint looked up and down the hall before closing the door behind him.

"Hey, we wanted to give you the heads up. We told James you wanted to ask him to join you for dinner tonight, so he might be looking for you to be your dinner guest." Ben glanced at his sister.

"Now, you tell me." Amanda scowled.

"You guys didn't have your communicators turned on." Ben tapped his ear.

"Oh, sorry." Amanda mouthed oops to Casey with exaggerated wide eyes.

"What happened?"

"James was here and started questioning Casey about her bruises and cuts being healed and kept walking toward her to try and touch the back of her head to prove it."

"He tried to touch you?" Ben took a step toward the door.

"He tried to, but she was pretty quick to dodge him and his questions. She did great."

"Did he believe you? What did you say?" Ben whirled to face Casey.

"Yes, or at least I think he did. Amanda said he did." She slid the toe of her shoe back and forth across the floor.

"She was great. She even had me believing what she said. Although when he kept walking toward her, I thought we were in trouble."

"What do you mean he kept walking toward her?" Clint clenched his jaw.

"Almost as if he was testing her to find out if he could scare her, or if she would fight."

Ben's shoulders tensed. "Don't turn off your communicators until we're away from him!"

Amanda snagged the marker and tape she had earlier. "We're headed to do my room before dinner. Did you guys need us to do your rooms after that?"

"No, we were coming to grab boxes for ours. We also informed everyone about James, so after we sedate and detain him, everyone should be packed and ready to go tonight so we might be able to move out our first group of boxes before morning." Clint marched to the door, opened it a sliver. He tilted his head, listening for any sound from the hallway before he opened it wide enough for someone to fit through.

Thirty-Eight

Several boxes later, both Ben and Clint's rooms were done. The contents consisted of their clothes with weapons nestled in, hidden among the fabric. They smiled as they listened to the girls talk on the other side of the warehouse as they packed Amanda's room. They both nodded to turn off their communicators.

Ben spun the ring around and around on his finger. "A couple of weeks ago, I wouldn't have thought Casey would be okay with this move."

"I told you to give it time. I don't think she trusts us completely yet, but she's come a long way since you first brought her here. She still has nightmares."

"She what?"

"When I walk the halls at night to make sure everything's secure on my rounds, I hear her. She still has nightmares."

"I didn't know that." Ben dropped on the edge of the bed with his elbows on his knees, his head in his hands.

"She's come a long way since then. She's still the fighter who wanted to slug you that day in the lab. I think she can take a lot, but I don't want to see the day she's pushed past her limit." Clint checked the hallway for the hundredth time.

"We need to take out James. The girls aren't safe with him here. The fact that he tried to touch Casey...just...makes me so mad." Ben lurched off the end of the bed.

"You and me both brother. We'll do it today. I don't like that no one knows where he disappears to. No one's seen him in a couple of hours. Ned said he was headed back from the empty side of the warehouse when we came in here." Clint pushed the last box he closed onto the pile.

Ben turned toward Clint. "What would he be doing on that side of the building? Didn't you tell him not to wander around and to stick to this side?"

"Yes. I can only assume he was contacting the Monarchs. We aren't safe anymore." Clint checked the hallway again. The hairs stood on the back of his neck. A shadow moved on the wall past several doors. He couldn't see who made the shadow, but something made him reach for his firearm. He firmly grabbed the butt of the gun and let his hand rest as the shadow moved. The girls being in the same building as this man they let into their lives irked him. The shadow darted farther down the hall, and Clint's hand pulled up on the gun, removing it from his waistband. His heart raced as it did every time he had a weapon in his hand as if it heightened his senses. Taking a step into the hallway, he focused his eyes on the elusive shadow that stopped.

The rustle of clothing as Ben stood from the bed reached Clint's ears. He didn't need to look back to know Ben had his firearm out, stalking toward his position. Clint raised two fingers and motioned toward the shadow. Ben's figure emerged in his peripheral vision as he nodded.

Clint took the lead and crept down the hall, knees bent. His hands held his firearm in front of him, finger off the trigger. Only because of his military training could he tell Ben's movements, but to the untrained ear, it would be hard distinguishing the noise of the fabric swishing as they approached the corner.

Just shy of the corner, Clint stopped. With his back against the wall, he closed his eyes and listened. Someone's feet shuffled against the floor as if they dragged something. Clint blew the air out of his lungs through his mouth as he counted to three. A quick peek around the corner, he ducked back out of sight. James was hauling a large bag through the door to the empty part of the warehouse.

The latch on the door caught as he closed it behind him. He jogged to the corner where Clint and Ben pressed themselves even flatter against the wall. He turned right at the junction where they were just to the left of him. He never saw them as he jogged toward the women's side.

Clint motioned Ben around the corner as he pressed his communicator. Ben pressed his as he reached for the door James just came through. A quick nod from his best friend and Ben opened the door.

Thirty-Nine

They were done with Amanda's room in less than an hour and had her name on her boxes with them stacked behind the door. They didn't want to show their hand before having a chance to play it.

"Ready to meet the guys for dinner?" Casey reached for the doorknob as Amanda joined her.

"Sure, let's go meet the boys."

"Hey." James startled her, and a small cry of shock escaped. "You didn't say what time to meet for dinner, so I thought I would check, but you weren't in Casey's room, so I's getting ready to knock."

Casey's hand covered her mouth. Ben and Clint raced around the corner. Her cry was louder than she thought. She laughed to downplay it as she tried to step into the hall with Amanda on her heels. James didn't move, and he blocked the doorway only inches from Casey.

"You startled me. I didn't expect anyone to be outside the door." Casey chuckled as she stopped short, and Amanda ran into the back of her.

"Sorry. I was gonna knock when you opened the door. Honest." Beads of sweat glistened on James's forehead. He was out of breath, and she was unsure why.

"No need to apologize. You ready to eat?" Amanda grabbed the back of Casey's shirt.

"Sure, let's go." James took half a step to the side. His haunting eyes came alive as Amanda started to pass him. When he tried to step forward again, Ben and Clint joined them.

Ben slung his arm around Casey's shoulders, she jumped, and her heart raced. His strong arm around her comforted her, and she tried to relax. She grasped his hand that draped over her shoulder with her trembling one. He steered her around James as they followed his sister. Clint whispered to Casey through her communicator, "Casey, don't leave Ben's side. He killed Mike and hid his body on the other side of the warehouse."

Ben squeezed her hand and tightened his arm around her shoulders. Casey tensed. Amanda slowed down, "No, Amanda. Keep going. We're going to take him out at dinner."

Ben guided Casey into line behind James. He wrapped his arm around her upper arms and kissed the top of her head. She hooked her hand over his arm.

James grabbed a bowl of chili, following Amanda to the round table in the corner. Ben and Clint both grabbed chili. They doused each with liquid from a vial Clint removed from the t-shirt pocket he'd hidden underneath the plaid shirt he wore over it. They kept their backs to the table as the servers took their spoons and gave them new ones. Ben nodded at Casey.

The final three sat at the table, with Amanda and James. He stared at the trays Ben and Clint carried that mirrored his own. Nodded his head at them as they sat on each side of him.

"Man, I forgot a fork, I'll be right back." Amanda stood.

James jumped out of his seat. "Let me. I'll be right back."

Clint had their bowls switched before James was halfway to the food. He switched James spoon that was in his chili and deposited it into the new bowl on his tray,

James came back to the table and handed Amanda a fork as Clint ate his chili, while Ben took an enormous bite of his cornbread.

"Thanks. Some men still know how to be a gentleman." Amanda nudged her brother, who only nudged her back and smiled.

"Sure, no problem." James stirred his chili as if he changed his mind and didn't want it. He took a bite, nodded his head. "Yep, without a doubt, glad I got the chili."

"Bitty makes the best chili," Ben mumbled with a mouth full of cornbread.

James pulled at the collar of his polo shirt and chugged his soda. After a few more bites, he placed his hands on the table on either side of his tray and stood, his skin flushed as he sweated profusely.

"You okay?" Ben rose out of his chair and put his hand on James's shoulder.

"A little dizzy is all." He shook his head and grabbed the back of the chair.

"You don't look so good. Do you want to lay down?" Ben's concern seemed genuine.

James blinked several times. "No, maybe I need some water."

"I'll grab you some. It is the least I can do since you got me a fork." Amanda rose but didn't move.

A hush fell over the room. James's knuckles turn white while he clutched the back of his chair.

Everyone in the cafeteria stared. James stumbled back several steps and pointed a finger at Ben and Clint, who rushed to him as his knees buckled. James lunged at Casey, who jumped out of the way, dumping her chair over. Clint bent at the perfect moment for James to fall over his shoulder. He carried him out of the room, followed by Ben.

Casey and Amanda grabbed their trays and dropped them at the wash station. Everyone else went back to eating and talking to the person sitting next to them as if nothing happened.

James bounced on the gurney Clint dropped him on. Ben and Clint used restraints that took Casey back to the image of the chair she was restrained in at the Monarch headquarters. She shivered. No doubt, these were also like the ones they used on her when she first got here.

CASEY STARED AT JAMES'S lifeless form. "How long's he going to be out?"

"We'll keep him sedated until everyone, and everything's moved into the new area." Clint seized the head of the gurney while Ben took the foot and wheeled James through the hallway to the infirmary.

"Come on, Casey. We can move our boxes out into the van." Casey tried to keep up as Amanda jogged toward their rooms.

Ben and Clint locked the wheels of the gurney and nodded to Hank, who waited for them at the end of the hall. Another tug on the restraints before Ben joined Clint. Hank wrung his hands as he stared at the gurney.

"Did you take care of Mike?" Ben strolled up to Hank.

"Yeah. Had someone take him through the tunnels to the garage where he was picked up by friends. They'll make sure he gets a proper burial. Doc said he did a number on him before he killed him. I'm not sure how we didn't hear it. He broke several bones, and Doc said he doesn't think it was from interrogation either, but instead, someone not only sick but pure evil." Hank stared around Ben and Clint to the gurney.

"Does anyone else know?" Clint leaned his hulking body against the wall.

"No, we kept it quiet like you asked. We didn't want to scare the families and kids." Hank jammed his hands in the front pockets of his jeans that had seen better days.

"Good, thanks for your help." Ben spun on his heels.

Clint snatched his gun out of his waistband, as Ben did the same. The hallway was quiet. Ben motioned to Clint. One hesitant step forward, James groaned, Ben shook his head at Clint. This man killed one of theirs today, and he wanted to crush him with his hands. Clint was right. There was something evil about him. His thoughts flash to the woman he loved and his sister. He would do anything to keep them safe.

"Ben, grab another dose from Doc." Clint tugged on the restraints yet again.

"I'm going to finish packing," Hank glanced at James before bolting through the hallway.

Ben sprinted down the hall toward the infirmary. Doc had his back to the door packing all the medical supplies they accumulated over the couple of months they had been in the warehouse. It was the longest they had stayed in any one spot for any length of time.

"Doc, we need another dose of sedative. James is starting to come around."

Doc jumped at the sound of Ben's voice. "Already made a couple of doses, grab the two injectors off my desk."

"Thanks, Doc. You going to be ready to go in a bit?" Ben surveyed pure chaos in the boxes that littered every square inch of the infirmary, from the floor to the cots.

"Yeah. Casey and Amanda are going to help finish after they put the ones from their rooms on the van." Doc didn't look up from his inventory sheet as he counted the supplies.

Ben snatched the injectors then darted out the door. Several turns later, he was back with Clint, who had his gun trained on James's chest. He drooled out of the side of his mouth as he laughed hysterically. "You're all dead!" Pure hate oozed from his cold, dark eyes.

Ben jammed an injector into his arm and depressed the plunger. Clint let out the pent-up air from his lungs and put his weapon back. James's head lolled to the side as he slipped into unconsciousness.

"Let's hurry everyone out of here. He said we would all be dead in a couple of hours. We can't wait to leave. They want Casey back. They take it personally when someone escapes from them. He also told them she had no injuries, and they want to know how that's possible." Clint grabbed a roll of tape off the box as someone walked past on the way to the van. He yanked a piece of tape off, tearing it with his teeth to cover James's mouth.

Ben checked the restraints again before racing to the other side of the warehouse for his and Clint's boxes. They were the ones that held any hope of them protecting this group if the Monarchs rushed in. Clint caught up to him, and they hurried around the corner to their rooms. Ben tossed a case to Clint, who quickly assembled the rifle and stowed it in the bag, slinging it over his shoulder. He concealed his own shotgun in another case he placed over his shoulder and head, so it sat slanted across his back.

Ben and Clint grabbed the three boxes of their clothes that also hid more weapons and raced to the underground tunnels.

Forty

Casey and Amanda's rooms were void of any signs anyone lived there. They made their way to Doc's infirmary, and Amanda let out a low whistle as she took in the clutter he still had.

"Doc, this is a mess. We need to be ready to go." Amanda peered into one of the boxes and wrinkled her nose at Casey, who laughed.

"I just finished inventory, and boxes are ready for each house plus the ones for the infirmary. Please grab the tape and start closing them. They are labeled where they need to go." Doc hefted himself off the floor, where he finished putting the last label on the box for his office.

"Casey, grab that cart in the hallway so we can load the boxes and transfer them to the van."

"Sure." Casey snagged the old rickety gray cart. One of its wheels spun freely as it didn't touch the ground when she rolled it into the doorway. Casey and Amanda froze when they heard James telling Clint that the Monarchs wanted Casey back. James said he told the Monarchs of her healing the wounds they had inflicted. They stared at each other for a couple of moments then worked faster to close all the boxes.

A roll and a half of tape later, the last box was loaded on the cart ready for transport.

Doc grabbed the cart from them and thanked them for their help as he ambled down to the van.

They were met by Ben and Clint. Casey eyed the soft-sided gun cases they had slung across their backs. She didn't say anything but shoved her hands into her pockets as her eyes widened.

"Okay. Ben and Amanda, go check on the male's side of the warehouse and make sure everyone is ready to go while Casey and I check the women's side." Ben and Amanda discussed their parents as they headed for their side of the warehouse. Clint glanced down at Casey, who studied him, waiting for him to say something.

Why would he separate her and Amanda and take her with him for this? She diverted her eyes as he shifted the gun case on his back a little to the left then took long strides down the hall. She hurried to catch up.

"Why did you separate Amanda and me?" Maybe he could at least answer a simple question for her.

"More than likely, the Monarchs know we're here. I always want someone armed to be with you. Once we're at the houses, I need to show you how to use a gun."

"No. I don't ever want to learn," she stammered.

Clint whirled around to her and narrowed his eyes. "Casey, we are at war here. You can't stay on the sidelines and wait for it to end. Our group of Chosen Ones is on the front lines of this. I would never forgive myself if I let you charge in without being able to defend yourself! You heard what James said, the Monarchs want you and are coming for you!"

"I don't want to be on the front lines!"

"I'm sorry. You're stronger than you give yourself credit for. I can also teach you how to fight."

She brushed past him. "I'm not strong."

"Hey," he grabbed her arm, spinning her back around to him.

She clenched her hands into fists as she drew back her right elbow.

"That right there says you're a fighter—the same fighter I saw weeks ago when you were ready to deck Ben." He gazed down at her, and his face softened. His smile showed his dimples.

Casey looked at her right fist. Was she ready to hit him?

"He isn't a bad guy." Clint marched past her but glanced back to make sure she stayed with him.

They reached the first set of rooms. The doors all stood open, and people milled in and out of the rooms at will. "We need to leave. We aren't safe. Please make your way to the loading area. The van will be back shortly to take everyone to the new place."

Clint smiled as everyone filed out of their rooms and murmured between themselves before they disappeared around the corner. Casey ignored the statement, not sure this was a conversation she was ready for, much less with Ben's best friend.

A quick check of the rest of the rooms showed their side of the warehouse vacant.

Clint reached behind his ear and nodded to her to do the same. "Are you okay?"

"Yeah." Casey diverted her eyes.

"You can talk to me. Nothing you say to me will ever be said to anyone else."

"I'll be fine." She searched down the hall, expecting someone to walk past.

"Casey."

She took a deep breath, closed her eyes, and then blew it out through her nose. "I'm working through a couple of things. No big deal."

"I think it is. I can see something bothers you." Clint stopped in the hall.

"You wouldn't understand."

"Try me."

Casey bit her cheek then cleared her throat. "I'm scared someone's hold over me may only end up hurting me like it always did in the past."

"What does the past have to do with the now? You can't compare them. This is an entirely different situation. Trust what's in here." Clint pointed to her heart.

She diverted her eyes. "What if I don't trust my heart?"

He put his hand on his chest. "Trust mine. This is real on both sides, but tear down that wall you've spent years building and let him in."

"I'm not sure I can." Casey took a couple of steps.

"Yes, you can. It will just take a leap of faith in your Heavenly Father." Clint's smile touched his eyes.

Casey locked eyes with Clint as he nodded. He reached behind his ear, activating his communicator. She did the same as Amanda and Ben laughed with someone else. Determined steps led them to the loading dock before the other two got there.

The van backed in, and the engine was left running while Hank opened the back doors. He joined everyone as they formed a circle, joining hands, bowing their heads to pray in unison.

"Dear Heavenly Father, please protect everyone on the next journey You're sending them on. Let them be a witness to the non-believers in the world. May we find favor in Your eyes and Your protection here on earth. Send Your heavenly warriors to place a hedge of protection around us to hide us from Satan's armies tonight and to make a safe journey to our new homes. Thank You for our lives that You touch every day in one way or another. We count our blessings we have You. Until we meet in Heaven, we are here to do Your work here on earth. Thank You for all You give us, in each other and in Your providing for our needs. In Jesus's name, amen."

Her heart raced, and she tried to memorize everyone's face as they loaded into the back of the van. Everyone except the four of them and James scrambled to leave. They pulled out of the warehouse. If only they didn't need to make the journey they were headed out on. She knew God would protect them and keep them safe. But until she saw them again safe in their homes, she wouldn't be able to breathe normally.

"OKAY. LET'S GET READY to go." Clint didn't wait for the other three. He reached the hallway where they ditched James earlier as the rest trailed behind.

"He's still sedated, but Doc left a couple of doses in case we need them." Ben grabbed a couple of injectors and placed them above James's head along with one that was already on the gurney.

Straps held James down as Clint and Ben pushed the gurney, his profusely sweating face caused the tape to come loose as it lay barely attached by the edge. Halfway to the loading dock, Ben snatched a sedative to give James another dose to be on the safe side. He barely grabbed the injector when James's eyes flashed open. He yanked his arms, thrashing against the restraints. Clint pointed his gun at him, finger on the trigger. Ben jammed the injector onto his arm, pulled the trigger to make sure the dose was administered then jumped back.

"You'll pay for this," James slurred, then reached as far as he could in the restraints and grabbed Casey's wrist in a death grip. She screamed seconds before the unmistakable sound of bones breaking filled the air. Ben jumped at him, prying his white-knuckled fingers from her wrist one by one. Clint landed a devastating blow to his jaw. James cursed as his eyelids drooped, and his eyes rolled back into his head. "They're coming for you! They will kill you, and I can't wait to be there when they cut you open to find out what makes you tick."

They stared as James slipped into unconsciousness. Casey shivered at his words.

"Casey, you okay?" Ben moved and blocked her view of James and held her hand gingerly. It swelled as her wrist turned several shades of purple, then black. Ben cringed at the odd angle her bones were now positioned.

"I'm okay," she blurted out as she grabbed Ben's upper arm with her non-broken hand and leaned her head against his chest as her face drained of color.

Clint stormed back to the gurney and jabbed another injector in James's neck. Ben wrapped his arm around Casey's shoulders as blue filtered through her eyes down to her wrist, where bones righted themselves and snapped back in place. Ben grimaced.

"Casey, do you need Doc?" Ben cradled her wrist.

"No, I think I'm good." The blue faded back into her skin as the swelling and purple bruises disappeared. Red marks lingered on Ben's arm when she released it from her death grip.

"We need to move." Ben pulled out the relics, handing the bracelet to Amanda. He put the ring on then tossed Clint the weapon.

Amanda's bracelet wound its way up her arm camouflaging with her skin. "Casey, turn your communicator on in case we get separated."

"It is."

"We aren't sure how we'll do with the small amount of practice we've had with the relics. If we come across the Monarchs and need to fight our way out, these are our backups." Clint handed Amanda a gun, and Casey's eyes grew wide. He motioned with one for her. She shook her head. Ben was okay with that since they hadn't shown her how to use one yet.

"Casey, you go with Ben and make sure the living quarters are sterile at the women's end of the warehouse.

Amanda and I'll take the other end then work our way back here." Clint and Amanda jogged off toward the men's side.

Forty-One

"We need to look for anything personal left by anyone from our group," Ben explained as they took off in the opposite direction. Maybe this would be a good way for them to finally have a heart-to-heart talk.

"Personal, such as a photograph or something?" Casey glanced down the empty hallways.

"Yes, but we don't have photographs anymore. They're image sequences. Something as simple as a hairbrush can be tested for DNA. We can dispose of what's left in the incinerator in the basement."

"Got it." They started with the women's rooms, and when they checked hers and Amanda's, it bothered her that they were void of any personal touches. They opened drawers, lifted mattresses, looked under cushions on chairs and couches, under the beds, armoires, and dressers. They turned every room upside down, not missing anything, including the dust bunnies in the corners. The women's side was clean, with nothing left.

The lab was closer to the women's side, so Ben and Casey went to sterilize it, which took longer than all the rooms combined because there were so many filing cabinets and drawers to be checked. About halfway through one of the cabinets, Casey found papers and literature on the relics and thumbed through them. A clear plastic film was tuck between the pages. She turned it over, and an image of two small boys and a young girl materialized.

"Ben, is this what you called the uh, image something. Is this you guys?"

He joined her, looking over her shoulder and reached around to take the picture. "Image sequence." His fingers brushed hers and lingered for a split second. She turned around to face him, and his eyes locked with hers. Lifting his hand, he pushed behind his ear. Her heart caught in her throat. Her attraction to Ben was unmistakable. He lifted his hands slowly while his eyes never left hers. His hands cupped each side of her face. He pushed behind her ear, leaned in, and kissed her. She pushed against his chest but not hard enough to separate them. Her emotions tugged at her heart, and light-headedness hit. She curled her fingers into the front of his shirt, and before she knew it, she kissed him back.

"I knew you had feelings for me." Ben's voice was a husky whisper. "I knew it."

"No, I don't. I can't." She pushed back from him, but he wrapped his powerful arms around her.

"Yes, you do. You don't kiss someone like that if you don't."

"Please don't. If I can go back...We may be able to repair the sphere." She stopped pushing and let him hold her. She was comforted by the safety of his arms around her.

"We can't repair the sphere. I haven't been able to stop thinking about you ever since the first time I saw you." Ben tucked her hair behind her ear.

"You think about me?" Casey closed her eyes and listened to his heartbeat.

Amanda was right.

"Yes."

He kissed her again. This time she didn't fight it. Her arms found their way around his neck as his strong hands around her waist pulled her close. Did God choose him for her? Was this why she was so hesitant to let anyone in before? She might never know the answers, but for God to choose this guy—this strong, amazing, handsome guy—for her, made her feel as if she didn't deserve this, she wasn't worthy. She couldn't begin to understand or how to even ask the question. Was he for her? Was she going to be happy? It was worth the wait. But her family. How could she not want to go back and instead want to stay here?

So much had changed in the last few months. She couldn't believe this was her life. There were no more boring jobs where they never changed and had the same mundane tasks every day. She finally found her place in life. She knew she was needed here. Granted, it was thirty-five years in the future, but she was home, at peace with herself and her relationship with God. Who was she to deserve this much happiness?

"*Because, my child, I love you. And these are the gifts I set aside for you and waited for the moment you were ready for them.*"

"What?" She lifted her head off Ben's shoulder.

"I didn't say anything," Ben said as he pulled back from her.

An explosion shook the building. Ben grabbed her by the waist and pulled her to the doorway. They both pushed behind their ears at the same time. They hunkered in the doorway as another explosion hit. It collapsed part of the wall in the lab, knocking over several of the cabinets and desks they worked at in the previous days.

"You guys okay?" Clint's voice was in her ear.

"Yeah, you?" Ben held his right arm above their heads

Clint's thundering footsteps sounded in their ears. "Yeah, too close. We need to leave. I think they know we're here."

"Casey and I'll meet you at the dock. How'd you guys do?" Ben tugged Casey's hand and sprinted down the hall.

"Fine. Didn't find anything. Meet you in a few," Clint answered.

Another explosion rocked the building. Ben threw Casey to the ground. The weight of his body on her as he covered her pressed her to the floor. Ben's dead weight crushed her as she was unable to move.

"Ben, you okay?" He didn't answer. She rolled to the right. Blood covered his face and neck. Scrambling to get out from under him, she pulled her knees under her and pushed off the floor.

"Guys, Ben's wounded. I need you over here now! We're outside the lab."

"Ben?" Amanda called out for her brother, who wouldn't be answering.

"Hey, Ben. What's your status?" Clint's breath came out in quick gasps.

"How bad is it, Casey?" Amanda's voice broke.

Finally, able to crawl out from under Ben, she rolled him over to find a large gash in his neck with more blood than she thought the human body could hold. Unable to swallow past the lump in her throat, "Guys, you better hurry—" Warmth started at her heart. She glanced down at the pinprick of blue at her chest. It winked out.

She grabbed the end of her shirt and tore off a large piece, applying pressure to his open, gaping wound, which appeared to never run out of blood to push through the opening. No, this couldn't be happening, not to Ben.

"Ben, you need to talk to me." She placed her hand on the side of his stubbled face.

Nothing. She grabbed his shoulder, shaking him with one hand, while blood seeped through the shirt and fingers of her other hand. She trembled. Where was her healing ability?

"Ben, open your eyes and look at me." Frantic, her shoulders shook as she searched for a pulse. It was slow and weak. Tears landed on Ben's shirt, making dark, damp dots on the fabric as they absorbed into the cotton blend. "Father, help me." She cried out in an anxious, muttered prayer. She laid her head on his chest, listening for his heart. There was no warmth, no blue aura. Why couldn't she heal him?

"He needs you as much as you need him."

"What?" Her eyes darted up and down the hall, sure someone was there.

"You need to let him in."

"Who?"

"Casey, is there someone there with you?" Clint whispered as she heard the slide on his gun pulled back.

"I chose him for you."

"Clint, is that you?" Were the Monarchs messing with her? She spun around on her knees.

"Casey, we're several hallways away. What's going on?" Clint's voice was strained.

"Open your heart, child, and let him in. Then you can save him, but you need to let him in."

She gasped and closed her eyes. God was here with her, speaking to her. With her left hand still plastered on his neck, and the other one on the side of his face, she tilted his face to her. Warmth filled her heart.

"Ben, you need to open your eyes."

She stared into his beautiful blue eyes—ones she'd first seen in her dreams so many months ago—as they fluttered open. Their gazes locked as the world around them disappeared. He reached for her face and wiped her tears away. She tore down the walls she'd worked so hard to build around her heart. She let him in, this man in front of her who she couldn't stop thinking about even when apart. This man who God chose for her. For her, someone who was a nobody and didn't matter, who was now part of a prophecy. She slowly kissed him. "I love you. Ever since the first night I dreamed of you."

Warmth rushed from her newly opened heart racing down her arms, even to her lips as she kissed him again. Quick, steady footsteps approach behind her as Amanda cried out. She could only imagine how bad it looked. She didn't acknowledge them.

The blue aura became brighter as her love for this man flowed through her and engulfed them both. Amanda cried out her brother's name.

"No, leave her alone. Let her finish." Clint soothed Amanda. He held her back as they squinted from the bright light that engulfed Ben and Casey.

Blood no longer poured through the torn shirt. She yanked the fabric off his neck. The wound was almost closed, and she placed her hand over it. Ben's pulse strengthened under her hand as the wound closed. The blue glow subsided, and she fell back against the doorframe, exhausted. Her arms fell limp at her sides.

"Ben, you okay?" Amanda called out as she reached for Ben, pushing away from Clint.

"Yeah, I think so. I don't remember much of what happened except I threw us to the ground and covered Casey. I woke to her kneeling over me and telling me to open my eyes."

Clint helped Ben stand. Amanda cried, and she threw her arms around her big brother. Ben returned Amanda's hug. Casey tried to stand, but her legs wouldn't hold her weight.

"Casey, are you alright?" Ben cupped her face in his hands.

"I'm tired, and I can't stand."

"Are you hurt anywhere?" Clint was on one side of her checking her arms and head for injuries.

"I don't think so. I didn't check."

Ben grabbed one arm while Clint grabbed the other, and they pulled her to a standing position. While the guys held her, Amanda checked her back and legs for injuries finding none other than minor cuts and scrapes. Her head was heavy, so she laid it on Ben's chest as he held the back of her head with his hand.

"Ben, you need to change your shirt. You can't go out with blood all over." Clint tugged at his plaid shirt, then yanked off his t-shirt. He stuffed his arms in his plaid shirt then buttoned it. Clint and Ben exchange positions and Clint held Casey while Ben changed shirts.

"Much better. I don't ever want to see you like that again. You scared me half to death." Amanda's voice cracked, and no one argued with her.

"Hey, Casey. Who were you talking to before Amanda and I got to you?"

Exhausted, she blurted out before thinking it through, "God talked to me."

"What did He say?" Ben had changed his shirt and stepped over to Clint, who still held her and bent his knees to look her in the eye.

It was personal, and she wanted to keep the memory to herself a little longer. She didn't want to be selfish, but she didn't want to share it with anyone yet. A smile touched her lips. "I don't want to talk about it."

"That's okay. You don't have to. Casey, I owe you my life. Thank you. I could never repay you."

"You don't owe me anything. Shouldn't we be getting out of here?"

"She's right. We need to move before this whole warehouse collapses. I don't know if it was luck or God's hand that had everyone gone before the explosions or if the

Monarchs didn't know exactly which building we were in." Clint put his arm under hers and around her back while Ben took the other side. With guns drawn, they raced to the dock.

Forty-Two

Clint transferred Casey to Ben as they approached the dock and held his hand in front of him with the relic in his palm. He shook his head at Ben, telling him something was wrong. A few steps further, James was no longer on the gurney, and it was pushed against the opposite wall. The doors to the dock were blown in. Smoke rolled off the paint toward the ceiling.

Ben wrapped his other arm around Casey and again shielded her with his body ready for another assault.

The shield burst out and enveloped all four of them. Amanda clung to the back of Clint.

Clint turned to face them. "Amanda, did you—"

She shrugged as her fist clung to his shirt.

"No, keep doing what you're doing. I think this is the reason for the protective shield the parchment spoke of." Clint nodded.

"I'll try, but it may be running off pure fear." Amanda released Clint's shirt from the death grip she had on it and flexed her fingers.

Clint turned toward them. "Let's move to the underground tunnels and the car before anyone catches us."

"Sure. We need to move fast. I don't know how long I'll be able to hold this shield."

Ben swung Casey into his arms and kissed her forehead as he whispered, "Hold on."

Clint took the lead and sprinted toward the stairs. Down three flights of stairs, Ben breathed easier. If they were going to be ambushed, it would've been in the warehouse.

The secret entrances and doorways were a blur as they rush through tunnels, through doorways, and flights of stairs. Once they made it down the final five flights of stairs to the parking garage and the disabled cars, Clint stopped and held up his hand for them to take a breather.

They were at the top of the stairs and ready to race to the car when Clint froze midstride. The shield, which had retracted during the last part of the trip to the car, suddenly reemerged enveloping all four of them. Clint held up his hand while his other pulled his menacing handgun from his waist. Ben's hair stood up on the back of his neck as he turned in a full circle.

Ben moved in behind Clint, pulling Casey closer to him. "Did you see or hear something?"

"Thought I saw movement between two of the cars out there, the opposite side of where we're headed."

Amanda moved in behind Ben, her eyes wide. He glanced down at the panic etched on the face of his little sister.

Ben lowered Casey from his arms but kept her pulled in close. He kept one arm protectively wrapped around her shoulders while his other hand grabbed his own gun.

After what felt like an eternity, Clint motioned for the backpack Amanda carried. He pulled sparkplug wires from the bag and had them in his hand, ready. They moved as one staying in the bubble and made their way to the car. No one was in sight when Amanda jumped behind the wheel to pop the hood. Ben opened the back door to help Casey into the backseat. Amanda retracted the protective shield from around them. Ben walked around to the other back door to the car and had it open when Clint closed the hood. Ben slid in beside Casey while Amanda walked around to the passenger door as Clint climbed into the driver's seat.

A shot echoed in the garage, reverberating off the cold concrete walls as Amanda collapsed half in, half out of the passenger door. Ben lunged over the seat and pulled his sister into the car, slamming the door as Clint lurched out of the seat and spun on his heels. The relic sent a yellow pulse out, expanding as it flew across the span of the parking garage knocking out the men who fired the shot. Clint jumped in the car. The engine caught with the turn of the key and roared to life. He threw it in reverse and backed out of the parking space. Tires spun on the pavement.

Amanda looked down at the gaping hole in her chest and attempted to wipe the blood away. Casey yanked the first aid kit Clint had used on her a few days ago out from under the seat. With a stack of bandages, she applied pressure to Amanda's chest wound and closed her eyes. The blue aura spread from her arms to her hands. Ben nodded, at least they had Casey to heal Amanda. Everything was going to be okay.

They raced past buildings as Casey's hands glowed, and the flow of blood slowed to a trickle. Clint nodded. Casey's eyes closed as her head dropped forward into the back of the front seat. "Casey!"

"Ben, hold me up." Casey blew out a breath.

Ben grabbed her and held her forward with one hand on her back. He put her hand on Amanda's chest. Blue light flooded the car but grew dim after a minute. Amanda's eyes fluttered open, and she looked at Ben.

"Amanda, I'm here. You hang in there, okay! Hang in there while Casey heals you." She smiled at Ben.

Gasping, Amanda was unable to pull in air.

"Hey, big brother...you need to look out for Casey. Keep her safe." Amanda winced as she breathed. "Clint, you were always there for me like a real brother. Ben's going to need you to help him through this."

"No, what are you talking about. You're going to be fine. Don't you dare say goodbye! We're not finished with the bad guys yet." Ben tried to smile through the tears. Blue filtered down Casey's arms but didn't reach Amanda's heart.

"I'm tired, Ben...I can't." Casey closed her eyes and leaned her head against the back of Amanda's seat.

Amanda closed her eyes, then opened them wide. "Ben, I know where I'm going. And we knew this couldn't last forever without some casualties. We've talked about this before."

"Mom and Dad can't lose you. You hang in there." Ben leaned in and kissed her forehead. "Come on, Casey, you can do this." Ben held her up with one hand while his other hand held Casey's over his sisters' heart.

Clint continued at the deadly speed at which they left the warehouse. He checked the rearview mirror to make sure no one followed. "Amanda, I'm sorry. I should've checked the garage better before we left the stairwell."

"CLINT, THIS ISN'T YOUR fault. Don't blame yourself. Ben, tell him. Ben—" Amanda gasped for breath as she scrunched her eyebrows. Short shallow breathes told Clint it won't be long now. He had seen it too many times in battle when his friends died. She coughed again as blood trickled from the corner of her mouth.

"I'm here, sis." Ben wiped tears away, and his words caught in his throat. He grabbed a bandage from the first aid kit and wiped the blood from the corner of her mouth.

Casey's hands no longer glowed. Ben laid her back in the seat, and her head thudded on the window. Clint watched him in the rearview mirror. Ben finally found love today, but this loss could overshadow that.

"Ben, I love you. You're the best big brother," Amanda's eyes closed again, "anyone could ever ask for. Tell Mom and Dad how much I love them." Her eyes opened wide as they locked on Clint. "If you had any sisters, they would be able to say the same thing about you. You were there for me growing up as if you were my brother. I love you guys."

"Amanda, I love you too. But hang on. We're on the way to Doc, so you hang on." Clint turned and stared out the windshield, not able to stop the tears.

"Casey, I don't think I need to know what God told you. I think I can guess, can't I?" She looked at her brother then nodded at Casey.

"I wish I could've gotten to know you better, Casey, we have so much in common." Amanda's voice caught as she coughed, blood flowed out of the wound in her chest. Casey's body was lifeless against the back door as tears rushed down her cheeks. She would struggle with this. She knew so much loss because of them, and now with this on her conscience.

"Amanda, I'm sorry I can't heal you," Casey said with her eyes closed.

"Casey, I'm okay. Don't blame yourself. I'll see you in heaven." Amanda's face contorted in pain, and she closed her eyes.

"Please, Father, I can't lose her. Please don't take her from me." Ben's tears fell as he prayed.

"I'll be at Heaven's gates and will show you around." Amanda smiled as her face relaxed, and she stared at nothing. Ben kissed her forehead. He gently closed her eyes.

Ben sobbed and pulled his sister partially over the center console, but stopped when the lower part of her leg caught between the seat and molded plastic of the console. Clint checked the next intersection before turning on a residential street. Clint choked back a sob as he gingerly unwedged her leg from the side of the seat and helped Ben pull her into the back seat. The bracelet on Amanda's wrist unwound, falling off. Clint picked it up. It was the final tell she was gone with no soul to keep it attached. Clint quietly cried, holding back his sobs as he punched the steering wheel.

A jerk of the wheel took them back on the road as Clint punched the accelerator. Tears blurred his vision as he raced through town. A glance in the rearview mirror made him realize there were still others in this car who he swore to protect. He eased off the gas.

Clint pulled into a garage. Ben cradled his sister's body, and his sobs tore through the night. "Ben, I'll be back."

Clint darted through the door into the dark cavernous house. Minutes ticked by as Ben pulled Amanda out through the back door of the car. He held her close as Clint and Doc emerged through the door.

"No, how did this happen?" Doc searched for a pulse.

"It's too late for that, Doc. Help Ben take her downstairs." Clint brushed Amanda's hair off her forehead and kissed her. He clasped a hand tightly on Ben's shoulder.

Since Casey leaned against the door, Clint opened it enough to reach a hand in to support her so he could open the door all the way. "Casey?"

He checked for a pulse and exhaled loudly. He dropped his head forward when he found one. With one hand under her knees and one around her back, he scooped her out of the car. He kicked the door shut as he made his way around the car to the house. They disappeared into the dark stillness inside as he mourned for his friend.

Forty-Three

"Amanda!" Casey scanned the room, her stomach fluttered. Ben was in a chair next to the bed, and Clint rose from a chair by the footboard.

"Casey, we're here." Ben leaned forward.

"Did Amanda—" Casey cried.

"She's gone," Ben choked.

"I'm sorry, Ben. I tried, I'm so sorry. I can understand if you're upset with me. Clint, I tried. I did," Casey stammered and hung her head, unable to look at the man she fell in love with, knowing how much pain she could have saved him from if only she healed his sister. Would they ask her to leave the group? She wouldn't blame them if they did. She couldn't imagine watching a family member die.

"Hey, now you listen to me. I don't blame you or hold you accountable for this!" Ben sat on the bed and put his arms around her, pulling her to him. "You did more than I could. It was in God's timing for her to go home and be with Him."

"I wish I saved her. I'm so sorry, Ben." Guilt laden sobs shook her.

Ben put a finger under Casey's chin and gently turned her face toward him. "Look at me." He smiled when her eyes locked onto his. "You took a big risk trying to heal her after healing me a few moments before. It drained you and scared us that we might lose you, too. Thank you for trying to save her, but don't do this to yourself. God's in control of everything. If she were supposed to be saved, she would still be here."

He wiped her tears away and stared into her eyes. She finally broke from his stare. She couldn't help the emptiness that engulfed her. Fresh tears fell as it dawned on her that Amanda wasn't going to be around to confide in anymore.

"Are we at the houses?" She eyed her boxes in the corner.

"Yes, we've been here for a couple of days." Clint moved the chair he was using to the corner.

"A couple of days?"

"Yeah. That's why we were worried about you. You were comatose. We thought you'd never wake up," Clint said as he leaned against the wall next to the door.

"Is everyone else okay?"

"Everyone's okay. They made it safe and sound. We took a roundabout way to make sure we didn't bring unwanted guests once we knew Amanda couldn't be saved."

She scooted back against the pillows and headboard when an IV in her arm tugged at the skin where it was inserted.

"We didn't know how long you were going to be out, so Doc put in an IV to pump some fluids into you. I'll grab Doc to remove it." Ben disappeared through the door.

She glanced at Clint then back at the door. "How's he doing?"

"He's taking it hard, but he'll pull through. He has people to fall back on and talk to when he needs to." Clint took a deep breath and clenched his jaw.

"How are you doing? You were as close to her as her brother." Casey fidgeted, wringing her hands.

Clint looked at the floor, then raised his head. "I'm okay. We know where she is, and we'll be together again, but I miss her."

"I'm sorry."

"You don't need to apologize. You lost so much as a direct result of us, so we should be the ones apologizing to you. You saved Ben. Jason wouldn't be here today if God didn't work through you to heal him." Clint tilted his head.

Casey stared down at her hands. "I still wish she was here. I miss her more than I thought I could. I can't imagine what you and Ben are going through."

"We have each other, including you, and everything is in God's hands. We'll make it through this."

"Was I really out for that long?" Casey jerked her head up.

"Yeah. We got to the houses, and Ben took Amanda out first through the tunnels so Doc could prepare her for the funeral. Ben stayed with her while I got you out of the car and carried you into the lower level of the house. It was a few minutes before Doc checked on you, said you were exhausted, and to let you sleep it off." Clint glanced down the hall and shuffled his feet.

"What about Amanda's funeral?" She didn't want to think she missed it. Although she was sure she wouldn't want to watch Ben and Clint cry again. It was hard enough to listen to it in the car and not able to do anything about it.

"Yes, the same day we got here. One end of the tunnels is set as a burial chamber in case we lose anyone and knew we needed to be prepared for such an occasion. We never thought we would use it so soon." Clint pressed his lips together.

"If only I was able to spare Ben the pain of loss, and you for that matter," she cried.

Clint moved over, sat on the side of the bed, and put his hand on hers. "Everyone's given choices in life, and those men in the garage chose murder. I could go over and over it in my head. If I only waited or checked out the garage by myself before we entered an unsecured area, maybe she would still be here. But I can't think that way, or it will eat me up inside."

Casey straightened her back. "We need to put a stop to them and take back our country." They ran around like rats in a maze with no way out. No matter how much they fought back, nothing changed.

"Oh, trust me, I know. We need to show everyone else what we know to be true about President Polson. He needs to be removed from office so we can live without fear of being caught and executed in our own neighborhoods and backyards." Clint turned toward the sound of footsteps in the hall.

Doc entered the room with Ben. "Okay, guys, leave us alone for a minute."

"Sure thing, Doc." Clint met Ben outside the door, closing it behind him.

"Hey, Doc." She didn't know what else to say.

"You gave us a scare being comatose for so long. Sorry for the IV, but we didn't know how long you were going to be out of touch with us here." Doc removed the IV catheter, applied pressure with a cotton ball, and had her bend her arm. He listened to her heart and lungs, then took her blood pressure.

"Do I get a clean bill of health so I can move around and get out of this bed?"

"Everything looks and sounds great. Those two hardly left your side, or if one did, the other one stayed, except for the funeral. That's the only time someone didn't sit by your side. They care about you, Casey. But anyway, you're good to go if you want." Doc slid off the side of the bed, put all his medical instruments into a bag, then shuffled toward the door. When he opened the door, Ben and Clint leaned on the wall across from it. "She needs to walk around guys. She may be a little unsteady at first." Doc gave her a quick wink and left.

Clint lingered in the doorway. Ben offered her his hand. "Shall we take a tour? We'll show you where everything is. You were going to share this house with Amanda. Clint and I are next door, but we aren't sure now on the living arrangements. We're trying to find someone to move in with you."

Casey's hand hovered over Ben's "Why would I need a roommate? I can take care of myself."

"Well, we didn't know if you'd be okay being by yourself in a place where you don't know anyone." The blue of Ben's eyes darkened.

"All the houses are connected, right? I'll be fine." Casey took Ben's hand and pulled herself up.

"We can see how it goes. If you want someone to share this house, we'll talk to everyone about it," Clint suggested with a smile.

Casey nodded as they exited her room. The hallway was short, and they passed a closed door opposite hers. Clint reached around the corner, flipped the light switch, and the bathroom flooded with light.

"The bedrooms are at the end of the hall, and the bathroom's here. The kitchen's the next doorway on the left, which leaves the right open to a living room and dining room area," Ben explained as they continue their tour of her new home. She had dropped his hand by the time they were through the kitchen and into the dining room. The dining room housed a large bookcase with several items on the shelves, including pictures—pictures of her family from what looked like newspaper clippings? She spun on her heels to Clint and Ben.

"We didn't have any real pictures, so we found those in the library's archived newspapers and thought it'd at least make it more like home." Ben shrugged his shoulders.

"Thank you." She picked up one of the frames. It was from a newspaper who published a family portrait at some time during one of their stories about her family. Whether it was from her disappearance or their deaths, it meant the world to her to be holding the memories of the day when the picture was taken.

"Sorry. Are they too painful to look at?" Ben joined her as she traced her finger over the frame while tears spilled on the glass distorting part of the picture.

She quickly wiped at her tears with the back of her hand. "No. I was remembering this day. Thank you so much for these."

"If you move the clay elephant on the second shelf to the left, you can access the tunnel to our house." Clint grasped the elephant. It slid slightly to the left.

Behind the bookcase clicked as if tumblers of a lock had been activated before it slid forward from the wall. Sure enough, light illuminated the edges of a door through the ajar bookcase that moved effortlessly away from the wall to expose the door behind it. Dank, underground, earth-laden tunnels lay behind the hidden door illuminated by single bulb lights secured into the ceiling by hooks.

"If you take the first right and go to the end, you'll find another door and a coded keypad to our house. Clint and I share a house. A list of codes and maps of the tunnels are in a hidden drawer if you need before you memorize them."

"Whose idea was it to put this all together? Much less the ability to build this network and make it secure at the same time without being caught." She was amazed by the ingenious way they connected the homes and the security within.

"It's been in the works for about a year, and God put the right people together at the right time to make it work," Clint boasted.

"Food is in the refrigerator and cabinets so you can cook when you want, and there should be plenty there for you. A cell-link system is hooked to all the houses. It is off the grid, so not all the features work. Swipe your hand over the panel and select the house you want to talk to on the map."

Ben motioned to a small clear glass square on the wall in the kitchen.

"Well, if you guys don't mind, I would like to take a hot shower. Wait, is there hot water?" She didn't want to boil water on the stove to add to a bath.

Clint chuckled "Yes, there is."

Ben stood there for a few minutes after Clint gave her a quick hug and charged through the tunnel. Before turning to go, he hesitated. "Thank you for trying to save my sister and for saving me. Casey, I don't blame you at all for her not being here. God's timing is always perfect. Please don't beat yourself up, okay. We're glad you're here, and I wouldn't be if not for you. Thank you." He walked over and placed his hand under her chin and looked into her eyes as he said the last sentence. Ben enveloped her in his arms, giving her a hug she wished would never end. He turned. "I heard what you said to me in the hall when you healed me." The tumblers reset themselves after he closed the bookcase before she could say anything.

BEN STARED AT HER DOOR from the tunnel. She was all alone in there. This was nothing like her living alone in a regular world. This world was so full of evil. He saw Clint out of the corner of his eye but didn't move.

"We're here if she needs us." Clint stood in the doorway to their house.

"What if she needs us and can't ask for help." Ben's shoulders slumped.

"Ben, she's got this. Remember? I said she's stronger than she looks. I think she'll be okay. Plus, we are just down from her. We can be there in a fraction of a second, and with our communicators, we'll know something's wrong before she has a chance to say it." Clint leaned his broad shoulders and upper back against the tunnel wall crossing his arms. "I understand your protectiveness toward her. And now with Amanda gone...it isn't wrong to want to protect her. It's our job as the Chosen Ones to keep the Key safe. I'm not sure what it means that she's the Key, but I know our lives have drastically changed since she came into them."

Ben turned from the door and lumbered back to their house as if in protest. Ben knew Clint also suffered, and there was nothing he could do to help him through this. He missed Amanda so much it ached. He found himself awake at night, staring at the ceiling when he sat with Casey. He would be there for his best friend, but he admitted he looked forward to getting a full night sleep tonight with Casey awake and one less strain on them. Maybe they could both sleep decent tonight.

He edged around the door. They needed a break from the dire circumstances of their stressful lives. With energy in his step, he rummaged around in the kitchen, pulling ingredients out of the refrigerator while Clint lurked in the doorway.

"Dinner with friends is exactly what this group needs," Ben insisted.

"You're right." He glanced at the bookcase.

Ben shook his head as he yawned. The long nights took their toll on Ben, who had slept less than a couple hours a night as he sat in the chair next to Casey's bed.

Forty-Four

Casey took in her new home. It was quiet without noise to break the ominous silence. On the way to her room, it brought to mind they never showed her the room across from hers. The hinges creaked as she eased the door open. She fanned her fingers over her chest. It was identical to the room in the warehouse for Amanda. All her boxes and pictures were set out, with the Bible next to her bed. A few steps into the room, she ran her fingers over the letters of Amanda's name written in her handwriting on the boxes. Quiet sobs escaped. She missed her more than she ever thought she could. She closed the door as she stumbled to her room.

The hot shower did wonders to make her feel human again and wash two days of sleep off her. She was almost ready when the phone rang. Hesitant, she stared at the panel, raised her finger to answer the incoming call. She clutched her hand to her chest, sure the Monarchs had found her.

Ben's face filled the screen. "Casey?"

"Yes." She covered her mouth and almost laughed at herself for being so scared.

"Clint's making dinner, and we're having Doc and Chloe over. Did you want to join us?"

"Sure, let me grab shoes, and I'll be over." Casey started around the corner.

"Do you remember where we are?" She jumped back in front of the panel and saw Ben tilt his head. His eyebrow inched up.

"Yeah, see you in a few." Casey smiled.

"Okay, bye." Ben disappeared.

She ran as if catching a second wind to finish her hair, threw on a pair of tennis shoes, and bolted to the bookcase. She slid the elephant to the left. It disengaged the lock, and the shelves moved slightly forward. She gripped the edge and yanked it forward, almost falling when it moved easier than she thought it would, exposing the door to the underground tunnel. Several items tottered back and forth on the shelf. She steadied them, took a deep breath, and stepped through the doorway. They said they were at the end of this tunnel, so if their house was next door, that must make it the last house in the tunnel system this direction. Reaching their door, she clenched her fists and shook them slightly. She'd forgotten about the code, so she knocked. The door opened, and Clint stood there, tongs in hand, smiling.

"Sorry, I forgot to look at the code before I came here." Casey pointed toward the direction of her house.

"No problem. Come on in."

Their house layout was like hers. They must be in a neighborhood with cookie-cutter houses since the floor plans were the same. Doc and Chloe were there with the table set.

Ben placed a plate full of rolls on the table, joining the green beans and potatoes and gravy. Ben took a seat in an empty folding chair next to Casey. Chicken baked to perfection sizzled in the dish as Clint placed it on the table.

The aroma made her mouth water as her stomach gave away her hunger with a rumble. Heat rushed up her neck and across her cheeks as she nervously laughed.

Everyone else laughed, but a good laugh. Clint sat in his chair, and they bowed their heads. "Dear Heavenly Father, we thank You for the food You put before us, and the company of our brothers and sisters in Christ. Please watch over us as we fight for our freedom to worship You in the open. Keep a hedge of warriors around our homes and not let the eyes of the enemy find us. We thank you for all You bless us with and each other. In Jesus's name, amen."

They all replied in unison, "Amen." The food was passed around the table with generous helpings piled on everyone's plate.

"Casey, I'm glad you're okay." Chloe had a timid voice to match her frame. Here she was in hiding when she should be enjoying her teenage years in high school or college with friends sharing stories of their outings.

"Thank you, Chloe." She smiled, and Chloe smiled back.

"We invited you here, Casey, for your input on something we've been working on for a while now—a plan to ambush Polson out in the open and expose him for the terrorist he is. People at news stations and other media avenues around the U.S. are ready to air the story as soon as we collect concrete evidence about him," Clint explained in between enormous bites.

"How are you going to find him out in the open? Does he go to the Monarchs's complex that often? It was full of guards, and now that someone escaped, they'll more than likely increase security or move it all together, right?" She devoured a piece of the chicken on her plate.

"You're right. I would do the same, either move the operation or step up security. We hope they're arrogant enough to think we aren't a big enough threat to them and leave everything as it is."

"But we still need to break in there when Polson is back in town," Ben added.

"A friend at the airport knows his schedule and says he'll be here within the week." Doc peered over the rim of his glasses.

Chloe shook her head. "I still think it's too risky to try to get to him, though."

"We need to try. It may be the only way to get to him, especially since he's been there before," Clint reasoned.

"Yes, but I think we need to lay low for a little while until things cool down. James has seen us. He'll be dangerous to our cause." Chloe's knowledge of the everyday happening's shocked Casey, but she had to remind herself she had seen more than Casey had in her life and at only half her age.

"What if you confront him when he's in his car? Would he be in an armored motorcade if he's trying to stay under the radar?" Casey swirled a green bean through the gravy on her plate. "How many people does the president trust enough on his administrative staff? Would he trust his employees with a secret about his ties to a terrorist group?"

"We're not sure which route he'll take to the complex. We don't have the manpower to put the number of people it'd take to monitor all the possible routes to and from the airport." Clint studied her face, raised an eyebrow waiting for her response.

"But, Doc, you said you have a friend at the airlines?"

"Yes, but he may not know which vehicle he'll take."

"Okay. If he can find out which one, can't we tag it with a tracker we can follow so we won't put people all over the city in harm's way?"

Clint sat back in his chair and crossed his arms. "That would be a good plan, but they sweep the vehicle for bugs, bombs, and a multitude of other scenarios that pose a threat to the president."

"Okay. All these wonderful people help build our Fort Knox here. Can't they build a bug to be undetectable until turned on? After the sweep and the presidents on his way, someone at the airport can turn it on?"

Clint and Ben looked at each other. "Might work. Doc, can you contact your friend to find out if the vehicle would be something he can get close to before he's in town to plant the bug, then he can activate it by remote once he's on his way out of the airport?"

"I don't see why not." Doc nodded as he smiled. "I'll check with him tomorrow."

"Chloe, call your uncle and find out if he can make what Casey is proposing and a remote to activate it at a far enough range so we won't jeopardize Doc's friend."

"Sure thing, Clint."

Ben grabbed plates from the table, and Casey stood to help. "No, you're our guest, so sit."

"Well, a friend once told me the first time is being a guest, and every time after you are family to help yourself. So, remember the next time I'm invited to dinner. By the way, who cooked? It was delicious."

"I did. I learned a few things in the military besides deadly force operations." Clint smiled and winked.

"Well, I need to get back in case anyone needs me." Doc rose out of his chair and shuffled out.

Clint helped Ben clear off the table as Chloe and Casey sat in the living room. It was sparsely furnished with a couch and a couple of chairs. "So, your uncle is the genius to thank for the safe homes we live in?"

"He was a computer programmer for the military, but they honorably discharged him after the Monarchs group invaded and knew he was a proclaimed Born-Again Christian, devout in his faith. He chose to work in God's army and help us out when he can. He still has access to some of his old contacts and can obtain anything he needs to do a job. He's outfitted more than this compound. One north of here has been operational for over a year and hasn't been detected. They still make the usual food runs, but other than that, they're self-sufficient." Chloe beamed.

"Wow. How long does it take to outfit a group of homes like this?" Casey motioned to the room.

"About eight months or a little longer, depending on the availability of the components he needs for each one. He always tests them out before letting anyone move in. He scans with an old satellite the government thinks crashed in the ocean years ago. He reprogrammed it to work only under his code key and to hide if anyone else tries to access it besides him." Chloe tucked her feet under her.

Casey leaned toward Chloe and lowered her voice. "Isn't he scared his contacts will give him up if questioned about what they give him to secure these houses?"

Chloe shrugged. "To a point, but no matter what happens, his soul is spoken for by our Father in Heaven. He hasn't had any problems so far, and the guys he has as contacts are people who devoted their entire life to the safety of the U.S., so they aren't too thrilled with our uninvited guests."

"Okay, Chloe. Can you find out from your uncle tomorrow on the status of making a bug smart enough it can be turned on and off from a remote location?" Clint kicked his feet up on a small table.

"Sure, with how intricate the work was on this place, there shouldn't be a problem if he doesn't have something in the works or already built." Chloe glowed when she talked about her uncle.

Clint steepled his fingers. "Great. Doc will let us know from his friend about how close we can get to the car before the president's here. Security will be tight from the Monarchs. It'd be hard for one of us since they know what we look like."

"Can't Doc's friend at the airport also hide the bug?" Ben swiveled his chair toward Clint.

"I don't want to take the chance someone's caught with the bug and the remote trigger. Chloe, can you check with your uncle if he can't build it into a keychain or phone and make two remote triggers so if something happens, we can be under the overpass when they leave the airport?" Clint met her eyes.

Chloe smiled, and red flashed across her cheeks. "Sure. Nothing's come across his plate that he hasn't been able to do, so we should be fine."

"Good. I think we should be able to take out the contingent of Monarchs protecting him so we can record the confession Ben will force out of him while wearing the ring." Clint smiled.

"Okay, I have a question. What if he retracts what he confessed to, that he was under duress when he said it to save his own life and keep us from killing him?" Casey sunk into the pillows on the couch.

"Good point, but it may be enough to interest people and start an investigation into his actions and who he's been hanging out with lately. Or to spark interest in the right person who'll follow it through and come to the truth through all the legal channels, making it so he won't be able to lie his way out of anything." Clint seemed willing to risk this to motivate someone on the other side to remove Polson from office.

"Okay, guys. I'm heading home. Casey, you coming?" Chloe rose from the couch and headed toward the bookcase.

"We're going to go over a few things. We'll see you tomorrow," Ben answered for Casey.

"Goodnight."

"Goodnight, Chloe," they said in unison.

Ben strolled to the bookcase, pulled a crystalline box from the top shelf, and sat in the chair leaning forward, and elbows resting on his knees. "We wanted to show you something. This fell off Amanda in the car, and it doesn't work for either one of us."

Inside lay the relic bracelet. She tenderly held it, remembering when Amanda died, it fell from her wrist. She frowned and glared at the bracelet while her hands shook. With a curt nod, she slid the bracelet on and waited.

She glanced at Ben and Clint. Then her shoulders dropped, and she cleared her throat. "Does this mean we need to find someone else? Oh, whoa!" The bangle snaked and intertwined around her arm.

"Guess this means she's in," Clint smirked.

"In? In for what?" Casey wasn't sure she was ready for what they would say next.

Clint dropped his feet to the floor with a thud. "We need someone there who can operate the shield in case we come under fire when questioning Polson. Even with the other relics, we thought you should use the shield while we do all this to keep us safe. But we need to test the weapon to see if it does more than what it did in the garage at the warehouse."

Ben's dynamic blue eyes cut through her. "Plus, we figure you wouldn't want to sit on the sidelines after what they did to Amanda since you're part of our family."

"You're right. I don't want to sit on the sidelines. Tell me what you need me to do, and I'll do it." Unsure how to make the bracelet work, she would go back to her house and work a little tonight to figure out a thing or two.

"Good, we need everyone working on this one. First, we send the confession out to the right people who can slip it into production on the news and the Internet, to as many audiences as possible for the biggest impact. A prayer chain to pray for the right person in Washington to take some action. If we're lucky, we get more than one to collaborate with each other so they won't be taking on the whole organization by themselves. We don't want them to back out thinking it's too risky to take on alone." She could see this was personal for Clint. His eyes gave it away. Maybe Amanda was more than just a surrogate sister.

"How many of Polson's group will be there, do you think?" Unsure how many they would take on, she hoped it wouldn't scare her away from wanting to help. She'd had a run-in with the Monarchs before and didn't want a replay.

"Not sure, but hope there's only a small entourage since he's been coming to town for a while now, and we didn't know it until they had you." Clint strolled over, then reached under the table for a few seconds. He pulled back, worn pages clutched in his hand.

"What are those?" Casey rose from the couch.

"This is the small amount of evidence we've collected so far on Polson to use as leverage, but we never had enough to use it," Ben explained, taking the papers from Clint.

"This is the first real lead we need to prove he's in league with the Monarchs. He said when he opened the borders, terrorist groups wouldn't be able to get in due to the screening process. But according to rumors, he had certain applications squashed and hidden to get them in. Yet again, they were only rumors, and we've been unable to find any good, solid proof of any involvement with Monarchs," Clint added. "A couple of applications show his signature for the top three Monarchs leaders when Polson put on a huge show on television of him signing a couple for the cameras. What no one knew at the time was who they were, or that he had personal ties to them."

"So, if he'll admit it on camera, we can prove he's been in league with them all along, and they can remove him from office. He's past his term anyway, right?" Casey recalled they said he'd been in office for ten years.

"Right, and if enough people in Congress believe us, they can overturn the bill he signed to keep him in office indefinitely." Clint went to the kitchen and brought back water for everyone.

"Thanks. So when is he scheduled to come back into town?" Casey's pulse raced with an adrenaline rush, and she couldn't wait to try and help bring down this evil man.

"Well, that's what we need Doc to verify, but it should be within the next couple of weeks. We'll be able to put our plan into play, so long as Chloe's uncle can supply us what we need." Ben leaned back in his chair.

Clint pushed up the sleeves of his shirt. "We also think, since they don't want to draw attention to the fact that they're escorting the president to their headquarters, there may not be a large contingent of men to drive him, leaving him open for us to put our plan into place."

"What do we do if he has a large contingent of personnel around him from Monarchs, and we can't get to him?" Casey wasn't ready to go head-to-head with a terrorist group and lose anyone else—especially Ben. She clutched at her chest at the thought of losing him.

Clint raised an eyebrow at her. "We thought about that and will let him go about his trip, as usual. We can track the car when it heads back to the airport, where it will be all or nothing. We can't take a chance that we'll miss him while he's here and lose any more of us."

She stared with wide, disbelieving eyes. "Clint, you said all or nothing. There has to be a safer way to make sure we don't lose anyone else."

"Casey, no passage in the Bible says being one of God's children doesn't come without trials and tribulations. We have faith in Him and know we'll be taken care of either in this life or the one after." Clint leaned in, his hand on one knee.

"I don't want to lose anyone. I'm not sure if I can handle losing anyone else—first, my family, my friends, then Amanda, I just—I don't want to let you guys down." She hung her head, and her hair fell around her face.

Ben rushed to her side, putting his arm around her. "Casey, we're right here with you. I'm so sorry for taking you from your life, but I'll spend the rest of mine making up for it."

She stared into his eyes and leaned away from him. "Not if you lose your life."

Ben pulled her to him. "That's a possibility in the world we live in. We can't go around afraid of every corner we round because of what might happen. I'm not going to do anything stupid to put myself or anyone I care about in harm's way, which especially includes you."

"And that goes for me, too, Casey. We're doing something to improve this situation. Do you want to live in the basement of abandoned houses for the rest of your life, not knowing from one day to the next if we'll be found and killed?" Clint interjected.

"No, I don't. I don't want to be alone here if something happens to either one of you, or both of you, for that matter." Casey clenched her jaw.

"Now, what are the odds of something happening to both of us?" Ben smiled at her.

"Slim to none if you ask me. Casey, I've been thinking, maybe you were brought here to save you." Clint's frown deepened as he stared at her.

Casey glanced at Clint. "Save me?"

"If Ben hadn't brought you here, more than likely, you would have been the one killed when your house exploded." Clint nodded.

"So...if I wasn't here, I would have been there." Shivers ran down her spine.

"I think so. It could be why Chloe's uncle couldn't find you the first time before we brought you here. You were killed if you stayed in your time." Clint wouldn't look at her.

"I would have rather it had been me than my brother and his family. I'm going back to my house." Ben and Clint rose as she did and walked her to the bookcase.

"I'm sorry. I didn't mean to upset you. Call if you need anything—anything at all." Clint hugged her quickly.

"Well, I do need the code to my door. I didn't look at them before I left."

"Your code is easy. Ours is seventy-one seventeen. Yours is seventy-two twenty-seven. The first number for all the houses will be seven, and we numbered the houses according to the order they're in. We are the first house on this side, so ours is number one, then mirror that number," Ben clarified.

"Thanks. Have a good night. See you tomorrow?" It was a question she wanted to ask but didn't want to seem too eager. She hadn't talked to Ben since he said he heard her tell him she loved him.

"Of course. Tomorrow." Ben hugged her, kissing the top of her head before she strolled toward her house. Hasty steps took her home. She punched in her code and the lock disengaged for her to push the bookcase in. It was jarringly quiet as she stepped into her house. When she started to close the door behind her, she caught a glimpse of Ben in the tunnel. She smiled and gave a small wave with her fingers before she pulled the door closed, then pushed the bookcase in place. She thought it was nice of him to follow her to make sure she made it okay.

"I DON'T LIKE THAT SHE'S alone over there." Ben stalked to the couch.

Clint dropped onto a chair. "She'll be fine. You know how fast we can be there for her if we need to."

Ben stared at the bookcase. "Maybe we should take turns sleeping on the couch over there for a couple of weeks."

"Be my guest, but I'm sleeping in my bed tonight," Clint stated.

Ben gawked. "You aren't worried about her being alone over there?"

"Calm down. I never said that, but we both need sleep. We're exhausted. You haven't slept but a couple of hours over the last few nights. You need to rest. We *both* need to rest." Clint yawned.

"I won't lose her. I can't." Ben slumped into a chair.

Clint knew what he meant. He missed Amanda so much there was a tightness in his chest. He knew Ben wouldn't be able to function if he lost the woman he loves so soon after the loss of his sister. Their parents took it hard when Ben called them and broke the news of Amanda's death. They demanded that he move out by them and to bring Clint with him. They both knew they couldn't with the power of the relics released. They needed to stay and fight against the Monarchs who killed Amanda. They would get justice for her.

Clint knew he was Casey's guardian, and he knew God chose him for that assignment. He didn't take it lightly. He wouldn't ignore God again like he did the last time when he let Casey go on the grocery run. He knew if he kept Casey from going, James couldn't have given the Monarchs their location, and Amanda would still be alive. He lived with that regret every day. Maybe that was why he grieved for her as much as he did. He felt responsible for her death as if he had pulled the trigger.

"She told me she loved me." Ben stared at the ceiling as he lay on the couch.

"She did?" Clint twisted around in the chair he lounged in.

"Well, sort of. It was when she healed me. She told me she loved me when she thought I was unconscious." Ben had a faraway look.

"Congrats, brother. I couldn't be happier for you." Clint nodded and thought about Amanda. Would he ever find someone like that in his life?

Ben smiled. "I love her. When I grabbed her at her house, I never thought it would end like this. That, in just a matter of months, she would care for me."

"Maybe if we kick Polson out of office, you two can live a semi-normal life."

"Wouldn't that be something?" Ben sat up. "I'm going to crash. See you in the morning."

"Yeah," Clint didn't move. Instead, an urgency to protect Casey took his breath away. He pushed behind his ear and turned his communicator on and listened. He knew he eavesdropped on her, but something stirred in him. He dropped his feet on the floor from where they were draped over the arm of the chair. Something was wrong. His heart quickened as he pictured Amanda covered in blood in the front seat of the car with Casey unconscious in the backseat.

A pulse passed through the walls penetrating their house. Clint grabbed his weapon.

Forty-Five

While she brushed her teeth, Casey's mind drifted to Amanda. She smiled thinking about her when a lump formed in her throat. She placed her hands on the sink and dropped her head as the ache of her absence hit. Her shoulders shook. After a couple of deep breaths, she stalked to her room.

In her room, she glanced at Amanda's door. She turned her back as she closed hers. The weight of the thick comforter made her reminisce of home as she slid between the covers. Before she knew it, she couldn't keep her eyes open. She placed her Bible back on the nightstand, turned off the light, and pushed behind her ear. Images of her life before being pulled into the future flashed through her mind as she drifted off.

A crash from down the hall startled her, and she jerked into a sitting position. She strained to listen to the sounds of her new home. Was it a dream? There it was again, but she couldn't tell if it was someone or something. She pulled on her robe then slid on the bracelet. She took slow, unwavering steps as her heart hammered in her chest. She inched closer to the door as she listened for what made the noise. Wait, was that someone talking from the other side of the house? The bracelet came to life, enclosing her in an invisible shield she knew was there since she could sense the energy from it.

She forced herself to take slow, methodical breaths as she closed her eyes, not sure what to do as she kept her back to the wall and inched ever closer to the living room. The link something or other, hung in the kitchen so she couldn't call for help, or could she? With a quick push behind her ear, she turned on the communication device. She wasn't yet ready to call for help until she knew for sure someone was in her house. She continued toward the living room, her heart racing faster with every step. She clenched her hands into fists as she rounded the corner, reaching for the light switch. It wasn't there, which meant it would be on the other side of the doorway. She would be an easy target if she crossed the opening. Her head dropped, and she took a deep breath and blew it out, determined to go for it. Plus, this would give her a chance to test the shield on what it could withstand if there were intruders in the kitchen. Counting to herself, one...two...three, she lunged past the doorway and flipped the light switch.

Light rushed out of the kitchen and into the hallway, not leaving many places for shadows to lurk in the immediate vicinity. With a quick peek, she only saw the sink, cabinets, fridge, and stove—nothing out of the ordinary. The second doorway from the kitchen into the dining room was pitch black, and it beckoned her to come into the shadowy darkness. There was no use putting off going into the dining room. They knew she was looking for them. Now, pressed against the wall on the outside of the kitchen, she continued toward the living room to the corner where one turned left into the dining room where the second doorway to the kitchen was exposed. This light switch would be easier to get to, and when her hand crept around the corner for the light switch, a hand was already there.

A scream erupted from the depths of her. She was sure it would wake everyone. The shield shot out several feet and propelled the person across the room into the opposite wall, where they crumpled into a heap.

"Casey?" Clint's voice calmed her as it came across the communication device in her ear. "What's wrong?"

"Someone's in my house," she whispered.

"We're on our way." Pounding filled her ears as Clint bellowed, "Ben, Casey's in trouble!"

Her heart raced, and she gulped in mouthfuls of air as she stared at the man crumpled on the floor. She leaned forward, taking a closer look at the person lying there. He looked familiar, but she couldn't place where she'd seen him.

"Casey, we're outside your door on our way in. You okay?" Ben was out of breath.

"Come in. He's on the dining room floor," she whispered, never taking her eyes off him.

The bookcase swung away from the wall, and Clint and Ben joined her guns drawn and aimed at the unconscious man on the floor. Ben walked around the man and put his arm around Casey's trembling shoulders. "I'm here. You're okay."

"Ben, have you seen him before? I don't know who he is." Clint's squatted over the man.

"No. How'd he get in here?"

"Not sure how he'd know the code to open the bookcase, and if he did, why would he shut it and lock it behind him."

"Casey, did you hit him or knock him out with something?" Ben grabbed her shoulders in both his hands as he looked her up and down.

"No. Well, sort of." She pointed to the bracelet, never taking her eyes off the intruder.

"Wait, you're telling us you rendered him unconscious with the shield?" Clint tilted his head and glanced at her wrist.

"When I went for the light switch, my hand landed on top of his. I screamed, and the shield shot out with a pulse and pushed him back as if he ran into an invisible wall. It tossed him through the air."

"So, it sent out a pulse that knocked him out?" Clint smirked.

"No, it was a wall as if the shield was solid. I was scared, and it shot out in an instant, and he bounced off the wall and landed there." She pointed to the still unconscious man.

"What were you doing exploring the house by yourself instead of calling us?" Ben scolded.

"With the link thing in the kitchen, I had to leave my room to get to it, but I turned on my communicator. Luckily Clint was worried enough to leave his on tonight." She teased Ben, who hooked an arm around her neck, pulled her to him, and kissed her head.

Clint laughed as he pulled out plastic ties and bound the hands of the man lying on the floor.

"Hey, I worry about you, so don't you start," Ben yanked a chair away from the table.

They grabbed the unconscious man by his elbows and hoisted him into the chair. He moaned as his head flopped from side to side.

Clint smacked his cheek and shook him. "Hello."

The man drooled. "Whaaahhh happened?"

"How did you get in here?" Clint spun a second chair around then straddled it, so he faced the back of the chair and rested his arms across the top.

"I live here."

Ben, Clint, and Casey exchanged a questioning look.

Clint continued, "What do you mean you live here? These houses were abandoned for years."

"Yup, this makes them perfect for hiding from the bad men," he slurred.

"Bad men?" Ben asked.

The man tilted his head back and almost fell over. "Yup. The butterflies."

"You mean the Monarchs?" Clint slightly raised his chin toward Ben.

"Yeah, they's the one. They's mean and hurts you if they catch you, so I hides in houses so they can't ever never find me." The man's head fell forward and rested against his chest.

"What's your name?" Clint shook the intoxicated man's shoulder.

"Charles," the man hiccupped, "Sanders."

Casey gasped. She used to babysit a little Charlie Sanders for the neighbors across the street when they had a date night or were at retreats. That was why he was familiar. He was the spitting image of his father.

"What is it, Casey?" Ben put himself between her and Charles as he faced her.

"I used to babysit him when he was a boy." Casey peered around Ben.

Charles looked at her and smiled a lopsided grin. "Well, hello, Miss Casey. You look the exact same. Wow, must been a good batch I drank tonight because you should be, um...*old*."

"Charles, how did you get into the lower part of the house?" Clint grabbed his shoulders and turned Charles toward him.

"What?" Charles belched. Casey covered her mouth and nose from the stench of alcohol.

"How did you get into the lower part of the house?" Clint enunciated each word.

Charles shrugged his shoulders. "By the basement stairs."

"There aren't any basement stairs." Clint tilted his head.

"Sure are. You has to open the closet in the hallway. It's the bestest place to sleep. And whens I leaned against the wall to settle in for the night, it pushed back a little, and there were magic stairs." Charles leaned toward Clint and whispered about the stairs, "I figured I would be safest in the basement if the butterflies came after me again. They ain't gonna catch me. No siree, Bob, I tell you. Oh, wait, unless you guys are the butterflies, but you don't have any pretty wings." Charles cackled.

"Come on, Clint. We need to ask Doc if he can do something for him. We can't let him go until we secure upstairs." Ben winked at her. "Casey, we'll be right back."

Clint stood to take Charles under one arm while Ben grabbed the other one.

"Bye, Casey. It was good to see you again, although you must have found the fountain of youth. You're still the same as you were when you used to play fort with me. Can I has a drink of it? I's take just a little. Why are we leaving Casey? I want to talk to her some more. She's so purty." The conversation dwindled as they continued through the tunnel.

Able to breathe, she pressed her palm to her heart. The bracelet had retracted the shield when Ben and Clint came through the bookcase before their conversation with an inebriated Charles. She sank into the sofa's overstuffed cushions and waited for Clint and Ben to return. She didn't think she'd be able to fall back to sleep tonight. Unsure what time it was, she shuffled to the kitchen, hoping for a clock on the wall. Something for her to do tomorrow—explore every room of this house and find out what she had, especially in the kitchen. No clock.

In the bathroom, she swept her hair out of her face and pulled it into a ponytail. She couldn't believe Charles was in her house. Of all the people in this world to find their way into her house, how did the person she babysat some thirty-five years in the past find her? It may have been thirty-five years for him, but it'd only been a few months for her, and the fact he looked like his father took her back to memories of home and her family.

Clint and Ben came back through the bookcase as she sat back on the couch. They interrupted her thoughts, and she frowned.

"Are you okay?" Clint turned from the closed bookcase.

Casey shook her head and wrapped her arms around herself. "No. How do we secure the upstairs closet, so this doesn't happen again? Is he going to be able to remember which house and will the Monarchs find us if we let him go?"

"We're asking those same questions. Securing the upstairs will be no problem. The safety latches should've been engaged when we all came in but were forgotten in our haste."

"Okay, question—do we keep him against his will if he wants to leave so he can't tell anyone about us here? And if he is drunk, will he even remember this, or are we going to let him sober up, so he has a possibility to remember?"

"I know...I know. Doc's running a blood alcohol test to ascertain what his level is. Then we'll go from there to decide what to do with him. He passed out again before we even got to Doc's." Clint shrugged.

"Clint, you do realize he also said he hides from the Monarchs." Casey wrung her hands. "Do we offer him the safety of living here or put him out on the streets to possibly be caught, tortured, or even killed?"

"We don't want another James situation on our hands, which is why Doc's running a test to tell us his intoxication level. James lied to get into our group so he could spy for the Monarchs. We hope Charles is telling the truth." Then Clint spun around to Ben. "Oh, wait. Wait just a minute. Ben, can we use the ring, so we know if he's being truthful?"

"Good idea. I'll grab it so we can ask him some questions. But I do need to interject—I'm not sure how accurate it will be on someone that intoxicated." Ben took three steps toward the tunnel.

"Casey, you okay to stay alone while we question him, or did you want to go with us? Or go back to sleep?" Clint's brow furrowed.

Casey stood. "No way I can sleep after this. I'll go with you."

"Okay. We'll grab the ring. You throw some clothes on and meet us in the tunnel in what, say five minutes?" Clint joined Ben.

"Sure, see you in five." Casey was already halfway to her room.

A fight with jeans and a sweatshirt ensued as she dressed as fast as possible. Her clothes didn't cooperate. She yanked her shoes on as she hopped toward the bookcase. She peered in the closet as the hinges groaned when she opened it and found a ladder leading into the upper level of the house with the hidden door propped open. She climbed several rungs, slammed the hatch, and hoped it was secure enough for now. Then she jogged to join Ben and Clint in the tunnel.

SEVERAL TURNS THROUGH short tunnels brought them to a door with a keypad. Clint punched in numbers, and the door unlocked. Ben held the door for Casey to go in before him.

"Doc, how's the patient?" Clint peered around a curtain at an unconscious Charles on the bed. The living room had two beds with hospital curtains dividing the room down the middle. The dining room was Doc's office with his desk and chair pushed close enough to the wall to be comfortable for someone sitting there. Chairs lined the opposite wall as if in a waiting room.

"Intoxicated and passed out." Doc didn't raise his head.

"Can we risk taking him out of here and him not knowing how to access the basements of the houses?" Clint pulled a curtain back from the bed Charles occupied.

"Good question. I'm not sure how much he's retained, or if he's a blackout drunk no one would listen to if he were to say we're here." Doc peered over the glasses perched at the end of his nose.

Ben stood over Charles and lightly shook him. He stirred and squinted at Ben. "Charles, wake up." Opening his eyes more, he looked at Ben, confused. "Charles, do you know where you are?"

"In a house sleeping. What are you doing here?" Charles tried to roll over, but Ben stopped him.

Ben smiled. "How did you get here?"

"Through the front door." Charles closed his eyes.

This wouldn't be as easy as they hoped. With no definite answers, it was going to be hard to decide what to do with him.

Ben continued. "Charles, did anyone come in with you?"

"No. I stays to myself, thanks you much." Another hiccup escaped from Charles.

"Have you been here before?" Ben's ring glowed.

"No. I don't stay in the same place more than once. Otherwise, the butterfly people will finds you." Charles' eyes drooped before he finished the sentence.

Ben shook him again. "Hey, stay awake, Charles. What did you do when you came into the house?"

"I went to sleep until you woke me. I got in the closet to hide from the butterfly people. They don't like it when you walk around at night. They hurts you." Charles pulled his legs up and turned on his side.

"What do you mean they hurt you?" Ben glanced at Clint and pictured Casey when they rescued her from their headquarters.

"If they find you, you's never ever come back, or if they can't catch you, they shoots you and gets rid of the body." Charles tried to shrug out of Ben's grasp.

Ben's hand tightened on his shoulder. "How do you know this?"

"That's how I lost my friend, Pete. They shot him in front of me. They didn't knows I was there, but I watched 'em load Pete into the back of the van they's driving, and I hasn't seens him since." Charles's eyes closed again as he drooled.

"Did you hear them say anything?" Ben rolled Charles onto his back.

Charles fought to turn back onto his side. "Yes."

Ben sighed. "Charles, what did they say?"

"They couldn't wait to not have to wait until dark to shoot the people outside the designated areas, and as soon as the big guy gives the orders, they'd be able to do it in the daytime," Charles grunted.

Ben and Clint stared at each other, mouths open. "Charles, do you know who the big guy is they were talking about?"

"Yes, the big guy. He only runs the country. What other big guy would I be talking about? Sheesh, who doesn't know him?"

Ben shook him. "Charles, do you always get away from the butterfly people, or been caught before?"

"I never gets caught. I only go out when there's dark, and no moon so's I can dart between the houses real quiet-like and hide." Charles swatted at Ben's hand.

"Do you know the person standing at the end of the bed?" Ben's eyes locked with Casey's.

Charles half lifted his head, "The one standing next to my babysitter? No, never ever seen him before."

Ben's heart dropped. He still recognized Casey, but if he was this out of it, would he remember seeing her when he was sober? "How can she be your babysitter? Wouldn't she be older?"

"Yeah, well, I guess so. She looks like her, though. Wow, I must be plastered if I sees my babysitter from years ago standing at the bottom of my bed, especially when she died a long time ago. Although they never found her body. I remember when I was little, all the cameras were at her house after the big explosion, and they had to build a new house." Charles shivered.

Ben let go of his shoulder, cringed and mouthed "sorry" to Casey. "What do you think, Clint? Can we risk sending him out there?"

"I guess we can take him to the other site we first looked at and put him in one of those houses in the closet. When he wakes in the morning, it'll be a funny dream to tell people when he was drunk. If he's been able to hide from the

Monarchs this whole time, with his condition, I don't think anyone would believe him if he did talk about us?"

"I agree. Casey, you okay with us taking him out of here while he's still drunk?"

She nodded her head, yes. Ben knew she thought of her family after what Charles said.

"No one in their right mind would take him seriously," Clint smiled and added, "although we know it's true."

"Well, let's go. We need to move him upstairs and out of this neighborhood before dawn." Ben and Clint each grabbed one of Charles's arms, lifting him. Ben locked eyes with Casey. Her chin trembled, and he knew they had that connection—the loss of a sibling.

Ben glanced at Doc. "Do you mind if we use the car upstairs? It'll be a shorter distance to carry this guy."

"Sure, guys." Doc snatched a set of keys from a drawer in his desk and tossed them to Clint, who caught them mid-air.

"Casey, can you open the door to the closet?" Ben asked, but she didn't move.

"Casey?" Clint narrowed his eyes.

"Casey, are you okay?" Ben lowered his voice

Casey jumped. "Yeah. Sorry."

Hurried steps took her to the closet door. A set of stairs were there, and she climbed part of the way to unlatch the handle on this side, then gave it a shove to fold the door against the upper closet. She hopped down, then moved to the side for them.

All he wanted to do was wrap her up in his arms and hold her.

Ben searched her eyes. "We'll call you when we're back, okay?"

"Be careful, and hurry back." She stood on her tiptoes and pecked his cheek.

He did a double take and smiled as a blush spread across her cheeks. She raised a hand to the side of her face.

"We'll be right back, I promise. We won't take any unnecessary risks." Ben ran a finger along her cheek, never taking his eyes from hers. This time she didn't jump when he touched her. Hope sprang into his heart.

Forty-Six

She closed the hidden door behind them then the closet door. Doc's smiled when she turned around. "Stop it. Don't say a word." Casey held up her hand.

"I didn't say anything." Doc's grin widened.

"Which tunnel do I take back to my house?" Casey raised her eyebrows.

Doc dropped his glasses on the desk. "I'll walk with you."

Casey put her hand on the tunnel door. "No, no. I'll be fine if you can show me which way to go."

"Ben would never forgive me if I didn't walk you back, plus I promised him I would." He ambled over to Casey.

"I'd appreciate it if you walked me home." She smiled at Doc.

They left through the bookcase to the tunnels. Doc broke the silence. "How you doing? Any better?"

"Yes, although I would've loved a full night's sleep tonight." She stared at the ground.

Doc's slow steps stirred up dust. "I understand. At least you got help. But I don't think Charles was in any condition to do anything to hurt you. I'm not sure if he's like that, sober."

"He isn't. I think he fell on bad times and turned to drinking. He was a great kid when I used to babysit him, and his parents were raising him in a loving Christian home." She rubbed her hands over her upper arms.

"Take your next left." Doc pointed ahead of them.

She stopped and faced Doc. "Can I visit Amanda? Where's she buried?"

"Are you sure?" Doc raised his eyebrows.

"Yes. I need to say goodbye."

"I'd like to talk to Ben first." Doc patted her arm.

"He doesn't want me to visit her tomb?" She clutched her chest at the thought that he didn't want her to visit Amanda.

"It's not that. I think he wants to be with you." Doc placed a hand on her shoulder.

"Please, Doc. I need to see her alone." Casey fidgeted with the cuffs of her sleeves.

"Okay, follow me."

They backtracked, and Doc turned down a tunnel before his. They continued for a couple of blocks when he stopped at a door and punched in a code. The door opened much in the same way the doors to the homes did. Doc flipped the light switch on the other side of the doorframe. Several squares of concrete were in front of her, but only one with a name chiseled into it. It looked like a crypt at a graveyard except for the dirt floor and the concrete front to the crypts instead of marble. Walking forward, she extended her hand to Amanda's name, tracing each letter with her fingers.

"I'll be in the hall." Doc made her jump even though he whispered.

She smiled at him, then turned back to Amanda's name. She still couldn't believe she was gone. She wanted her to be here to laugh with and to confide in. Amanda would've thought it funny out of all the houses a drunk would've found his way into, it would be theirs since Casey had once babysat him. Casey could hear Amanda's laughter in the living room as they relaxed before bed, retelling the details of the story.

Tears trekked down her cheeks, and she swiped at them, smiling. She thought of Ben coming here to talk to her and the comfort of coming here when he missed her. She was in a better place, and Casey was jealous of that, but she knew in God's timing she would see Amanda again. In the short time she knew her, she made such an impact in her life. Casey pictured how Amanda would concentrate if she were interested in something you were talking about, or the concern in the always expressive features of her face. She didn't wipe away the tears anymore. It was a futile effort.

Amanda was so intuitive about Casey's attraction toward her brother. And if she was right and he liked Casey as much as she did him, Amanda would've loved that. Amanda would cherish Casey telling her what God told her when she healed Ben. Amanda would have talked about dresses for a wedding, making sure Casey knew no one else on the face of this earth could be her bridesmaid. Casey laughed out loud and placed her hand on her name on the cold, granular concrete it was carved into.

"I miss you, Amanda." It was the first thing she said out loud since Doc left her to herself in the room, and she jumped when it echoed off the walls.

"I miss her, too." She jumped again and spun around toward Ben's voice behind her. Her trembling hand flew to her mouth to keep from screaming.

Hastily she looked away and wiped her eyes as Ben wrapped his arms around her. Not wanting to break this moment, she relaxed and leaned into the hug, breathing in his intoxicating scent.

Ben rested his cheek on the top of her head. "I would never want to keep you from visiting my sister."

"I wasn't sure when Doc said he needed to ask you." Casey closed her eyes.

"I just wanted to be here if you needed me." Ben kissed the top of her head.

"Did you move Charles to a house without him knowing?" She didn't want to, but she pulled back.

He released her from his bear hug, cupped her face in his hands, and kissed her forehead, then took a step back. "Yes. He didn't regain consciousness, and we took him several miles away, so he won't even know where he is when he wakes."

"And no one saw you?" She peered up at Ben.

"Nope. Clean getting in and out of the houses, even made sure your closet wouldn't be a trap for unwanted visitors." Ben smiled.

"Where's Clint?" Casey glanced through the doorway.

"He went to bed after we found out you were here, and I told him I would make sure you made it home." Ben motioned Casey to the hall.

Once they were in the hall, Ben closed the door behind them as she glanced up and down the tunnel.

"If you're looking for Doc, he went home." Ben smiled.

"Yeah. I'll need to apologize for leaving him out here for so long. I'm not sure how long it was but, since you guys are back, I'm sure it was longer than he wanted to stay out here." Casey sighed.

"No, he's fine. We were only gone for about thirty minutes." Ben kicked his feet along the ground.

"Thirty minutes? I asked him to take me to Amanda before we were back at my house. It was at least twenty minutes. Okay, now I feel bad." She raised her hand to the side of her face and shook her head.

Ben leaned toward Casey. "It's okay. He knows you two were becoming close friends."

"She was like the sister I never had." Casey gave Ben a wavering smile.

"Yeah, she was great as a sister. She could push my buttons when I was younger and get me going, but I still loved her and always protected her." Ben stared down the tunnel, a smile playing at the corners of his mouth.

Casey glanced up at him. "I would say a typical big brother role, and you stepped right into it."

"Yeah, you could say that. Clint was with me when she needed both of us." Ben stopped at her door.

He waited while she punched in the code. She turned to say goodnight.

Ben shoved his hands into his pockets. "Do you want me to come in and make sure the house is secure?"

Casey backed into her house. "No, thank you. I'll be fine."

"Are you sure?" Ben's eyes studied hers.

"Yes. I'll call if any more unwanted visitors come by." She smiled.

"Okay, you leave this on." Ben motioned toward her ear. "Mine will be on."

"No problem." She smiled as heat rose in her face when she pictured kissing his cheek and told him to come back safe. She had no clue where that came from.

His eyes seemed to laugh at her as he smiled and stepped back. "I'll see you tomorrow."

"Goodnight." She quickly closed the door, pushed her bookcase back into place, and listened for the click of the lock engaging. She turned and took in the rooms of her house. The silence was deafening. She turned off the lights as she shuffled to her room, but left on the bathroom light. With her door open a crack, she curled under her blankets and listened to every creak and groan escape from her house as she settled in for a more productive sleep.

BEN LAID IN BED AND listened to Casey breathe. Long, deep breaths told him she finally fell asleep. He couldn't erase the image of her trembling after she had found Charles in her house. He wanted to be with her and wished he could sleep on her couch to be closer to her if she needed him. He tossed over on his side as he sighed.

A few minutes later, he swung his legs over the side of the bed before he lumbered down the hall toward the kitchen. Chugging water, he drained an entire glass. He set the glass in the sink upside down.

He shuffled his way to his bedroom, hoping he didn't disturb Clint. They were both in need of sleep. He was wired after being that close to Casey in the tunnels. She was so small and fragile when he held her. With the covers pulled up over him, he tossed and turned for several minutes. The blankets tangled around his feet, and he kicked out, wrestling them free before shaking out the blanket, so it covered him again. He listened to her breathing and imagined when the Monarchs had her.

His heart raced as he tried to shake the image of her battered and beaten as he and Clint worked on her in the back of the car to stop the bleeding from all the wounds she suffered. No one could ever guess the trauma she had since she was able to heal herself, and all the scars had melted away in the blue aura.

He imagined how she grabbed onto him and shook when she healed him. He heard the words again as she told him she loved him. That was the last thought he had before he drifted off into a fitful sleep.

Forty-Seven

Her fingers brushed the headboard as she stretched to remove any sleep left in her body, unsure what time it was. With only being able to live in the lower part of the houses, it was hard to tell the time of day with no windows for light to enter in and give away any sort of reasonable clue of the time. She shuffled across the room with the help of the bathroom light she had left on the previous night. The light in the room blinded her as she squinted until her eyes grew accustomed to the brightness in the normally dark room. Chilled from the coolness of the basement, she pulled out a sweater and grabbed a pair of jeans.

Steam rolled out of the shower as she locked the door behind her. The shower eased the tension she had in her neck from the stress of the previous night. They had a big day ahead of them to plan the interception of the president. The clock on the sink announced it was after eleven, and she did a double take. Was that the right time? Would they plan the mission before she got there?

She tugged on her sweater then brushed her teeth. Running her fingers through her hair, she ran the dryer over it then pulled it into a ponytail while her stomach growled.

The refrigerator held so much food that it could feed several families for a couple of weeks. She wouldn't be able to eat it all before it went bad. Eggs, bacon, biscuits, butter, milk, vegetables, fruit, and countless other items were packed in her refrigerator. She would check with Ben and Clint to let someone else use some of the food, considering they put enough in here for her and Amanda, plus some.

She grabbed a banana and yogurt, devoured them as fast as she could while thinking about the time and the fact she slept so late.

Casey started to open her mouth, then closed it. She blew out a breath. "Ben?"

Nothing.

"Ben?" She tossed her banana peel into the trash.

Nothing.

She looked at the panel and pushed the option to call Ben and Clint. It rang several times, showing bubbles dancing and bouncing across the screen that disappeared when Clint answered. "Hello?" He was out of breath.

"Hello, did I wake you?" Casey tried to see if Ben was in the background of the image.

"No, I was in the other room." Clint's voice sounded more like himself now.

"When did you want to get together to work on everything?" Casey tugged on the sleeves of her sweater.

Clint smiled. "You can head over now if you want. Doc and Chloe will be here in about an hour."

"Sure, see you in a few." Casey gave a small wave at the screen.

"Did you want one of us to walk you over?" Clint's concern oozed through the display.

"No, I think I can handle walking next door. It isn't like I'm going to be outside in the dark, and a stranger will come and offer me candy, Dad." Casey laughed.

"Just get over here." Clint's finger filled the screen as he disconnected.

She stopped midstride to the bookcase and turned as if she forgot something. Wait, the last time she left a home she lived in, she had always made sure Mason had fresh water and anything he needed while she was away at work. Her heart had a hole in it for him, but not as much as the one for her family. She closed the bookcase behind her and pushed the door shut. Would the guilt of her family's deaths ever go away? Especially since Clint's revelation that maybe she was the one who was supposed to die in the explosion instead of them.

A few steps shy of Ben and Clint's home, her chest tightened and breathing accelerated. Why did he affect her so much? As she closed the last couple of feet, her heart raced, and she closed her eyes and told herself to take deep, slow breaths. She wanted to turn and run back to her house. With her fingers poised over the keypad, she hesitated then punched in the code. The tumblers unlocked, and she opened the door to push the bookcase away from the wall. Their house appeared to be void of anyone.

"Hello," she called from the dining room.

"Hey." Ben popped his head around the corner with a toothbrush hanging out of his mouth.

"Good afternoon." Clint came out of the kitchen and joined her in the dining room. Several street maps lay on the table. "Did you sleep okay after all the excitement last night?" Clint studied her out of the corner of his eye.

"Slept like a baby. Why didn't someone wake me?"

"We wanted you to sleep as much as possible. Plus, Ben here slept until two hours ago. We're just getting around, ourselves."

"What are we looking at?" She motioned to the maps on the table.

"This one's of the airport garage where Polson will come in. Doc's friend won't have access but has someone he trusts who can get to the car during detailing and plant the bug."

Casey glanced at Clint. "So, Chloe's uncle can make one for us?"

"Not only *make* but already *made* and fully tested. He's always thinking ahead and was in research and development for the government, so he has all sorts of projects like this he didn't hand over before they gave him the boot." Clint nodded.

"Good to know there won't be a problem with Polson's people knowing what to sweep for or having found a way to detect the bug while it is turned off." Casey ran her fingers over the bottom edge of the slick gloss finish of the map.

"Smart girl. Chloe said he has several different types, but one in particular, we like." Clint looked up.

Ben loomed at the table before he sat in the chair opposite of where Clint and Casey stood. "Where are you at in the plans?"

"Not far. Casey and I were talking about the bug but didn't cover any details." Clint hooked his thumbs in his belt loops, tugging on them.

"Which one are you interested in?" She slightly tilted her head and raised her eyebrows.

"He built one into a lightbulb that will work like a normal bulb, but when activated, a secondary component in the base has a GPS locator in it." Clint bobbed his head up and down.

"Nice, and we don't think they'll be able to detect it?" A smile crept across her face.

"No, Ben will be able to activate it from under the next overpass on the freeway so I can follow them. Ben will catch up to me when we pull Polson over." Clint lifted the first page of the maps and pointed to a second page.

"How are you going to make a motorcade pull over?" This, she knew, would be the part she wouldn't like—the dangerous part.

Ben shifted in his chair and looked at Clint, who continued, "We're going to use the pulse weapon to disable his car. We think it will shut down the electronics."

"How do you know?" Her voice rose an octave. "It's too dangerous to try when you're out in the open with the Monarchs around."

"Well, it works on appliances, because Ben here had the bright idea to try testing it in here and I may or may not have shorted out our kitchen appliances. The center stone turns and can be used for different types of pulses besides knocking someone out." Clint pressed his lips together, suppressing a smile.

She stepped back. "Whoa?"

"Yes. Ben and I discussed that I needed to practice, so when I put it on, I pushed on the center gem, and it rotated inside the relic. I thought it possibly had more than one setting when a pulse shot out from the dining room and disabled several appliances in the direct path of the pulse." Clint sat on the chair in front of him.

"Was anyone hurt?" She didn't like the thought of Ben being in harm's way.

"No. Ben was in there when it shot through the kitchen, and he's fine. We even had Doc check him out." Clint swept his hand toward the kitchen.

A quick glance at Ben, and she raised an eyebrow, knowing he could have been hurt.

"I'm fine, promise." Ben raised his hands as if in surrender.

"Yeah, well, you used your one and only get-out-of-jail-free card," she teased.

Ben winked then returned to studying the maps.

Clint checked the top map. "Doc's friend at the airport, along with a buddy who works on the vehicles, will access the vehicle to replace the bulb without any suspicions. He's not loyal to anyone, but he's also not a friend of the president—a little on the rebellious side of authority. We don't know him, but Doc trusts his friend, and if he vouches for him, we're going to run with it. This may be the only chance to grab Polson."

"Once the vehicle's been bugged, I'll be here." Ben pulled out a map of the airport, including surrounding highways, with a red dot not included in the original print of the map. "Once the limo passes this ramp," Ben pointed at the red dot and a ramp close to where he would be, "I'll activate the bug and wait to hear from Clint to make sure it tracks."

"We'll be by the highway here." Clint pointed to a blue dot on the map on a side street located next to another ramp to gain quick access to the highway. "We'll wait with the GPS scanner for Ben to say he's activated it. Then we'll let Ben know the status of the activation and jump on the highway from the ramp right next to our location. Ben will join us, and if they exit on any side streets, I'll give him directions as we go, or you can, whichever is more convenient."

She looked at Clint, glad they were including her in the plans. "So, I'll be in the car with you?"

"Yes. Ben and I thought if you were in the first car with me, you could help with the shield the bracelet gives off if I come under fire while disabling their car."

"Okay. I'll need to start practicing so I can control the shield." She couldn't live with herself if something happened to either of them because of her.

"Once we disable the car, Ben and I'll be able to take out the guards and grab Polson. You'll then drive the one we're in, and Ben will follow. We'll meet here." Clint opened the map a little more, pointing to a section of streets a couple of miles away from the airport. "Chloe will be here, all set for our arrival. We'll record that he's a fraud and planned this whole terrorist act since before his inauguration."

Ben sat back and put his hands behind his head. "We'll leave to come back here while Chloe makes a side trip to drop off the video chip to her uncle. He'll send it out to the news stations to not only air it on live television but also to leak it out to the web. They say once something is on the web, you can never get rid of it. People will download and send it in emails. They won't be able to stop it from going viral."

"We'll need a lot of prayers for this to go off without a hitch." Casey dropped into the chair in front of her and stared at the map.

"Hank's working on the prayer coverage now, so there's enough when we need it. We know God's behind us, but the power of prayer is unbelievable when enough people are praying together." Clint sat next to Casey.

"Casey, did you want anything to drink?" Ben stood.

"I'll take water if you don't mind." Casey smiled.

"Me, too," Clint chimed in.

Ben headed into the kitchen. Cabinet doors thudded, and glasses clinked together.

"Wow, service with a smile." She took a glass, brushing his fingers with hers and leaving him with one in each hand. He placed one in front of Clint before he sank into his seat across from them and smiled at her. Did he realize she did that on purpose?

Forty-Eight

Clicks from behind the bookcase startled them. Doc and Chloe stepped inside.

"Hello, everyone." Doc was always so chipper.

"Hi." Little, petite Chloe sheepishly smiled as she joined them at the table.

Ben grabbed a folding chair out of the closet to place at the end of the table. He faced it the wrong way then sat, his arms crossed over the back of the chair. He slid his glass across the worn grainy top of the table, so it sat in front of him.

Doc and Chloe sat in the two chairs opposite of Casey and Clint.

"Did you want something to drink?" Ben offered.

"No, I'm fine." Doc turned to Chloe, who shook her head, then studied the maps.

"Is Casey up to speed on our plan?" At Chloe's young age, Clint hated that she was involved in the dangerous plan of kidnapping a president.

"Yes. She's seen the maps, and we discussed where everyone will be. I'll ride with her," Clint answered.

"Well, I spoke with my uncle, and he had the bug ready to go. He's meeting with Doc's friend out at the airport tonight to pass it off, and then he'll meet me after to give me the remote to activate the bug. It should be in place in the next day or so." Chloe clutched her hands together.

"Yes, my friend who's meeting Chloe's uncle said the car's ready to go and will be sitting in the secured garage for Polson's visit. He did say they called a large meeting for tomorrow evening's staff, and he thinks they'll announce the exact time Polson will be here. He'll let me know when." Doc pulled his glasses off the top of his head and peered through them at the maps.

"Sounds good. Chloe, did he say what the range is on the reception of the remote?" Clint chugged from his glass.

"No. I told him about our plan, and he said for what we need it for, there'd be no problem with reception. He said even if we activate it early, there shouldn't be any detection of it to alert them. He said all electronic items give off some sort of frequency, and he's been working on a GPS chip, which doesn't give off any more of a frequency wave than the object he hides them in. According to him, he said all it'd show as would be a short in the bulb itself, or it would be mistaken for a short in the wiring. They may not even acknowledge it," Chloe explained.

"Great. If all goes well, we'll meet you at the oil change shop. Did your uncle tap into the surveillance system of the garage and loop a digital frame to run so no one will be aware of us coming or going?"

Chloe nodded. "Yes. He ran a loop for the timeframe of six hours from a week ago and will start the loop at the same time when you follow Polson. Their system doesn't use a date stamp on daily imaging. It only logs the time, showing continuous images, and they'll be stored into the library as the current day."

"Perfect. Doc, when your friend contacts you tomorrow after their meeting, make sure his friend's able to do his job and put in the bulb Chloe's uncle will give him. We'll know to go ahead with the plan. If he isn't, we'll change to plan B." Clint caught the shock on Casey's face.

"We'll follow him the old-fashioned way, which is more dangerous since we can't stay as far back and take the chance of them spotting us before we make our move. They'll more than likely call in reinforcements who will be there in no time. We're trying to avoid that, but will attempt it if the original plan doesn't work." Clint's jaw clenched for a split second. Casey would be in danger while in his car if the original plan failed. He couldn't let that happen.

"Casey, the GPS will allow you two to follow at a safe distance. He can tell me where Polson is so I can catch up and help when you guys come under fire." Ben locked his eyes on hers.

"Right. I just wasn't aware of there being a plan B." Casey's eyes were wide. She dropped her hands and gripped the sides of the chair, her fingers white.

"We hadn't had a chance to tell you yet. But it will be okay. Our military brain is on this mission, and he's the best." Ben mock saluted Clint, who saluted back.

Chloe laughed and looked at her watch. All three men rose out of their chairs when she did. "I need to meet Hank to put in a call to the northern group and get them on their knees, praying, and spread the word out to their subgroups."

"Okay, see you later?" Clint turned to her.

"Yes. As soon as I leave to meet my uncle, I'll give you a call, so you know when to expect me back. If something happens, you'll know how to proceed to the next step." Chloe gave a small wave and left through the bookcase.

"I would still like to go with you guys in case anything happens." Doc sat back as Ben folded his chair and took the seat Chloe had vacated.

"Doc, we talked about this. What if something happens and the group needs a doctor here to take care of them? Casey will be able to heal us if one of us gets injured."

"Yes, but last time she couldn't save both you and Amanda. If I was there, maybe Casey could've kept her alive long enough for me to work on her, and she'd be here today." Doc put a hand on Ben's arm.

"This was not Casey's fault. She was too weak from healing me to be able to save my sister." Ben lashed out toward Doc, putting Clint on edge. He knew he would never strike out at him, but Ben's raised voice bothered him.

Doc backpedaled. "Oh, Casey, I didn't mean it that way at all. You're the reason we still have Ben. I hope you know that."

Casey reached across the table for Doc's hand. "I didn't take it that way. I knew what you meant. You wish you could have been there to possibly do something to save Amanda with me keeping her stable for as long as I could."

"Exactly. Clint, are you sure I can't come with you? What if there are two people hurt again? The last time I was sure Casey wouldn't come out of it. I thought we were going to lose her." Doc gave Casey's hand a squeeze.

Clint shook his head. "I have to side with Ben. If something happens to, let's say all of us, we can't take the risk of you not making it back to the group. What if someone here gets sick?"

"I don't want to lose another one of you. You're like my kids, and I feel responsible for you." Doc pushed his chair away from the table.

Ben put a hand on the back of Doc's chair to keep it from tipping over. "You're like a father figure to so many here in this group, and I'm not sure how we would've survived without you through the years. I don't want you to not be able to take care of the ones who are staying here."

"We'll have prayer coverage, and the best thing you can do is to be ready in case one of us needs you." Clint held his ground.

"You guys be safe and don't take any unnecessary risks out there. That's an order." Doc's voice caught in his throat.

Clint took Doc's hand in a firm handshake and smiled. "We will. Thanks for the concern. Pray for us, and with God's will, we'll do what we can to come back in one piece."

"I'll call when the car's ready and with an exact time when Polson will be in town." He hobbled through the door, closing the bookcase behind him.

"Did you want to practice with the bracelet?" Clint raised his eyebrows at Casey while a smile played at the corners of his mouth.

Forty-Nine

"Sure, I'll go grab it." Casey jumped out of her chair.

"Okay." Clint leaned back.

Casey jogged to her house and let herself in. She took the time to freshen up, grabbed the bracelet from the nightstand, then headed through the tunnel.

Energy coursed through her since she hadn't practiced before now, unsure if she could work the bracelet by sheer will. Why did Clint smile when he asked? What was he up to? She could only assume Ben was in on it.

Punching in the code to their house, she entered a dark dining room, barely able to make out the furniture from the light in the tunnels. The hair stood on the back of her neck. A gut feeling told her the Monarchs had found them. The bracelet intertwined and laced its way from her wrist and up her forearm. Before she knew it, the shield deployed as her heart raced.

She called out, "Ben? Clint?" Movement to her left caught her eye as an object hurtled toward her, she instinctively put her hands out to block the object when the shield shot out several feet and deflected it across the room. A second object came at her from the kitchen, this time with her mind, she threw the shield out, causing it to rebound back at the one who threw it.

Ben and Clint put her under pressure like this to help with the training. Her heart rate slowed as she started to relax. From the living room, something else came at her, but she couldn't make out what it was, except it wasn't an object but more of a wavering field. Wait a minute, did Clint shoot the weapon at the shield? Before she could finish that thought, her instinct was to brace for impact because there was no dodging or deflecting this one; it came right at her. She braced as the shield went opaque just before the pulse from the weapon absorbed into it. Static electricity sparked and traveled around the shield before it rushed through the bracelet and her whole body.

The light in the living room turned on as Clint's stood next to a floor lamp smiling, proud of himself. She knew it had to be his idea to plan this ambush. The kitchen light flickered on as Ben stood there with the roll of paper towels he used as his weapon.

"Nicely done. I don't think we need to be concerned about Casey and the shield." Clint waited until she withdrew the shield before extending his hand to shake hers.

She reached out to shake his hand when a static spark discharged from her hand to his, even though their fingers were several inches away from each other.

"Ouch!" Clint looked at his hand as Ben laughed.

"Don't look at me. You started this by shooting me with your weapon." She beamed. It was fun to pay him back from his ambush.

Ben gaffed, holding his hands up as if in mock surrender. "Did the pulse get absorbed into the shield?"

"Yes. It was like what Clint got in the static discharge, and as a matter of fact, my hand and arm are still numb." She frowned when she looked at her hand, wriggling her fingers, and gripped her forearm with her left hand.

"You okay?" Ben took quick, long strides and took her hand as he threw a look at Clint.

"It was on stun. Nothing more." Clint took a step closer as Ben checked out her hand. "Does it hurt?"

"No. But it's numb and tingly as if it fell asleep," she reassured them.

"Sorry. I didn't know it'd do that." Clint frowned.

"It doesn't hurt, and I'm sure that's all anyone feels when they're stunned."

"Weird." Ben still held her hand but let it go after giving it a squeeze.

"So, are you happy with yourself and the little ambush you set up?" She scowled at him.

Ben laughed. "He couldn't wait to spring it on you when he found out the bracelet worked."

"Oh, nice. So you were conniving and planning this for a while?" She spun to Clint and narrowed her eyes as she stepped forward when a spark ran across her outstretched fingers.

"It isn't as bad as Ben makes it sound. I knew we had to test it, and I thought if it were in the moment, it'd be a true test of what you're capable of." Clint stepped back, eyeing the sparks

"Are you planning on doing the same for testing your weapon?"

Clint frowned at her. "I can't plan a surprise test for my own device, now can I?"

"No, but you do have two people here who could whip something up for you." She winked at Ben.

"Hey. I'm sure we could, just for you." Ben jumped next to her and put his arm around her shoulders. Goosebumps ran rampant up and down her arms. She hoped it never went away.

"Yeah, I'm sure you could." Clint laughed. He gawked at her arms.

She crossed her arms, uncrossed them, then crossed them again as she fidgeted. She wished Amanda was here to draw the attention away and misdirect Clint from what he saw, although she would've been drilling her later about her attraction for her brother.

Ben's eyes met hers, and she got lost in them. He quickly removed his arm from around her shoulders. Was his reaction the same as hers toward him? Amanda said he liked her, but she was still unsure of how deep his emotions went for her. She knew she didn't have the courage to talk to him about it yet, but she also couldn't shake the memory from the day she saved him and what God spoke to her heart about him being the one for her.

CASEY RUBBED HER HAND and arm. Clint was supposed to be her guardian. He was mad at himself for wounding her. Although, if the relics were able to talk to each other, would they ever really put her in danger?

A real situation would be completely different, but he was pleased with the testing of the bracelet. Her instincts impressed him. She was a natural.

"So, with the surprise testing done on mine. How do we test yours without taking out any more innocent appliances?" Casey teased.

"Thanks." Clint mock glared at her.

"She has a point. We need to find out what the other setting does and how potent this device is, so we don't kill someone with it when we only intend to disable vehicles and people."

"I was thinking about the house we never occupied at the end of the far tunnel. It's vacant, so we won't be destroying someone's home since it was never finished. It's underground, so no one will be able to hear us." Clint gave a crisp nod.

Ben turned to Casey. "Sounds good to me. You up for a walk?"

"Sure. Do I need to bring anything?" She glanced from one to the other.

"Nope. Just the lovely bracelet you're wearing. Maybe we can test it some more." Clint stalked to the bookcase, unlocked it, then swung it back.

"Well, let's go. Wait." Casey stopped in front of them, causing Ben and Clint to almost run into her. "Isn't Doc or Chloe supposed to call?"

"No, not for several hours, which will give us time to do some testing before dinner when they return." Clint shooed Casey with his hands to keep walking.

Clint took the lead with Ben and Casey on his heels. The far end of the tunnel was unfinished. Dirt was held back by boards with two-by-fours wedged against them. To the left was a door without a combination lock. Clint opened the door, then shoved the bookcase in.

They stepped into an unfinished basement, and Casey's eyes grew wide. She stopped in front of Clint after he motioned her and Ben into the basement. She eyed the dark far corner. Clint placed his hand on her shoulder from behind, and a small yelp escaped as she jumped about a foot off the porous concrete floor.

"Sorry, didn't mean to scare you." Clint studied her.

She laughed yet didn't take her eyes off the ominous corner as he walked around her.

"I thought we could test the pulse that took out our appliances earlier on several items here. We use this for the storage for extra appliances but also the appliance graveyard. Some of them don't work well enough to use daily, so we can test this out on them." Clint motioned to the relic he pulled out of a pouch, placing it in his palm.

"You know what we also need to test, don't you?" Casey glanced up at Ben and Clint, who towered over her.

"No, what?" Ben was the first to answer.

"If the shield can withstand bullets, the Monarchs won't have weapons like what Clint has, so we'll need to make sure the shield can withstand a barrage of bullets flying at it with us behind it. I also need to know if it will drain me like the healing relic."

"No, I don't like it. We aren't shooting at you!" Ben spun on his heels and marched to the other wall.

Casey held up her hands. "No, not shooting at me. I can extend the shield a little so you can shoot at the extension. But we need to make sure you two are safe. I don't know how solid the shield is, or if there'll be ricocheting bullets flying at you two."

"I think that's a great idea. Ben, did you want to go for a firearm, or did you want me to?" Clint crossed his arms and stood with his feet shoulder-width apart.

"I still don't like it, but we need to make sure we have cover for Casey. I want her behind something in case they either go through the shield or glance off the concrete back toward her. Clint, why don't you grab what you think we'll need while Casey and I work on building some shelters we can hide behind."

"Sure thing, I'll be right back." Clint disappeared into the tunnel.

Fifty

Ben turned and snatched several pieces of wood, stacking them in a pile nearby. Casey took his lead and did the same while Ben grabbed a hammer and nails out of a toolbox that he pulled from under a workbench attached to the far wall. In the meantime, Casey splayed a trembling flashlight she found on the workbench across the corner. No spiders or critters scurried around, and she blew out her breath.

Ben arranged plywood and two-by-fours on the concrete floor and nailed them together so that there were several layers with the two-by-fours in a crisscross pattern between sheets of the plywood. When he was finished, Ben set it across the corner of the room and surveyed his work.

"Will that work?" Casey wasn't sure what bullets could penetrate.

"I'll be back there with you, so you'll be fine," he huffed.

"What about Clint?" She turned away from the corner where he had placed his handiwork and came face to face with Ben. She was unaware he stood next to her. Casey inhaled sharply as their eyes locked.

Ben reached to touch her cheek, and she flinched. His eyes dropped to the floor. "You're never going to trust me, are you?"

"I do trust you. It's—well, I—Never mind, you wouldn't understand." Casey inwardly berated herself for jumping.

Exposing her feelings to others wasn't something she had ever been good at.

She searched for enough lumber to make another barrier for Clint for when they tested the shield. Ben turned her around to face him and stared into her eyes. "Casey, I would never hurt you. I'm going to do everything I can to keep you safe."

She looked at the floor when his hand cupped her chin, guiding her face to his. "Ben, I know—"

He brushed her forehead with his lips, then enveloped her into his comforting embrace. She took a deep breath. Safe in his arms, she didn't want this moment to end but knew Clint would be back any moment. She wrapped her arms around his waist and laid her head on his chest as she closed her eyes and relaxed her shoulders. If this was who God had chosen for her, he was better than anyone she could have ever hoped or dreamed for, and she wanted to cry. She closed her eyes. On the verge of tears, she was amazed at God's enduring love for her.

Ben slowly unwrapped his strong arms from around her shoulders and stepped back, but continued to study her with his piercing eyes. Ben gently swiped his finger across her cheek and showed her the smudge of dirt.

He walked around her snagging several two-by-fours and proceeded to make a barrier similar to the other one. Clint walked into the room with a gun tucked in the waist of his jeans while he placed one on the bench by the door. Clint glanced back and forth between them, then raised a single eyebrow. She smiled as Ben finished with the last few nails on Clint's barrier.

Ben stood and leaned Clint's barrier toward him. "Will this work?"

Clint checked it over. "It should. We're going to be shooting at an angle, so even if it ricochets, it should hit several objects, such as the concrete walls before it'd make it back to us."

"Okay, you ready?" Casey called from behind her barrier.

"Wait, I told you I'm going to be with you behind yours. Clint, if a possibility exists that the shield is able to stop a bullet, I want as many people behind it safe and secure."

"Good idea. Casey, when Ben's in place, go ahead and put up the shield, try to extend it to this point." Clint pointed to an opening of a hallway to where the bedrooms would be if they had finished this house like the others. "It will be a good spot. If the shield doesn't stop the bullet, it will continue down away from us."

She concentrated and created a shield around herself and Ben. When Ben put his arm around her, the shield shot out well past the hallway. Heat flooded her face as she concentrated on the shield, ignoring Ben's arm and retracted it, so it only covered the hallway.

Clint took aim from behind his barrier and squeezed the trigger. The gun fired off a round. The shot was deafening, and she jumped at the sound, which only made Ben tighten his arm. The bullet stopped mid-air in the shield. It held it in suspended animation. She rose and retracted the shield, and the bullet fell to the ground. The sound of the metal hitting concrete echoed in the basement. She glanced over at Clint and smiled. Could this keep them bulletproof?

Ben strode to where the perfectly shaped bullet lay on the ground, unmarred from not encountering anything to cause it to fragment or become unrecognizable. Ben picked up the bullet, almost dropped it, then tossed it to Clint, who snatched it out of the air.

"Whoa." Clint almost dropped it as he tossed from one hand to the other.

"What, is it still hot from being fired?" Casey's eyes widened.

"No, ice cold." Clint walked over and placed it in her palm. It was cold as if it had lain in freshly fallen snow and was outside in sub-zero temperatures.

"I have a question. If it can stop one bullet, will it stop a whole barrage coming from different directions?" Her eyes darted between the two. She knew this meant they would both have to fire from different directions at the shield to test it. She wasn't sure how Ben would react to the idea.

Clint raised his eyebrows and looked at Ben, who never tore his eyes away from her. "Well, let's try and find out."

Ben glared at Clint then back to her. "Did you bring more than one gun?"

"Sure did, different calibers, too."

THEY PLACED THE BARRIERS to form a V shape in the middle of the back wall. "Okay, in you go." Ben stared down at her, his hands on his hips.

"It stopped the first one." Casey marched over to them and stared up at the two. "I'm more worried about you guys.

You need the barriers more than I do. I'll be safe behind the shield."

Ben didn't hesitate. He wrapped his hands around her waist, picked her up, and deposited her behind the barrier. Clint smiled and strolled to the wall, which met with the hallway while Ben stalked to the back wall opposite of Clint. They both knelt, and Clint nodded at Casey to raise the shield.

Concentrating, she extended the shield to the same distance it was before. Ben motioned to her to kneel below the barriers. He refused to fire until she was completely hidden. Her head peeked over the barrier as Ben and Clint nodded to each other and raised their guns. He saw her plug her ears as they fired.

Ben rose from his position and stared at the bullets that hung in mid-air. He nodded and had hope for the first time in a long time that they finally had a chance against the Monarchs.

The bullets hung in the shield as Clint walked over and reached for one. "Clint, stop. It may hurt you." Casey threw her hand out.

"Wait, let me try something." Clint touched the outer part of the shield that was extended to the hallway. He slowly pushed his hand into it where the bullets were suspended. His fingers reached one of the bullets, and he grabbed it. Once he pulled his hand free, he glanced at her, wiggling all his fingers after dropping the bullet into his other hand.

"Are you okay? Any pain in your fingers?" Casey marched over.

"Yes, and no, to answer your two questions. I'm fine, not even cold like the bullet. It must react differently with human tissue than with inanimate objects."

Ben joined them and snatched the bullet from Clint's other hand, rolling it from one hand to the other. It was still cold from being in the shield. Casey grabbed Clint's hand and turned it over and over. Ben smiled at her concern.

"So, question—can someone walk through the shield to shoot at us? Or will it stop someone from even walking through the shield?" Casey frowned. "Or is it because of the different velocities of the two? The bullet has such a high velocity. Maybe it senses that, and since you slowly placed your hand in the shield, it didn't sense you as a threat."

"So, do we have someone run into the shield to test it?" Ben tilted his head toward Clint for him to try it.

"You go first, and we'll watch what happens," Clint quipped back at Ben. "Casey, grab some popcorn. This could be a pretty good show."

Chuckling, Casey shook her head and stepped away from them. "Leave me out of it."

"Or is the shield tuned in to the person using it, and you aren't a threat, Clint, but when an intruder was in her house, it treated them as one."

Clint nodded at Ben. "Maybe how the person using the shield thinks of the shield. In our house, you deflected the objects with the shield, but in here, you're in a different mindset. You don't want anyone to be injured by a ricochet, so it suspends any flying objects."

"Makes sense. Now Clint, what can you do with your relic?"

Clint engaged the safety on his gun, then held his hand out for Ben's and did the same, rendering both guns safe. Clint placed the guns on a makeshift workbench then turned toward Ben. "Help me with one of these refrigerators."

Ben and Clint moved one close enough to an outlet to plug it in to make sure it was operational. Ben glanced at Casey, whose mouth hung open and whose eyes were glued to his arms that strained under his shirt while moving the appliance. He smirked as she clamped her mouth shut. Red spread from her neck up across her face. Ben walked around the front and opened the door, and the light came on inside. He took a couple of steps back and joined her behind Clint. "Ready when you are."

Clint pulled out the relic from his pocket, placing it in his right palm. The tendrils formed rings and wrapped around the outside of Clint's hand. Looking at the triangular stone in the middle, Clint, satisfied with its setting, pointed his palm toward the refrigerator and concentrated. A small pulse of a red energy wave shot out toward the refrigerator as if someone took a picture with a red flash.

Ben walked over to the fridge. The light inside didn't come on as it had before. It was rendered inoperable. "Great job, Clint. If killer mutant refrigerators attack, we now have a defense weapon to keep the women and kiddies safe."

Clint slugged his friend in the arm as Ben walked past him to Casey's side. "Gee, thanks, buddy. Not sure what this other setting is for, but we now know the other two settings work and can use them."

"Yes, it works on appliances. How will it work on a vehicle?" Ben gazed down at Casey as she said it. She had a point.

"CASEY'S RIGHT. IS THE old junk car still parked in the garage upstairs?" Ben turned toward the closet in the hallway.

"I think it is." Clint was right behind Ben. "We need to make this fast since we won't be under the cover of the houses up there."

"Well, you two stay here until I'm sure the car will start." Ben reached for the hidden lever to release the ladder and disappeared into the upper level.

Clint and Casey waited at the bottom of the stairs. She shifted from one foot to the other, listening for Ben to give them the go-ahead to join him in the garage. Her lips were slightly parted, her mouth dry when he gave the all-clear. Clint went up first and waited at the top for her to join him. It was weird and creepy being in the upstairs of the house. All the furniture was still in place with heavy layers of dust so that you couldn't tell the true color of anything. Pictures hung on the walls that showed idyllic families. This was someone's home, and it was as if she intruded on their lives, peering in a window without their knowledge. She couldn't believe people were driven out of their homes and taken away from their lives because of a terrorist group. It disturbed her. She half expected someone to walk in and ask why they were in their house.

She followed Clint as goosebumps marred her smooth skin. She rubbed her hands up and down her arms. Once in the garage, a vehicle idled that looked to be in mint condition, but according to Clint and Ben, it was an ancient piece of junk.

"We need to do this quick before they scan this area and find three heat signatures and alert the Monarchs' headquarters." Clint paced in the garage around the car.

"You're right. Come on, Casey. We'll watch from the doorway." Ben grabbed her hand and pulled her to him.

Clint stood one step lower. He aimed his palm toward the car, and a red pulse illuminated the garage. The engine sputtered then died, which left them in a deafeningly quiet garage. "Well, I guess it works." Clint smiled at himself.

"We better get downstairs." Ben trudged down the two uneven, dilapidated wooden steps into the garage, took the keys out of the ignition, then placed them under a block of wood on a dusty shelf by the door.

They made their way back into the secure basement and locked the hidden entrance from their side. Chloe stepped through the doorway to the tunnel seconds before they reached the entry. "We're set. Doc's friend received the bug and will pass it on in an hour, and they plan to have it in the car in less than half an hour after. There isn't anyone supposed to be on duty tonight, and Polson is flying in tomorrow. They moved the meeting with Doc's friend to today." Chloe was out of breath as she relayed the details of her meeting with Doc.

"Tomorrow?" Ben peered at Clint. "Glad we were able to do a couple of tests today."

Casey glanced at her bracelet. The realization that they would be taking on the president made her hands shake. She didn't realize she would react this way. Even though she volunteered for this duty, she trembled like a little girl facing a giant on the playground.

"We need to gather everything together and go over the streets we'll be traveling before we try to sleep. We'll make an early start so we won't raise any red flags with vehicles not there when the Monarchs go to pick up Polson." Clint snatched the guns from the counter. Handing one to Ben, he stuck the other in the waistband in the back of his jeans and pulled his shirt over it.

Swift steps took them to Clint and Ben's house, where Doc waited. Doc had two small ominous black plastic boxes sitting on the dining room table in front of him.

Fifty-One

"Hey, Doc. How did everything go? Chloe said they are all set on her end, and Polson will be here in the morning." Clint held a chair out for Chloe.

Ben reached for the chair next to Doc and found his hand covered Casey's as they reached for the same chair. A beautiful flush flashed across Casey's face and down her neck as she pulled her hand away. When Ben pulled out the chair for her, he noticed her hands shook, and as their eyes met, he caught the dread there just before she lowered her gaze and sat down.

Was she scared? Ben wanted to wrap her up in his arms and keep her safe. This world was unlike anything she had known, and she hadn't yet been exposed to the vast evil this world faced as he and Clint had.

"We're ready. My friend will have the taillight switched out by his co-worker within the hour. This is the remote to activate the GPS chip hidden in the light." Doc handed the smaller black box to Ben with the one small, simple button in the middle. One push and Clint and Casey would be able to follow Polson's car.

"This will be your GPS locator, tied to Polson's bugged vehicle." Doc handed Clint the slightly larger black box, which housed a screen with one button at the bottom.

"My uncle said he built into the chip a certain code only these two remotes will be able to activate and track, making it not only simple and easy to use, but it will also keep anyone else out, who may have a scanner to pick up the signal to tip off the Monarchs of an ambush." Chloe beamed with pride for her uncle.

"Sounds simple enough. Ben, you'll be here." Clint pointed to the red dot on the map under the overpass. "Doc, did your friend know when Polson would be coming into town?"

"He said he's on the Red-Eye, and he's supposed to report to work at five."

"Okay, we'll need to be in position at three to make sure we don't miss Polson in case his flight comes in early." Clint studied the map.

"No problem. It's five now, so if we go ahead and eat and pack a breakfast, we'll have no problem waking at two in the morning to make sure we're there in plenty of time." Concern etched Ben's brow as Casey remained silent.

"Chloe, will that give you enough time to set up in the back of the shop here?" Clint pulled a separate, more detailed map of the city, placing it on top of the state highway map he had marked with his and Ben's locations.

"Sure, no problem. When I was on my way back, I took a detour to the shop and set everything up so we can be out fast." She smiled, and her eyes twinkled. She seemed proud to be a step ahead of the military brains on the small part she would participate in.

Clint smiled down at Chloe, who blushed. "Good. Casey, you'll ride with me, and as soon as we take out the vehicle, I'll need you to raise the shield to protect us from the gunfire we'll undoubtedly take."

Casey nodded, not taking her eyes off the map.

"Okay. Now, if for some reason we can't grab Polson, we'll use these streets to come back here." Clint had a highlighter tracing an already yellow line on several streets.

"What time do we need to use as a cut off?" Chloe studied the yellow highlights.

"If we aren't at the shop, let's say by seven at the latest, you get out of there and make your way back here. We'll figure something out for us." Clint stared at Chloe, and the lines around his eyes deepened.

"Sure thing." Chloe didn't look up. Ben caught Clint giving her a look of concern. He didn't like Chloe being intertwined in the danger.

"Good. Let's grab something to eat." Ben rose from his chair.

Clint rolled the maps as Casey joined Ben in the kitchen. "Anything I can do?"

Ben smiled down at her. He loved having her here with him. "Sure. If you can peel some potatoes and start them boiling on the stove, that would be great."

The kitchen was small, and with four of them preparing dinner, they bumped into each other several times. Then they would laugh and excuse themselves for it. While the chicken simmered in savory juices in the oven, they put the salad on the table and sat.

Ben prayed, "Dear Heavenly Father, thank you for the friends in Christ and the close family we have here. Please send a host of Heavenly warriors to watch over us, placing a safe hedge of protection around us to bring us back victorious from our oppressors tomorrow as we fight for You and our right to worship You in the open, and not fear for our lives in doing so. Let everything go according to Your plan and not ours as ours will always be flawed, and Yours is always perfect. Thank you for the wonderful meal we are about to eat and everything You have given us to help us through these trying times. In Jesus Christ's name, amen."

"Amen," everyone replied in unison.

Ben grabbed the salad bowl and handed it to Casey to start. She helped herself, then passed it on to Doc. They enjoyed the salad while Clint and Ben checked the rest of the meal every so often. They made small talk, asking about each other's families and friends and how they each got into the professions they had before the Monarchs took over.

Clint and Ben brought out the rest of the meal of chicken, mashed potatoes and gravy, along with a side dish of corn—the aroma filled the house. Ben was glad no one brought up the subject of Casey's family. He knew at times she struggled with what happened to them because of him. He hated that he aroused the memory of fear and pain when they were together. He would never give up on her, she was here for a reason, and he would trust God to handle everything.

FINISHED WITH DINNER, they migrated to the living room. Doc excused himself for the night. There was a patient he wanted to check on who had a bad case of the flu.

Chloe, Clint, Ben, and Casey sat in the living room talking about tomorrow and what a big day it'd be. About an hour later, Chloe excused herself and left to try and sleep. It was seven, and they needed to be awake in seven hours to leave to track and interrogate Polson.

"Should we pack breakfast, then try to sleep, ourselves?" Casey had never fallen asleep this early before.

"Sure. I figure something simple like some fruit and granola," Clint hopped out of his chair.

"Sounds good to me. Do you have some containers? We can put them together, so they're ready to go." Casey wandered toward the kitchen. Ben grabbed containers out of the cabinets while Clint grabbed apples and oranges out of the refrigerator.

Clint snatched a cutting board, sliced apples and oranges, tossed them in a bowl, took half of an orange, and squeezed it over the apples, tossing them again. He filled one of the containers, cut more apples and oranges. Clint smiled as Casey closed the first container when the knife he used, sliced into his hand. Jumping back, he clapped his hand over the one he'd cut and dashed to the sink as blood dripped on the floor.

"Clint, you okay?" Ben jogged out of the kitchen, only to reappear with a first aid kit.

"It went deep. I don't know how bad yet." Clint hung his head as he held his hand over the sink and blew air out through his mouth with his cheeks puffed out, closing his eyes.

Casey's heart grew warm as flecks of diamonds and blue flooded her vision. She placed her hand over Clint's as she looked into his eyes and nodded. He removed his hand, and she was astonished not only at the size of the cut but how deep it was as blood oozed into the sink.

"Oh, man. Do we need—" Ben took a half of a step and turned back toward the kitchen.

"Wait, it'll be okay." Casey placed her hand over Clint's palm. With how deep it was, she was stunned she couldn't view the sink below. The warmth flowed through her arm as she closed her eyes and pictured his hand healing in her mind and prayed, *God, help me heal him. He's one of Your disciples, and we need him to help restore Your children's place where we can worship without fear of persecution.* The blue aura surrounded them, and Clint's cut closed under her hand.

The warmth subsided, and she opened her eyes and peeked under her hand. Clint rinsed his hand and rubbed the spot where only a small scar remained. She washed her hands and dried them on a towel as Clint held his hand, pressing his thumb into his palm where his injury once was. Ben strode over and examined Clint's hand, too.

They gawked at her, then Clint wrapped his arms around her and lifted her off her feet. "Thank you, Casey. I can't believe I was dumb enough to cut myself." He made a fist, then flexed his fingers.

"Yeah, pretty dumb. I mean, you're only human, and Satan's against us winning this thing tomorrow, so yeah. It was all you," Ben quipped. "But what Satan didn't take into account is our little chosen healer sent by God, which trumps anything he can throw at us."

Casey's eyes drooped as she stifled a yawn. There she went again, being tired. It wasn't the same as when she healed Ben then tried to save Amanda but tired enough that she knew she wouldn't have any problems falling asleep. She worried about waking on time.

"What's wrong, Casey?" Clint put his newly healed hand on her shoulder.

"Tired. I'll head home to sleep. I don't want to oversleep for tomorrow. Can one of you wake me?"

Ben guided her by an elbow out of the kitchen. "How about if you slept here, and we'll wake you when we do?"

The color drained from her face as she braced herself from walking further. He took a couple of steps back and held up his hands. "You can sleep in my bed, and I'll take the couch."

"No. I can't. I just need someone to wake me tomorrow." She sank heavily onto one of the dining room chairs.

"Yeah. I don't think you'll make it that far."

Clint knelt next to the chair and lifted her chin. "How about if you take the couch, and we'll wake you in the morning?"

"No!" She stood but teeter-tottered back and forth with wobbly steps toward the bookcase.

"I'll walk you home. Clint, I'll be right back." Ben wrapped his hands around her waist and steered her toward the door.

"See you in the morning, Casey. Thanks again for this." Clint waved his hand at her.

She smiled and waved back.

"Come on, stubborn. I'll help you home." Ben walked through the door after Clint pulled the bookcase into the dining room.

"I don't think it's appropriate to sleep at a house with two men. It'd look bad. I would know nothing happened, but I wouldn't want anyone else to think otherwise." Casey yawned.

"Casey, you don't have to explain it to me. I was going to call Chloe and have her come over to your house to stay with you tonight if you were adamant about not staying at our place. Since we are all involved in this thing tomorrow, you wouldn't have to agonize about the wrong impression getting out," Ben explained.

Casey scuffed her feet across the uneven dirt-packed tunnel. "Thanks for understanding."

"We're all close here, and I don't think anyone would question it, but I understand where you're coming from and wouldn't want them to think the wrong thing of any of us." Ben gave a small nod.

They reached her door, and she punched in the code. Ben pulled open the door. She shoved against the bookcase, but it didn't move far.

Ben laughed and pushed the bookcase in far enough for them to walk through. They entered the dining room, then the living room where he steered toward her room.

"I got it from here." She stopped him.

"You sure? Can you walk?" The sparkle in his eyes told her he was teasing.

"Yes, funny man, I can." Ben's hands slipped from her waist as she turned to face him.

"I'll call you in the morning," Ben tapped his ear, "so, leave your communicator on."

"Yep."

Ben placed his hands on either side of her face and kissed her. First on the forehead, then delicately brushed her lips with his. "Sweet dreams." He turned, walked through the bookcase, and closed the door behind him.

Her head spun as she stood rooted where he left her. Her heart raced as she touched her lips. Shaking her head, she dragged her lead-filled legs into bed. Her shoes and socks lay on the floor, where she dumped them before she crawled under the blanket.

Fifty-Two

"Casey? Casey?" Ben's voice was gravely this early in the morning.

"What?" Casey yawned.

Ben smiled when she finally answered. "You awake?"

"Yeah, what time is it?" Ben heard the light switch click through his communicator.

"Two-thirty, we let you sleep but need to leave in half an hour. Will you be ready?" Ben sat on the couch and laced up his boots.

"Sure will. I'll be with you in about twenty." He heard her turn on the shower then the communicator was turned off.

Ben went to open the door to the tunnel for Casey. Doc ambled toward him with Chloe in tow once he opened the door.

"Good morning," Doc called out as if it was later than it was, and he'd been up for hours. Ben couldn't grasp how people could be so energetic early in the morning. Casey joined them a few minutes later.

"There she is and right on time." Ben smiled. He loved how she looked with her hair piled on top of her head in a messy bun.

Chloe walked out of the kitchen with the containers of fruit followed by Clint, who carried several covered cups with milk or juice.

"We ready to go?" Clint watched as the milk and juice he held sloshed up the sides of each cup ready to breach the rim.

"I think we have everything," Chloe answered.

"Let's say a prayer and do this, so we can have you guys back safe and sound." Doc held out his hands, and they joined him in a circle.

"Dear Heavenly Father, please watch over and protect Your warriors who are trying to re-establish freedom of religion. Send Your Heavenly warriors to surround them and keep them in Your protective grasp. Let Your will be done today as they fight for You and Your other children here in the United States to be able to worship You. Thank You for always being there, and this is a time when You'll need to carry them through this. They come willingly to You to do Your work and surrender all to You. Keep their strength and courage today, so they may be able to withstand Satan's attacks so You may reign victorious over this battle. Bring them home safely. In Jesus's name, amen."

"Amen."

With a final squeeze of hands, everyone hugged each other. Casey's slight tremor when Ben let her go bothered him. He wanted her in his car with him but knew she needed to be with Clint.

Chloe grabbed a cup and container of fruit as she headed out of the house. Doc ambled to the tunnel toward his house, and Ben followed.

"CASEY, WE'LL USE THE car in our garage, and Ben's going to use the car in yours. He will join us once we have Polson's car disabled and his guards incapacitated." Clint headed toward the closet in the hallway.

"Does he have the ring and remote?" Casey grabbed their breakfast.

"Yes, he's wearing the ring, and the remote's in his pocket. He'll be fine." Clint placed his hand on her shoulder and gave her a quick squeeze. He studied her face. Tendons stood out on her neck as she rapidly blinked. He knew she might not be ready for today.

"Okay." Casey diverted her eyes and pulled out the bracelet. She put it on, and it wound its way around her arm.

"You ready?" Clint had one foot on the first rung of the ladder in the closet.

Casey blew out a sigh. "Yes. Let's do it."

"I second that." Clint climbed the ladder first, and she handed the bag with their breakfast to his outstretched hand as he leaned through the opening at the top of the closet. Then she mounted the ladder herself. Clint took her hand, helping her the rest of the way once she was only one or two rungs from the top. She took the bag out of Clint's hand and followed him into the garage. He cautiously opened the door. His breath steamed in the cool brisk air, and he rubbed his hands up and down his arms. He checked both directions for any signs of life. Content with the silence, he climbed into the driver's seat. Casey followed his lead as she climbed into the passenger side and closed the door. The car edged out past the side of the garage when he saw her looking at the full moon. He put the car in park and jumped out to close the garage door. To the west, Ben nodded his head to Clint. He knew Ben would be anxious about Casey until they were back home.

Clint climbed in and pulled the door closed with a small click, then yanked on the door handle to finish securing the door. Casey jumped. Her head was turned toward Ben. Once on the street, they headed east while Ben headed to the west. Out of the corner of his eye, Clint saw Casey clenched her hands in her lap. His top priority was her today to make sure she made it back safe.

They crossed through neighborhoods. Clint's eyes darted between every house and down every side street. The smallest movement caught his attention. He clenched the steering wheel until he recognized what moved—from a piece of trash to an animal skittering across the road. Once he knew what moved, he then loosened his white-knuckled grip. Clint took the next off-ramp, crossing over several side streets and alleys that connected like a spider web as Clint pictured the map in his head.

He backed up past the on-ramp half off the road to appear to be an abandoned vehicle, "we're in position. Ben, you there yet?" Clint's military training kicked in. He turned his emotions off.

"Will be in about five. All's quiet over here." Ben's voice filtered through their communicators.

"Okay, tell us when you're settled in." Clint stretched his neck from side to side.

"Will do."

"Hungry?" Clint opened the bag Casey put behind her seat and handed her a fork along with a container.

"Yeah, I am." She smiled.

Clint held up two cups, "Milk or juice?"

"It doesn't matter. I like both." Casey glanced out of the window.

"Which one do you like better?" He arched an eyebrow at her.

"Milk," she admitted.

He tilted his head to her and handed her a glass. "Milk it is."

"Thank you." Casey settled back in the seat and took a drink.

"Okay, I'm in position. You guys eating without me?" Ben teased.

"Well, we can't wait all day," Clint quipped.

Her fork shook as she ate her breakfast. Clint wanted to reach over and grab her hand to let her know it'd be okay but resisted showing his concern for her.

"Why are none of the streetlights on?" She stared out the windows.

"The Monarchs found it was harder to steal electricity to live on if they shut off entire grids. They hoped it would break people's spirits if they couldn't have the necessities of life."

"Did it work?"

"For some, yes. A lot of people turned themselves in to live in the designated areas for the comforts of utilities. But it made us more resolute to show them they can't run us out of our country and our homes. We defiantly stay and set solar panels to support our lives and to have heat and air conditioning, so we don't have to deal with the harsh elements—although living underground helps with that."

It was only four-thirty, and they still had who-knew-how-long to wait. If Doc's friend was supposed to report at five o'clock, Polson could be in as early as a half an hour from that point to even longer.

"How are we supposed to know when Polson's flight comes in?"

"I'll be able to watch flights come in, and Air Force One is distinctive," Ben answered.

"Makes sense."

"It'd be harder if Polson hadn't cut travel in the United States. Most of the travel's restricted. You have to go through rigorous screening processes to fly." Clint popped the lid back on his container, having eaten everything he brought.

"Is there anything Polson hasn't taken over?" Casey's shock made him only want to protect her more.

"Nope, which is why we need this to work today so we can alert the American people to who they elected into office. They're the only ones who can lift the ban on electing in a new president. Polson made a mistake with that one, but he also knew if he didn't give the American people the choice to reverse the ban on electing a new president, they would've never gone for the new law in the first place. Once it did pass, he kept his nose so clean that no one, except those who are in the designated living areas, knew he was behind everything, and he's as dirty as they come." Clint glanced at

Casey, monitoring how she was doing without her knowing it.

Fifty-Three

Casey's nerves got worse with each passing minute, and she wondered how people did this for a living. She wanted this over. It was as if she had a bull's eye painted on her and was left out in the open ready for someone to take her out. How would she hold up under pressure? Or would the shield fail, and she be responsible for getting someone killed? She didn't want to lose anyone else and couldn't imagine if she lost Ben. She liked having him in her life and couldn't fathom one day without him. This was something she had never truly dealt with before—love. She couldn't picture Ben not being here and hoped it was the same for him. She would need to talk to him after this. She wouldn't put it off any longer.

She didn't pay attention to anything Clint and Ben talked about. She'd better listen if she wanted to be an asset to this plan they devised. How could someone live in this country and know what the military did to keep this country free, then sell it out when they were elected into office? It was un-American to her, and she guessed loving this country as she did, she wouldn't want it any other way.

"Polson's here. His plane is landing as we speak." Ben broke her train of thought with the news flash.

Her heart raced as her hands started to sweat, knowing they would go ahead with the plan, and it may end one—if not all—of their lives. She closed her eyes and took deep breaths, slowly releasing them through her mouth. She hoped Clint wasn't aware of what she was going through, trying to keep her nerves under lock and key as nausea built up. She glanced at the clock in the car. It read five-fifteen. At least Doc's friends had good information for when Polson was due into town.

"Plane is making its way down the runway." Ben's updates only increased her churning stomach.

"Great. At least he'll be here today. No patrols through this area, so we should be good on our end." Clint sounded calm. She was glad they didn't ask her anything because she wasn't sure she would be able to answer without having a small coronary.

Panicked, she remembered a test they didn't perform with the relics. They never tested the theory of Clint being able to use his weapon inside the shield and penetrate to the outside without affecting what was inside. What if it absorbed into the shield, and it only affected her? The memory of the static charge that she took flooded her thoughts, and she fanned her fingers back and forth. What would the consequences be if he shot from the inside toward the outside of the shield? Would she have to raise and lower the shield every time he needed to use his weapon? And would she be able to raise it again every time before an assault came from the Monarchs?

"Ben, any movement with the vehicles yet?" Clint's question made her jump. She had been so intent on the thoughts and questions running through her mind. They would need to address those before they got in too deep and couldn't escape.

"Nope, nothing yet on this end."

"Um, excuse me, but I have a quick question." She was relieved her voice was steady with no hint of the panic that had her stomach in knots.

"Sure, what is it?" Ben answered.

"Well, it's more for Clint. Do you think you can use your weapon through the shield and not affect us in the shield since we didn't test that in the basement?"

Ben whistled in her ear. The realization of her question hit home. They didn't have a weapon to disable the car if they needed the shield before they were to that point. If the Monarchs found them before they could approach Polson's vehicle to disable the electrical systems, and she had to deploy the shield to keep her and Clint safe, that derailed the plan.

"I THOUGHT OF IT YESTERDAY, but forgot after Chloe found us to let us know this was on for today." Clint dropped his head into his hands.

"Clint, do you have time to test it?" Ben murmured.

"Not now. If we try, we'll have to leave the car and expose us to whoever may be watching. I don't want to try it in the car and take a chance we kill our own vehicle." Clint chewed on the inside of his cheek.

"Casey, do you think you'll be able to drop and raise the shield in a split second if you need to, so we're able to switch weapons, whether it is the relic or our guns?" Ben questioned.

Casey shook her head and glanced at Clint. "I'm not sure. I don't want to leave us vulnerable. If they have the firepower that you and Clint say they do, I won't be able to stop a few bullets from getting in, if I have to continually raise and lower the shield."

"We'll have to take the chance we can disable Polson's vehicle and have Casey put up the shield then go from there. We'll find out if bullets penetrate the shield from the inside with no fear of ricochets since firing from the outside, the shield stopped them." Clint placed his hands on the steering wheel.

"Two cars are leaving the airport and heading this way. I'm going to activate the tracker when they're overhead," Ben alerted them.

"Okay. Let me know so I can switch on the scanner." Clint's steady hand grabbed the monitor Doc gave him.

"Wait for it. I can see the headlights overhead. Wait...okay. I activated the remote. They should be at your location in less than three," Ben whispered.

The second hand ticked by on Clint's watch. He glanced at Casey, nodded, then turned on the scanner. Nothing. She trembled as she stared at the monitor. He had to tell himself this wasn't her world or what she was used to.

Beep. Casey jumped. The dot moved on the screen, and Casey blew out her breath. "Guess we're in business."

"I take it, it works?" Ben probed.

"Yeah. We're going to follow at a distance until they exit on Eighth Street. Then we'll close in and activate the relic to disable their cars and go from there."

Casey held her breath. Clint was sure she would pass out before she exhaled. He was ready to put a hand on her shoulder when the dot moved, and she jumped again, deploying the shield around the car.

"Sorry. I'm not used to this." Casey's hands trembled.

"What happened?" Ben snapped.

"Nothing," Clint quickly answered as Polson's motorcade passed them. He flashed a reassuring smile at Casey and nodded. He gave her hand a squeeze before returning his hand to the steering wheel's tattered vinyl finish, worn smooth in several places where people's hands had rested on the many trips taken in this car.

Taillights ahead of them in the night alerted him to be ready as their own car ran without lights to warn them that they were being followed. Brake lights brightened the area, piercing through the morning the sun wouldn't visit yet for a least another hour. Tires gripped the pavement below as they exited off the highway.

Clint pulled the relic out of his pocket, and it came to life and wound around his hand. He was about to test her resolve at being able to handle the war they were in. "Take the wheel and keep following them at this same distance until I tell you to stop."

Casey stared with a rapidly blinking, unfocused gaze at him. Her mouth fell open, and she shook her head. "What?"

"Clint, you can't be serious. You can't expect her to drive." Ben's gruff voice came through his ear.

"Ben, I didn't tell you or you wouldn't have let her come with me. You knew I'd have to have my hands free and on the passenger side of the car to effectively disable their car and shoot." Clint motioned for her to take the steering wheel.

Casey took a deep breath, grabbed the steering wheel then slid over on Clint's lap pressing the accelerator to keep the speed as Clint asked of her. Clint let go with his left arm after she took the steering wheel and landed in the passenger seat. Content that it went as smoothly as it did, it gave him hope that she'd be able to find the fight in her that they would need today.

Clint rolled the window down as he saw the cars stopped ahead at the end of the off-ramp. Casey glanced at him and started to push the brake. She clenched the steering wheel in a death grip that turned her knuckles white.

"Turn off the engine and coast behind them."

Doing as Clint asked, Casey popped the car into neutral and turned off the ignition, only using the brake. They were almost silent as they rolled toward what could be a devastating outcome. About six car lengths between them, someone jumped out of the second car, pulled a gun out of his holster. Clint fired the relic; both sets of taillights went out as the engines died. The shield shot out as Casey stomped the brake all the way to the floor, stopping only two car lengths from Polson's crew.

Clint drew his gun with his left hand, laying it in his lap as he switched the stone to another symbol on the relic still wrapped around his right palm. "Casey, hold on. If this doesn't work, we may be in trouble." Holding his right hand out, he shot a yellow pulse. It penetrated the shield and raced toward the men who exited the vehicles.

There were nine men in all, plus the driver of Polson's car in addition to Polson himself. The six men who jumped out of the vehicle behind Polson drew weapons and aimed at them when Clint shot off a pulse from the relic. Before the pulse traveled through the shield, they were assailed by a salvo of bullets from the Monarchs. Several of the bullets hit the front of the car they were in. She extended the shield to protect the engine before they were caught in a fiery inferno if the engine blew. The yellow pulse from the relic hit three men on Clint's side, where they fell to the ground the instant the yellow field passed around them.

Clint glanced at her, unable to believe it was able to penetrate the shield. Casey nodded to him that she was okay. Bullets riddled the shield's outer layer. Headlights illuminated the interior of their car from behind, and tires squealed on the pavement as someone slammed on the brakes.

"Behind us!" Casey yelled.

"Casey, it's me." Ben's calm voice interrupted them. Clint placed a hand on Casey's leg.

The men in front of them were now trying to flank them and started shooting at Ben's car. Ben threw himself into the seat, disappearing from her rearview mirror.

Fifty-Four

Casey didn't think about what it'd do, but she extended the shield instantaneously to include Ben's vehicle with hers. Ben raised his head when the bullets no longer ripped holes in his driver's side door and smiled at her. Ben climbed out of his car, joining Clint and Casey in theirs as bullets followed him the entire walk, not hitting their intended mark.

She pulled the shield back to their vehicle after Ben folded himself into the backseat, and the bullets caught in the gelatin shield fell to the pavement, ringing as they bounced off the asphalt. The Monarchs yelled and cussed at their partners to do something, blaming each other. Clint reached across the seat to turn the key. She looked at him. "Roll down your window."

Another pulse shot toward the three on her side of the car through the driver's window. They didn't have a chance to outrun the yellow field when they were overtaken and fell in midstride while trying to escape. Only the three who jumped out of Polson's vehicle were left who still fired at their adversaries. Half their team being unconscious didn't deter them.

"Can you reach them from here?" Casey asked as Clint angled for a better shot.

"No, I'll have to get out of the car. Can you extend the shield to include me if I go around the front of the car to take out the three remaining guards?"

"I think so. It hasn't been a problem to make it do what I want so far."

She extended it several feet past the passenger door, so when Clint opened it, he stood in the safety of the shield. Leaving the door ajar behind him, he started to make his way around the front of the vehicle. She extended it out to keep him covered when someone ran toward them on their left. They had talked about if someone ran into the shield if it'd stop them, but they hadn't had the guts to test it in the basement yesterday. She didn't know what to do but knew she would do anything to save the two men with her. The shield turned opaque as it met the sweaty man in the wrinkled gray suit, his face twisted and contorted in anger. The man not only bounced off the wall but was propelled back several feet, and his arms pinwheeled in the air. She cringed as his bones cracked when he hit the pavement, rolled a number of times, then lay there motionless.

Shocked that she hurt someone, she had to remind herself these were bad guys, and in wars, people not only were wounded but also killed. Her breathing increased as she tried to slow her heart rate. She shook, inhaling as Clint and Ben stared at her and did a double take.

Ben placed his strong hands on her shoulders and gave a small squeeze. "Shh. Smooth, deep breaths. Slow your breathing. We need you for this, Casey."

Clint turned around and fired off another pulse, and the three men at Polson's vehicle collapsed when the field reached them. That should only leave Polson and the driver. Not sure where the other man came from, she wanted to grab Polson and leave before reinforcements arrived.

"Casey, pull next to Polson's sedan." Clint climbed back in the car.

Her hands shook as she gripped the steering wheel and put the car in drive. It was a relief to have their car moving again. They approached the dead vehicles in front of them and pulled next to the rear door on Polson's vehicle

"No, they're all taken out. I'm alone here. Send reinforcements, and I mean now! No, I don't have to tell you what happened. Send someone to help me! What do you mean they're out on patrols, and it will be a few minutes until you can send someone in our area? No, that isn't good enough! Get someone here now, or I'll make sure you're punished for your insubordination!"

"Casey, extend the shield to the car window?" Clint rolled down his window and had his gun drawn. Still in the safety of the shield, Clint tapped on Polson's window with the barrel of the gun.

"What do you want? Leave me alone!" Polson's voice was shrill and whiny, no longer the strong political voice you heard in the radio broadcasts issued weekly.

"We want to talk, Polson. You might as well give up. You aren't going to make it out of this one," Clint chided.

"We need to grab him." Ben checked the rear windows with his gun drawn.

"I have access to money. Tell me how much to make you go away." Polson's voice cracked.

"Do we need to open the door and drag you out?" Casey flinched at Clint's stern voice and hoped he never directed it at her.

"Come on. Everyone has their price. Tell me yours." Polson's shrill voice broke.

"Polson, if we have to open the door ourselves, you won't like us," Clint barked.

Without warning, the driver's side door opened, and two hands pushed through the opening. "Don't shoot. I want to go home." It was too much for the driver, and he was not about to take one for the team.

"Where are you going? Don't leave me!" Polson screamed from the back of the car as the driver bolted from the vehicle. A shot rang out. The driver collapsed as a bullet tore through his back from Polson.

"Clint, let's grab him and go. Can we break the window and knock him out with the pulse?" Ben looked around for approaching vehicles to rescue the Monarchs' liaison.

Clint pulled back his hand, then lowered it, shattering the glass as the back window exploded from impact with the butt of the gun. Several bullets flew out of the shattered window, stopping dead as the shield enveloped them. Clint ducked out of reflex and pointed his own gun at Polson through the open window.

"Throw your gun out of the car!" Clint yelled.

"Okay, okay." The gun flew out of the window, lodging in the shield. Clint took the gun and handed it to Ben in the backseat.

"Polson, out of the car!" Casey flinched as Clint yelled.

Another shot rang out, but the bullet fell short of hitting its target and hung in the shield's outer wall. Clint stretched his hand out with the relic and shot a pulse toward the president's car. The pulse passed through the shield and spanned the width of the car in front of them then dissipated. Clint turned and looked at Ben, who only shrugged.

Clint opened his car door, turning toward Casey. "Can you keep me in the shield without including the president's car until I can find out if they're still conscious inside?"

"No problem." Picturing Clint in her mind and keeping the shield in front of him, she only advanced it with every step he took as he edged closer to the car. Clint stooped to glance in the back window and gave the thumbs-up sign that all occupants of the vehicle were no longer conscious. Clint reached through the decimated window, opening the back door.

Once the door was open, Ben joined Clint to drag Polson to the rear of their car and slid him into the backseat behind Casey. Ben climbed into the front while Clint kept Polson company in the back.

"Casey, drive straight toward the next couple of intersections. You'll want to take a left on Ashford Drive," Clint instructed from the backseat as he scanned the area for any other vehicles that would respond to the mayhem they left.

With a left on Ashford, she waited for the next set of directions. Her heart raced, and her palms sweated. Were they going to be able to pull this off? Was everyone going to make it through this? She knew it was only because of

God that this was possible. No one could have this much luck. And the fact her side found relics with such power and protection all in one, the only answer was this was all part of His plan.

"Turn left on Marin Circle."

Casey kept a watchful eye for the correct street when there was a groan behind her. She clenched the steering wheel and glanced with wide eyes to the backseat. Clint put handcuffs on Polson, so his hands were restrained from doing any damage. Ben reached over covering one of Casey's hands with his. She relaxed and smiled at Ben, who intently watched her with his piercing blue eyes. Changing gears and concentrating on the road, she saw the street where they needed to take the next left.

The shops were deserted on either side of the street. It was as if the world outside of the car ceased to exist, and they were the only survivors of some horrendous war.

"CASEY, TURN LEFT AT the next alley and pull around behind the auto repair shop. Chloe is set up in the bay on the left so we can pull into the one on the right and keep hidden until we're done." Clint's voice remained calm in his instructions. Casey did outstanding and was there when they needed her. He knew the fighter he saw in her at the lab was still in there just waiting to find her way out.

Pulling behind the building, the door to the bay on the right opened, so Casey pulled in and shut off the engine before the door closed behind them. Chloe approached the car.

Ben was the first one out. Clint yanked Polson out of the back of the car by his armpits. Ben grabbed one of his shoulders as Clint held the other, and they heaved him into the chair in the bay on the left side of the garage. The zip ties' ratchet system echoed in the garage as they tightened them around Polson's ankles and through the handcuffs to the lumbar support on the chair. Ben slid the ring on his finger.

"Who are you?" Polson snapped at them.

"We'll ask the questions." Clint took charge, and he wanted Polson to know he didn't have any leverage here.

Ben approached Polson, while Chloe steadied a flat-panel clear tablet and tapped an icon on the screen. She gave the signal that Ben was out of video range, with Polson the center of attention in this production. Ben slapped his hand on Polson's back, who tried to jerk away but remained secured to the chair.

"What's your name?" Clint's voice was gruff with no hint of the true man he was.

"I am the president. You know who I am!" Polson's conceited arrogance filled the air.

"Good enough." Clint took a breath and looked at Ben, who nodded at him to continue. "Polson, are you in league with the Monarchs?"

"Yes."

"Did you or did you not plan, from the time you ran for president, to open our borders and let known terrorists into this country?" Clint's monotone voice filled the garage.

"I did. What of it?" Polson glared at Clint. He twisted his shoulders back and forth under Ben's hand.

"Polson, how long have you been in league with the Monarchs?" Clint continued.

"Since I was sixteen," he spat out.

Clint raised an eyebrow. "So, about forty years?"

"Yes." Polson tried to wriggle free from the chair but didn't accomplish anything. Clint saw the evil on his face as the anger of not being able to control the situation surfaced.

"Did you initiate the bill that was passed to do away with freedom of religion?" Clint didn't falter with the line of questions they had decided on.

"Yes, the world is a better place without God in it. There isn't guilt for all the wrongs in today's society." Polson's face reddened.

"If you say there is no guilt for the wrongs you do, doesn't that mean the things are wrong? That you don't want to have the reminder from God and His people that they're wrong, and that you'll have to answer for those wrongs on judgment day?" Clint raised an eyebrow at Ben.

"Yes. If we did away with religion, we could do as we please, and none would be the wiser."

"None would be the wiser? What about everyone who lost their lives standing for God and trying to protect their First Amendment rights? So, they lost their lives to make it a less guilt-ridden place to live for you and your terrorist group?" Clint glanced at Casey and shook his head.

"Well, yes, in a way. America is seen as the strongest country, and what better place than here to start this terrorist group's world domination?" Polson sat straighter, squaring his shoulders.

Clint's face flushed red as the muscles strained in his neck, and his shoulders tensed. He was done with this man who didn't care about lives. "So, you admit to putting this whole plan into motion to be elected President by lying to the American people about your beliefs and what you stand for so you could pave the way for your terrorist group to take over America?"

Polson smirked. "Yes."

Clint took a deep breath, then continued, "So, what about the designated living areas and the martial law set in place?"

"Well, how are we supposed to rule this country with religious fanatics like you ruining our plans? If you would just come over to our way of thinking, the world would be amazing. No guilt for the things you do, and no worry about being caught in inappropriate activities because all guilt has been done away with. Once we perfect our conversion process, it will be a better place to live." Polson glared.

Clint leaned forward. "Conversion process?"

"Yes, we're trying a type of selective memory erasure method to take away the memories of the Bible's teachings and get people in line with our views on life. There have been some casualties, though, so we went back to the testing phase to minimize some of those losses. There are some of you who, no matter how hard we try, don't let go of your God, and we can't have you influencing others, so you're done away with." Polson wriggled against the zip ties.

Clint took a breath, then slowly blew it out. "Done away with?"

"Well, you seem like you've experienced a little military. I don't need to go into detail with you, do I?" Polson raised his eyebrows.

"No." Clint's mouth hung open at the man's audacity. His eyes narrowed as he tried to process the pure evil in front of him.

Fifty-Five

Casey saw Ben flinch, but he stayed to the side of Polson and kept his hand on his back. She saw the anger flash across his eyes as it coursed through him. Ben closed his eyes as he prayed, she believed, for the strength to keep from killing this man who caused his sister's death.

Vehicles on the road outside alerted them that it was time to go. Chloe snatched the chip out of the tablet, tucked it in a small hidden pocket in the waistband of her jeans. Chloe jumped in the passenger seat since she couldn't reach her own car to make a safe retreat and placed the tablet under her seat. As Clint slid in behind the wheel, Casey jumped in behind him. Ben slammed his hand on the garage door button then bolted into the backseat next to Casey. Clint threw the car in reverse, punching the accelerator.

"Hey, you're going to pay for this! We'll find you! You won't make it out of this alive!" Polson yelled as he tried to get off the chair he was tied to. He bounced the chair several times, which only caused it to tip over.

As Clint backed out of the garage bay, he scanned the area before they made their way through the alley, taking the first side street as brakes squealed seconds before car doors slammed.

"Polson must have a tracking chip on him." Clint checked the rearview mirror.

A shot rang out, and Chloe's head snapped back against the headrest as the windshield shattered in a spider web of cracks around a small hole.

"Chloe!" Clint screamed. He yanked the steering wheel, and they careened into the next alley over, then he punched the gas pedal.

Casey jumped, and the shield deployed seconds before she grabbed Chloe and covered the hole in her forehead with her hand.

"Chloe, look at me!"

There was no response. Warmth flowed from her heart and raced through her arms. She refused to lose anyone else in her group. She wouldn't let anyone else go. If it took every ounce of energy and life she had, she would use it to save this girl.

BEN STARED IN AWE AS the blue light surrounding Casey grew brighter with each passing second. The car slowed, and Casey whispered, "Don't stop. Get us to Doc." Clint accelerated again.

Casey closed her eyes and dropped her head. Ben glanced around as Clint checked side streets for Monarchs. The blue aura grew and enveloped Chloe. He knew Casey wouldn't let go.

"Father, use me to heal Chloe. Please don't let us lose another one from our group." Tears streamed down Casey's face as she clung to this young, lifeless girl.

"Come on, Chloe. Please!" Clint glanced at Casey.

There was an explosion of light as the aura filled the car when Clint pulled into the garage. Ben yanked the garage door closed behind them. Clint bolted from the garage as Ben shielded his eyes.

"Come on, Chloe. Please come back to us."

Several minutes later, Clint reemerged with Doc, who whistled at the amount of blood on Chloe. Casey moved her hand, and a bullet fell in Chloe's lap. Casey put her hand back over the wound.

"Casey, let me check her." Doc opened the passenger door.

"Not yet, Doc. I need to finish."

"Casey, if you run yourself down, I'm not sure it won't kill you. Let me check her, please," he pleaded

"You'll need to check her while I try and save her. I refuse to lose anyone else." Casey focused on Ben.

"Casey, let Doc in there. We don't know the consequences if you push yourself too far. Everyone has limits." Ben shielded his eyes. Casey wouldn't let go until Chloe was out of danger. His heart raced at the thought of losing her. He loved her, and if he needed to, he would yank her out of the car, kicking and screaming to save her.

"Guys, please let me do this. Now stop interrupting me." Casey closed her eyes and lowered her head.

Doc checked for a pulse when Clint and Ben yelled in unison, "No!"

Doc yanked his hand back as if he touched something hot. "What? What is it?"

They forgot no one else could see the blue light.

Chloe's hand moved slightly, then her leg.

Doc checked for a carotid pulse. "Guys, I thought you said she was shot in the head. She has a strong, steady pulse."

Chloe grasped Casey's hand as she opened her eyes. The blue aura rushed back into Casey.

"Casey?" Tears sprang into Chloe's eyes as she looked down at all the blood. She threw her arms around Casey. "Thank you, thank you, thank you."

Casey's eyes closed as her arms fell from around Chloe. Ben rushed to her, and he held her head in his hands. "Casey? Casey. Hon, can you hear me?"

She smiled. "Yes."

Ben hung his head and pulled Casey to him. His arms worked to un-wedge her from between the two front seats from when she'd healed Chloe. He slid her to the edge of the backseat by the door. "Hold on," he whispered.

She wrapped her arms around his neck. He lifted her as she lay her head on his shoulder and closed her eyes. Ben passed her off to Clint, who stood at the bottom of the stairs in the closet and held her until Ben joined them. Once the stairs were secured, he headed toward the bookcase.

"Want me to look at her?" Doc asked.

"No, thanks." Ben cradled her. "I think she needs to sleep like she always does after healing."

"Well, I'll send this to my uncle so he can distribute it over the Internet and email it to his friend at the news station since I couldn't meet with him in person. Not sure what will happen from here. I think it went well and hope something good will come out of this." Chloe darted through the bookcase before Ben.

Ben carried Casey to her house from his. Clint opened the bookcase as Ben carried her to her room. She was unconscious before Ben set her on the bed, and he strolled to the kitchen, pulling a bowl from the cabinet and filled it with warm water. On the way back to Casey's room, he grabbed a washcloth from the bathroom. He placed the bowl on the nightstand, soaked the washcloth, and wrung it out. Ben gently wiped the blood from her left hand, then picked up her right. The water turned pink has he washed the blood from Casey. He carried the bowl to the bathroom and dumped the water down the sink, then refilled it with cold water and placed the washcloth in it to soak. Ben placed the covers over her and felt behind her ear for the button to the communicator, shutting out everyone and everything. He sat with her as Clint loomed in the doorway. He didn't care. He wouldn't leave her again.

Fifty-Six

There was a sound of the link system jingling in the distance, but Casey didn't care. She rolled over as the darkness engulfed her again.

Deep sleep evaded her as nightmares stalked her. Both Clint and Ben were injured, and she couldn't save them both. She had to choose between the two which one to let die and which one to heal and save. The kidnapping of Polson wasn't going according to plan. The bullets, instead of being caught in the shield, were still coming through at their intended target but at a slower pace and pierced the skin of Ben and Clint. She was unable to stop the bullets this time and now had to choose which one to save. It wasn't right to let Clint die because she loved Ben, but she couldn't imagine Ben not being here. Clint reached for her as his eyes pleaded to save him.

A squeak in her room startled her out of the dream into a sitting position. Ben bolted to the bed. His weight pushed the mattress down to half its thickness as he sat on the edge.

"Ben?" She grabbed his arm to make sure he was real.

"Casey, what is it?" Ben placed his hand on her shoulder, which shook as tremors racked her small frame.

"Ben, where's Clint?"

"He's at our house. He's fine." Ben pulled her to him and circled his protective arms around her.

"Are you sure?" She pushed back from him, and her eyes searched his.

"Yes. You're trembling. Are you okay?" Ben brushed the hair from her forehead.

"Yes, it must have been a dream." She clung to Ben so hard her fingers turned white.

He placed a hand on her back. "Dream? Sounds more like a nightmare."

"Yeah, well. Wait. Chloe!"

"She's fine. You saved her, Casey." Ben placed an arm around her back and gave her a squeeze with his hand on her shoulder.

"Wait. She is?" Casey shook her head.

"Yes, she's fine," Ben reassured her. "Did you want to tell me about it?"

Casey frowned. "About healing Chloe?"

"No, the dream." Ben smiled.

Casey sighed. "No, I want to forget it if it isn't real."

"Sorry. I didn't mean to wake you. I opened the bookcase to check on you since you didn't answer your link system when Clint called. I heard you talking and thought someone was in here with you," Ben murmured.

"I was talking?" Casey didn't remember saying anything.

"Yes, you were frantic. But I couldn't make out what you were saying because you were mumbling."

Her shaking subsided, so she released her death grip on Ben and sat back.

"You slept for a while, so we were worried about you. Go back to sleep and call us when you wake." Ben stood.

"I don't think I could go back to sleep now if I wanted to. Give me a half an hour, and I'll meet you and Clint over at your place." Casey swung her legs out of bed.

"Okay, sounds good. We'll have lunch ready." Ben sauntered to the doorway.

Casey snapped her head up. "Lunch?"

"Yes, sleepyhead. You slept for a whole day." Ben raised his eyebrows.

"Are you serious? Why didn't someone wake me?" Casey looked down at her hands and turned them over. They were clean.

"I stayed last night. We checked on you a couple of times today, but let you sleep." Ben leaned against the doorframe and crossed his arms.

"We?" Casey pulled open drawers and grabbed clothes.

"Yes. Clint and I took turns coming over to check on you today when you didn't wake up this morning." The blue in Ben's eyes deepened when she glanced up at him.

Her cheeks flushed red. They went to the trouble to keep checking on her. "I'm sorry. You should've woken me instead of coming over here and checking on me."

"It was no big deal. You needed sleep. Anyway, see you at our place in about half an hour and we'll have lunch for you." He continued to lean in the doorway.

"Okay." She walked up to him, expecting him to move.

Ben leaned forward, and his lips brushed her forehead and lingered. He traced her cheek with his finger, then sauntered down the hallway and disappeared. The bookcase locked a few seconds later.

She cringed as she peered in the mirror after her shower. Dark circles lurked under her swollen, puffy eyes. She hung her head. There was nothing she could do to change it unless she got more sleep. She trudged down the tunnel and punched in the code to their house. She was greeted at the bookcase by Clint. "Well, if it isn't sleeping beauty."

"Stop it. I feel horrible that you kept coming over to check on me." Casey blushed.

"Oh, no big deal. I wish I could sleep like that after a mission, but I'm too wired to get any kind of quality sleep." Clint peered down at her.

She snickered. "You should use the healing stone. It'll knock you right out."

Clint smiled. "Well, someone, I think, cornered the market on that relic."

"What's for lunch, and can I help?"

"Sandwiches and nope. It's all out and ready to go."

Ben strolled from around the corner and joined them at the table as they bowed their heads to pray.

The sandwiches tasted good as if she'd never eaten one before.

"So, have you heard anything on the recording we made of Polson yet?" She hoped their efforts paid off.

Clint swallowed his bite. "No, not yet. Chloe sent it to her uncle, who sent out multiple emails. So far, they've blocked it from getting to the intended targets. Chloe's uncle is working on a program to hit every email on a given server, so they won't be able to stop a massive email attack. He's also writing into the program a virus so it can't be deleted no matter what the other person tries."

"I can't wait to find out what develops. Do you think he'll try to deny it and say it was a recording pieced together from speeches he's given? Will he try to run?" Casey glanced into the empty living room. Would they ever live normal lives?

"No one can be sure, but I say he'll try to deny it and have his technical staff debunk the recording by saying we digitally enhanced it." Clint didn't make her feel any better with all the work they put in and the danger they faced to remove the president from office.

Ben clenched his jaw. "I say he'll run and hide like the rat he is."

After lunch, they invited others over for a Bible study. It was great to hear God's word in a group of people who loved Him as much as she did. She couldn't wait until they could celebrate their freedom out in the open and tell everyone about God's love without the fear of being killed for their beliefs.

The Bible study ran later than planned. As she said goodbye to everyone, she noticed Ben and Clint weren't there. She was so absorbed in the study that she missed them leaving and wondered if it had something to do with news on Polson.

The tunnels were quiet as she strolled back to her house. Almost to her door, she saw Clint step from her house. His eyes grew wide as he stared at her, then diverted his eyes before hustling past her.

"Clint, what's going on? Did something happen with Polson?" She wanted to know how much longer they would have to live in these tunnels.

"No, nothing yet. I'll catch you tomorrow. I have something I need to do." Clint hurried past. She pictured the day Chloe's search on her family led them to her brother's and father's deaths.

She punched in the code to her house, pushed open the bookcase, and was greeted by Ben.

Fifty-Seven

Candles offered a soft, flickering glow over the dining room table. He held out a single rose made of thin, translucent, variegated paper, crafted so meticulously that it looked real. He waved his hand toward the table for her to come in. A soft melody played from a radio.

His heart pounded as a lump formed in his throat. She looked beautiful. Ben held out a chair for her, and she cautiously sat.

Ben vanished into the kitchen. The springs on the oven door groaned as a delicious aroma filled the air. Ben's hands were insulated in oven mitts as he carried the dish into the dining room. The sides of the sauce still bubbled and sizzled on the lasagna with the lightly browned cheese on top. Casey's stomach growled as Ben dished out two huge helpings on their plates.

Ben reached over and took her hand as he bowed his head. He thanked the Lord for bringing everyone back safe from their mission for Him and thanked God for bringing Casey into his life. His voice broke when he saw her dab her eyes with the coarse napkin he had placed next to her plate.

Ben released her hand to grab his fork. "Casey, I wanted to tell you for a long time, how much you mean to me."

Her eyes widened as she stared at him. His heart raced, and he cleared his throat.

"Casey, I fell in love with you the first time I saw you on the sphere and knew you were the one. The one God chose for me. You're so amazing, and I want you to know I hold so much guilt for taking you away from your family and everything you've been through because of it."

"Ben, you don't need to...I don't hold you responsible anymore." Casey stammered. "I'm sorry I blamed you, and I couldn't take it back."

"Wait, let me finish. I was only able to let go of my guilt when I asked God to save me if I was the one for you when I was injured. God spoke to my heart and told me He chose us for each other, and I needed to keep you safe. The secret from the day when I took you was God spoke to my heart and told me not to let you go, even though I wanted to. I hated that I was the cause of all that fear. When I saw you leave, I had only gone back to grab a toothbrush or something with your DNA on it. When you came back in, I couldn't believe you were there in front of me." Ben cleared his throat as he stuck his fork into the sides of the lasagna on his plate.

"God spoke to me and told me not to let you go. It broke my heart. You were scared, and it was because of me. I held you tight, so you wouldn't be injured fighting against me. I couldn't believe you were in my arms. God told me again not to let go. So, I'm sorry, but I couldn't. It was what God wanted. When you were here and got away from us, and I thought you got outside, I was scared I lost you after God put you in my care."

Ben looked at his plate again as Casey reached over and took his hand. Tears trickled down her face when he looked up. Ben flinched when he saw her tears and carefully wiped them away.

"That was the secret I kept from you. Clint almost told you the night the sphere broke. I didn't want to scare you off with the thought that God told me to bring you with me, and you'd think I was some weird stalker or something."

"BEN, I HAVE A CONFESSION to make also." Her voice caught. She cleared her throat as her heart raced. "I guess I should start at the beginning. A week before you brought me here, I dreamed of you every night. It was as if you were there with me, and I could sense your presence, but I couldn't find you or get to you. I would wake every morning and swear I could still sense you. One night in my dream, you looked right at me with your amazing eyes, and I memorized everything about you."

Casey sipped water from the glass as condensation dripped off the bottom onto the tablecloth. "I'm not sure why I dreamed about you, but you were always trying to keep me safe. Someone chased me the last night I dreamed of you. You were there in front of me, urging me on when you grabbed my hand and helped me escape. Ben, I still remember the touch of your hand from the dream. I didn't know you were the one who grabbed me and pulled me here until you turned me around, and I saw it was you. I didn't know what to do. I couldn't understand how you could be real. I didn't want to be away from you. It scared me, so I pushed you away. I loved you the first night I dreamt about you."

"I keep people at a distance, no matter who they are. I knew there was someone out there for me, but I put up walls to keep them out. You made my walls crumble little by little. I wasn't in control, and it scared me more than being taken. The day you were injured, it terrified me that I could lose you. God spoke to me." Tears fell as she held onto the moment God was there with her beside Ben.

She smiled as she finished her story. "God told me to let you in, that He chose you for me, and I needed to give you my heart to heal you. I wouldn't have been able to save you until then. So, I let you in. I let you in when I was used to keeping people out and keeping my heart safe from harm. I had to give you a part of me, and I did. But then I couldn't heal Amanda—" She choked as her voice caught.

Ben pulled her out of her chair and pulled her to him, wrapping his safe, strong arms around her. "Casey, I don't blame you. You're going to have to let it go."

"What I was going to say was I now know what you went through when you knew my brother was going to die because you brought me here. It was no more your fault than Amanda dying was mine. It tore me apart when I look back at how rude I was and how upset with you I was when I couldn't go back to save him." Casey placed her hand on his chest.

Ben placed both hands on either side of her face and lowered his face to hers until their lips met. The thought of God picking Ben—this adorable, sweet, great looking guy—for her, was as if she cheated. Her knees wanted to buckle, but Ben's strong, safe arms kept her from collapsing.

"Let's eat. Our food's getting cold." Ben pulled away first. She'd forgotten about dinner.

They couldn't keep from smiling as they enjoyed their first date together, hidden in the basement of an abandoned house, hiding from people who wanted them dead. It was a bittersweet moment, but she didn't care about the latter because she was with Ben. They made small talk while enjoying each other's company.

Ben left after dinner, and she couldn't believe she was tired and headed toward bed. She knew she would have good dreams tonight—no more choosing between her new friends who should live and who to let die. The link system jingled. She stepped back to the doorway of the kitchen and answered it.

"Casey?" Ben's face filled the screen.

"What? Miss me?" She laughed.

Ben laughed. "Of course. Can you come over? Clint wants to talk."

"Sure." Hesitant, she hung up, returned to the bookcase, and walked the short distance to their house.

The door was open, and several voices joined Ben and Clint's, and by the sounds of things, something big happened.

She was greeted by Ben, who held her hand and walked with her over to the group of people gathered around a computer. Chloe was at the helm and hushed everyone.

"Ladies and gentlemen, this is a breaking news announcement. We have received a report of dire circumstances. We have video of President Polson as he's being questioned by an unknown group regarding his ties to the Monarch terrorist group. We suggest you watch the tape in its entirety. Some of the conversation will be disturbing. We have it on good authority that this is a legitimate recording and has not been doctored or changed in any way." The newscaster turned to her monitor as their video of President Polson in the garage was played.

Everyone kept hushing others during the broadcast, so anyone who didn't know what was on the recording could listen. The spirits were high. Everyone hugged and rapidly talked. After Polson answered the questions, the news broadcaster sat at her desk with the camera zoomed in on her with her mouth hanging open, her eyes narrowed.

"Ladies and gentlemen, we apologize if any of you lost the signal. We are told there were several towers shut down as the broadcast was being aired. Still, we hope enough of you were able to watch what we were trying to tell the American people of the harrowing ordeal our fellow Americans have gone through because of one man and his ties to a terrorist group. The thought that our current president could be so cold and calculating in his quest for world domination starting in America is shocking." The news broadcaster pushed on her earpiece and glanced down.

She tried not to smile but continued. "We have received word that the FBI, CIA, and several other organizations in our government are in the process of locating the president, who happens to have disappeared. Also, as we speak, the central hub of this terrorist group has been hit by the military. Everyone in the command post has either been captured or killed. We received anonymous reports they were holed up in an abandoned high school in the Midwest. Several individuals who were being held against their will have been rescued from apparent interrogation rooms. With the Monarchs in custody, they're confirming with authorities they had one-hundred percent cooperation from President Polson and, in fact, took their orders directly from him."

Cheers broke out in the room, and Casey smiled. Was this happening? Was this man being taken out of office, and his terrorist group dismantled? She couldn't picture a happier group of people. Everyone hugged as Chloe closed her computer and approached them.

Clint gave her a big hug, then stepped back. She smiled and blushed three different shades of red. Ben quickly hugged her, then Casey gave her a long hug.

Clint beamed at her. "Good job, Chloe. We couldn't have done this without you."

"Well, the video's out and authenticated so no one can refute the fact Polson's dirty and in deep with the Monarchs. This broadcast airs every half an hour and, according to my uncle, several of his friends give him updates as they come in. He said Polson went underground as soon as the story aired, but at first, he tried to deny it. When he saw the copy hit the White House email system, he disappeared." Chloe smiled and waved goodbye to everyone as she left.

Everyone else filed out shortly after congratulating them on accomplishing the nearly impossible task of removing Polson from office. They reiterated to everyone it was God's will, and He was the one to thank, and they didn't need any acknowledgment on this.

The thought of the school used as an interrogation site being raided and everyone who was tortured there getting rescued made Casey smile. She was only in there for a short time and didn't have to endure any real pain. "Wait, who leaked the school location?"

"Well, when Chloe told her uncle where you were held when she got the recording to him, he included the address to his friends in Washington. With the recording and the information on their headquarters, there were several military personnel eager to go since they fought to keep this country free. They had a mission in place before the first news broadcast was aired, so the Monarchs didn't have time to think much less plan an escape." Clint stood taller as he spoke of the military. Casey knew he would've loved to have been on the mission since it hit so close to home.

Ben and Clint bowed their heads, and Casey joined them. Ben prayed, "Dear Heavenly Father, thank You for the win in this battle for You. To be a part of such a great day in history and to see You victorious is a blessing to us. We are proud to be Your children and can't wait until the day when these small battles are done, and the entire war is won for You, and we'll be in Heaven with You for all eternity. You're an amazing awesome God, and we thank You for sending Your Son, the one perfect sacrifice, to die for our sins so we may have a way to Heaven. On our own, we couldn't make it to Heaven. Thank You for the love and blessings You send us every day. In Jesus's name, amen."

"Amen," was echoed by Clint and Casey.

"So, how was dinner?" Clint smiled.

Casey smiled as Ben put his arm around her shoulders. "Fine, how was yours?"

"You guys look great together. Hey, Casey, anyone else from your time we can try to find for me?" Clint tilted his head and raised an eyebrow.

"Sorry, I hear the way back has been destroyed. Some crazy chick broke the sphere," she teased. She'd never been happier.

"Great. I guess I'll have to wait for who God has for me because if my soulmate and I are as close and perfect as you two are for each other, I can't wait for God to introduce her."

"Yeah, maybe one of these days, buddy, before you're old and decrepit, you'll meet her." Ben gave Clint a playful punch in the arm. Ben steered Casey toward the closet stairs. "If you don't mind, I'm going to take Casey for a walk under the stars and show her what freedom looks like."

Clint grabbed the doorknob. "Do you think that's wise? Monarchs could be out there ready for revenge."

"Clint, we're fine. We're not going far and will stay in the shadows." Ben patted Clint on the shoulder before he tugged down on the ladder and motioned that he would go first.

"Wait, take some sort of protection in case they're still out there." Clint jogged to the living room and handed a gun to Ben, who tucked it into the back of his jeans. No doubt, Clint also had one hidden.

Several minutes passed, and Casey cleared her throat and clasped her hands together when Ben poked his head through the opening and smiled. "You two get up here." Ben grinned from ear to ear.

Clint motioned to Casey. "Ladies first."

She climbed the ladder, then waited for Clint to join them.

"Ready for this?" Ben opened the door, and Casey gasped as she saw people wandering around outside.

Clint smiled and followed as Ben grabbed Casey's hand to lead her outside.

Several people greeted each other as they milled about and looked at the stars. Who knew how long some of these people had been hiding from the Monarchs? The news broadcast reached people faster than she thought possible.

Casey smiled at Ben as he put his arm around her shoulders, pulling her in tight. She slipped her arm around his waist and followed him out of the house as they were greeted by smiling individuals with upturned faces enjoying their freedom.

Energy filled the air. People exclaimed joy at their freedom for the first time in years, and they knew it was from God. He was here with His children enjoying the victory with them. A tear glinted in the corner of Casey's eye, and she looked at Ben and smiled. Clint, the military spokesman for their group, clenched his jaw.

"I wish Amanda was here," Clint's voice broke.

"She is," Ben murmured. "She is."

Casey held onto Ben—the man from her dreams—the dreams God gave her.

Don't miss out!

Visit the website below and you can sign up to receive emails whenever K. A. Moore publishes a new book. There's no charge and no obligation.

https://books2read.com/r/B-A-MAMI-WOGGB

About the Author

K.A. Moore, born and raised in Kansas, is a retired 911 police dispatcher with over thirteen years of service and will be the first to tell you dispatchers are a special breed all their own. Her real passion is writing and putting her imagination into works of fiction. Faith-based Christian suspense is her preferred writing theme, with wild, crazy dreams as the backdrop to many scenes that seem to come alive in her writing. As she writes, her Chihuahua scampers for the coveted position of curling up in her lap while creating her stories.

www.ingramcontent.com/pod-product-compliance
Lightning Source LLC
LaVergne TN
LVHW050915080826
845145LV00001B/90

* 9 7 8 1 9 5 7 2 2 3 1 3 1 *